George's Head – Kilkee

Who Occupies
This House

Who Occupies This House

A Novel

Kathleen Hill

TRIQUARTERLY BOOKS
NORTHWESTERN UNIVERSITY PRESS
EVANSTON, ILLINOIS

TriQuarterly Books
Northwestern University Press
www.nupress.northwestern.edu

Copyright © 2010 by Kathleen Hill. Published 2010 by TriQuarterly Books/
Northwestern University Press. All rights reserved.

Printed in the United States of America

10   9   8   7   6   5   4   3   2

Library of Congress Cataloging-in-Publication Data

Hill, Kathleen.
    Who occupies this house / Kathleen Hill.
        p. cm.
    Includes bibliographical references.
    ISBN 978-0-8101-5211-3 (cloth : alk. paper)
    1. Irish Americans—New York (State)—New York—Fiction. 2. Families—New York (State)—New York—Fiction. 3. Loss (Psychology)—Fiction. I. Title.
PS3558.I3897W46 2010
813.54—dc22

2010016967

∞ The paper used in this publication meets the minimum requirements of the American National Standard for Information Sciences—Permanence of Paper for Printed Library Materials, ANSI Z39.48-1992.

Elizabeth Sarah Kathleen

Leah Anna

And within its depths I saw ingathered,

bound by love in a single volume,

the scattered leaves of all the universe.

—DANTE, *PARADISO*

Contents

Ann Catherine Weber	Robert Ethridge		Alice Quinn
b. Frankfort, N.Y., 1820	b. Frankfort, N.Y., 1814		b. Co. Limerick, 1•
d. Frankfort, N.Y., 1902	d. Frankfort, N.Y., 1873		d. Mohawk, N.Y., 1

Married, Frankfort, N.Y.,
1834

Married, Co. Lime
1838

Mary Ethridge	John Carmody
b. Frankfort, N.Y., 1850	b. Mohawk, N.Y., 1843
d. Washington, D.C., 1908	d. Pelham, N.Y., 1917

Married, New York City, 1872

Robert Carmody	Deirdre Carmod
b. Mohawk, N.Y., 1873	b. Mohawk, N.Y., 18
Lost at Sea, 1899	d. Pelham, N.Y., 19

Married, Washington,
1905

Bert Aubry	Kate Conroy
b. New York City, 1904	b. New York City, 1907
d. Pelham, N.Y., 2004	d. Pelham, N.Y., 1994

Married, Pelham, N.Y., 1936

Charlie Aubry	Narrator
b. Pelham, N.Y., 1937	b. Pelham, N.Y., 1940

ichael Carmody
Co. Limerick, 1817
ohawk, N.Y., 1873

Patrick McDonough
b. Co. Roscommon, 1797
d. Frankfort, N.Y., 1847

Bridgit Fitzmaurice
b. Co. Roscommon, 1799
d. Ilion, N.Y., 1881
Daughter Bridgit, age 8, died crossing the Atlantic, 1846

Married, Co. Roscommon, 1824

Mary Elizabeth McDonough
b. Cloonfad, Co. Roscommon, 1834
d. Ilion, N.Y., 1913

Michael Conroy
b. Elphin, Co. Roscommon, 1823 or 1825
d. Ilion, N.Y., 1893

Married, Ilion, N.Y., 1850

William Conroy
Ilion, N.Y., 1869
New York City, 1944

Eleven Other Children

Mary Conroy
b. New York City, 1910
d. New York City, 1911

Grace Conroy
b. New York City, 1910
d. San Francisco, Calif., 1980

Maddie Aubry
b. Pelham, N.Y., 1943

Who Occupies
This House

Prologue

Ginkgos

That July there had been a spate of clear days and nights so softly luminous that people in Morningside Heights where I live hung around on stoops and street corners during the long twilights, reluctant to go inside. Returning home alone one evening, I passed a dark-haired young man who was stopped in his tracks, staring west toward the Hudson a few blocks away. The rays of the setting sun were lying in low even shafts along 120th Street, and the ginkgos lining the sidewalk floated so eerily in the light you might have thought a storm was brewing. A gleaming shadow was pressed against the far side of each tree, outlining its bright edge of silver bark and shining foolish limbs. It seemed you could see straight through each leaf to its ragged underside, could see around each nubby branch to its hidden spurs and stems. Not a stir of air, not the faintest breeze, and yet the dreamy fan leaves appeared to be advancing in the light, to be turning toward a moment still to come.

Is there one day of the year when the tilt of the earth, its distance from the sun, causes light to stream from every direction? When the last rays of evening are permitted to give back what has not yet been lost? When there descends a clarity so forgiving that everything is revealed at once?

The young man turned to look at me as I passed and swept out his hand in a wide gesture that offered it all, the boundless earth itself—just as if it had been his to give. When I got to the end of the block and looked back, he was gone, but the intensity of the light on the trees, if anything, had deepened, and the sky was the tender blue usually seen only at the winter solstice. *This* is the life we cling to, I thought.

Troubling the Waters

—The life we cling to?

My own life had become eclipsed by fear. My mother had died seven years earlier and now it was my turn to stand at the edge.

—Were you ailing?

Not in any way I could name. I taught my classes, saw my friends, drank my morning coffee with Martin. Spoke on the phone with our three grown daughters. Following my mother's death I'd wanted a life I could call my own, wanted to draw breath without having to look backward to the lives that came before. But instead of rejoicing in my freedom, I found myself alone and afraid. Chilled to the bone. One day I came across a line from an Emily Dickinson letter written soon after the death of her eight-year-old nephew: *I do not know the Names of Sickness. The Crisis of the sorrow of so many years is all that tires me.*

—Did you fear a child's death?

Always. There'd never been a time when this wasn't so. But now the ghosts of every age were crowding at my back: insistent, clamoring. And I would not turn and look at them, I would not. I was frozen in place. Terrified. But of what? From the time I can remember, of breaking the connection with my mother. Now she was dead. As for my children, I above all needed reassurances that they were all right, wordlessly pleading with them to spare me the tale of their sorrows. After all, panic makes a poor listener.

Almost seven years passed. And then the climate changed in the second year of our new millennium. There had been a day in early September that ended in forked lightning and shifting curtains of rain, a storm that cleared the air for a dawn of liquid light.

—We know the rest.

It was the death of small things I observed in the days after: a yellow-shafted flicker lying on an iron grating, the updraft from the subway stirring the red feathers at its neck. The grass around the tombstones in the cemetery of Trinity Church covered in white ash. A ginkgo leaf astray on the sidewalk, brown at the edges. Despite the continuous drone and chop of helicopters, it was the silences that compelled me, in the streets, in the places where people assembled. Waking to the first night of rain later that week, I imagined those buried beneath smoldering ribs of iron and wondered if they heard the rain falling out of the sky. Were they listening, those who in order to escape a wall of fire had themselves fallen from so great a height? And if so, was this the last time we the living and they the dying would know something of the world in common? Or did the drum of rain come to them as if from a time already past? And what of the cell phones in their pockets ringing at all hours? What of the ones making the calls, the ones punching the numbers more and more desperately? Did they listen as the phone rang on, listen to the gulf, the space like death, opening between? I imagined some who wanted only to say they were sorry for the angry silence of the Saturday night before, or perhaps the preoccupied silence of the last ten years.

It was the silences in my own life I was listening for. Some were my own to address, others were not. For example, my mother's! What was the connection I'd always feared would be broken if not a shining web of silence?

—Did you wish to say you were sorry to someone?

My three grown daughters, without a doubt. For lapses too many to name. Not so much Martin, who was away during that week in September. With him it's a matter of professions of love followed by upsets followed by reconciliations followed by more professions. But no, I'm not aware he's waiting for me to speak. It was the empty spaces that troubled me in our apartment during that week when I was alone and wakened by the rain: the floors no longer strewn with sneakers and book bags, with jackets flung off in haste; the silence of the long hall, of the door into which no one fitted her key. Silences that translated into a question: what have my daughters been waiting to hear me say? What have they been waiting for me to listen to? It was time. And yet I did nothing. I brooded on the tide of fear, fear of the stranger, rising all around me. I fell into deeper despondency.

So I remained—too dispirited for the task—until almost an entire year had gone by and then one evening in July on my way home saw the ginkgos turning in the light.

That same night, laying my head on the pillow, I had a dream. In the dream I know that very soon I'll be carried swiftly down the river and out to sea. I'm writing, feverishly writing, on a piece of burgundy brocade: there is news I must confide while even a moment remains. If I delay, my three daughters will be left without the single thing in the world I have to bequeath. My pen moves on and on, but when I stop to read I see to my horror that the brocade is soaking up my sentences, the rich fabric is swallowing the ink. I might just as well have not written a word. My daughters arrive and I tell them I'll be leaving soon. They nod and ask if I have anything to say. I answer I have nothing, a fact which bothers no one but which seems unbearable to me.

I am my own mother being carried out to sea, I am my daughters asking for a word at the very last, the fortifying word that will perhaps even now allow me to listen to their sorrows. Because the question is this: is it possible, finally, to soothe and restore, to repair the damage? Stir the waters and dip my hand in the pool?

—What pool is that?

It's the pool of suffering I'm speaking of, the concealed anguish of the generations that came before. The pool that lies within myself, all that I contain of the past. My mother, Kate. Her own mother and father. And their parents as well. My great-grandparents. Those who arrived from starving Ireland and never returned, those who came to call themselves Americans. Their lives stamped by poverty, by faith. The pool in whose depths I hope to find the measure of my claim to our own passing moment, our place in time.

For it's this I want: to break free of the inherited fear that lies behind my own failures to speak and to listen, lapses I know nothing about. If it were possible to give utterance in some small, even mistaken way, to that legacy of lost children who fell into the sea, fell into the earth, wouldn't that constitute some modest stab at repair? It's the miseries endured in solitude, the words left unsaid, that bloom darkly from one generation to the next.

—And have you forgiven your own mother, Kate? She whose death set loose the swarm of ghosts?

At the time of her death, it seemed to me I'd forgiven her. But if that were the case, then why should the night of the ginkgos have left me with the brimming sense that the dawn of forgiveness was breaking only now, that everything was still to come? And why should the young man on the street offering me the beauty of the world have struck me as the angel of annunciation?

When it comes to my daughters, my question is a different one: I ask how those we've harmed can forgive us if we don't look to our own wounds, to our own stern judgment of those who came before. Because how can we receive mercy if we've bestowed none? We all know there's no respite from fear, no lasting peace, without first having extended some measure of pardon. Without some attempt to understand. Otherwise, everything frets the soul, scrapes it raw. Yet how does it happen, forgiveness? In a flash? Over long years? A promise to be fulfilled only at our deaths?

—What of your children's children? And in time to come, theirs as well? Does your wish to soothe and restore extend into the future? What's more, do you mean to release the clamoring ghosts, the parade at your back?

All. All. With so little to lose, why not cast a wide net?

—So now what must you do?

Invoking the spirit of poverty, set out to decipher, to read. Find a blank page on which to write. At my elbow, papers and notebooks, letters and diaries. They lie scattered on the table at which I write. From my chair at the table, I look out at the wide city through the bare branches of an elm, through the arms of the ginkgos farther down in Morningside Park. The moon rises white in the window, the evening sun strikes a glowing band of orange on the tops of the brick buildings below. A flock of pigeons turns in the light, a white seagull drifts past. Five times a day the call to prayer from a mosque slices the hour. At dawn, the morning star. Only a few blocks away, the Hudson flows to the sea, old men sit fishing, buckets beside them.

Of course, there's the matter of time. And the house, the vanishing house where the secret that overshadowed my childhood was lived out day by day. The silence that opened to all the others. Only one occupant now remains and after he's gone the house will be sold. The ghosts will stay or go as they choose, but I will no longer be able to sleep in their midst. And they, I fear, will no longer be free to flow through my dreams like water through reeds swaying on the sandy bottom of a river.

Part One

Inmates of the Air

Of nearness to her sundered Things

A coral necklace, white, with a gold clasp. We had always thought coral was pink, but no, this coral is the color of eggshells. The beads are round, like pearls, and in size grow from the size of a pea to twice that where they must have hung between her breasts.

An ivory knife she used to open letters or cut the pages of a book: along the upper edge of the blade, a string of elephants lumbering toward the pointed tip.

And last, a little gold watch with spidery roman numerals and hands that point.

These are the objects Deirdre left behind. When we ask where the ivory knife came from, Kate says she's not sure, perhaps it was her mother's. She keeps the knife on her desk, using it to slit an envelope along the top long after everyone else rips open their mail with their fingers.

Objects, that was all. We, Kate's children, grew up in a house where a woman had lived and died, then disappeared without anyone's being able to say a word about her. She was neither mentioned nor made a character in a story nor spoken of as having been this kind of person or that. She was nobody's anything—Kate's mother only by name; our grandmother, not even that. No one would ever have thought to say to us, "your grandmother." Her name was never pronounced: Deirdre.

Daybreak in January: the hoarse blast of the foghorn carried on a southeasterly wind, conjuring black rocks shrouded in mist, boats rocking in the icy waters of the Long Island Sound. But for us, the children sleeping in the house in Pelham, the lonely sound of the horn is the muffled boom of the house itself, a long breath exhaled.

A little later the fierce knocking in the coils of the radiators, the spit and hiss of steam escaping from silver valves, the commotion of scalding water coursing through pipes: the struggle to remove the chill, to warm the place up a little. Water at the boil rising from cellar to kitchen and downstairs hall where Bert, our father, is shrugging on his coat before leaving for work, into the rooms upstairs where, shivering, we were getting dressed for school.

But all that clanging and banging, that rush of steam condensing in the cold air, if we stopped for a moment and listened, fell like the echo of other winter mornings, the echo of other rumblings heard long ago by those who'd lived in the same spaces before us, sounds we might listen for but never quite catch.

Always the sense of other hands on the banisters, other feet on the stairs; that we were living only to repeat what others had known firsthand, our lives a pale reflection of what had gone before.

The hickory tree still stands beside the house, shading the screened porch that runs along the south side. The tree must now be at least seventy feet tall, twice as high as the house. The lowest branches reach toward the three dormer windows that extend in a shining row beneath the slate roof. But this was not always the case. The tree must have been half its present size when Kate, five years old, moved into the house she would never leave.

Standing in the pachysandra beneath the tree in springtime, staring up at the shaggy dark underside of the bark spotted with moss, we know that the others have taken it in before: the whole dizzying length of trunk to the branches at the top. There in a high wind the branches are tossing and rolling, leaves are flung in and out of the sun. They blow open to let in a sky streaked with watery light. The sky is the element in which the branches move, it is the silence in which they flail and tumble. Against the thrashing of the branches, the silence is something to listen for. It is the motion of the tree that makes it possible to hear the silence waiting on the other side of things.

Those others, a generation before us; ourselves, now. Kate was the link, Kate who once had been a child among them, who had been one of those now gone: Deirdre and Willie, her parents, and the little sister Grace.

Of Deirdre we know almost nothing. Of Willie, a little. First of all, by the objects he too has left behind: books shelved on the landing, in the hall, volumes with dusty jackets whose titles we can barely make out on the backs of their spines:

Parnell's Faithful Few, Margaret Leamy

Famine, Liam O'Flaherty

Deirdre of the Sorrows, J. M. Synge

The Man Called Pearse, Desmond Ryan

The Angler's Guide to the Irish Free State, Ministry of Fisheries

Representative Irish Tales, compiled with an introduction and notes, W. B. Yeats

Kate takes down a book from a high shelf and shows us the title: *The Interpreters: The Candle of Vision,* A.E. She opens the book to the flyleaf on which has been written, in an inky scrawl: *Constance Markiewicz from her friend A.E. 25. October. 28.* The stem of the *E* leans sharply backwards against the *A*.

Or: *A Book of Saints and Wonders,* Lady Gregory. This last one is inscribed, again in ink:

> To Theodore Spier-Simon from A. Gregory—at Coole, where the memory of these Saints still dwells—May 17, 1922

Kate tells us these books along with the others were acquired by her father, Willie, over many summers on the fishing trips to Ireland he began making almost immediately afterwards. By "afterwards" we understand her to mean after the death of her mother.

Of Course – I prayed –
And did God Care?

In the stories told by Kate, stories featuring Willie, Deirdre figured always as the missing one: Deirdre, the woman dying upstairs; Deirdre, the woman dead. Take Kate's account of one summer's morning, a morning it seemed we might recall ourselves if only we tried hard enough.

Yet how could we have known it? We weren't even born in 1923. But the long-ago people in the story had been assembled that morning on the same porch where we were scattered decades later listening to Kate pick words out of the air, the same screened porch where summer after summer—against the rattle of passing trains, the horn at the fire station hiccuping at noon and at six—Charlie and Maddie and I whiled away the hours, elbows dug into a glossy straw floor mat, staring at a Monopoly board, at tiny red houses placed on Boardwalk or Park Place.

It was there that Kate, sixteen years old, and her younger sister, Grace, had been told that very soon *the awful door should spring.* They had sat in the same wicker chairs we pushed aside to make room for our bare legs, had sat there one Sunday morning in July, gathered solemnly by their father on their return from Mass. He had something to tell them, he said, and he knew they would ask God's help in their hour of need.

It might be, he asked, that they still held out some hope? Of course by "hope" they knew he meant that the woman upstairs—by turns shaking the bed with chills, soaking the sheets with sweat—this woman, their mother, would survive her terrible ordeal. But no, it was his painful duty to tell them it did not seem that the will of God was to be accomplished in that way. He sat there in the rocking chair, one leg crossed over the other, propelling himself back and forth, to give them the facts. Their mother was suffering from Hodgkin's disease and the doctors believed she would not recover. None of the remedies known to them—blood transfusions, arsenic placed in the veins, radium applied to glands in the throat—had brought the return to health they'd hoped for.

Kate, listening, had gazed through the screens into the rhododendron bushes that ran the length of the porch—or so she might have, we were free to imagine anything we liked—into the bushes that shaded our long afternoons. Rhododendrons as refuge. Anywhere to avoid the sight of Willie's blue eyes that swam alarmingly behind the magnifying lenses he wore, pince-nez, his flat, sensitive fingers thrumming the wicker arm of his chair. As Kate sits with her feet hooked around the legs of a chair in the silence that follows Willie's announcement, thinking nothing, feeling nothing, the shrill note of a cicada lifts in the late morning air, holds for a long moment of shattering intensity, and falls back into silence.

Had Willie been with them at Mass that morning or had he been to another? Had he knelt beside them under the window dedicated to St. Catherine and her spiked wheel? St. Catherine, hair waving back from her face like a Botticelli angel's, green robe struck by the sun to a glassy emerald blaze.

The wheel is intended to be the instrument of her torment. But see how she is unharmed, see how her hand rests lightly on its highest point. As if the wheel had been her plaything, as if she might, at a whim, tap it into motion, whirl it down a hill.

Willie is at a loss. Sitting there with his daughters on either side of him, disconcerted that the announcement he has prepared so carefully has been greeted without question or any show of grief, he is uncertain what to do next. Impulsively—wanting to shock these stony-faced daughters into some display of feeling—he decides to tell them a story he has confided to no one, a story he had earlier determined that under no circumstances they should hear. He comments, by way of preamble, that he is sure their mother's illness had been a sad surprise to them all.

And yet, he says, looking from one to another, at Kate with her dark eyebrows drawn together, green eyes staring off into the rhododendrons, at Grace hugging her elbows, flaxen hair falling around her lowered chin, their mother herself had not been surprised. She had seen her death approaching even before she had fallen ill. Yes, they might be interested to hear that she had known it all from the first, before anyone else could perceive the slightest sign.

A little more than a year ago, on her birthday, April Fools' Day, he had woken and first thing reached over to wish her many happy returns of the day. That was the expression he used, Kate said: "Many happy returns of the day." But instead of looking pleased, Deirdre had suddenly sat upright in bed and burst into tears. "In a year I'll be dead," she had told him, "and not a soul will have known what ails me."

Willie had tried to laugh it off, had called her his April Fool. But she would have none of it. And now see. There had been only one return, and that one had not been happy.

Hopeless, the muddle of what Kate tells us and what we imagine.

Fact: The announcement, made in July of 1923, that their mother would be dead within a month.

Fact: Willie's story of her prevision, of her appalling knowledge.

Fact: Her death three weeks after the announcement on the porch.

But all the rest is made up, invented from bits and scraps, conjecture, shaky interpretation, and certainly some prejudice against Willie, who is the only one of that generation we ever met, appearing—before he too was removed by death—long enough to figure as a creature who would point a finger at a child playing on the floor and ask her if she was a good girl, ask her if she was not a trouble to her mother, who would hide a penny in a fist held behind his back and ask her to guess what was in it.

Is it true that we were scattered about in the same wicker chairs—listening to Kate relate to us some version or other of this story—where she and Grace had sat that July morning? We may have been, but it scarcely matters. The hard back of the rocking chair where Maddie or I might in turn spend a morning reading, pushing ourselves back and forth with one bare foot, was felt along our spines, against our skin. And so it must have been felt along Willie's as he sat motionless, trying to compel his daughters' tears. He had sat in the chair, one leg crossed over the other, watch chain lying across the smooth white linen of his waistcoat, the last button alone undone because even on the hottest days of summer he will not appear in shirt sleeves: Willie Conroy the banker, and quite a successful one at that, who when he was a boy in the Mohawk Valley picked strawberries at daybreak to sell for a few cents to the shops.

While Willie and his daughters are sitting downstairs on the porch, each waiting to be released from this moment, the woman they're talking about is upstairs shaking violently from a chill. She is also tortured by thirst, and the bed is pitching from side to side upon a restless sea. At first it had been rocking gently, reminding her that a soothing hand is looking out for her comfort and release. But soon enough the pitch and fall of the waves grows more intense until she fears being tumbled over the side. A fever, a delirium, and then over the top, over into the churning waters below.

The waves have risen on one side, then the other, she could feel the swell rising beneath and then the drastic fall. It had been like that, the pitch and drop, the plunge.

"Poor man," Kate always ends her story. "Now that I'm an adult, I'm able to imagine how hard that must have been for him. Left alone with two daughters. And of such a difficult age!"

But why should we imagine any such thing? It was the woman dying upstairs who invited compassion. It was Kate herself, and her younger sister, Grace, left motherless.

It was only the final exhortation, the plea for Willie, that moved Kate to energy. As for the rest, she spoke not as one who had been present, slouched in a clean middy blouse, dark brows drawn fiercely together, but as someone trying to recall a tale she had been taught to recite.

Safe Despair it is that raves –
Agony is frugal

But Kate did not leap to this story. It was pried out of her like all the others. More likely, we pressed her and she declined.

"What was she like, your mother?" we asked from time to time, curious because we never heard a word. We'd forget the dead woman for months, even years, and then she'd suddenly fill the air. We had no name for her, this stranger who'd died upstairs in the room where Kate and our father, Bert, now slept. The phrase itself, "your mother," which we pronounced otherwise only in the company of friends when we wished to refer to their mothers, seemed to make of Kate someone our own age. Which of course we were asking her to become, the girl who had once lived in this house with a mother going up and down the stairs.

"I don't really remember," she said.

"You don't remember? But that's impossible! How could you not remember your own mother?"

"I must have some kind of a block," Kate replied. "I know it's odd, but I don't seem to remember her."

"But you were sixteen years old when she died! If you were to die now, don't you think we'd remember you?"

We were indignant as well as in sore need of reassurance. The present was even more precarious than we'd thought. We might like to think our mother was the one person on earth who could be relied on to keep us firmly in mind. But that was clearly wishful thinking.

"Well, I'm with you more. You know, she wasn't very well."

"What was wrong with her? She wasn't sick, was she? Not until that year before she died?"

"No." Kate was vague.

"Well, why wasn't she with you, then?"

"I don't think she was very strong."

"Why not? What was wrong with her?"

"Not after the death of that baby. You know, Grace's twin."

In the upstairs hall—above the shelves holding *Parnell's Faithful Few* and *The Well of the Saints*—hangs a photograph in a gold oval frame. A woman with glossy dark hair is sitting with head bowed, a newborn twin sleeping raptly in each arm. Her face is in shadow, she is gazing down at one of these babies. But which one? The one who is to die a year later, falling from a carriage onto her head? Or the one who has seventy years more to live? Kate, three years old, an enormous white ribbon in her hair, is pressed alongside, craning her neck to see.

When night comes this happy family group is illuminated by an electric bulb covered by a milky glass shade, a white porcelain tube swirling above. It is the same light that makes a sliver of reassurance beneath the bedtime door closed against the quick steps retreating down the stairs, the ring knocking on the banister.

The Sun and Moon must make their haste –
The Stars express around

Timepieces:

The nautical clock that sits on the bookcase just beneath the photograph of the man with the epaulettes and the sad eyes, its double pendulum weighted with mercury to preserve the balance needed for accurate measurement against the roll and pitch of the sea.

The grandfather clock in the downstairs hall, moon smiling down on the child playing on the floor, silver pendulum swinging a leisurely tick-tock, the quarterly play of its chimes, hourly wheeze and bong, the massive clock that later on Grace would ask for, the only thing from the house she wished to claim as her own.

The little French clock in the sitting room, its tiny silver hammer jiggling up at the half hour and again at the hour.

The clock on the mantel in the dining room, hooded with a glass bell, the kind used to cover cheese against a swarm of flies. At the base of the clock the golden balls that swish all the way round, then all the way back, this way, that, indefatigable, a kind of soundless metronome. Here, too, the hammer rises and falls.

But none exactly coincident with the others, so that all night long, the chime and wheeze and bong of clocks, upstairs and down, the high clear ringing notes, the muffled boom, the silence created by rings of sound vanishing into thin air.

Not to speak of the gold watch with spidery roman numerals, with hands that point to seventeen minutes after three, face looking up from a jumble of coral beads in the back of Kate's drawer.

With the exception of the watch that ages ago stopped dead on hours and minutes and seconds, all are noisy, all insistent, merciless.

Always the moon, exactly on time, falling through the windows, into the mirrors, drowning in sliding silver depths, passing over the backs of books, over people lying asleep in their beds, people lying awake listening to the approaching whistle of the train pounding through the darkness to New York City half an hour away. Glazing the gray slate of the roof, the high brick chimneys, flooding the grass, running silver over the curled oak leaves clinging to winter branches. Released at last from the crisscross of trunks and limbs and forked bush and bough in January, sailing above the house, shining.

The silent flash of stars in the windows: fall, Orion rising in the east each evening exactly four minutes earlier than the night before, not a minute more nor less. By the time the leaves are off the trees, we can see it before we go to sleep, a signal aslant, a scabbard, bright buckle at the hunter's belt. In spring the Swan beginning its long flight across the summer sky.

The sun stirring phantoms at noon, ghosts of a kind to numb the brain, hit it broadside: dust curled in a corner, paint splintering on a windowsill, the ring of rust around the drain in the bathtub on the third floor, a nick in the wicker rocking chair that reveals a coat of green paint beneath the white.

Filtering through the high slice of cellar window, a dusty chink of light that touches the two black burners of the little cast-iron range once used for boiling starch, the raised letters stamped across it: *Michigan Stove Co. Detroit Chicago.*

Refracted in the beveled edge of the mirror in the sitting room—during the winter months, when the sun rises 45 degrees south of its summertime spot—throwing trembling prisms of light onto the ceiling.

Gilding on October afternoons the Buddha who sits cross-legged, eyes closed, palms together, atop a box in the living room, tracing the gold in the loose folds of his gown, shooting a shadow up the wall, the elegant slope of his shoulders, the incline of his neck.

But whatever the season, throwing oblongs into the rooms this way and that, exactly on time, showing up the bare places in the carpets, the tattered yellow shades lowered against the heat in summer.

The last Night that She lived
It was a Common Night

Kate's refusals were not to be tolerated. A woman had lived in the house and vanished without a trace. Her disappearance was disturbing, uncanny, as if you'd been looking into a mirror and as you stood there gazing, maybe a little absentmindedly, the image of your face had faded away and was gone.

"Don't you remember anything about her?" we ask.

It is Sunday morning, we are back from Mass, and Kate is standing in the kitchen at the stove, an old-fashioned affair propped on four slender gray legs, each of its three ovens stamped in black letters with the word *Oriole*. She is slowly raking a fork through the eggs she is scrambling.

"She loved children," she says at last, as if offering a gift we will be unable to refuse. But what can this mean? It incenses us, the idea of a mother loving "children," as if Kate might have her eye on a child we've never met, or that her heart is otherwise engaged.

"Were you in the house when she died?"

"I was sleeping up on the third floor. In one of the brass beds."

"But did she say good-bye to you? You know, during the days before?"

"No, I don't think so."

"Did someone call you when it happened?"

With one hand Kate is lifting the thickening eggs, with the other she is holding onto the handle of the frying pan.

"I mean, how did you know she was dead?"

"It was during the night. I heard doors opening and closing. There were voices in the hall."

"Did you come down then?"

"No, I don't think so."

"Did someone come upstairs?"

"No."

For the moment we let the matter rest. But after breakfast, when Kate is standing at the sink washing the dishes, while we are drying them and putting them away, we take it up again. It is Kate's stunning vagueness about the past, her aloof removal, her startling capacity for expunging and forgetting, that we can't reconcile with our own clamorous need that as the mother of ourselves she be none of these things.

"What happened then? You must remember her funeral. Was there a wake?"

Kate raises the wrist of one dripping hand to push back a lock of dark hair.

"Yes, a wake."

"Well, where was it?"

"It was here, in this house."

"The wake was in this house? You mean they brought the coffin in here?"

It had never occurred to us that there was once a dead body lying in one of the rooms where we came and went all day.

"Where did they put it?"

"In the living room."

"Where in the living room?"

"Along that wall. The one that faces the porch."

So that anybody sitting in the wicker rocking chair must have been able to look straight in and see the long polished box, its brass handles.

A Day! Help! Help! Another Day.
Your prayers, oh Passer by!

If we are to picture Kate during those days of her mother's dying, we must start with something we know: the room at the top of the house. The beds, these at least we can get hold of, solid brass and very heavy, built for hard use, not gleaming at all, but dull and scarred. Horsehair mattresses that squeak when you turn over in the middle of the night. For the last couple of weeks Kate has been sleeping on the third floor because she is sick to death of the smells below, the mingled odors of ammonia and rot.

Three o'clock in the afternoon, maybe, and Kate is sitting on the floor, cross-legged, playing solitaire. The cicadas are hammering in the trees. She is laying out in rows cards limp with heat, gathering them up in her hand. The house has been silent for hours, but at last she hears the nurse who always shuts the door in Kate's face go along the hall and down the back stairs into the kitchen. Immediately Kate gets to her feet and stealthily creeps down to the second floor and into the room where her mother is sleeping. Standing there, looking down at the face lying on the pillow, she can't make any sense of what she sees. Is this her mother? This one with the purple eyelids sunk in craggy sockets? The spidery hands lying as if they had been arranged on the dazzling white sheet?

The long mirror on the closet door is throwing into the room the heavy green underwater light of the hickory; on the little mahogany dresser two cut-crystal scent bottles, each plugged with a round stopper, are flinging wobbly splashes of blue and purple onto the ceiling. One of the knobs of the bed is looped with a black crucifix. While Kate is standing there, feeling more and more as if she is about to topple from some absurd height, the eyes of the sleeping stranger are suddenly staring straight into her own. A flash from the depths, an uncanny beam of light. Kate's heart leaps forward. This is the "once and for all" she has longed for. Now she will at last collapse in a sobbing heap and her mother will beg forgiveness for all this dreadful time.

But even as she stands there, certain that here at last is the one whose call she has listened for day and night, she is beset by doubts. The blaze of her mother's eyes burns with an intensity that terrifies her, a flame that might burn her alive. Is this the desperation of the dying? Or is it the furnace—the great roaring furnace—of love?

In her confusion, her fear of scorch and burn, Kate thinks perhaps she should do something in response: take in her own hand the hand lying on the sheet? Or lean down and kiss the forehead? But before she can decide to make any move at all, before she can so much as feel the itch of tears behind the lids of her own eyes, her mother's eyes close and she is once more standing there helpless and alone.

A Clock Stopped –

One day I take from its shelf one of Willie's books—*The Big Fellow: Michael Collins and the Irish Revolution* by Frank O'Connor—and opening it see a photograph fall from its pages. Who are they, this group of young people sitting in twos and threes up and down the stairs of a summer porch?

Kate looks and says, pointing, that one is her mother. All the rest are caught turned toward each other, laughing, talking. But she is sitting with one hand on the railing, looking straight out at the camera. It is before the days when people are told to smile, to arrange an expression that will tell their descendants who may look at the picture, however many years hence: see how happy everyone is, see what warm, good-hearted people they are, your ancestors, how at ease with each other, see how their arms are draped around each others' shoulders, see how their arms are linked.

The young woman in a white dress whom Kate is pointing to has dark brows, and her eyes may very well be gray. But what is her expression? What is it possible to say about her state of mind? Something in her eyes perhaps a little lost and bewildered, some odd tilt of the head as if she has just been dazzled by a sudden burst of light.

Kate remembers a dress her mother wore, that's true. Remembers it in detail: at the neck, white; but gradually moving through every shade of gray until around the knees the skirt floats black. But of course all this must have been later. In the picture the women are wearing long dark skirts and white blouses that clutch the neck. Long strings of beads are knotted between their breasts. The young woman Kate is pointing to is wearing what looks to be a watch on a chain.

Over and over, like a Tune –
The Recollection plays –

On summer evenings, when we are still little, Bert teaches himself to play
the piano. He uses a book with a gray and red cover, the John Thompson
method, and after he's worked his way through the scales and arpeggios,
gives himself up to the song from *The Bohemian Girl* he's determined
to learn: "Then You'll Remember Me." It is full of trills and runs and
complicated fingering, and his arms swing back and forth from one end
of the piano to the other as he hurries along, trying to keep up with the
melody playing in his head. Then, breaking off suddenly on a mistaken
chord, he steps out through the screened door of the porch and walks
meditatively up and down in the night. Maddie and I have been sent to
bed long ago, but from the window of the room where we sleep can look
out over the slated roof of the porch and see the red spark of his cigarette
moving slowly beneath the trees.

Bert keeps his John Thompson music in the piano bench that holds as
well a book covered in green silk, white cotton showing beneath: *The Irish
Melodies* of Thomas Moore. We have heard some of these melodies sung
on the old Victrola, a relic from another day. The Victrola—that starts up
when you wind a handle on its side—sits in a corner of the room at the
top of the house, the room with the brass beds. There are piles of records
with a Victor Red Seal to go with the Victrola, some in paper sleeves,
some lying about naked in the dust. On rainy Saturday afternoons when
there is nothing else to do, we sometimes listen to these, John McCormack
singing "The Minstrel Boy":

> The minstrel boy to the war is gone.
> In the ranks of death you will find him.
> His father's sword he has girded on
> And his wild harp slung behind him.

All this is sung in a low steady voice, but when the time comes for "Land
of Song, sang the warrior bard, though all the world betray thee," John
McCormack's voice rises in shrill anguish before it sinks again.

> One sword at least thy rights shall guard
> One faithful heart shall praise thee.

This is the song that Charlie favors; but John McCormack also sings "Believe Me If All Those Endearing Young Charms" and "Mother McCree":

> God bless you and keep you, Mother McCree.

On these words his voice wobbles with the record dipping and falling on the turntable.

A Spider sewed at Night

"A cold house," Kate pronounces, tucking a Kleenex into the sleeve of her sweater. "That's what Grace used to say."

We know Grace mostly by reputation. She lives at a distance and seldom returns to the house. We are in the sitting room, Maddie and I, supposedly doing our homework. Maddie is in fact playing with the ivory elephant letter-opener on Kate's desk; I am stretched out on the floor doing nothing at all. Kate is darning socks. Kate doesn't often sit sewing. She doesn't like it and says she doesn't know how. Even so her finger with the pocked silver thimble on it is raised delicately above the sock stretched across what she calls a darning egg. Behind her chair, against the wall, a bookcase stands on four legs, glassed in with doors you can lock with a key. Inside, more books bought by Willie. This time a set of Thackeray; a set of Dickens: a sheet of filmy paper in front of one volume protecting a picture shows Miss Betsey Trotwood chasing donkeys with a stick.

"And this the warmest room in it," Kate continues, glancing at the radiator beside the chair where she sits.

Maddie and I know that the radiator's dark frame looms larger than any other in the house—rises almost to the windowsill—because many years ago the man with the sad eyes and drooping moustaches was subject to cold. This man looks out at us—like it or not—from the other oval picture frame hanging in the hall, at a little distance from the woman tipsy with twins. He is wearing epaulettes and a jacket buttoned in two brass rows up to his chin because he fought in the Civil War, and afterwards traveled with the navy, among other foreign places, to China and Japan.

He is that woman's father, John Carmody by name. Our own great-grandfather. When as an old man he came to live in this house, when this room was made his own, his daughter and Willie, out of respect for his old bones, had a smaller radiator replaced with the large black one hissing nearby.

We know it is he who brought with him the Buddha who sits on the dark wooden box inlaid with blond belted figures raising swords to each other like crescent moons. Inside the wooden box is a smaller box of tooled metal. It has a lid with a small ivory knob that opens on a sheaf of folded papers covered with Chinese characters. These papers are both tough and very thin, almost transparent, and when we unfold them, release the subtle odor of smoke.

"Did your grandfather die in this house too?" Maddie asks the question: a leap, a subterranean move—surprising neither to Kate nor to me—designed to renew conversations separated by months, sometimes by years.

"Yes, when I was a girl, in the room at the end of the hall."

"He died in my room?"

"Yes, the room you're sleeping in now."

"Oh."

Through the window of the room where we are sitting, the red winter sun is slipping down behind the black bulk of the house on the hill. It is spilling rosy light on the snow. There is a sun like it in the little oil painting that hangs on the wall above the mahogany chest of drawers at the other end of the room. In the painting a pond in the middle of a snowy wood looks as if it has caught fire. Not far away a sun of molten gold is dissolving in a mesh of black branches. What is important about this scene is that no one is there to see it.

The sunset in the picture at times seems more real than the one out the window. Because sometimes it's as if in fact you're not there, even when you're looking out the window at the sun aflame in the winter afternoon, at the shadow of the house on the snow. As if there's another house, another flooding winter sun, another spitting radiator waiting behind this one, and that it would all suddenly blaze before your eyes, like the pond in the woods, if you could only turn and catch it by surprise.

Here is what we know about this man, John Carmody: first, of course, that he is the dead woman's father. We are aware too that he is also someone else's father: a young man we have heard about named Rob, brother of the dead woman. As children, this sister and brother lived in Washington, D.C. We have never seen a picture of Rob but we remember him very well because he was the one who died when he was still a young man. The story of his death is the only thing we know about him. Rob had some kind of fever and was on a ship sailing for Japan, just as his father had sailed years before. One morning very early he was seen walking on the deck of the ship; the next moment no one could find him. This event that no one was there to witness took place in the Pacific Ocean when Rob was in his twenties.

"And your grandfather's wife?"

The silver valve of the radiator is spitting little puffs of steam.

"That was my grandmother, of course. I think she died not long after I was born. Before we moved into this house."

Kate's use of "we" is striking. Before Bert and Maddie and Charlie and I were part of her "we," she had another one that included a whole other set of people. They would be the "we" who had once gone in and out of the room where we are now.

"And did you ever see her?"

"If I did, I was too little to remember. But this thimble belonged to her. Her name, you know, was Mary Ethridge. She's the little girl on the bookcase in the hall."

We know this photograph too. Not a big one hanging from the wall but a very small upstanding oval. Every day we pass the little girl with the pointed chin and dark eyes, but we have a hard time keeping track of who she is. Of course we've been told she is the mother of Rob and of the dead woman, just as John Carmody is their father. But it's confusing because this child who grew up to be our great-grandmother has always seemed younger than ourselves. By the time we are tall enough to take a good look

at her, we have already passed her in age. The little girl on the bookcase seems about five years old. In the photograph she is wearing a dress with a scoop neck. Her hair, smooth and parted on top, gives way all round to a thick cluster of black curls.

"No, certainly I couldn't have seen much of her because at the time I was born, in New York City, she and my grandfather were still living in Washington, D.C. In the house where they'd all lived for many years."

Kate's lips are sealed when it comes to her own mother, but it seems she can find words easily enough when it is time to speak of a grandmother she's scarcely met.

"In Washington where your mother and Rob grew up." We pronounce this fact sternly, because we know Kate has chosen to say "they'd all lived for many years" as a way of avoiding the words "my mother."

Then, perhaps as a way of covering up a lapse she is aware we've noticed, as a way of distracting us from our pouncing appraisals, she rushes to give us information we haven't asked for. "They always said Mary Ethridge fell ill because of the terrible thing that happened to her son." We are intrigued but maintain a reproachful silence.

"They said," Kate pursues recklessly, wrist turning in, turning out, as her needle weaves a crisscross of thread where the sock has worn thin, "that Rob's letters kept arriving long after his parents received the telegram saying he was gone." She looks into our cold eyes and pushes further. "Can you imagine? His mother kept all his letters. And later on gave instructions asking that they be buried with her."

The mind recoils. What kind of people would think up such a thing?

Letters in the hands of a skeleton? Or scattered loosely over a dress of a rich burgundy color, perhaps, a lustrous silk. The dress would now of course be turned to dust. The envelopes mottled with spots of dark mold, not stiff and white, as they had been when the young man had leaned over them, dipping his pen in a jar of ink, scratching the words he had no way of knowing would be his last. Suppose someone had informed him, as he sat there scribbling the address, they'd end up not on a desk or in a drawer, but in a coffin.

"Did your mother tell you all this?"

"No, I don't think so."

"Well, she might have. This was her brother, after all. This was her mother. She might have talked about them."

"She might have." Here Kate is once again in the land of supposition. "Apparently someone must have told me."

Babies pitching over the sides of carriages, young men over the railings of ships into the deep-moving waters of the Pacific. A fall. A fatal fall. Then down into the wormy earth, down onto the silent ocean floor where sharks nuzzled and poked.

The Frost of Death was on the Pane

Kate has scratched her initials and the date—November 18, 1918—into the windowpane of the room where her parents slept. She could not have known at the time that the room, the windowpane, would compose the scene of her own married life, that year in year out she and Bert would go to bed in this room and wake up in it just as those others had done. She could not have known that for the rest of her life she would catch sight of her own initials coming and going. But she must have been aware—as she painstakingly pressed the stone into the screeching glass—of the hickory tree standing on the other side of the pane, of the November sunlight filtering through the yellow leaves still hanging from its forked limbs.

In 1918 Kate would have been eleven years old; November 18 of that year marked the one-week anniversary of the signing at Compiègne of the armistice that ended the Great War. Is it possible Kate had the historical moment in mind when she chose that particular day to cut her initials into the glass?

But the uncanny thing about this event, the truly staggering fact—

recalling her own mother's prescience—is that Kate inscribed on the pane the very day and month that she herself would die in the same room, seventy-odd years later.

Talk not to me of Summer Trees

Kate speaks, always, as if the house is an irritating fact in her life that she continually has to come to terms with, implies that she lives between its four walls only because against her will it has turned out that way. In winter the house is too cold; in summer, it is shrouded in trees.

"No, I never would have chosen a house like this one," she says on rainy summer nights. "All these dripping leaves." Here she shudders and a moment later looks wistful.

"What I've had to do for a mere nothing of a garden! For a few miserable daisies and a clump of peonies."

Bert likes to sit on the porch listening to the smack of drops on the leaves, likes to feel the tulip trees rising in the night around him. "We can cut one down if you like," he says, sitting in the rocking chair with a drink in hand. But it's clear he means only to be obliging. "At the time of the Revolution," he says, "all this must have been a grove. These trees may have been saplings during the days when patriots were hung on Executioner's Light."

Executioner's Light is home to the foghorn whose bleat we hear at daybreak on winter mornings, the foghorn that Bert has told us worked overtime during World War II when convoys leaving Block Island hugged the protection of the shore before passing through the Long Island Sound and on out to sea.

Bert, who moved into the house a little more than a year following his marriage to Kate in 1936, who rakes the autumn leaves and burns them, who unhooks the screens every October replacing them with storm windows, who hauls wood from under the cellar stairs to make fires on winter nights and on Saturday afternoons winds each clock, who climbs a ladder and putties and plasters and paints the crumbling walls and ceilings in one room after the other, over the years making the rounds, is seldom in the land of supposition. He shows us newspaper clippings. He gives us the facts.

The house was built in 1910, only two years before Kate and Grace and their parents moved into it. It was designed by an architect named Orchard. The first owners were Dr. Newell and his wife and they broke the house in by introducing it to unhappiness. After living between its walls for little more than a year, they decided to separate, she to move in with her sister in the next block, he to remain in Pelham as well, but to marry someone else.

The house then was rented to Deirdre and Willie, who signed a one-year lease on April 15, 1912, the day after the prow of the *Titanic* came into violent collision with a massive block of ice. Deirdre and Willie were hoping for a year of recovery "in the country," as they would have put it, following the death of their infant daughter Mary the September before. It was she who had received a fatal blow to her head falling from her carriage onto the marble steps of the Chatsworth, the "residential hotel" where they lived on 72nd Street and Riverside Drive.

And following, as well, a second calamity that occurred one winter morning only four months after the death of little Mary. In the early hours of January 9, 1912, as freezing temperatures overtook the city, Willie found himself trapped in his own safe deposit vaults during the fire that destroyed the Equitable Building at 120 Broadway, directly across the street from old Trinity Church graveyard.

A clipping from a newspaper—yellowed, crumbling at the edges—
describes his rescue:

> Seneca Larke, Jr., a full-blooded Indian of Company 20, advanced un-
> falteringly into the peril zone and sawed through two one and one-half
> inch bars behind which William Conroy was imprisoned. A stream of
> water was played over Larke's head continuously while he worked to fight
> back the flames that threatened to envelop him. Stone and debris were
> falling around him but he never faltered in his efforts until he had saved
> the man.

Willie was taken directly to the Hudson Street Hospital and the next day
brought home in a state that can only be imagined. His shattered nerves
made rest imperative, and no one even considered a return to work until
spring. On the night of May 22, having arranged for the removal of their
belongings from the Chatsworth, Deirdre and Willie—along with John
Carmody and their two remaining children—walked around the corner
to the Ansonia where they spent the night. The following day they took
the train out to Pelham.

It was almost five years later, not long before his death in one of the
rooms upstairs on St. Patrick's Day, 1917, that John Carmody bought the
house for sixteen thousand dollars and hung the deed, bearing Deirdre's
name alone, on the Christmas tree. When Deirdre herself died six years
later she left a will stating that the house was to be held in trust, her
daughters named as the beneficiaries.

Bert likes to describe the evening in October in 1934 when he entered the house for the first time, a windy wet night that was bringing down the leaves. He'd only recently met Kate—she was twenty-seven—and they'd been to the movies to see *It Happened One Night* with Claudette Colbert and Clark Gable. Afterwards he'd escorted Kate home. They walked in together and there was Willie giving a dinner party, white napkins scattered up and down the long table, tall candles burning. In the living room Kate made the introductions: the Morrisseys, the Fitzgeralds, the Riordans, and a sprinkling of priests. As well as Willie himself, who Bert recalls giving him a sharp look from behind twinkling glasses. Someone at the piano was pounding out "The Wearing of the Green." The rest of them, glasses aloft, were singing at the top of their lungs:

> Oh I met with Napper Tandy and he took me by the hand
> And he said how's dear old Ireland and how does she stand?
> She's the most distressful country that I have ever seen
> For they're hanging men and women for the wearing of the green.

About two years later, Kate married Bert and they moved into a small apartment in nearby New Rochelle. But not before Bert had mounted the stairs one Saturday morning, made his way past the books in the hall and entered the room where Willie was waiting "like an emperor on his throne": not before Bert had answered to Willie's satisfaction questions put to him regarding his savings account.

Then, during the summer of '38, accompanied by the infant Charlie, Kate and Bert returned to stay in the large room on the third floor, sleeping in the brass beds. Willie had decided at last to take an apartment in the city and Grace to look for a life on the West Coast from which she was never to return, putting a continent between herself and her losses. The plan was that Kate and Bert would spend the summer in Pelham, looking after the empty house, while it was decided what was to be done with it. As summer turned to fall, they stayed on. These were the years of the Depression and although Bert was employed in the city as an engineer— as he would be throughout his working life—money was scarce and he and Kate could live in the house as cheaply as anywhere.

In 1941 a man named Kennedy came along who was buying up houses in the neighborhood for a song. Bert told Willie—who was apparently handling his daughters' finances, the trust in their name—that whatever Kennedy offered for the house, he, Bert, would top by one thousand dollars. So it was decided: the house was purchased for nine thousand dollars.

It was Bert's name alone that appeared on the deed for more than half a century. Finally, during the fall of 1994, as Kate lay dying in the room upstairs but was still able to handle a pen, she signed the papers that changed the deed of ownership to include her name. This alteration was made at Bert's urging, for tax purposes.

Back from the Cordial Grave I drag thee

When Bert is ninety-five, he likes to sit in the living room with a drink before he goes into the kitchen to cook his dinner. Kate has been dead for five years and he lives on in the house alone. He sits there in the winter evenings, listening to the six o'clock news, swishing the ice cubes in his glass with his finger. He tells us that after he's turned off the radio, he remains there for a while thinking about all the people who have passed through the room—all the people he has seen and talked to, early and late. But there is one, a familiar of the house, that despite his more than sixty years in it, he has never laid eyes on. He thinks about her, too, imagines her passing through the room, stopping for a word.

One September afternoon we help Bert turn the wicker furniture upside down on the screened porch and cover it with plastic drop sheets. We tumble the rocking chair on its face, leave it to the mercy of wind and snow, scimitar rockers slicing the hour.

Afterwards we stand with him beneath the hickory, look up into the branches as into a great height and see the sun winking there between the leaves. The leaves haven't yet begun to turn, but the sun is already pulling in. For once we can see how the sun might appear a star in someone else's constellation.

I learned – at least – what Home could be

The *heavenly hurt* traced to the stab of light on a windowsill, to a netted shadow on the wall: this obscure anguish, in one form or another, may have been bequeathed along with the floors and windows and walls. But is it possible that—just as we are suddenly impaled on some shard of pain left lying around from the past—those who came before were once visited by intimations of the future, by glimmerings of things to come? Could old John Carmody, for example, sitting beside the black radiator in the sitting room, have looked up one drizzly day from the book he was reading with a premonition of happiness, have been visited by a moment still three generations distant, that split second when Maddie would look up from her own book with exactly the same expression of joy?

A Wounded Deer – leaps highest

"You say she wasn't very well, your mother, but it sounds as if maybe she wasn't very forceful. Did you ever think that's why you don't remember her? Because she didn't make much of an impression?"

We took what there was and returned to it—sometimes deliberately overstating the case—so that Kate might be involuntarily stung into revealing some new fact. Theories, any theories we might offer, were sure to provoke her. But particularly those that implicitly exonerated her from the sin of wiping her own mother clean from memory. Because we felt it a terrible fault in her, this forgetfulness, this sublime erasure, and were eager to offer excuses that would place the blame elsewhere.

"She was very forceful, my mother. Very." Kate shot us her green-eyed glare.

"It doesn't sound that way."

"Well, she was, I can assure you."

"It's not to find fault with her, but don't you think there are some people you have a hard time remembering? You know, who don't make much of an impression? I suppose you could say they don't have much personal force, if you want to call it that."

"I don't see why you press me, when I've already told you things you don't seem to remember."

"What things?"

But Kate will say nothing more.

We understand only that she will not hear her mother criticized, nor will she countenance any theories that would excuse lapses of her own. When pushed to the wall, she will make us the perpetrators, the ones guilty of forgetting.

We are careful not to goad Kate again. It occurs to us for the first time that there might be a dark space, a gap in perception, between what Kate in fact remembers and what she says she does. Is it perhaps a matter of will, a stubborn reluctance that drives her silence?

Or is it possible that the failure of memory is in fact our own?

I see thee better – in the Dark –

A dream belonging to someone in the house. Or maybe to each of us, one at a time, at intervals of years. In the dream the one dreaming is five years old and is standing in the room upstairs where she takes her afternoon nap after coming home from morning kindergarten. She's tired of staring at the pictures in the book—Babar and the old king who has sickened and died after eating a poison mushroom. She's looking around for something else to do.

Suddenly, but not at all surprisingly, there appears at the window open on the fall afternoon the immense head of an elephant, an elephant so large that one of his wise old eyes fills the entire window. The child and the elephant regard each other for a long moment. Then he puts his trunk through and tenderly wraps the end of it around her hand.

But the dreamer says nothing of this to anyone. For one thing, she isn't sure what she's dreamt. Sometimes she thinks the elephant hasn't been so benevolent after all. No, his ears are fanning back and forth in fury, something has been taken from him, his tusk, his precious ivory. He is beside himself for want of what he cannot do without.

Or maybe the elephant isn't in a rage at all. Maybe she just imagines he *could* be in a rage if he wanted to be. It may be that to her everlasting woe it was she who couldn't give herself up to his perfect kindness, that this has been the cause of all her grief, that at the last moment she had been beset by fears that she would not survive the heat of his love. What she thinks she may have dreamt is that even while his trunk was sweetly wrapped around her hand, even in the midst of a moment of surpassing peace, she had been seized by the suspicion that he might suddenly pick her up and smash her up against the wall. And so her fears and doubts had spoiled everything.

Uncertainty, that's one reason for silence. Could it be, too, that the dreamer's reluctance to tell the dream has to do with some blind loyalty, some unshakable confidence in its seductions? In its heart-stopping appeal? Hence the fear that to haul it up, dripping, would be to risk its spectacular charm?

It's enough, waking, for the dreamer to find herself in a place where she has become a stranger, the rooms where she was last at home with the beloved, the one now hidden away, who against every hope she discovered waiting there in the afternoon beside her, available for tender looks, for sorrow and tears, for the boundless joy of tomorrow.

To announce her dream may be a sure way to become someone who is looking through the bars of a locked gate at a house she no longer has the right to enter. Why should the elephant at the window who puts his trunk through and tenderly, confidingly, takes her by the hand be regarded by her daytime self as ridiculous? Or worse, be assigned meanings, be tagged, rendered commonplace, torn limb from limb?

Her difficulty in remembering what happens in the waking world may involve a fear of disloyalty. Instead of turning them in her fingers, she drops the precious beads over the side of the boat, allowing them to return from whence they came, to rest at the bottom of her own fathomless sea, undisturbed. There they are safe from the gradual erosion of recorded memory, from the vagueness that comes with touching something too often, from the insidious betrayals involved in fitting the tale to the expectations of the listener.

Me, change! Me, alter!

And then, in a moment, all our notions, our ideas, are overturned. We are making beds one day, changing the sheets, when Kate, in a sudden burst of gaiety, does something unprecedented. She offers us a story, unasked.

"She said we'd play a trick on my father. That we'd make his bed with one sheet short. 'A French bed,' she called it."

What?

Maddie and I, by then old enough to make something of this, are quick to interpret. She didn't like him in bed, that much was clear, wanted to keep him from getting in between the sheets. Or was it just the opposite, was it that she wanted to prevent his crawling into his own bed so that he would get into hers? We knew practical jokes always involved some impulse to cruelty, the wish to see someone undone. Willie the banker, we decided, was a prig, laced in by fear of his own desire. Safe deposit boxes. Things locked away. Precious things behind bars. And she was punishing him for punishing her.

Or could it have been this was their kind of joke? Some bizarre come-on? That they would laugh their heads off at this sort of thing and then collapse into each other's arms.

And there is something else as well. Although we are old enough to imagine Willie as impossible in every way, a pious old scoundrel, we are not old enough to know that to make of someone else a villain is to leave oneself wide open to the possibility of becoming the very thing despised. Because how can you see as a danger to yourself the qualities you are so firm in condemning?

Who occupies this House?
A Stranger I must judge

One evening I'm standing in the hall with Kate, contemplating the photograph of herself as a child looking over her mother's elbow at the infant twins.

"Do you remember when that was taken?" I ask. I'm fourteen, now, and old enough to have learned at least one tone of voice in which to invite confidences.

It's a rainy Saturday night in early November and Charlie has gone into the city to see the Rangers play at Madison Square Garden. Bert sits reading by John Carmody's radiator, and Maddie is staying overnight with a friend. There's nothing for me to do, nothing except sort laundry and put it away in closets and drawers, the stack of folded shirts and socks and underwear that Kate has carried upstairs and put down with a sigh on the chair beneath the picture. The skirted light with the swirling porcelain top hat fixes the woman with the dark glossy hair.

Our ordinary life that carries us up the stairs and into the rooms and down is at low ebb. Last week Bert fit the square key of each clock onto its peg and wound the hands back one hour so that now night falls early. This is a season between seasons. The few remaining leaves are falling with the rain onto sodden grass. Soon the branches will be stripped. But in the morning, there is still no frost along the edges of the windowpanes to scrape with a fingernail, no jab of pain as a sliver of ice pierces beneath. Tonight only the rain lashing the dark windows, falling dully on the slates of the roof. If it didn't seem too much trouble, it would be time to ask certain questions. What is the difference between last night and this one? What is the difference between this year and next? Is this our life we are living? And if not, whose is it?

Kate is pensive. "I think I do remember," she says. "The photographer told me to look at one of the babies and I deliberately looked at the other. I suppose I didn't like being told what to do."

"And look at that huge bow in your hair," I say. "You must have hated sitting still while someone fussed with that."

"I didn't want anyone to touch it. But that was another time. When I was older, maybe eight or nine."

"You probably hated them yanking at your hair."

This has become my canny new way of encouraging Kate to talk. Heartily agree with her, push her forward a little in the line she seems to be pursuing, nudge her along. If in doubt, say nothing. And never pronounce the words "your mother."

"No, it wasn't that," Kate says.

"Oh."

"I didn't *like* it, but that wasn't it."

"No."

"I was determined that no one else would touch it."

"Oh?"

"It was because she'd been the last one to tie it."

This is startling, but I take a moment before responding. We are still standing there brooding over the photograph in its oval frame, at the woman with the averted face, at the slumbering babies, one in each of her arms, at Kate in her little white boots with the buttons up the side.

"It would seem so easy."

"What would seem so easy?"

"Well, she might have just tied it again."

"Yes, that's what you'd think."

"Yes."

"But you know it wasn't so easy."

"No."

"It wasn't always so easy."

"No."

"Deedy wasn't always very well."

"Deedy? Who's Deedy?"

Kate is bending down to pick up Charlie's brown corduroy trousers, folded at the top of the pile. "That's what we called my mother."

And from the simplicity of her answer, the matter-of-fact quiet with which she speaks, as if explaining something plain as day to any stranger, I realize I know less than nothing about anything that has come before.

The Sheeted Dead

By heaven, I'll make a ghost of him that lets me!

I was fifteen, home from school recovering from the flu, upstairs on the third floor in one of the brass beds. Thoroughly fed up with it all. Everyone was out that winter afternoon—Maddie and Charlie in school, Kate somewhere, Bert in the city—so the house was empty. What was I doing? Reading *Hamlet* for my tenth-grade English class. When I reached the end of Act I, I got out of bed and started downstairs.

From the landing I looked down at John Carmody staring sadly out from his gilded frame, imagined his sloping eyes following me as I descended the last step or two. May have been reminded, that day, by the creak of my bare feet on the stairs, of "the gibber and squeak" of those others, the sheeted dead. But I recall quite clearly that looking around the corner into the sitting room, where icicles hung in the window, everything struck me as fixed for all time. In silence. Immobility.

For instance, the massive mahogany bureau standing on clawed feet, the shiny round knobs of its drawers unblinking in the afternoon. Idly, thinking of nothing at all, I pulled open the little side-by-side drawers at the top, first one, then the other. Everything again just as before: paper clips and rubber bands, a pair of scissors in the shape of a stork, a silver gadget used to puncture holes in paper.

Next I yanked at the knobs on one of the huge lower drawers below and it swung open, tipping down. Here again, the same old mass of confusion: yellow legal pads, untouched; notebooks bound in stiff cardboard mottled green and white; folders with ragged newspaper cuttings spilling out of them; pince-nez in a case that clapped open and shut; a green enamel

43

ashtray; tiny opera glasses in a silk case. I'd seen all this before, had looked into the drawer and closed it, dismissed its clutter as part of the deadly ennui that covered every surface of the house like ash. Boredom, that was the mood of it. As if a volcano had erupted long ago and everything had been left exactly in place, frozen for all time, transfixed.

I dipped my hand further into the drawer and pulled out a ledger, long and narrow, bound in canvas the color of moss. It was written closely with numbers, long rows extending down the page. Not in Kate's handwriting or Bert's. I put it back, continued rooting amidst the crumbling edges of old paper. Rising from my fumblings, the scent of dust, ancient exhalations.

Then my fingers closed on something that had the feel of velvet, of soft suede. I drew it out and discovered in my grasp a thick fawn-colored notebook held together with a dark red string tied firmly in a knot. The string had been wound several times one way, then the other, so that the book's soft brown cover was stamped with a blood-red cross. I took the stork scissors from one of the little drawers and with its sharp beak worked open the knot, untangled the string.

The pages of the book that fell open—and there is no suppose about *this;* if I like I can at this instant hold the book in my hand—were covered from top to bottom in bold handwriting, long flat strokes linking one word to the next, as if the writer had been going at full speed. But the curious thing was that on many pages there were pencil sketches, as if someone had first made the drawings on the bare blank paper and later filled in the space around them with writing. On one page, a sketch of two infants lying side by side, curled in sleep; on another, a dormer window poking out from a roof. There were watercolors, too: a child in a crimson cap; yellow daffodils in a clump, some still sheathed in cool green, others with their trumpets raised against a sky washed gray.

Then I turned a page and found there drawn in painstaking detail an object I thought I knew intimately but couldn't place. What was it, anyway, this swirling column standing like a candle in a saucer? And from where did I know it?

With a chill I realized I had only to lift my eyes to find it just as always fixed on the wall next to the door. Someone had made a close study of what I thought of as the porcelain top hat that spun above the frosted skirted shade on the electric bulb. The light fixture identical to the one in the hall lighting up the woman with twins.

At first I couldn't make out a word. I contented myself with looking at the pictures. Beneath the child in the crimson cap, dark curls winding beneath, the word *TATIE* was written in block letters. On a page further on, an ink-and-wash sketch of a child—again with dark curls—sweeping with a small broom, head lowered with intent.

Long horizontal dashes flew across the paper—*T*s were crossed with a line of two inches, a word was carried into the next by a flat, firm extension of its final letter—so that the page with all its strokes up and down, the letters *y, p,* and *f* each with a mast of its own as well as a plunge, looked as if it were driven along by a strong wind, like a ship in full sail. That was the impression. There was one letter that appeared frequently and standing by itself that looked like a capital *L.* But on closer inspection it turned out to be an *I.*

I wish I could describe Tatie exactly as she is today on her third birthday so in years to come she could see herself as her mother sees her now.

That was the first sentence I made out. Then:

An energetic little maid full of life and health. She has a loving sunshiny disposition, which includes an occasional April storm. Her eyes are green, fringed with long black lashes. I dislike seeing the baby looks fade but a sturdy independent little character is emerging, and I am already looking forward to the companionship this will mean in years to come.

I was glancing to the date at the top of the page—April 12, 1910—when I was roused by Kate's key in the back door, the sound of her feet crossing the kitchen floor. Quick as a flash, I thrust the book to the bottom of the drawer and made my way stealthily up to the top floor so that by the time I heard Kate's voice, calling from below, I was back in the brass bed and had already opened *Hamlet* to Act II.

—But why the secrecy?

Because I'd glimpsed, written in bold black letters on the flyleaf, the word *Carmody.* That was her name before she married Willie and became Deirdre Conroy. Although of course she must have been married already if she was writing about Tatie, whom I immediately took to be Kate.

The fact is *Carmody* is my name as well, my middle name, given to me in unspeaking memory. My uncanny bond with the woman no one could recall. If I was her walking girl, she was my ghost, my indispensable passport to the world of the gone. It was Kate who had made me Deirdre's

45

namesake, and Kate who had allowed Deirdre to go down into the pit like those forsaken among the dead, like those you remember no more. Left her own mother without a snatch of story to cover her white bones with. Tapping at the window, crying at the lock. So. The two of us together, unclaimed.

—In reading Deirdre's journal you imagined you were reading the book of yourself?

Of course the Deirdre who'd kept the journal had been a grown woman, a mother writing about her child. All that seemed very far away. But turning the pages I felt the shiver of a ghost at my side, woke up to the fact that the world I lived in, the house itself, had been written down years before I was born, inscribed.

—And reading, did you think the ghost wanted anything of you? Was making an appeal?

Not till years later did I feel the urgency of an appeal, on an afternoon I'll soon tell you about. But in those days, I thought nothing of that. I wanted only to read a book written by someone whose name was my own. To read a book with *Carmody* written on its flyleaf. Someone, moreover, who'd gone up and down the stairs in the house where I lived, the house I'd grown so tired of. Perhaps, after all, I did hope to find myself in her book?

What's certain is that in the days that followed I furtively returned to the bureau again and again. At first it was only to the fawn notebook tied with the red string, it was to gape and feel: *here* her fingers had touched as mine did in this instant: above *this* page her pen had hovered and dipped into a pool of words. Then it was to trace the words, to make sentences of the flying script, to turn the pages with no consciousness of what I was doing. And after weeks of gawking and stroking and fumbling with the red string, after the journal had been consumed in secret moments when no one was aware what I was up to, I reached further into the drawer and one by one, over months of secret sessions and finally years, drew out tablets and tattered notebooks with the pages loose in them, albums and ledgers, scrapbooks into which letters had been pasted, address books, pages held together at the corner by a bright gold pin; copybooks crammed at the seams with loose poems cut from newspapers; articles, invitations, calling cards, train schedules, maps, menus, postcards; a leather-bound daybook with a little loop on the side to hold a pencil; packets of letters tied with string, letters loose all over the drawer.

Who had put them there? The dead. The dead who at the time they were on their feet had lived in the house: Deirdre, of course. And Willie Conroy and John Carmody as well. But not all composed, compiled, within the house. Not by any means.

The opening pages of the fawn notebook, in fact, the notebook in which I'd discovered the house incarnate, were written in New York City, in the apartment building where Willie and Deirdre and her father all lived before moving to Pelham. Where Kate had been born. And the twins, too.

And where, so many years later, I would have a startling encounter.

The Chatsworth

Despite the fact that Martin and I have lived in Morningside Heights for almost thirty years and 72nd Street is only a few subway stops away, I'd never set foot in the place. At some point, sifting through the contents of the drawer, I must have come across this loose newspaper clipping advertising the building when it was new. But had paid little attention.

Designed in the most lavish Beaux Arts Style with finely carved stonework and ironwork. Apartments of 5 to 15 rooms renting from $1000 to $4500 a year. Views are panoramic and cannot be duplicated in New York. The Chatsworth combines elegance with every modern convenience boasting its own electricity generator, refrigerator plant, conservatory, billiard parlor, café, barbershop, valet, hairdresser, and tailor.

—Was your decision to visit the Chatsworth a sudden one?

It was not. There had been the evening in July of the ginkgos turning in the light, and then the dream that night of death by water. The next morning, waking slowly, it was the Chatsworth I thought of, for no apparent reason. But I see now the dream had pointed the way.

Because the images my dream made use of were not the stuff of my own memory, not things I myself had seen and remembered. They were fragments belonging to the memory of someone I'd never laid eyes on, someone who was drawing me forward. Without my knowledge, it was a scrap of burgundy brocade I went in search of: the piece of fabric that was swallowing my ink, consuming the written word I wish above all things to bequeath to my daughters.

Although I didn't know it at the time, my dream life had never been my own. I was a territory occupied by strangers who swarmed my imagination by night, had their will of me by day.

—What brought you at last to the house of dreams?

Could it have been the tide of fear rising in the city around me following that September dawn of liquid light? The imperative to name the stranger? After all, who could they be, these faceless ones? And how had it come to be we'd all been seized? Or perhaps what started me was simply the sight of the ginkgos, what Kate would have called "grace." The unbidden moment when the world reveals itself to our wandering, distracted gaze.

—And what had kept you away for so long?

Above all, I'd wanted to forge a life separate from Kate's, separate from all those others she couldn't remember. I wanted to believe my life was of my own making. Martin and I had lived in Africa, in Europe, and when we returned to this city in our thirties I didn't like to think that my forebears had preceded me here. Although the city allows anonymity, it's true that most of my adult life I have lived only a half hour's ride—by car or train— from the house where I grew up. I kept an uneasy distance. Yes, perhaps it was after all Kate's death, my own children's transformation into adults, that propelled me that July afternoon to do what might have seemed so simple: to take the subway down to 72nd Street.

Of course I knew the Chatsworth by sight, even from the earliest times. As children, on the excursion we made into the city every Christmas with Kate and Bert to visit some old cousins who lived at One Fifth Avenue, we'd be asked to pay homage. Somewhere on our way down the West Side

Drive—soon after passing the roller coaster that hung out over the cliffs of the Palisades—Bert would break his customary silence. "It's coming up on the left," he'd call out. "Bow your heads as we pass." Hunched in the back of the black Chevrolet, sullen and silent, protesting the tyranny of a family outing, as adolescents we declined.

But when we were children, Maddie and Charlie and I had eagerly strained to look and there it would be, rising like a lonely specter just on the edge of Riverside Drive, its towering rows of bay windows gazing up the Hudson. At that time I may not even have connected the Chatsworth with a photo I knew well, a photo taken of our infant mother in long white baby clothes, held in the arms of that unnamed one, the woman who had called her baby Kate. Behind them, in a mirror hanging above a little dresser on which rested two cut-crystal scent bottles, each plugged with a stopper, is reflected the back of the figure sitting with the baby in her lap, the slender waist, the row of buttons running straight down her spine.

If Charlie and Maddie and I had recalled the story of the little lost twin as we sat slouched in the back of the black Chevrolet, the story would have spun differently in each of our imaginations. Even in the unlikely event that we remembered it. Because the story had been told to us in fits and starts, over years, so that at last whatever there was of narrative seemed to have no necessary sequence, no beginning and no end. Rather it was all a grab bag of "it might have been" and "they always said" and "no, you wouldn't think so, would you" that could be arranged in any order you liked, according to the day or hour.

The only constant in Kate's telling of the story was the scene where it had taken place: the steps of the building where they'd lived. That was certain. But to us the event described seemed to have occurred in some atmosphere of myth, to have happened to people who were as unknown as any of the dead in some legend from long ago. So that if we had been told that the catastrophe could have been helped, if by some freak chance we had been given the power to say, "No, let this not happen," it's not at all sure we would have chosen to prevent it.

Over time the story had come to seem the shadow pressed against the back of the trees, the brilliant dark outlining.

One sultry day in July Kate's little twin sister had tumbled from her carriage and hit her head. The carriage had been on its way down the steps of the Chatsworth and Mary had been in it. She was just short of fourteen months at the time. The dying had taken many weeks.

We knew that Deirdre, the twins' mother, had not been present. This fact was stressed. But she had given careful instructions. She had told whoever it was taking the twins out to be very careful going down the steps. She must leave Mary and Grace at the top and then, after the carriage was at the bottom, securely settled on the sidewalk, she must carry each one down separately with every care. This is what she had not done. She had put the twins in the carriage and bumped them down the steps and one had fallen out and hit her head on the marble step. The carriage may have been one of those wicker affairs sitting high on enormous wheels you see in old photographs. It may have been wobbly on its wheels; its lofty balance may have been precarious.

The twin fell from quite a height. At one moment she was sitting in the carriage, rosy-cheeked and blue-eyed, tucked into a white cotton sweater, perhaps. The next her skull was cracking against a surface with the hard brilliance of ice.

What's certain is that Mary died more than two months later, a lingering death that allowed plenty of time for visits by numerous doctors, for daily records of weight loss, for sudden, recurring convulsions, for nights of frozen bedside watching, for snatched promises and prayers, for wild hopes disappointed time and again, for a slow collapse into disbelief and horror.

So it happened that—compelled by visions of a lost child, by a dream of brocade—I found myself one hot July afternoon taking the subway down to the old 72nd Street station with its swinging mahogany doors and brass fittings. And what did I see, coming up from below, there at the intersection of Amsterdam and Broadway?

In the distance, at the far end of 72nd, the vast Dakota, a crouching shadow. To the north—above the dusty sycamores in Verdi Square—the Apple Bank for Savings: in digital numbers, the time (3:46) and temperature (87). And beyond that, the glinting white brilliance of the Ansonia, its gables and arches, its turrets and towers, rising against the blue.

Crossing to the sidewalk, following the gentle slope of 72nd Street west to the river, I caught sight of the Chatsworth itself: even in profile, all Beaux Arts exuberance. Cherubs lolling on cornices, antlered heads of deer peering out at the park. A cornucopia spilling what looked to be pomegranates, clusters of grapes, fruits of the earth in stone.

Drawing closer, I examined—above the entrance, marked with the number 344—the serene stone face of a woman, hair waving back from her forehead in the manner of Athena, staring with blank blind eyes into the afternoon. On either side of her a cherub rested a chubby arm on the scalloped shell that framed her face like a fan. But in terrible contrast with her blithe beauty, as if they had seen what she could not, these children had abandoned themselves to grief, their mouths pulled awry in energetic weeping.

And then, looking down, I saw the steps: marble of a slightly pinkish cast, speckled and glinting in the harsh afternoon light. But only three— and rather low ones at that, not steep at all.

After the glitter of sunlight on stone, the interior was dim. But here again, the same impression of studied grandeur: the high hard glaze of parquet floors offset by dark mahogany walls that absorbed the shadows, by walls broken at intervals by the shining arch of a mirror, by a panel of old silk brocade the color of burgundy.

The place was deserted, not a soul in sight. At the far end of the immense lobby, a mosaic floor replaced the parquet, tiny squares of black, white, and orange tile jostling each other at odd angles, like teeth that over time have rearranged themselves inside a mouth. Two elaborate elevator cages waited nearby. Above them, a single dusty ray of sunlight pierced the air shafts.

I'd looked around and was on my way out when I paused in a space I'd scarcely noticed in passing, a long transept of sorts. At one end a little tufted sofa covered in the same silk burgundy brocade squatted in the shadows, white cotton spilling out through slits in the old silk. Above it, a worn mirror glimmered blank and stupid in a gilded frame, the zinc plate showing through.

In the distance, at the opposite end of the transept, an immense baronial fireplace loomed in a dark recess. For a closer look, I crossed and saw that the fireplace was made of the same pink marble as the steps. Was it possible that yellow and blue flames once leapt between its massive andirons? That someone on a cold night stood listening to the crackle and hiss, the deep underwater roar, pondered how at any moment the fire might escape and shoot up the walls, run along the ceiling? Light up with a transfiguring blaze this unholy pile of marble and glass and stone?

Turning my back on the fireplace, turning once again toward the recess from which I'd come, I became aware by degrees that from across the way someone was looking out at me, a pale face was flickering there in the brightness. For a moment I was seized by the old fear of walking into a room familiar from birth and only slowly coming to realize that I was not alone. Without my noticing, someone had been there all along, someone I'd never laid eyes on, watching me from afar and now awaiting my return.

Then, in the still flat light of afternoon, in a silence thick with smothered voices, I saw that the face looking out from the other side, the face of the stranger, was neither more nor less than my own. And yet this face, the one I was contemplating in the mirror filling up with shadows, was not the face I called mine.

Part Two

Willie and Deirdre

I had seen the Hudson River flowing alongside the Chatsworth, was aware it was carrying us all out to sea. A river swept by tides. That much was clear. But the dream had also told me I was writing in ignorance, that the tattered brocade of a century ago was absorbing my ink, that my words were being swallowed by a detail someone else had observed in one of the supreme moments of her life: Deirdre. Or so I imagined following my afternoon visit to the Chatsworth. But who was she, this woman who like myself had given birth to three daughters? And where had she come from? Because it seemed that if I could attempt to answer these questions, even in some small, mistaken way, I would be responding to what I'd at last recognized as an appeal: *Remember me!* And I knew without a doubt that it was only by honoring some promise from long ago—a promise I have no clear memory of making, the promise itself perhaps some forgotten legacy—that I had any chance of stumbling on a speaking language of my own.

So I begin with Willie, my grandfather, and the story he told of how he came to know Deirdre: Willie, who for reasons still obscure to me I've appointed the foil, the false paragon, the villain of my tale. Willie, the terrifying specter who stands in wait. The typescript before me—his life-account from which the story is taken—is undated. If there was once another version in Willie's own handwriting, it has been lost.

The first time I recall seeing Deirdre is as a little girl of five or six, in Ilion, coming down West Street with her brother, the two children followed by their father and mother. Both her parents had grown up in the Mohawk Valley and often returned from Washington to visit.

John Carmody's sister, Elizabeth, was married to Edmond Roche of Ilion, and later, of Utica and it was he who for many years was my brother John's business partner in the coal business.

The next I recall of her was when she was about fourteen and visiting her cousin Agnes Roche in Utica. She and Agnes came down to Ilion to go with a party on a picnic up the Gulph from Ilion. She stopped at my brother John's office to see him. I was there sitting behind a high desk and paid no attention to her until John called to me: "Will, don't you know Deirdre Carmody is here?" Then I went out in front and spoke to her. After we were married she used to tease me, saying John had had to make me come from behind my desk to greet her.

In the summer of 1895, when I was twenty-five years old and she was twenty, her father wrote me asking if I would meet his daughter at the Pennsylvania Station in Jersey City and escort her across New York to the Grand Central Station where she was to take the train to Utica. At that time I was working at 120 Broadway in the Equitable Building and I had only to walk a few blocks and take the ferry across. I met her at Jersey City and we came over on the return ferry to Cortlandt St. There I wanted to take a cab but she was not willing and we went by the elevated. She was a stylish girl, a bit shy, and I certainly was attracted. She, too, was agreeable, for she told me she was expecting, on her return from Utica, to visit her aunt, her mother's sister, in Brooklyn, where her uncle, David Gregg, was pastor of the Lafayette Avenue Presbyterian Church. She promised to let me know when she arrived at the Greggs, and asked me to come over to call. Which I did.

I had never been to Washington, so late that fall I decided to go and once there went to call on the Carmodys. Perhaps it would be more accurate and truthful to say I went to call on her. From that time on I continued to see her in New York when she visited the Greggs, and we wrote once in awhile but without any regularity. I was fond of her and she seemed glad to see me. But I had only a small amount of money saved up from my salary. I knew she had been carefully brought up and was accustomed to good living and I knew I could not afford to marry her and give her the comforts she had at home. I was not in a hurry to marry and was unwilling to become engaged until I had accumulated some money and felt able to support a wife in some comfort.

I suppose the first real shock that made me realize how much she was to me and how much I cared for her was January 9, 1903, when she sent me a telegram saying she was to be operated on that evening for appendicitis and asking me to pray for her. At the moment I received the telegram, I was getting ready to go to a dance. It destroyed all interest in the dance and instead I went to bed worried and distressed. She had a good recovery from the operation but was left weak and tired. Nor was her mother at all well following the death of her brother a few years earlier. The summer after her operation she and her parents left for Ireland and I went over to Philadelphia to see them off.

I had already made my own first visit to Ireland a few years earlier, in fact during the summer of 1896, accompanied by my good friend Stuart Chambers who later became a priest. The circumstances of my first trip abroad were these:

By June of that year I had my tickets and the whole trip outlined. One day about ten days before I was to sail, Mr. Henry B. Hyde, president of The Equitable Life Assurance Society, sent for me and said he understood I was soon to go on vacation. I told him that was my plan and asked what I could do for him. He then said not to worry about my vacation as he would see that I got it but perhaps not at that time. He told me he wanted me to go to Chicago to acquire some information for him. He gave me the instructions and I went the next day. I spent four days in Chicago, then telegraphed that I was leaving for New York.

The day I returned was a very hot day, all the awnings were down. When I arrived at the office there was a message that I was to go up to see Mr. Hyde at once. I found him with his coat, vest, collar and tie off, trying to get cool. He asked me if I had the information and I showed him a pencil report I had written on the train.

He read it over and turning to me put his arm around my shoulders. "Conroy," he said, "there isn't another man in the country who could get that information in the same amount of time. I have been trying for six months to get it. When were you planning to go on vacation?" I told him and he asked if I had ever been abroad. I told him I had not. He called his clerk and told him to give me a sum of money. This sum was sufficient to pay the cost of the trip.

But to return to my story: I went to Washington in 1905 to spend Deirdre's birthday with her, April 1, with the intention of asking

57

her to marry me. On her birthday she and I settled the matter between us and the next day talked it over with her father and mother and received their consent and approval.

But there is an occasion before we were married that I particularly remember. One summer she was visiting friends in New London and I left New York Saturday night to spend Sunday there with her. She came into New London where I met her. When I saw her walking toward me that morning I thought she was the loveliest girl I had ever seen. She was dressed in a summer gown of a lilac color with lavender sweet peas at her waist and she carried a white parasol. The summer after her death I went to Ireland and called on my dear old friend, Mrs. Murray, at Rostrevor. The reception room was filled with sweet peas ranging from white to lavender or purple in color. At once I remembered the lovely girl with the lavender sweet peas.

We were married October 25, 1905, in Washington. The bride looked lovely that day and I was very proud of her. I remember that the programme of music included her favorite song, "Believe Me If All Those Endearing Young Charms." We had a jolly time at the reception and then about five o'clock started on our honeymoon. We went to Martinsburg, West Virginia, to a farm. It was raining most of our wedding day but when we arrived at our destination it was pouring. Deirdre always made a joke, saying that I immediately went to sleep when getting on the train and snored most of the way there.

Fawn Notebook

Did I mention it's beautiful, the fawn suede? A beautiful book? The scarlet string, wrapped one way, then the other, crisscrossing the soft brown, makes you think of blood-red oak leaves in November. And then, opening the book, turning the pages, you marvel at the flying words, the lovely muted wash of the watercolors.

Her entire collection of journals and sketches shows how keenly she felt along her nerves the vanishing moment. But the fawn notebook—a lengthy address to her children at a time when they were still too small to read, an address begun in the Chatsworth—makes clear that her need to remember did not stop with herself. She was quite consciously working to establish a memory bank in her children's name.

Here's an entry for another of Kate's birthdays:

> *April 12, 1911*
> *I wonder if you will remember this day, your fourth birthday.*
> *Although the rain was falling this morning on the gray river, by*
> *afternoon a green mist along the trees was shining in the sun. We*
> *had a white cake with four pink candles—and Mary and Grace*
> *sitting on the sofa for guests! Another year they will be big enough to*
> *enjoy the day with us. For now they are still little babies only eleven*
> *months old today and have never seen a birthday yet.*

The fawn notebook is addressed directly *to* the children, a letter the length of all its pages. She's invested in selecting their memories, shaping them. She's laying away images as in a cedar box protected from moths.

September 11, 1910
Is it possible that tomorrow, twins, you will be four months old?
It has been a comfort watching you grow as you were once so tiny,
Grace 4½ lbs and Mary 4 lbs even. Indeed we were afraid of
losing you in your bathtub so Lillian and I bathed you in our laps
and rubbed you with olive oil. We fed you with a glass medicine
dropper—five drops made a meal. Twice weekly we weighed you and
kept the chart you may someday like to see.

Grace was fair and had a voice like seven lions howling in the
woods, and Mary was very dark and cried like the little lamb who
had lost her mother. You had to lie in your big basket surrounded by
five fat hot-water bottles to keep you snug and warm.

I wish you could see yourselves as your mother sees you today in long
white dresses lying on the bed kicking your feet and turning your
heads to and fro in your excitement to take in everything in this big
new world!

How can you help noticing—what would you call it?—something cloying in the tone, something altogether too delighted with itself. Bespeaking ambivalence, I think. The mark of all she forbade herself to say. Oh yes, in writing with "us" constantly in mind—because it's my further conviction that she wrote not only for her children but for theirs—she censored herself. That's clear. She emphatically did not wish to bequeath a record of anguish.

There's nothing in the fawn notebook that would even faintly require a lock on the drawer: the drawer, as it turned out, in the massive chest in the sitting room where her book ended up, ignored. Deirdre meant her book to be preserved, the official story, a family account. And so—with a book so lavishly prepared—fear of an audience must have broken in. Fear of the eyes looking over her shoulder, reading her words so many years in the future.

—Could Deirdre have been the conduit of an inherited fear like your own? Was she subject to her own hauntings?

Perhaps she was afraid, like myself, of losing her innocence, of betraying others: her own mother, recently dead; Tatie, the twins, whose care must certainly have roused feelings of exhausted frustration and anger as well as delight. And yes, I believe she was aware of her own ghosts. Aware that she was caught between the need to speak and fear of the consequences.

—What are those consequences? And do you fear them yourself?

I do fear them. What I imagine is this: I'll make an urgent call, the phone will ring and ring but no one will pick up. Will they disown me, the living? My children, for instance. Will I die before I can reach them to make amends? As to the dead, I fear the revenge the ghosts may take for my betrayals. Something has been stolen from the kindly old elephant. His tusk, his precious ivory. He wraps his trunk around the child's waist and bashes her head up against the wall. But it may be that I will take revenge on myself. In a paroxysm of grief, of regret.

—So Deirdre bequeathed these fears to you, and to Kate before you. At this instant are you aware of a grief you cannot speak of?

Yes. I will try to set it down now before it's too late. I leave my baby daughter—barely a month—in the middle of a large low bed. I am in the next room, tending to my other small children. The baby is crying. She cries and cries and then the crying stops. I go into the room and to my horror see that she's fallen, she is lying on the floor, face down. Her tiny lip has a drop of blood on it. I snatch her up, terrified. I am wild with fear. I tremble. I cannot sleep that night. I have dreams.

—And then?

The baby wakes in the night and I nurse her. She is "all right." There is nothing to say she has been injured. No trace of her fall the next day. I say to myself that she did not fall on the back of her head but on her face! Her face! The demands of the next morning sweep me into what will be the rest of my life. But there have been other mornings that have swept me into what will be the rest of my life. Even now I don't know if the fall—of which my daughter has no conscious memory—has made the least difference in her life or if it has marked her in some unknown way.

—Are you lost now in a spasm of guilt and anxiety?

What I thought could not be said has been said. I shall not forget.

—Deirdre was perhaps the same, resembling anyone who, against all odds, wants to rescue from obscurity a moment that has lain across her life like a sword.

Then she was like the man on his way to the guillotine? You know the story? He cried out, asking as his dying wish that the tumbrel be stopped and he be allowed pen and paper. He was given them, on the assumption he had a final word to address to someone. But no: he wished to make a note for himself of something that had caught his eye. On the extreme margin of life, this condemned man feels the urgent need to record in ink the black-haired woman who raised her hand to him as he passed. A woman in a blue woolen cloak standing on cobblestones glazed with rain.

So Deirdre paints her fluted daffodils. Records a catastrophe. And in doing so, leaves undeniable evidence that she too passed this way.

The Fall

October 1, 1910
Dear little Mary plays with her little silk shirt sleeve all day long.
With her right hand she holds fast the sleeve of her left and tugs and
plays with it whenever she is not sleeping or eating!

October 10
My dear little twins were christened today—or rather the ceremony
was completed for they were hurriedly christened the day they first
came to us, and today names were given to them at four o'clock
this afternoon at the Blessed Sacrament Church at 71st St. and
Broadway. As the day was warm with only a suggestion of autumn
in the air we all walked out together. For Tatie nothing would do
but that she help push the carriage with the twins in. Father Stuart
Chambers (Daddy's friend) christened them. Mary was wearing a
long dress that was worn by Uncle Rob who died in the Philippines
in 1899. This dress was made by my own mother, for whom little
Mary was named.

November 12
Six months old today. Since last I wrote in this book a few weeks ago
you have outgrown your long dresses and are now kicking your pink
feet in the air all day long. Grace is as merry a baby as you could
find. She has a bright smile for everyone and should be a great social
favorite a few years from now. Mary is more reserved and only smiles

at her few chosen friends, but with them is altogether winning. She is dark, like my own mother. I wish you could see yourselves, babies dear, holding hands in your crib and talking to one another.

March 17, 1911
We observed Mary's first accomplishment today. She claps her tiny dimpled hands whenever Lillian sings "Patty cake, patty cake, baker's man." Grace blows bubbles and makes funny faces when we ask her.

April 3
Today Grace surprised us by showing two first little points of teeth. Lillian discovered them this morning and gave her a rubber doll, as she says the first person to find the baby's tooth must give it a present. Mary's will soon follow, and we are all interested to see who will find hers first.

May 11
Tatie had her hair cut today for the first time. We wanted to surprise Daddy when he returns and pretend she is a boy. Today was a warm day, so we called Paul the barber in the Chatsworth and he sat her in a high chair, put a big sheet around her neck and snipped off all the baby hair. Mother saved the locks as most mothers do.

May 12
One year old today, dear twins, and many happy returns to you both! Each night when I come in to kiss you good-night, I thank God and pray your lives may be blessed with faith, health, and happiness in all the years to come. Grandpa gave you a new twin baby carriage, larger than your old one, as you are both growing so fast there is danger of your kicking one another now.

July 7
Little Mary had a bad fall from her carriage today. She struck her head on the steps and was quite bruised. I was frightened and had two doctors at once to examine her. They tell me she is not badly injured and will be all right soon.

July 10
Grace stood up on her feet today for the first time.

July 17
Our baby Mary does not seem well today and sleeps most of the time.

July 19
Mary not so well.

July 20
Dr. Keeley and Dr. Chace examined Mary today and say she is not seriously ill but is suffering from the shock of the fall ten days ago, which has upset her very much. I am taking care of her in our apartment at the Chatsworth.

July 26
Mary is pale and weak and has lost two pounds. She has two new teeth (her first ones). Grace already had her two first lower teeth a few weeks ago.

August 6
Little Mary has been quite ill. Today she had slight convulsions all day and Dr. Chace remained overnight with us. The dear little soul looks so weak and ill and I am almost heart-broken.

August 12
Daddy and I brought our little Mary to Mrs. Juletta Wilson's sanatorium (15 W. 46th St.) today. She loves children dearly and seems to do wonderful things to make them well, so the doctors advised our coming here. I have a room right next to Mary, so I can be near my little one. Everyone is earnestly praying our baby may be spared to us.

August 19
Mary weighs only 11 lbs. 12 oz. She has lost five or six lbs. The Dr. and Mrs. Wilson today assure us she is going to recover, but it may be many weeks as the disease "bacilli colitis" is very slow. We feel her sickness was indirectly the result of her terrible fall on July 7th.

An obituary—dated September 30, 1911—is pasted at the top of the next page:

CONROY—At New York, N.Y. September 24, 1911.
Mary Ethridge, infant daughter of Mr. and Mrs. William Conroy, granddaughter of Pay Inspector John R. Carmody, U.S. Navy, retired.

August 20, 1912
It is almost a year since your mother has had the heart to take up again the history of her little ones in this book. It is so lonesome to go on without our gentle Mary. Even a year has not served to stop your mother's silent tears when she is alone. You can never know—nor do I want you to know—my suffering. Instead let us remember the great happiness we all had together, our walks in the park under the trees or the birthdays we enjoyed with cake and candles. God sent her to us, and it seems He has taken her away. I have made the effort to give her up as all true mothers should—with willingness in God's ways.

I earnestly hope you will keep the faith your father and mother have tried to give you. Let everything else come second and the great sorrows of life will not draw you to despair of God's goodness. Although I say to you truly that sometimes you may find yourself rocked on a sea of doubt.

There are many things to record in your lives from the year past. Tatie saw the great Hippodrome with her grandfather who had much happiness in taking her to her first theatre. Nor must we forget to note the progress of Grace who stood for the first time, without support, on Sept. 26, 1911. On Dec. 13, 1911, Grace walked alone.

Nor must we forget: As if the easiest, most natural thing, might be to pass over an event which must have followed Mary's death by two days. The tone of this entry makes quite a change from the effusions of an earlier time. As far as I can make out, Grace first walked alone at the age of nineteen months. Signs of early sorrow, surely. In fact, a year later, when Grace was two and a half, Deirdre writes:

Grace is making a very rapid progress in talking. She has been quite backward until recently but now is trying hard.

Did Deirdre's grief allow her to imagine the highly colored absence that must have become Grace's closest companion? Is there any evidence she lamented the wrenching of one twin from the other? There's this: a little envelope, fastened to the page with a pin black with rust, labeled *Grace's and Mary's hair—September 15, 1911*. That date would put it nine days before Mary's death. Inside is a paper torn from a ledger, ruled on each side and folded in three to enclose a single lock of hair tied with a scrap of blue silk ribbon. Written on the paper, again by Deirdre: *Mary's hair—dark, Grace's hair—light.* To tell the truth, it's almost impossible to make out the difference. Although yes, you can distinguish—if you look carefully, under a strong light—a few strands of fine hair that might be called dark mixed in with the flaxen. So here they are, twins indissolubly united in the notebook for the first and last time.

Deirdre, it's plain, was aware of the terrifying nearness of things. If you turn the page stuck with the rusty pin, and then the next, you find a sheet of faded blue paper folded in a clever way, first in half, then narrowly at the edges, to make an envelope where there wasn't one. On the outside, in Deirdre's handwriting:

Sunday, September 24, 1911
Last flower that little Mary looked at with any pleasure.

Mary died the same day. But the extraordinary thing is that it's possible to unfold this paper, slip apart the careful arrangement of creases and flaps, and find inside—a perfect rose. Desiccated, of course, but strikingly beautiful. As if now, almost a century later, the rose had at last become a thing you might contemplate without anxiety: an object of elaborate beauty, fixed, frozen. In fact, it might have been fashioned by human hands, resembling something made, a piece of art: the tender twist of the stem with the tiny cilia standing upright all along its length; the points of the stamen curling with elaborate intent; the leaves sharply notched, their flat surfaces flashing silver on one side, moss on the other. And running through each ruddy petal, startlingly visible, as they could not have been in life, an intricate network of dark veins: like Virginia creeper on a winter wall, like the blue tracery on an infant's chest.

For an afternoon and evening, moist and fragrant, the rose stood in a glass of water beside a child's crib. If you'd found yourself in that room, beside that bed, you might have marveled at the living flower itself, the elusive touch of petals on your mouth, a spicy scent that carried a hint of cinnamon and sweat. Might have pondered its eventual course from bud to blossom, an unfolding so gradual your attempts to catch the motion of the thing would surely have been baffled. Might have begun thinking that very soon the petals—released with every tick of the clock—would curl, drop one by one, the pollen begin to scatter. You might, in fact, have begun obsessing on the rose's decline. Because it had all become too much, simply too much, sitting there and waiting for it all to happen. In the end you might have wanted only that the rose die, succumb quickly to what must appallingly follow. Embrace death and be done with it.

Nothing survives of that once-solid room on 46th Street, not bed or table or door. But what we *do* have, so strangely, is the perishing flower itself. And we only have *that* because Deirdre's passion attached itself to the rose, *became* the rose, that single particle in all the universe where she had looked on her living infant daughter for the last time, had faintingly touched her.

—So close but no closer. Can you not give us Deirdre herself?

A moment! What I've been trying to say is that this faded scrap of beauty—the preservation of it after they're all lying deep in their graves, Deirdre and Willie and Mary and Grace and Kate—reflects a lover's obsession. It's clear this flower was pressed by Deirdre before it had entirely opened. Perhaps removed dripping from a glass in the room on 46th Street the morning of Mary's death. Because if you've lost what you love most in the world, you keep some memorandum, don't you? Hold on to something solid so that in moments of anguish you can reassure yourself you haven't made the whole thing up? That your lover once looked out on the world with you, that together your eyes lingered on the blossoming moment? That your misery is motivated, so to speak. Although, really, do you know a single misery that isn't?

✦

Doubling the blue sheet of paper once, twice, slipping one corner into the folded flap of the other, hiding away at last—a small burial in itself this first bereaved Christmas—the rose that ever since those shattering days in September she'd kept pressed flat between the pages of a book, Deirdre remembered Ireland. Remembered how during that fortnight in Kilkee on the Atlantic coast where she'd gone on holiday with her parents, she'd stopped one morning, on her way out for a solitary walk, to cut a rose blooming at the door of their rented cottage. It had been a windy day in July, she'd drawn her collar up around her neck and stood at the seawall, inhaling the sea, the crimson rose, watching the waves run up the beach and out again, seen how each wave as it advanced almost to the wall just at the last moment before it drew back spread across the sand a light film of shining water that for an instant gave her the sky. Because that's how it had been, she'd seen the sky in the mirror of the sea, in the thin glaze on the sand, had seen the sun moving behind the racing clouds, black ones and white. Had stood there beguiled for some minutes watching to see how each time the waves ran up and fanned out over the shore the sky reflected there looked to her somewhat different from the time before, the clouds were not the ones she'd seen only seconds ago, were not the same white clouds flying across patches of blue: the baby curled tight in on itself for instance had become a stallion with a streaming mane. And as she stood watching—thinking that's what she'd never be able to catch with her watercolors, that irresistible push across the sky, that wind at the back of everything—she'd thought of snapping open the watch she wore around her neck, of looking at the little face set in the other with the racing single arrow, to ascertain how long it was between waves, between momentary flashes of sky. To clock, as it were, how quickly it all changed because looking at things straight you could never actually catch what you wanted, you had to look and then look away to see the difference, time incarnate.

But then with little Mary's fall it seemed as if that weren't true anymore, it was the stupid clash between trying to see the world as it was when no one was looking—as in the glaze spread across the sand, the sudden vanishing glimpse one had—and then the event that "happened," the something brutally shoved in your face throwing open the door on unspeakable landscapes of sorrow that all the time had been waiting within. As on that sunny October morning in Washington, for instance, while they were at breakfast, her mother peeling a yellow peach and she herself marveling at the ripe dark bruise on one side of it. Then the telegram had arrived and been placed in her father's hands, and it was as if a human being had entered, a person, and the slack-jawed presence she'd always taken care to twist her head away from had crept around on the other side of her when she wasn't looking and was suddenly staring her wild-eyed full in the face. So last July 7 was not the first time she'd stood appalled. But this time she'd found that along with grief—waiting there in the trees, the shine of the floor throwing back the sun—there had been guilt, the crushing sense that if she'd been a different person, less taken by her own thoughts, more attentive to the demands of the day, then she'd have been able to keep the brigand from plundering their lives, the thief, the pillager of all their happiness.

She revisited that morning—how often, how often!—the twins waking in their room overlooking the river—the river that would so early have been shrouded in mist—and then at some point later Tatie wanting to haul Mary out of her crib and she herself preventing her, and then not long afterwards giving Mary into the care of Lillian who God knows for how long had been taking the twins out in their carriage. But then they had a new carriage—the one bought for them by her father on their first birthday less than two months before, a bigger one by far—and what she wasn't sure of was whether she had remembered to tell Lillian what she knew she had told her so many times before when it was a question of the old carriage, that the twins must be left at the top of the stairs until the carriage was at the bottom—there weren't very many steps, it wouldn't take a minute—but perhaps that had been the problem, Lillian had decided only a step or two, what can be the harm and on such a hot day and the park just on the other side of the street waiting for them all cool trees and lovely shaded walks, that's what Lillian may have been thinking. But however that may have been, she could in no way imagine how it was that she, the twins' own mother, had herself perhaps forgotten to remind Lillian—she didn't know if in fact she had done so—but even if she had reminded her once, then she should have reminded her a second time, should never have forgotten, not ever, when Lillian went with the twins down the elevator and out, should have spoken to her, instructed her to stay with the twins at the top of the steps and ask Michael at the door to lift the carriage onto the sidewalk.

So she tried to remember if she'd said anything that morning to Lillian and went over every waking moment, recalling a little more each time. How she and Willie had woken in the dawn as they did often these mornings in July so near the solstice and talked quietly—knowing the twins would wake at any minute—spoken of how in a week's time they would go down to the house they'd rented in Belmar on the Jersey shore, how he would come on weekends because he didn't really like to take off more than a day or two at a time from work—not since as long as she had ever known him but now particularly when he was in this new position and in charge of the vaults and every paper in them in the bowels of the building where he worked: she of course didn't say anything but in truth she didn't like to think of the vaults, all shining bars and sliding doors, keys rattling and so on, no—and soon she'd heard Grace making little cooing sounds in her crib and Willie had gone back to sleep for a few moments but she'd gotten out of bed and there was Tatie already up trying to pull Mary—who'd been lying there so quietly not making any sound at all—out of her crib.

Then how long after she didn't know Willie was rushing about trying to fasten his collar pin in the mirror of the little bureau, snatching up his cuff links—how awkward he always was with these especially right after he'd first clamped on his glasses in the morning and his eyes were going from wide to narrow—and she'd helped him with one of the links slipping it through the starched holes and folded his handkerchief that he'd then hastily tucked with two fingers down into his breast pocket, she remembered that, and then he'd dashed out and for a moment she'd followed him in her thoughts disappearing in his straw boater through the mahogany doors of the new subway at the corner with the beautiful tiles and polished brass. And then when she'd looked into the twins' room again there was Tatie trying to pull Mary out of the crib. No but that must be wrong because she'd caught Tatie at the crib earlier, while Willie was still there and she'd tried to keep things quiet while he slept a few moments longer because although she knew he tried hard for her sake he flared up without meaning to. But anyway what had happened next she couldn't remember, she and Lillian always bathed the twins after their morning orange juice—after Tatie had had her breakfast and she her coffee—and now the terrible place was rushing up to meet her the junction when she might or might not have reminded Lillian about the carriage, Lillian who was already getting things together for the outing, a little early as she remembered as a way of soothing Tatie who had been in a temper ever since that moment when she herself had spoken to her, probably too sharply, as she thought of it now, to her grief yes much too sharply: no she must not haul Mary out like that, she'd told Tatie that before, after all she was a big girl, already four, and knew that these little sisters were delicate. And herself knowing how Tatie hated all this talk about the need to be careful, this everlasting fuss around these small creatures—knew Willie hated it too but of course didn't like to say so, their lives at first had hung by a thread—and was aware too that it was precisely because Tatie felt herself so much older that she'd wanted to show herself as belonging to another order entirely, to be of some help, in her own small way.

So, seeing Tatie's outrage she had thought to herself today I'll send Lillian on a walk with the twins alone instead of our all sailing out together, today I'll spend the time upstairs with Tatie, the two of us, will read her new book to her, I'll draw a picture of herself beautifully helping with the twins. But as they'd at last sat down together, companionably plumping the pillows behind them, there'd been a knock at the door—oh terrible! terrible!—and there stood Paul, the barber—Paul who'd cut Tatie's hair a few days before with so much ceremony, talking to her with a seriousness she knew Tatie had loved, inquiring into the mirror if now she didn't have a twin of her own, a boy, a boy named Tom, he'd said—there Paul stood telling her that Lillian was downstairs with the little girls but that one of them had taken a tumble, he was sure nothing serious but all the same perhaps she'd better come and see. And then when she'd gone down with him and Tatie in the elevator knees trembling violently the ocean roaring in her ears and crossed the lobby with all the people milling about streaming this way and that, there between those panels of shimmering red brocade she'd caught sight of herself in the mirror distraught, distracted, as if she were passing—as she flew by—some self she would never see again, as if she were bidding the only self she knew good-bye.

Afterwards she and Lillian in a fright together—little Mary unable apparently to catch her breath hiccuping deep in her chest—and then the whole thing had begun the doctors and all the rest she and Lillian weeping together in the days following knowing that Lillian who had been there from the very beginning helping her through the nights with the medicine droppers and hot water bottles would have to leave. It wasn't she who had suggested it but it was taken for granted between them—as if the presence of the other was too much, simply too much, as if they were looking into a certainty there in the face of the other they saw reflected nowhere else, not in the doctors' faces or in Willie's—and so Lillian had gone and afterwards alone in the apartment without the one who more than any other in the world had taken pride and pleasure in the small landmarks that had allowed them to rejoice these frail lives were at last out of danger, the daily record of weight in pounds and ounces—and she all the time thinking: but who could actually *see* the gains except in leaps of time, one week against the next, for example—she felt the door on the happy past slide closed like the door of one of Willie's vaults. She observed Tatie standing in a corner sucking her thumb and was seized with horror that on top of everything else Tatie might have things turned around and believe that her own small attempt to remove Mary from her crib that morning for which she'd been so roundly scolded had somehow caused the fall, that Tatie had gotten it all mixed up in her head, how maybe she'd thought she herself had dropped Mary on the floor of the nursery and that was the cause of all the rest. Oh she didn't know, anything was possible, anything at all.

So the horror grew and grew and finally Willie suggested she speak to his old friend Stuart Chambers, who before he'd become a priest had traveled with Willie to Ireland, who had been, Willie said, at one time quite a favorite with the ladies, who after all had christened Mary and Grace.

But now she was suddenly wondering with terror why she'd dressed Mary for the christening in Rob's baby dress, Rob, oh my brother, what could she have been thinking, knowing. But so she had, weeping a little as she carefully put the tiny arms through the sleeves and fastening the buttons and then consoling herself—as she observed Mary's baby right hand tug at the left sleeve—here after all is new life and if only her mother had been here with her to see little Mary and then weeping again that she wasn't and that this child named for her mother was quite wonderfully like her, dark of hair and brow. And thinking that here and now whatever else this little namesake was adorned in the dress her mother must have worked on so hopefully for Rob—stitch by stitch, in that far-off time when her mother was only twenty-one so much younger than she herself was now and so clever with a needle again unlike herself who'd always preferred a paintbrush—she had gone smiling and weeping into the day.

But she hadn't gone to see Stuart Chambers right away, hadn't gone until everything was over, until after she'd purchased the rose on that final day—although of course she didn't know it as the very last until later—placed a coin in the hand of the woman standing in a black shawl on the corner of 46th Street, a woman who had a child with her and whom she hoped she'd be forgiven for envying. Yes, she'd envied the woman from whom she'd bought the rose for the healthy child with curly red hair and green eyes standing beside her, she couldn't forget either of them— neither the woman with the kind smile nor the child whose green eyes had immediately reminded her of Tatie's—and followed them past their encounter on the corner into the tenement where she imagined they might live, one of those full of coughing and illness. Because she knew, she'd seen a woman like her in one of the new moving pictures, a woman carrying a sick child down into the street on a sweltering summer evening to give it some air, a sick child, a child in fact probably dying of tuberculosis and she'd pitied that woman with all her heart had thought about her for days afterwards and thought how she'd known what lay ahead, yes surely known even as she walked with the child's head on her shoulder hoping for her little one the luxury of a breeze, a last moment of comfort—just as she who was so much more fortunate had bought the rose—both of them desperate to give a dying child something, oh anything at all that might afford the least snatch at pleasure.

Now the woman selling the rose and the woman walking the child in an alley where laundry hung from window to window far above her head, these two were all mixed up in her head—although she'd come to feel that the division between rich and poor was of less consequence than the division between women with sick children and women with well ones because what difference had it made the doctors she and Willie had been able to afford and this woman's child who might be as old as eight stood there beside her with her red curls and pink cheeks looking oh God forgive her the picture of health—and yet wasn't that the point after all the woman with the blooming child might very well be the same woman she'd seen in the picture what was to prevent that especially as this woman with the kind eyes was wearing a black shawl possibly in mourning and then she knew she must ask forgiveness of everyone in the universe with a suffering child for not remembering that Tatie and Grace would present to any passerby a picture of privilege and health and how was it that she had become in her own eyes in no way a woman whose good fortune must be remembered every day with gratitude but instead—ever since the fall the collapse into despair—a mother bereaved, a woman whose nearest companion day and night was desolation.

Would this terrible recoil from naming her blessings she wondered have been any different if Grace had not been Mary's twin, if as she watched the flesh fall from Mary's bones she had not with measured eye observed Grace grow day by day in strength? There they both had been, babies with plump creased thighs at long last, chubby wrists that looked as if a string had been tied at the joint and then—as the spinning earth lurched away from that extreme point of its ellipse where it had hung during the solstice, as the leaves of the city trees acquired a film of dust—Mary before her horrified eyes became a pitiful little soul with damp hair clinging to her scalp, faint breath, little wandering sticks of legs and arms she didn't even want to think about or find words for, eyes looking out from sockets that made her think, like it or not, of a skull. And all this while Grace, she couldn't help noticing, flaxen-haired, rosy-cheeked, each day exerted herself more and more strenuously to stand alone, hoisting herself up on any ledge she could get hold of, crowing with delight, slapping with a flat hand the table or chair she had mastered.

Mother of both, she was deeply deeply ashamed to have had such thoughts—involuntary as she knew them to be—and would rather have died than to have whispered them to another living soul but precisely because she jealously kept this guilty watching to herself knew her fascinated scrutiny had become more intense, more absorbed, as if she couldn't help but turn to look at a spectacle she knew she should turn away from. But no it wasn't observing the process that was wrong because of course she was helpless not to, but the fatal meaning she gave it of an equation, a bargain, a balance struck, as if some god of destruction demanded Mary's life if Grace were to grow into adulthood, as if she herself were being chastened for earlier thinking herself doubly blessed—even going so far as to evoke a time when these babies would have children of their own and so forth—when she should have known by her long and intimate exposure to her mother's grief that no happiness would be permitted to last, no joy left untarnished. Yes, when she had even by some logic come to believe—without knowing it until her fallacy had been appallingly revealed—that her own children were protected by the sudden calamity of that other death, Rob's, as if lightning would surely not strike twice, as if her mother's overwhelming misfortune, her own terrible grief at losing the companion of her earliest days, would somehow protect her from the worst. Even so, she thought, at least her mother had been spared the torment of neat comparison, both she and Rob had been grown—he twenty-six, she twenty-four. But twins! Her own courage had failed entirely when a couple of days after Mary's death Grace had stood alone for the first time—hoisting herself into the air, precariously to be sure, but proudly pulling herself to her feet and letting go for seconds at a time of the shelf she had always clung to—only a few hours before she and Willie had set out for Ilion to be present, high on that hill where her own grandparents were buried, as Mary's small white coffin was dropped by ropes into the earth that day in late September.

But that had not been all. No she'd also felt her heart wrung painfully—on Grace's behalf—as the days passed and for instance she'd looked in at her lying alone in her crib, vaguely disquieted, turning her head from side to side, at first slowly, and then more quickly and yet more quickly until it looked at last as if she were making a frenzied gesture of "No"—or when she heard her chattering away, sending her gurgles and coos into the air like solitary balloons. And when Grace opened her mouth in a wail that opened to further and further reaches of desolation the sound struck her at the core as did no other. One afternoon—it was the middle of September she remembered and she'd been on her way down to Mrs. Juletta Wilson's on 46th Street to be with Mary—or rather not to "be" but to pad back and forth snarling like a tiger sleepless, at large, protecting its young—she'd walked out of the Chatsworth down those terrible summer steps onto the sidewalk and had immediately looked up and for the first time it seemed really taken in the white façade of the building, the tumbling cornucopia spilling the fruits of the earth the sculpted sightless woman with that benighted look of equanimity staring out into a day she had no idea of, the cupids on either side, those fat twins, those equally thriving children, abandoning themselves to paroxysms of grief, eyes streaming. And she'd thought as she walked up the incline of 72nd Street to find a cab on Broadway and then as she waited there at the corner glancing up at the Ansonia—its gables and turrets, its bays and balconies, where Pons herself may well once have stood because she'd heard opera singers when performing in New York liked to stay at this hotel with its thick interior walls, its dazzling display of comfort all designed in the service of a carefree enjoyment she knew was now forever closed to her—decided that today she must snip a lock of Mary's hair she must carry it back with her and similarly snipping a lock of Grace's twine them together so that at least in this very small way there would be something to touch and see, some earthly evidence, some irrefutable proof that just as they had entered the world one after the other, tumbling forth as did that ripe fruit from its cone, so would they she imagined someday fall together through this earthly membrane— this frail skin that kept us here rather than there—and in those vast silent spaces awaiting us all make the same slow swimming motions first performed in her own inner cavity, the two at last wordlessly reunited, buoyant, at large, released from every law of gravity, recovering—after Grace's life had run its course—that first boundless joy.

One rainy afternoon in October she had gone to see Stuart Chambers. Although of course she'd met him many times she'd never sat with him alone and she saw how it was that women liked him, his quiet attention, his air of waiting without any hurry at all for one to speak. So after a time she had told him—because like herself and her mother he hadn't been a Catholic always and had a different manner from Willie of speaking of these things—told him that she wanted to die: that was it quite simply, she wanted to follow Mary down into the earth. Despite Grace's early morning cries, despite Tatie who appeared in the dawn like a silent apparition by the side of their bed, she couldn't seem to wake in the mornings, she opened her eyes to Tatie standing there her face level with her own, Tatie whose old rages it seemed had for the moment been driven underground, looked into her small face and put out an arm to enfold her, to draw her close, but Tatie wasn't fooled and drew away.

As for Grace, caring for her was a more exquisite torment, when she touched her small body she did so fearing that a terrible wave was about to break over her own head, that she would be overwhelmed and drawn with her brother Rob down into the deep. But truth be told that's where she wanted to be, under, somewhere beneath, jostled about on the floor of the ocean or rigid under the floor of the tired and trodden earth. She supposed this was what they called the sin of despair but she couldn't really see what to do about it. It was all very well to talk about accepting the will of God but what if it wasn't so much rebellion you felt as simply the wish to close your eyes once and for all and let go. They'd all prayed that Mary might live, there'd been no lack of prayers, Willie had written to this one and that, she didn't even know who they all were, but what had been the use and what kind of a God anyway would snatch one small child from death because a lot of prayers were said and condemn another because no one was thinking of her. From what she'd seen in Ireland poverty and prayer went hand in hand—and here she for whatever reason remembered that clear July afternoon eight years ago again at Kilkee when she and her parents had sat on a rock and looked across at the Cliffs of Moher, her mother eating chocolates, her father doing nothing at all, both dedicated to silence as they brooded over the silver shining sea—and she told him she thought it must be some other kind of God entirely who could be called good not one who put prayers in a sort of bank and used them for credit when there wasn't any other kind available. No, a God rather who looked on those who didn't pray with particular compassion child spared or not and really she didn't know what that meant anyway a good God she had nothing to put in that place and preferred to think of the woman she'd seen in the moving picture carrying her baby out of the tenement to allow it the luxury of some passing breeze and who was now drawing rasping painful breaths just as she was herself, tasting the salt of her own tears.

No, she probably hadn't said all this to Stuart Chambers but what she had said had been enough because after a time he'd answered, sitting there in that ugly room in the rectory with the bleeding Sacred Heart in the corner, that she mustn't be afraid of her unhappiness, mustn't regard it as a sin, because then there would always be the temptation to find someone to blame for her misery others certainly but most of all herself and he thought her right when she cried out against God because it was there the trouble lay and hadn't Christ himself dying on the cross pronounced as his last words my God my God why hast thou forsaken me. No she must regard her unhappiness as she would anyone else's—something to be honored and pitied rather than condemned—and must herself look for an opening in paying close attention to the love other people bore for her and in the ways they tried to show it however failingly. And then he told her the story of how the resurrected Christ had prepared a breakfast for Peter and the rest who'd been out fishing all night on the Sea of Tiberius without any success at all and how he'd told them to throw the nets on the right side of the boat rather than the left and they'd caught 153 fish— surely they hadn't counted!—but then when they came ashore there was Christ with a little charcoal fire going and a fish or two on the coals and a loaf of bread waiting. But the strange thing was that they hadn't been entirely sure it was he, just as Mary Magdalene in the dawn had mistaken him for the gardener. But perhaps that was the point he was the gardener as he was anyone at all putting your breakfast before you and that she must look carefully for these gestures, these gifts, these ministrations, because they would restore her to faith in God's goodness, would lead her away from blame and guilt and to her own exercise of love however mingled with tears because those tears for a time were her portion, her lot, her own bitter prayer.

What she hadn't been able to say to Stuart Chambers because she would have considered it disloyal was that Willie was drowning his own grief in more and more work, he now was gone longer hours than ever and when he arrived home at the end of his day and when they at last sat down to dinner after the little girls were asleep he tried she could see to do what he thought best for her by telling her about his own day, about the notoriety in which the company had been enmeshed by Mr. Hyde's son who had taken his father's place and whom Willie considered vain, something of a snob, whom she knew Willie envied, but whom Willie found woefully lacking in the moral fiber of his father. Willie told her stories of this one and that thinking to distract her—told her about the woman he'd given his seat to on the subway who had been astonished, after she'd thanked him and said how glad to be sure she was to be off her feet, when he tipped his hat and asked which town in Mayo she came from—went on and on because, she imagined, he thought her own tears morbid, exaggerated, as if she might have a flair for self-drama he hadn't noticed before and so didn't inquire about her own day lest the question provoke tears. And so left to her own silence she sat stony-faced trying to interest herself in the stories she'd found so entertaining in Washington when her own mother was grieving and she'd desperately wanted only to live! to live! yes, even if her beloved brother had drowned. But now as they sat eating their dinner in their own apartment in the Chatsworth she felt the gulf widen between them as the stories floated over the waters of talk and sometimes as Willie lifted his glass for a swallow she suspected that of course although he grieved, grieved terribly, still one less nuisance about the house wasn't altogether to his disliking. But no she knew this suspicion was doing him a terrible injustice and so she ended up thinking for relief, for comfort, once again of the woman in the tenement whose arms also ached with loneliness. Or thought for consolation—but of this she had to be careful, very careful not to think too often or the effect she feared would wear off—of that final day when Mary had looked out through half-closed eyes, breathing very shallowly, barely at the last able to meet her gaze and so she'd brought the rose close as she lay there and for a moment her eyes had focused on it and she had stared as if all the world was contained there in its crimson folds, had stared cannily as if she knew and then had turned her gaze from the rose to herself and oh miracle had started the beginning of a smile and looked into her eyes a last time before falling a moment later into what had turned out to be her last sleep.

Nor did she tell Stuart Chambers that on that warm day in late September on the lofty hill overlooking the Mohawk Valley with its view of shining river and of trees touched in places by sunlight or frost she couldn't tell which—where they'd planted their own small broken seed and where she and Willie had asked that in the days following two young hemlocks be placed in the ground to mark the spot—in that high place listening to the long sorrowing whistle of a train wind toward them through the valley she'd imagined lying down beneath a tree, or perhaps she'd even done so although when she came to think of it that of course seemed unlikely but whatever the case, desire or deed, she'd carried an impression with her since that day of lying flat on the ground beneath a tree, perhaps, looking up into its low overhanging branches, into its high high heart watching the leaves lightly shift between shadow and sun, of sinking into the tall grass where she lay gazing upward, of sinking further and further into the place of hiding in the earth and had thought: oh a house what would it be like to live in a house with trees standing around it where she could lie down on the ground anytime she liked, get close to the earth, lie against it, in it, if she liked, the deep silent earth that now had replaced Mary's crib as her bed.

Kate's Diary

And so the next spring, the spring of 1912, they all moved to Pelham. Seven years later, Kate began the only diary I'm aware she ever kept. She was twelve and a half years old at the time. Writing in a green student's notebook—into which she pasted stamps and clippings from newspapers and the stray bit of ivy or wool—what can we imagine were her own fears of betrayal? What accommodations did she make with her own urgent need? Kate's first entries are written in a still uncertain inky scrawl. By the time she reached the end, four years later, her handwriting is fully formed.

November 18, 1919
A week ago today was the anniversary of the end of the Great War when the armistice was signed and men lay down their guns. On this day a year ago I put my initials in the window. Here is a piece of ivy that I took from a wreath placed at the foot of the honor roll in Pelham.

New Year's Day, 1920
Today we begin all over again because it is the first day of the year. Last night there was great celebration and everyone was up to see the Old Year go out and the New Year come in. The first day of the New Year is dark and foggy and the trees around the house are black and bare. There is some snow but it rained and everything is slushy. The skies are also dark, but we hope the New Year won't be like the weather.

January 10
Everything is taxed in order to pay off the great debt of the war. This is one of the stamps. Everything is taxed according to its value, some

things even as high as four or five dollars. A request has been made that everyone should wear overalls if possible, all college boys and girls, waiters in hotels and restaurants, and in fact almost everyone is doing so to reduce the H.C. of L. (High Cost of Living).

April 12
Today I am thirteen years old.

June 8
The whole family went to Utica and had a fine time. We saw all of our ancestors, Aunt Lizzie and the rest. Then we went to Ilion and up to Oak Hill cemetery and put flowers on the grave of our little sister Mary. There are two small hemlock trees growing nearby.

January 9, 1921
The other day I found this piece of yarn in the back of a drawer. It was out of this that I made my first sweater during the war. I wrote a note and put it in the sweater and later received a postal card from the soldier that got it. Some time I will put the card in here.

July 3
The big fight at Jersey City. This clipping shows many of the fights since 1882.

FAMOUS FIGHTS FOR HEAVYWEIGHT HONORS
SINCE JOHN LAWRENCE SULLIVAN'S HEYDAY

DATE	WINNER	LOSER	PLACE	ROUNDS
Feb. 7, 1882	John L. Sullivan	Paddy Ryan	Mississippi City	9
Sept. 7, 1892	James J. Corbett	John L. Sullivan	New Orleans	21
June 9, 1899	James J. Jeffries	Robt. Fitzsimmons	Coney Is.	11
Aug. 26, 1904	James J. Jeffries	Jack Munroe	San Francisco	2
July 4, 1907	Tommy Burns	Bill Squires	San Francisco	1
Dec. 26, 1908	Jack Johnson	Tommy Burns	Sydney N.S.W.	14
July 16, 1914	Georges Carpentier	Gunboat Smith	London	6
April 5, 1915	Jess Willard	Jack Johnson	Havana, Cuba	26
July 4, 1919	Jack Dempsey	Jess Willard	Toledo, Ohio	3
July 2, 1921	Jack Dempsey	Georges Carpentier	Jersey City	4

August 26
Here is a clipping from <u>The New York Times</u>:

Treaty Signed Without Ceremony
At the Foreign Office in Berlin

BERLIN, Aug. 25—The Peace Treaty between the United States and
Germany was signed here at 5:10 o'clock this afternoon. It was a cut-
and-dried formality of the utmost unpicturesque simplicity.

August 27
*Caruso died on August 5th. He had been ill many months. His
illness began when a blood vessel broke in his throat when he was
singing in the Metropolitan Opera House. Someone has written
a song called "They needed a songbird in Heaven." This is a great
loss for the entire world. He had his wish that he might die in Italy
because he died in Naples. His last words were "Let me sleep."*

*The ZR 2, the immense aeroplane that the U.S. was to buy from
Great Britain, fell today in Hull. 17 Americans and 27 British
officers were killed. The plane began to burn. That is what caused
the accident.*

September 13
Daddy, Deedy, and Grace went to Washington today.

September 14
*They returned. Went to Arlington and visited the graves of our
grandparents. The men of the ZR 2 are to be buried there tomorrow.*

September 19
*Grace and I went to school today at the Sacred Heart Convent,
"Maplehurst." We are going to board. Go on Monday morning and
return on Friday afternoon.*

October 25
*Daddy and Deedy are married sixteen years today. This evening
they had a wonderful dinner and last night Deedy took out her
wedding dress and veil, slippers, cake, and messages. My, it's so long
compared with dresses of today! It is beautiful. Satin with lace all
over it and a long train and the veil with orange blossoms on it.*

Nov. 4
Today the milk strike began. No milk to be had.

Nov. 8
They are distributing milk at different stations, real estate offices. Railroad stations, etc.

Nov. 11
The date will say what this day is. The third anniversary of the armistice. At a quarter to twelve we went to Benediction and from 12 to 12:02 everyone knelt down in prayer no matter where they were or what they were doing. Every denomination had some kind of service. The unknown dead man brought from France was buried in Arlington at noon.

Nov. 18
Marshal Foch visited our school today. He will remain in New York until Sunday. He is a fine-looking man and you are so impressed to think that he had charge of all our allied forces during the war. He spoke to us in French but it was so noisy I could not hear what he said.

Nov. 22
The milk strike is over. But two policemen go around with each wagon. Many men have been killed trying to deliver milk.

Dec. 6
Ireland's independence was acknowledged by England today at 2:15 P.M. Ireland is to be known as "Ireland Free State" after seven hundred years of struggle.

Dec. 8
I have been sick for about three weeks and today Dr. Newell came and said I had to be operated on for appendicitis as soon as possible. Deedy also had to have her appendix out years ago, before she married Daddy.

Dec. 24
I was operated on, December 13, at quarter to 8 A.M. and have only gotten home today. I expect I will feel better now only it will take me

a long time to get there. I saved a few of my stitches in the envelope I've pasted below.

Dec. 25, Christmas Day
Everyone except me went to Midnight Mass at St. Catherine's. We had a lovely day.

Jan. 1, New Year's Day, 1922
A lovely day. Lots of snow and a happy home. I am much better.

Jan. 7
Today Deedy, Grace, and I bought two parakeets. They are sweet little things.

Jan. 22
Today Pope Benedict XV died of pneumonia. "His Holiness" had only been ill a few days. He was Pope 7 years and lived through a time of great trouble in the entire world.

Feb. 5
Pope Pius XI was elected today.

March 27
We are not boarding at school anymore. From now on until June we are going to be day scholars. I am so glad.

April 1
Deedy's birthday and to celebrate she made a party for Grace and me. Afterwards all of us went to see "Forty-Five Minutes from Broadway" at the Pelham Picture House. When we got home I picked some violets for her from under the tulip tree.

April 12
I am fifteen today.

April 16
Easter Sunday. We had friends staying in the house and guests for dinner. Deedy didn't feel well at first but then she got up and was fine. We all had a lovely day.

April 22
Deedy is quite sick. I don't know yet what the matter is.

April 28
Deedy has pneumonia. She has been quite sick all of this week. I hope she will be well soon as this lovely spring weather is really too nice to have to spend in bed.

April 30
Daylight saving time began today. I am sure I have no idea how many more years this is going to continue. Deedy is about the same today.

June 2
Deedy sat up in a chair today for the first time since she has been sick.

June 4
Deedy's temperature has gone up again so she is back in bed.

August 3
Deedy is a little better. Still in bed. Alexander Graham Bell died today. The inventor of the telephone and a great scientist.

October 1
Today Deedy left for Atlantic City. She is doing very nicely and we hope the change will entirely cure her.

November 25, 1922
Since I wrote in this book we had Armistice Day and Election Day. Deedy has returned from Atlantic City and is feeling very well.

February 16, 1923
Since I last wrote here Deedy has been very well. She went to Palm Beach but two weeks ago she returned and now she is quite sick again. She had radium applied to her neck two days ago and I hope that is going to help her. She has been ill so long.

April 18, 1923
Tonight Deedy called me into her room and gave me a very
beautiful letter-knife made from ivory. She said that when her
brother's things were returned after he died in the Philippines, he
had marked a present for everyone but Grandpa. This knife did not
have a note with it saying who it was for so Grandpa always kept
it with him. Then when he died Deedy kept it carefully among her
precious things and now wants to give it to me. It is indeed very
beautiful, with the elephants walking along the edge, and I am
going to treasure it always.

August 3, 1923
Pres. Harding died of pneumonia today. Pres. Coolidge took office.

August 8, 1923
Deedy is now relieved of all her sufferings. She left us last night.

September 1, 1923
A horrible earthquake, fire, and tidal wave have occurred in Japan.
More than 10,000 people killed in Tokyo alone. The whole world is
trying to help alleviate the dreadful suffering.

Torn Copybook

Kate began her diary after they'd lived in the house for seven years. She discovered the value of a correlative: an earthquake, a milk strike, a war. These served her, at least for a time. But as we know, she would never again speak willingly of Deirdre's death.

As for the fawn notebook, in Pelham it dwindles almost to nothing, becomes more sketchbook than journal.

But I discovered another kind of journal in the confusion of the drawer: a ruled copybook with a brown cover, torn at the edges, the kind a child might use in school. On the front, the initials "D.C.C." Not so different from the one Kate employed for her own diary. Inside, the same strong handwriting, but written entirely in pencil, as if Deirdre wanted to be able to make free use of an eraser. A shadow notebook. In fact, on the very first page several words have been rubbed out. Thoroughly. The only figures discernible are "1914." But there are no dated entries as such, no chronicle of events. A catch-all, a receptacle to hold whatever she likes: little notices cut from newspapers or magazines—sky charts showing the position of the constellations for each season, the confluence of planets, timetables of solar and lunar eclipses, of high tides and low—these down to the minute. The kind of thing you'd find in a Farmer's Almanac. As well as articles recounting floods, volcanic eruptions, tidal waves, earthquakes. One relating how the incidence of suicide rises sharply following any kind of natural disaster, an earthquake or flood. Had Deirdre too learned the value of a correlative? Or rather was it Kate who'd learned it from Deirdre?

Deirdre seems to have used the copybook, as well, to store away loose writings of her own. Because from between the pages of the copybook I drew out yellow sheets taken from a legal pad, written in pencil, folded into three: the draft of an address Deirdre wished to make. But where? And to whom?

The first contribution that we have a right to expect from American laymen is a contribution of interest—that he or she be not indifferent to the social miseries that prevail among certain classes. We are hardly beings of fine feeling if we care nothing about what is going on in the workshops and the factories, the tenements and the tunnels, the mines and stockyards and steel mills. I shall not try your patience by attempting to paint in high colors the agonies to which many thousands of our fellow-beings are subjected by what is called the present social system—problems of unemployment, overwork, underpayment, unsanitary housing, occupational diseases, pensions, prices of fuel and food and clothing. But it is worth our while to recall that there is such suffering and that it is largely traceable to economic conventions for which you and I (if we are passive members of the comfortable classes) must be held in part responsible.

Science implies a conformity of the mind with the actual facts. In the interest of science, therefore, one must have a care not to be swayed by the gusts of passion, or the tides of greed, one must not be deafened by appeals to race loyalty, or handcuffed by religious bigotry. God visits punishment upon a board of directors as surely as upon a secret society of assassins, though the first may have let the victim's heart blood out with a majority stockholder's note instead of with a stiletto.

But surely this statement is entirely different from anything we've seen in the fawn notebook! Could Deirdre have had in mind the woman from the tenement? The one who'd come down into the street with her dying child on a summer's night? The woman in a black shawl selling roses? The only clue is a small slip of paper, the kind you might use for a grocery list, folded between the same pages.

Would you do me the kindness as a club member to read this before the club sometime in the near future? I am a new member and am not signing my name whereas to relieve any embarrassment on your part or mine. If members would give us more of the gospel, occasional talks on practical problems, I think the next generation would have a better chance. More bread and less cake is our need.

But what club had she recently joined? Who were its members? Clearly she believed her own ideas, if expressed by herself, would embarrass everyone involved. She wished to remain anonymous. With heat, she pleads for recognition of the injustices of *the present social system,* of the miseries inflicted by the indifferent rich on the poor. She makes clear who are the ones suffering, names the ones responsible. What's needed is more of the gospel. She is thinking of the entire next generation, not of Kate and Grace alone.

And so, one thought leading to another, she again takes up the legal pad, writes a letter and sticks it with the other between the pages of the brown copybook. This one is written in the month following her father's death in March 1917. If a good copy was made, I never uncovered it.

April 1917

Dear children of mine:

Out of the depths of my heart I want to write a few words to you, which in time may be a comfort and a happiness. I have always held that a will or testament is, at best, a poor and chilly legal document (even when disposing of untold wealth!) compared to the vast heritage of other treasure we may bestow.

I want to speak to you now of one of the legacies you are heir to. My father, removed from early influences by the war and by his marriage to my mother, did not practice his religion. My mother had been brought up in no particular faith but I fancy now she realized the lack of it sadly when we were children. I too had in my heart a longing to pour out my soul to someone for comfort in the great problems of life and death which were never discussed in our family.

When I was quite a large girl, in my teens, I was overjoyed one day to have my mother draw me closely to her side and confide to me she had received instructions and was on the eve of being baptized. With tears of emotion I heard the glad news, not knowing myself why it filled me with joy, and not long after accompanied her and a few relatives of my father's to St. John's Church, Utica, New York. I marvel now when I think of my dear girlish mother taking this great step alone, without the supporting hand of my devoted father, or even one of her own family to strengthen her timid footsteps into a new world. Then followed my own instruction a short time afterwards and the satisfaction and outlet it brought after my many years of spiritual craving.

These are the words I wish you to remember: "Blessed are the poor in spirit, for theirs is the kingdom of heaven. Blessed are they who mourn, for they will be comforted. Blessed are the meek, for they will inherit the earth. Blessed are they who hunger and thirst for justice, for they will be satisfied. Blessed are the merciful, for they will be shown mercy. Blessed are the pure of heart, for they will see God. Blessed are the peacemakers, for they will be called children of God."

But why is Deirdre writing a testamentary letter in 1917, when Kate was ten and Grace was seven? A letter in which she bequeaths the Beatitudes? Five years have still to pass before the April Fools' when she'll sit up in bed and announce to Willie that soon she'll be in her grave and no one will be able to say the reason why. Could it have been her father's recent death only weeks earlier that haunted her? Rumors of war? Could April, the month of her birthday, have been for her a season of prevision, a time when she looked through the clarifying light of spring and perceived her death looking back at her in the brash green? Did she foresee her children would forget her, I mean in some uncanny way? Because it's clear she was already living with some apprehension that she wouldn't be around, after they were grown, to tell them stories she feared they were still too young to understand.

Two little envelopes, again placed together between the pages of the copybook, tell a further story. The first, its two-cent stamp stuck in the corner—George Washington's white profile against a red background—is addressed to 131 East 57th Street, New York City. Inside is the letter her father sent to Deirdre from the house in Pelham where only a little more than a month later he would die of pneumonia in a room I would someday call mine. Perhaps the letter survives because it's the last he wrote her:

Feb. 6 1917

My dear daughter,

Your welcome letter of yesterday came promptly to hand through a driving snowstorm—far worse than any we have so far experienced this winter—and which prevented the children from going to school, or "sule" as Grace calls it. The trunks of the trees are buried in snow.

I can imagine how lonesome you must find your exile and pray God he may release you with restored health and strength. Your return will certainly rejoice this household. Rest assured that the

little ones are not forgetting their gentle mother; nor the children of
larger growth, I duly add. I assure you everything possible is being
done for my comfort. The good Will is untiring in his attentions and
I have much to thank him for.

I regret exceedingly we cannot be nearer one another so that
I could join you in your expressions of dismay. It looks as though
we are on the brink of disastrous times and will have a merciless
enemy to deal with if the situation results in warfare, as now looks
probable.

By the name you mention your new nurse I judge is French.
"Grace of God!" A good name in a time of trouble. With much love
and good wishes I remain, affectionately, your father,

John R. Carmody

P.S. I send you herewith your check, with much pleasure.

The other letter, its twin, is written only five weeks later by Deirdre herself. She has returned from the place where she was lonely in her exile: an exile populated by nurses, a place of which I know nothing. But now she is writing to her father's sister, Elizabeth Roche, two days before John Carmody's death. Perhaps Deirdre's aunt Lizzie kept the letter because it describes her brother's last moments, and eventually returned it to Deirdre for the same reason?

Thursday, March 15, 1917

Dearest Lizzie,

My dear father remains about the same but today he has failed
to ask for his tobacco all day and has not seemed to miss it. It has
been such a comfort to him that despite the pneumonia his doctor
has allowed him to use it constantly. On Thursday, Lizzie, he was
anointed. He seemed to realize fully and repeated clearly, "Sweet
Jesus, help me." Willie was suffering from fatigue and so went off
to Atlantic City two weeks ago (before my return) where I am in
hopes he will get a good rest and return restored. My illness has only
strengthened me for these days, and while there is much to attend to,
I seem to be strong and calm.

Now I must say good night to you. Remember, Lizzie, don't
worry, but go about your work rejoicing for God is good.

Devotedly, Deirdre

But isn't it strange that Willie should rush off for a few weeks' holiday in Atlantic City only days before his wife's return? Seize this particular moment in late winter to abandon his own house and fill his lungs with ocean air, leaving Deirdre to cope with her father's death alone? And what does it say of his feelings for his father-in-law? Although, of course, it wasn't exactly Willie's own house, John Carmody having only three months earlier hung on the Christmas tree a deed that carried his daughter's name alone.

Did Willie resent the exclusion of his own name? And for what reason was it excluded? Did John Carmody, having lived with him a number of years, know Willie to be—what would you call it—well, *close?* Was he fearful of leaving his daughter without resources of her own? Already, it would seem, he was supplying her with an allowance of some kind: *I send you herewith your check, with much pleasure.* Or, for all we know, Willie's ordeal in the fire had made him particularly susceptible to fatigue, to strain of every kind. Perhaps he fled to Atlantic City on the verge of collapse. Perhaps the spectacle of his father-in-law's pneumonia—contracted, it could be, when old John Carmody ventured forth to mail a letter to his daughter in the aftermath of a driving snowstorm—put him into a fever of his own.

And what of Kate and Grace in the midst of all these comings and goings? Kate whose tenth birthday on April 12, 1917, was spent waiting alone in the house where her grandfather had died three weeks before.

Kate told me a little story, once, when we were sitting together in the back of a car, a story I'm sure she'd never have confided or perhaps even remembered if we'd found ourselves talking inside the house. In fact it was her birthday and we were on our way to a celebration of some sort. As we drove along, each of us gazing out a window at the passing scene, I asked her if she remembered her birthdays when she was a child, perhaps remembering even then Deirdre's glowing accounts in the fawn notebook.

At first she said no, she didn't remember anything at all, any party or celebration. She wondered why she didn't remember but no, the fact was she didn't. After another moment's musing out the window, she corrected herself. She remembered her tenth birthday, she said.

What she remembered was sitting on one of the chairs in the dining room, a chair pulled up against a wall, sitting there by herself with a pair of new roller skates on her lap. She was fiddling with the skate key, trying to fit it onto one of the prongs that tighten the clamps of the skates.

"And was anyone there with you?" I asked.

"No, I don't think anyone was there."

"Were you about to try out the skates? Go outside?"

"No, I don't think I was very eager to do that."

"You didn't like the skates?" I asked after a moment. And then: "Had you wanted something else?"

And here something truly startling happened. Kate turned and—looking me full in the face—said she thought that what she'd wanted for her birthday was her mother.

Perhaps while Kate sat downstairs with her new skates in her lap, Deirdre was upstairs writing the testamentary letter to her children? Lying down on a bed? Or she may have returned to the place on 57th Street and so was beyond Kate's reach altogether.

As for the copybook, it was now a matter of loose papers, letters, cutouts, charts. She would no longer record the events of her day, store up memories for her children or anyone else. As if she'd renounced all that. No need of the eraser after all. There's only one entry in Deirdre's own writing. A single one. *How isolated we are even when two people draw as near as the strange fence of identity permits,* she writes. *To God alone does the soul reveal itself.*

After Mary's death it seems she no longer trusted the sound of her own voice. It was more a matter of breathing a cloud onto the glass. No question she believed, felt, all she wrote to her children: the legacy of faith she hoped to bequeath, her protestations to Lizzie of a good God. But it's the struggle breaking from beneath the lines, the records of natural calamities, the outraged lecture to the clubwomen, the ellipses and silences, the voice trailing off with no thought of an exclamation point, that finally overwhelm the rest. Her doubt had become the measure of her faith, there was no separating them.

—Is this true for you as well? Is your doubt the measure of your faith?

I scarcely know. The words themselves fall away. What hauntings of Deirdre's, of my own, compel silence? What griefs bequeathed by a parent? What fierce mourning following a mother's death? The decline of a father?

—And you? Are you too breathing on a glass?

I rush out to my old father wandering alone through the empty house in summer. Since Kate's death seven years ago, the tides of clutter have risen in the rooms. Her absence fills the house, overflows. I look for her in the closets and in the kitchen, on the porch where Bert sits in Willie's rocking chair at six o'clock, drink in hand. But it's only when I go in search of her that I can't find her. Otherwise she's there without the asking.

With Bert I watch flickering images on TV, a rolling ball of fire rising whoosh through a shining domino, a blaze up a chimney draft. Flaming columns, specks falling out of the sky. Bert sits with his head in his hands, eyes narrowed. He watches as the image is repeated. Then he rises from his chair, wordless, and retires for the night, closing behind him the door of the room Kate has vacated. Talking on the phone not long after, he says that on the day his family was celebrating his grandfather's eightieth birthday, June 28, 1914, the archduke Francis Ferdinand of Austria-Hungary was shot. The day after, the news came through on telegraph. Bert at the time was ten years old.

Then, perhaps stirred by his own memories of the early part of the century, he remarks that Kate's death has left a hole in his life the size of the *Titanic*.

I look into the torn book to see what I can find. Deirdre invites me in, opens the leaves of her book for any help I might discover there. In her silences asks me to consider the spirit of poverty, the miracle of empty hands. Reminds me that paradise lies within. She bids me wonder if isolation—or better, solitude—isn't only another word for the silence in which we listen, like Elijah on the mountaintop, for the murmur, the hum. The whisper heard in the high thin air after fire, earthquake, storm.

First curtains billowing into the rooms, the sky ripped open by fire, the crack and roll of thunder. Summer rain lashing against the screens. Later, in the night, dripping trees. The deluge of memory, the great stream rushing underground, snatching houses and trees and even people in its sweep toward the sea.

So now it's Bert alone who remains, and he's ninety-eight years old. He's become that frail leaf clinging to the branch that divides late fall from winter, is already becoming a ghost himself. Oh yes, I saw this very clearly one afternoon a few months ago when I was leaving the house to drive back into the city. Bert stood there in a window upstairs waiting for me to turn the key in the ignition and pull out from the curb. It was one of those days in late February when the season is turning and high winds are moving through the tops of the trees. Looking out from the car, I saw all across the face of the house the sky reflected in its broad windows, as if the house itself were ablaze, a dazzling sheet of blue with white clouds scudding across it, the sun gleaming at the edges of the clouds, about to break loose, about to turn the entire front of the house into a pond alive with the wind and spring sun on it. And there in the watery light, in the high brilliance of the afternoon, Bert stood hovering—clouds flying past his face—already disappearing, already a ghost. And at his back, crowding, the others.

Pressed by Deirdre between the pages of the torn copybook, a hickory leaf: sere, brittle, brown, but altogether whole, the desiccated veins rising as sharply as ever, the stem sturdy, nub intact where it was once attached to the branch. A leaf from the tree that Bert—one evening in early August when the sudden brilliant light on the back stairs appears like a summons—pronounced the finest tree of all. He made this remark standing beneath it, looking into its high branches where swollen nuts hung green and growing in their shells, marveling at what he calls the "backlight," at pure rays thrown by the setting sun onto leaves from beneath, leaves translucent in the last of the day.

And why was the hickory the preferred tree, the chosen one? Because its roots are deep and can withstand wind and storm, because its wood is hard and has grown "ring by ring." And then, turning from the tree, as if his thoughts had taken him elsewhere, Bert pointed out and identified—across an expanse of lawn lengthened by shadows—the twin yews he'd planted fifty years before: "sentinels of paradise," he called them.

—So remembering paradise we close the fawn notebook: close its shadow, the torn brown.

To God alone does the soul reveal itself. God the audience. God the reader.

In the Despairing Hour of Life

You call my gait spasmodic. I am in danger, sir.

She woke in the middle of the night to a pounding heart. The man lying in the bed beside her said everything was moving toward God and that sin was whatever held up the flow. She wasn't sure about that—everything moving toward God. By day, perhaps: shadows inching along the wall as if they meant it.

At night, crows walking beneath the trees.

They had made love in the night, the rain beating on the roof. The sound of the ocean in her ears, in his the roar and crackle of fire.

When she was a girl she had noticed that even on the quietest summer day trees were never still. Always some commotion in their branches, a faint stir of leaves.

One night she read to the children from a book that had been hers when she was a child. They all squeezed together on the little sofa under the frosted glass shade, ruffled like a skirt, and she read them the one about the misty, moisty morning when cloudy was the weather. She counted her children: one, two. Later on, kissing them good-night, she counted again: the same.

During her first days in the house she had tried to burn a new landscape onto the old. She carried a stone in her pocket to clutch in her fist. What she was trying to do was find all the high places where things held on. She had stood beneath the hickory tree that first May looking up at the crisp new leaves, veins standing out in startling relief. Then one night she saw in a dream a leaf, moist still, curled in on itself; she saw it turn before her eyes into the hand of an infant, fingers tightly coiled, then spread in sudden panic.

The roof was the same. Studying its gray slates, one fitting so neatly into the next, the chimneys rising sharply twice into the sky, moving rapidly through banks of white clouds, she lost her balance in the sheer tilt and pitch of it. The outrageous plunge into rushing spaces below.

So it was at last with everything: banisters, the windowpane where Tatie had scratched her initials, the bare blank walls of the rooms, even. There was always the steep tower of air.

"*Apogean Tide:* a month tide of decreased range that occurs when the Moon is farthest from the Earth."

As water in the desert flickered over her internal landscape—

"Oh yes," she said, "of course I'll try to keep still. Do you think I'm not aware of the children sleeping in this house? Do you think I know nothing about dreams?"

Through the windows of the house, in the evening, the sun tunnels down the sky, black branches watching, aghast. A little dog skids on brittle legs across the icy crust of snow. He smells what is there.

Her mother had been peeling a peach when it had arrived: the cable.

It was appalling, the steady throb in the tulip trees on summer nights, the chorus that rose to a shriek. One day she had seen the cast-off shell of a cicada clinging to a tree, brittle, crisp, like cooled butter candy, bulging eyes agog. She had lifted it from the bark with care so as not to break its legs, canny joints that shrilled in the night. She had placed it in the sheltering hollow of her hand. By making a fist she might have crushed it to bits, silenced the forests of the night.

When she tried to tell him of the clamor in her head he told her to pray for the grace to accept the will of God. She thought this was probably right but when she tried to remember to do so in the middle of the night felt only the clutch of fear tighten around her heart. As if she had looked out the window expecting to see her old father sleeping in his chair in the sun and had found it empty. What she needed to do was to make some claim on the future. Buy wicker chairs for the porch, plant some peonies.

She yearned over one, two, three, in silence. In solitude. Her thoughts never strayed.

The peach had rolled off the table onto the floor. Oh, Mother! Hold on to your grief. Do not let it run down the sides!

A pond deep in the woods: around it, snow, the skinned trunks of birches; an orange sun sinking fast, the pond on fire. Exactly here—at this forgotten point—the earth is turning its face toward night. But because no one is there to see, this brief blazing moment has happened only in the imagination. Or in another life.

In April, a purple pool of violets under the tulip trees. We'll press some in a book, Tatie, and when you grow up you'll always remember today.

And so she looks to escape yesterday morning, twenty years ago, the endless stretch of noons.

It didn't come naturally to her, prayer. What she meant by it was something he didn't, but she feared that speaking would only bring the flash of blue. Prayer had to do with injury, but not with death. It had to do with watching a breath, the in the out of it, but not with rot.

Despair, another name for the yawning sense that your only self is disappearing like water in the desert. Such a distance between one's face and one's feet! And overhead, an unforgiving sun. Nothing human anywhere around.

She sometimes caught herself thinking that if she could only see *around the corner,* as she put it to herself, she would have what she needed. A small extra angle of vision; that was all, but it would be everything. She knew, too, that if she *should* someday see what was hidden now, it would happen as if by chance.

On the table, covered with a white cloth, apples. The table is pitching beneath them, a boat on churning waters. But the apples refuse to be tossed overboard.

The room all gleaming planes: the mirror, of course, but also the glass doorknobs, centers stabbed by silver points. The windows growing shiny in the dark. When the light is at last turned off, the children will leave the room at their own risk.

Once she had used the word *love*. Now that word had broken open like a pod and was floating silver spores on the air. She yearned for his caress.

Her old father sitting at the dinner table between them. How slowly he swallowed his soup, this man who'd sailed the world. She could see the other quenching the blue blaze, flicking his napkin about.

At her father's request he had come to meet her at Jersey City. He had met the train from Washington. The thought that he couldn't easily say no had tormented her, and when she caught sight of him that July day standing in the crowd at the gate her heart had clamped shut. Then, lurched wide. They had taken the ferry across the river. She was alone with a man she scarcely knew, traveling, and her senses were flooded, she could see things only in pieces. In one blinding flash the gulls sitting on the waves. In another the plunge of rock at their back. And then the orange shore moving relentlessly toward them. She was lifted out of her body but was carried by the want inside it.

Stepping off the ferry she was again abashed. When he looked around for a cab, the fear that he should be spending money he couldn't spare urged her to suggest the Elevated. Besides, the little cars seemed less sedate, more open to hazard and chance, turned the journey into something wayward and risky. So they had walked up the steps and rolled along above the streets, their conversation coming in little excited bursts.

This was *before* the peach rolled to the floor.

The bleat of the foghorn: a full moon shining. But who could see? Tide sloshing in its black basin, stretched and pulled to the limit.

"If you will only try to come downstairs," he said.

And his own grief, she wondered? Soothed away at first by the smiling doctor: but as the weeks went by and the one they could not mention had lost weight ounce by ounce and then pound by pound, she could see him watching her. If they hadn't hired a nurse, she read in the blue blaze. If his own mother hauling the coal bucket up from the cellar before dawn and ten children to care for.

"You are breathing my air," he said. "You are swallowing all my sorrow."

At night when she curled toward him in bed, he reached for her hand as if she were a child he had determined to forgive.

The newborn twins had been laid side by side in little beds of cotton and fed a warm sugary milk, drop by drop. To everyone else, an everlasting trouble; to her, a purpose that reached and held. Eyes rolling back in their sockets, corners of mouths twitching up in something like a smile, though not in response to the world outside. The catch in the breath, the deep sighs. And then the eyes raking past her face as if trying to catch a glimpse of something that wasn't visible, squinting. The whole body suddenly catching itself, the little arms making those strange swimming gestures so moving in newborns.

December and circling in her arms one or the other she had watched the early sunset over the river. The flooding shadow on the face of the Palisades, and soon the new moon shining in the blue light. She could look for only a moment, as if staring might interfere with memory. For the second time she had felt at home on earth.

The first time: they had been sitting in a rowboat, she and her brother. Her brother was handling the oars. She had been watching the greasy roll of the oar in its lock, thinking of nothing, when suddenly she had seen them afloat in this moment of their lives and with amazement and gratitude had felt the kernel of her heart break open. Had glimpsed through the oarlock in the darting silver water a shimmering round O, an apostrophe to joy.

When it had arrived, the heartbreaking blow!

The hammer fell, iron on iron. The iron was the heart, the iron was the stroke of wrong, wrong, wrong.

He told her that true piety could be comprehended in the example of his grandmother who on the boat coming from Ireland during the Famine with all her children had buried one of them at sea. Yes, and only two weeks after her arrival, lost her husband to pneumonia, the one who in a December snowfall had stood in the station waiting to welcome her. Even so, he said, she'd worked the scrap of rocky farmland herself, raised the children, and on Sundays milked the cows before setting off. That would be for Mass in Utica. The farm several miles back in the hills; from Frankfort, along the canal to Utica, ten more miles. Afterwards, all of them home again in time to milk the cows at night.

"What can we learn from this story?" he'd asked. "I think we can learn something about faith."

She liked the wheel, though, the way the saint might suddenly take it into her head to roll it off into thin air.

The shaggy bark of the hickory tree outside the window curls out, like hair rising in a light breeze.

And you, beloved old father, sitting so quietly there eating your soup. What do you see? What do you hear?

"No," she said, "you'd better go down without me."

In the middle of the night, sometimes, she got out of bed and stood by the window. She tried to put herself into a swoon, gazing through half-closed eyes at the pale shadows of trees lying flat and motionless on the grass. She tried not to see the Swan tilting like the sail of a ship across the summer sky or even the invisible air. She pretended she wasn't standing there at all, that her heart wasn't pounding in the night.

"You must struggle with this," he said. "You must exert your will."

"*Vanishing Tide:* a mixed tide of considerable inequality in the two highs or two lows, so that the 'high low' may become indistinguishable from the 'low high.' The result is a vanishing tide, where no significant difference is apparent."

In the open spaces, ringed by trees, the summer evening flooded blue. The woman standing there thought that if she was completely still for even the merest fraction of a second she would fall past the place where she was into the place where she is. It was the silence of the tulip trees she was straining to hear, the trees standing all around her, as if about to speak. She looked down at the grass and tried to make her mind go blank. Then she glanced up quickly, thinking to surprise them, a ring of tongued flames singing in the twilight.

They stood before her: one, two. The shadow rising behind.

Whose Words Are These?

Whose words are these? What is the length of a single life? Where is its beginning, where is its end? How does grief feed desire, and how does desire seek relief in words? Like the vine cut down too soon whose roots grope a dark underground passage until one day a green blind nub cuts a hole in the stiff brown hickory leaf lying all winter next to the house, thwarted desire will up. Who are we when we wake in the night from the dream of the baby who will be taken from us? When we recall the smell of the damp scalp, the taste of the fine dark hair against our tongue?

Is it grief that rushes to meet us? Is it desire? The desire that falls into despair? The desire that falls into words? And for how long can one continue in silence? For that matter, who is it finally that forbids us to speak? And why do we imagine that words—the hope not of the elusive, forbidden thing itself, but of the wave of sound that summons it—will help us into one more stricken dawn? The words, often enough, we cannot find, the words too many or too few. The words that slip away, that fall in the air as they fly, that break against despair as against a seawall. The words that fall back into the tireless, silent, churning ocean of coral reef and pearl.

Part Three

John Carmody Has a Word or Two

I

Closer yet I approach you,
What thought you have of me now, I had as much of you –

And so I come to this: in imagining Deirdre in Pelham, I am never far from thoughts of her father, the man with the sloping eyes. As she moves about the house, meeting him everywhere, John Carmody is her own soon-to-be ghost: her own rapidly aging father, going up and down the stairs sideways as Bert will do, holding onto the banister, sitting with Willie and herself at dinner where he entertains them with stories familiar from her earliest days. Although Deirdre is still in her mid-thirties when they come to live in the house and her father not yet seventy, they are the survivors of a family that included a brother two years older than herself and a mother dead at fifty-seven. Did they speak to each other of their dead ones? Did they avoid the subject altogether for fear of rousing their own low-lying griefs? For fear of betraying feelings they would have kept secret from themselves, certainly from each other: rage at the arbitrariness of death, its irrevocability, rage at being left alone amidst the wreckage? Rage at their beloved dead for slights and omissions they'd been unable to forgive, for cruel lapses provoked by fear, by desire?

What is not a matter for conjecture is that in May 1914, a little more than a month before the assassination of the Austrian archduke that Bert remembers, John Carmody sat down to write his memoirs. For all we know at the very instant Deirdre inscribed her initials on the cover of the torn copybook. Perhaps they sat writing companionably in different rooms, upstairs or down, writing while the children were at school, Willie in the city, the two of them absorbed, oblivious, looking up at last from their papers at exactly the same instant, at the first shuddering bong of the midday hour, looked up a little wildly, each one distraught, elated: distraught because the words fell into confusion as soon as they were placed on the page; elated because each was at last doing the very thing that might ease, if only for a little, a strain around the heart.

It may have been to occupy her father—after he'd turned things over for a couple of years sitting beside the radiator—that Deirdre suggested he write down something from his store of memories. At any rate, he begins by disclaiming all responsibility in the matter of putting pen to paper.

May 21, 1914

My dear little Granddaughters:

Your good parents have been impressed with the idea that your old grandfather's life was possessed of sufficient venturesome interest to merit his leaving for you a record of same. While depreciating such ideas, he has been unable to withstand their flattering importunity, and trusts that when you grow up to an understanding of the big words used by "Grandpa," you may find these ruminations and recollections not entirely devoid of interest.

John R. Carmody

His life-account runs to almost fifty typed single-spaced pages. As in the case of Willie's, someone must have typed the original handwritten pages that have since been lost; however, unlike Willie, he corrects errors of fact here and there with the stroke of his pen, changes a word.

A Pleasant Shady Little Village

*I was born, June 9th, 1843, in Mohawk, N.Y., a pleasant shady
little village to which my father, Michael Carmody, and my mother,
Alice Quinn, came and settled about three quarters of a century
ago, having emigrated from the County of Limerick, Ireland. As
they soon acquired a modest, comfortable dwelling of their own and
prospered in a moderate degree, it would seem to show the wisdom of
their choice.*

*In the attainment of this home, however, I feel that Mother
must have been an active agent as she had excellent judgment and
was a most wonderful manager of her household—as industrious
as she was economical—and while my father was likewise diligent
and devoted to his business, he did not possess the forethought
and foresight of Mother. He was of a most generous and genial
disposition and always ready for a romp with us children. Mother
on the contrary was of a reserved, sedate nature and of most equable
temper, which I never saw ruffled. Both were charitable and liberal*

and on good terms with our neighbors. Of children there were five. Thinking of those early days I vividly remember the abundance of supplies for winter: barrels and barrels of apples, potatoes, turnips and other vegetables, beef, hams, etc. And with the woodhouse piled chock-a-block with stove wood, we could bid defiance to the winter's siege.

How one begins to create characters out of these long-ago people, to make them up! And that's precisely because of what is withheld. The silence is the shadow leaping on the wall. He allows himself not another word on the subject of his parents: it may have been that like Deirdre and myself, he was caught between the desire to speak and the consequences of doing so. Was prey to his own fear of disloyalty. Of the elephant slamming his head up against the wall, of harsh self-turnings, shame. And yet what wouldn't we give to draw near a single day, no, a single burning hour, in the life of the genial Michael Carmody of Limerick? The self-contained Alice Quinn?

As the domestic scene yields to a larger world, it seems there's less to wonder at: that is, as John Carmody's narrative moves away from his parents and turns to descriptions of school, enlistment at the Brooklyn Naval Yard in 1862, the Civil War, and so on. We're aware of something quite different in his accounts of public life: the long parade of people passing over the earth, the multitudes, the will to power: *the hell of war, the cruelties of creeds.* We thrill to the strangeness of having been born into a particular time, into these circumstances and no others, with just *these* people as compatriots. And so our secret life may be some baffling mix of the public and private. We wake and hear a dog barking in the distance, a voice calling out, tires swishing by on a wet pavement. We're aware we've entered *the propounded world.* We remember a face glimpsed years ago on a dusty moonlit street when we were sixteen. A hand holding tight to the railing of a ferry. Our very dreams draw from the common life. We see each other coming and going, we are each other's heart's desire.

The Eelrack

From the age of six to fourteen I attended school and had a different teacher for nearly every year, as such employment seemed to be only a makeshift occupation with most of them. The pupils suffered accordingly. Our old schoolhouse, popularly called the "eelrack" by the boys, is still standing but altered beyond recognition.

112

In wintertime quite a number of Erie Canal drivers used to attend and a turbulent lot they were, driving many teachers to resign. It was a settled policy that they must subdue the big boys or the big boys would eject them. You won't wonder now why my youthful bent tended toward a bellicose profession. On the first day of school (how well I remember it although I was only six!) I'm sorry to say I struck a big girl with a rubber overshoe for "making up faces" at me, and was sent home in disgrace.

One of the teachers, Mr. Randall, who had the unusual given name of Epaphroditus, was a rather advanced teacher for those times, calling his school an academy. I had the advantage of attending it for a while. It was there I first saw electrical experiments given; one day he became so absorbed in this work that it was long after the closing hour before he dismissed us. I remember the yelling and hooting the boys indulged in, rushing down the stairs shouting, "Epaphroditus! Epaphroditus! Come out to the woods and fight us."

About the time I was thirteen a great achievement was wrought by the village in its new brick schoolhouse with three teachers and three grades, so the old eelrack was abandoned. The new schoolhouse had a lofty cupola or belfry, which it was the ambition of the venturesome boys to climb and there carve their names at the highest point they could reach. This continued until one day, to the surprise of all, a reckless girl pupil surpassed us in the height attained. As the boys feared further defeat and humiliation at the girl's hands, the practice passed into desuetude, leaving the girl as victor. Only a few days ago an old schoolmate in Mohawk sent me a souvenir of those days, a slat from the blinds of that old cupola which had been removed for repairs. On it had been carved, over half a century ago, the inscription, "J. R. Carmody, June 11th, 1857."

In our community a boy who had reached the age of fourteen was expected to graduate from school and take up some employment. In accordance with this usage I sought and obtained work in a match factory at one dollar per week, out of which munificent salary I managed to save a little.

He was reading in his chair by the window, as I imagine it, when Deirdre placed the package in his hands one bright afternoon in late October, the radiator rattling and clanging because lately the days have grown cold. After she leaves the room, he carefully examines the writing on the brown paper, looks up and sees the last scrappy yellow tulip leaves hanging in the sun. Although tulips, he thinks, are not trees he's lived with; it's elms and their deep summer shade, their lightly trailing branches, he remembers from the days of his boyhood. He unties the string, loosens the paper, and then is holding in his hand a piece of splintered wood, gray, weather-beaten, rippled along one edge, is tracing with a finger the letters he remembers carving into the soft wood with his pocketknife to signify his name and a date that followed his fourteenth birthday by two days.

The school year was ending and the match factory waiting. He remembers the deafening clatter of boots on the wooden steps as he and his classmates were released from school that day, remembers someone calling out a dare and then his flinging himself onto the copper water pipe at the corner of the schoolhouse, shinnying up the pipe and scampering across the roof to the belfry where each morning the bell rang calling them all. Remembers looking out from his dizzying perch and seeing the valley tip up to his gaze, the river, the canal running beside it with barges standing in the locks, the swell of green hills beyond, remembers seeing the others insignificant below, all eyes on him, and felt—in this supreme moment, this solitary remove from everything that claimed him—ready to meet his destiny which he knew would be no mean one.

And were his expectations fulfilled? Did he become the character he imagined? Because that's the puzzle. We know, at least, that on March 18, 1893, the *Utica Saturday Globe,* with the flourish characteristic of its time, takes note of a visit he made to the Mohawk Valley when he was about to turn fifty:

> *Paymaster John R. Carmody of the United States Navy is one of the leading as he is one of the most esteemed citizens of the national capital. He was born in Mohawk and when 19 years old enlisted in the Navy. He served with the Mississippi and Gulf squadrons. He engaged in several encounters on the James and York Rivers, served under Porter on the Mississippi and was present in the operations on the Cumberland and Tennessee Rivers. He participated in the siege and taking of Mobile, and was present at the final surrender of the Confederate naval forces at the Tombigbee River in April 1865.*

II

Beat! beat! drums!—blow! bugles! blow!
Through the windows—through doors—burst like a ruthless force

Dire Resort

The year 1861 had now arrived and the country was seething with alarm and excitement—the South determined to secede from the Union and the North equally resolved to prevent it. All efforts to bring about a peaceful solution of the question had failed so the dire resort to arms quickly followed the firing of the first gun by the hot-headed southerners at Charleston, South Carolina, where they made their attack on Fort Sumter.

The following year, in June 1862, having reached the age of nineteen, I, together with some half dozen companions, inspired by the prevailing feeling, resolved to enlist in the Navy although none of us had ever seen salt-water. Why we chose the Navy in preference to the Army was due, I fancy, to the victory of our first iron-clad Monitor *over the Confederate iron-clad* Merrimac *in Hampton Roads which occurred about that time and gave great encouragement to the North, making popular the Navy.*

Equipped with light hearts and lighter baggage we proceeded to New York City, a journey then of fourteen hours from Herkimer, and to nearly all of us our first visit to the great metropolis. On arriving we lost no time and the following morning, bright and early, proceeded to the Navy Yard in Brooklyn. There we presented ourselves—probably the greenest bunch of young countrymen that ever aspired to the nautical profession—and notwithstanding all of us very confident that eventually we would attain fame surpassing that of Commodore John Paul Jones and Admiral Horatio Nelson.

A Capt. Richard W. Meade, an old time executive officer, received us in a brusque but kindly manner on the old line-of-battleship <u>North Carolina</u> which was used as quarters for recruits. At first he seemed inclined to decide against enlisting us on the ground that the old hardened sailors would be too rough for us to associate with. He summed up by saying, "Young men, if it is your intention to join the Navy for pleasure you might better enter Hell for happiness."

In fact, Meade was persuadable:

He finally decided to receive us when one of our fellows, Ralph Bell, a clever, cheeky boy, remarked that our finances were in such condition that it was a case of enlistment or walking back home. Within a few hours we found ourselves proudly arrayed in a man-o'-war suit and each detailed for duty in some department of the ship of which we knew not the stern from the bow. I was placed in the Paymaster's office to act as messenger and get experience to qualify myself for a clerkship on an active seagoing ship. As a novice for a month or so I encountered a rather hard existence where all my surroundings, personal and material, differed widely from my home life. The <u>North Carolina</u> had at this time over two thousand recruits on board, mostly experienced sailors, man-o'-wars' men, merchantmen and whalers, hailing from all parts of the world. The number included many foreigners unable to speak the English language, but who had been quietly encouraged in foreign ports by our secret agents to come to this country and join the Army and Navy.

Most of the days were devoted to drilling and whipping into shape this incongruous body. However, ships were being rapidly built and converted at the ship yards and crews transferred from the Receiving Ship to man them for active service on the coast and rivers of the South. I acquired knowledge of and experience in Paymaster's accounts, which embraced the clothing, subsisting and paying of the officers and crew.

In addition, I underwent instructions in the manual of arms under a very amusing drillmaster, one Sergeant Paddy Doyle of the Marines, who impressed his instructions and orders so forcibly that for many years I had a tendency to keep step and mark time. The Sergeant took greater pride in drilling his awkward squad than a Major General in his command of a division of troops.

116

I hear now his short sharp orders given to a squad of recruits to "Mark time! Right foot! Left foot! Halt!" "Take your position as a soldier." "Stand erect with your chest thrown out and your fingers resting on the outside seam of your trousers." "Eyes resting on the ground fifteen paces to the front." "Feet forming an angle of forty-five degrees—toeing the seam in the deck." The physical transformation was so great after the thorough "setting up" the recruits received that I doubt if many farmers' boys would be recognized by their own parents.

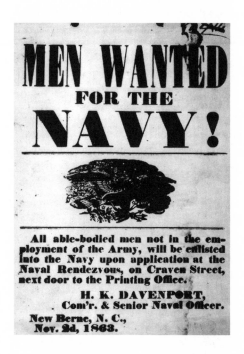

A timely escape from the match factory. However, I'm reminded by this story of enlistment that Emily Dickinson's brother, Austin, never went to war, nor did either Henry or William James. Three hundred dollars apiece took care of that. It was the Jameses' younger, more ordinary brothers, Wilkie and Rob, whom Henry Sr. allowed to go.

They were exact contemporaries, Henry James and John Carmody: born within a couple of months of each other, dead within the same year. And yet they arrive—for all their differing experience of war—in the same place. *It looks as though we are on the brink of disastrous times:* so her father writes to Deirdre on the day after the snowstorm, February 6, 1917, when glittering icicles are hanging from the gutters and he is looking down the dark corridor of our now-vanished century. Henry, staring into the same abyss, calls it a nightmare from which there is no waking save by sleep.

And yet at the age of nineteen, John Carmody exhibits a decidedly romantic turn of mind, fashioning himself on Commodore John Paul Jones and Admiral Horatio Nelson. One hundred and fifty years ago, naval heroes were all the rage. The young cadet looks out with sloping eyes from an early photo, fingers tucked inside his uniform jacket, a self-styled Irish Napoleon. The war gives him a chance to see himself as the hero of his own life. And so allows him, in the life we call "public," to discover the hidden, the unspeakable, waiting to be given language or image.

Incident on the Tennessee River

We know that 2,300,000 men fought in the Civil War. More than 600,000—that's one out of four—died. And thanks to Mathew Brady we know what the killing fields looked like. Does John Carmody strike the personal note as he looks around him? Does he break the silences surrounding war? Here he describes events leading up to the siege of Mobile, *black ships fighting on the sea envelop'd in smoke:*

> *Early in March we commenced in Mobile Bay operations in dredging for torpedoes which the Confederates had, in addition to strong fortifications, planted in the channel under the superintendence of French officers. At that period the use of torpedoes was modern and strongly denounced as a factor in civilized warfare. This was tedious and dangerous work, mostly under fire of the enemy's batteries. One day I witnessed the blowing up of three of our vessels, and the following day our launch and crew was struck and destroyed, instantly killing several men.*
>
> *On a dark night I volunteered to accompany a boat's party from our ship fitted out to pull into shore to do a little scouting, and as we found their Navy Yard looking very inviting and unguarded, we quietly rowed in with muffled oars, without disturbing its occupants, and captured a newly finished torpedo boat. We towed it off to the* Cincinnati *with great pride, which, however, was offset by humiliation when we were reprimanded by the commanding officer for exceeding our instructions. This action was a fair illustration of the old nautical maxim—"obey orders if you break owners."*

Early in April 1865, the enemy found their fortifications reduced by our constant bombardment and surrender was formally made of Mobile to our joint Army and Navy forces. The Confederate Navy vessels escaped a few days previously up the Tombigbee River where we found them and received the surrender of some twenty vessels of all sorts. We then steamed up the Alabama River to Selma, convoying General Steel's army corps but with no resistance offered except an occasional rifle shot from bushwhackers concealed along the banks who killed and wounded several of our men. As a measure of warning and reprisal the General commanding ordered the burning of two or three beautiful old houses belonging to the culprits, after which the firing ceased.

And is he emerging as the hero of his life? A war hero? He's careful to record the capture of the torpedo boat: an achievement of *great pride* that ended in humiliation. But here is something more to the point:

An incident occurred on the Tennessee River which gave me "une mauvaise quarte heure." In scanning the shores with my glasses I discovered one of the enemy on horseback and impulsively drew my revolver and fired at him. Much to my dismay I saw him fall from his horse down among the tall weeds, and with my heart in my throat feared I'd killed him. In a few minutes I was happily relieved to see him dart back into safety like a gray streak. My action, under the conditions of warfare prevailing, was justified but nevertheless I felt for the moment like an assassin.

Not a glorious hero at all but an assassin, the hired killer of a man sitting in his saddle among tall weeds. And here is something else:

While steaming up the Alabama River one night we stopped in front of a prosperous plantation and made fast to the bank in order to secure a supply of wood for our furnaces owing to our coal's having been exhausted. We found the place abandoned by all save the house servants and field hands numbering a hundred or more slaves who had got the idea that Lincoln had come to liberate them. Loading themselves with plunder, they had assembled with lighted torches at the ship's landing, singing songs of jubilee and glory. Finally, when we had cast off our lines and got the ship under way, a piteous, heartrending wail of disappointment went up from the crowd. The weird sight of the flaring torches reflected against the dark background was a sight I never shall forget. Had I been in command I should have taken them on board, notwithstanding regulations forbidding. One can imagine the punishment they received after our disappearance and the return of their owner!

Oh, terrible! No wonder he has premonitions of disaster. Years later the old man gets up from his chair to adjust the gas jet burning in the porcelain cylinder and sees before him the ship's landing, the torches flaming in the night. Hears in his granddaughters singing up and down the stairs a surge of voices, a wailing that he sometimes wakes to in the night, shuddering. In the book John Carmody is reading of his own life, he, the protagonist, now appears in a changing, fitful light. It seems he's becoming a character to himself—one among others—rather than an "I" shooting like a firework into dark skies, alone and particular.

—And have you become a character in your own life?

I have not. I speak glibly of his becoming the protagonist in the book of his life, but who am I in the book of my own? Is my book not merely the book of these others? Even now I'm as adrift as once as a child, standing in front of the closet door in the sitting room, staring into the same mirror he looked into every day of those final years: slipping buttons through the holes in his shirt, combing his hair, searching his face for traces of the one who climbed the water pipe, who blithely cast his lot for war.

—And do you despair and call out for help, standing there in front of the mirror?

I am bidding farewell to the year. It is New Year's Eve, a dripping white winter morning, and I am six years old, suddenly overwhelmed by the notion that the year that had seemed in no way distinct from the ordinary flow of life, nothing to consider or think about, is in fact particular, perishing, and that I am losing it forever. A piercing loss, and I speak to the passing year as if it were my dearest love, calling out to it as it departs, assuring this moment that I'll never forget, ever.

—You look for yourself in the vanishing years?

It's not so much that. It's rather that in my struggle to say, yes, this is who I am, no, this is who I am not, I'm over and over swept beneath by the undertow, by swift bleak currents threatening destruction if for one instant I permit my gaze to stray. A love affair, of a kind, because the sweet seductions of the past allow me to step out of ordinary life altogether and surrender to longings that shatter time. Oh yes, there's a kind of voluptuous enchantment in keeping my eyes fixed on these perilous depths. A dangerous enchantment. And so for fear of slipping I plunge.

Sadly Astounding News

On arriving at Selma we found that our General Wilson of cavalry fame had passed through and left the Confederate arsenal and other public buildings in ashes. From our intercourse with the citizens, we plainly saw the bottom had dropped out of the Confederacy and its end was near at hand. The people of the South had made terrible sacrifices for their cause, but their prolonged and heroic struggle against our superior number, and greater resources, finally met with a most disastrous and dismal ending.

Upon our return from Selma to Mobile we learned of the surrender of General Lee, the capture of Richmond, and the general collapse of the Confederacy, together with the sadly astounding news of the assassination of President Lincoln. That great and good man's tragic death spread a pall over all of us. I saw tears in the eyes of strong men that night whom I thought had become callused to all sentiment through their familiarity with the heartrending events of the war.

Bert, moving sideways up and down the stairs in the house in Pelham at the age of ninety-seven, hanging onto the banister, remembers hearing a woman—who'd been taken to see it as a child—describe the progress of Lincoln's funeral cortege up Broadway. The throngs lining the streets, each one having risen from a bed that morning or, if not a bed, a pallet or nest of newspapers; each having peed in a pot or against a wall, clapped to their feet shoes or boots or rags, shrugged their shoulders into some garment or other. Drawn outside each one to their own kind, out onto the street, out with the others, away from the rooms or alleys or doorways they'd slept in. Each with a private anguish, you may be sure, each with a single burning hope.

III

Hither my love!
Here I am! here!

The Greatest Good Fortune of My Life

In December 1868, while I was sailing in the West Indies on the
Yantic, that dire scourge yellow fever made its appearance on board
and I contracted a milder form of the disease, the dengue, from
whose effects I never fully recovered. It wasn't until April 1871, that
I was ordered to the store-ship Relief, which was fitting out to convey
provisions to the suffering French after their disastrous defeat by the
Germans. On our voyage across the Atlantic we were unfortunate
enough to be overtaken by a terrific cyclone, which lasted five days.
These storms are of vast extent, rotating about a calm onward
moving center of low atmospheric pressure, and are exceedingly
dangerous to ships drawn within their vortex. Our poor old sailing
craft found herself almost helpless under the circumstances but
escaped finally in much damaged condition with our beds and
clothing, our quarters and stores, thoroughly drenched by the heavy
seas which pounded our decks.
*   At Plymouth I made some pleasant acquaintances among the*
British naval officers, one of whom, a son of Charles Dickens, I had
known previously when he was our guest on board the Yantic at
Colon and waiting for his ship to arrive in Panama.
*   After my return, the greatest good fortune of my life came to me*
in the person of sweet Mary Ethridge, my precious wife, your dear

mother's mother. We were married in New York City on January 25, 1872, after a correspondence of several months and a courtship of more than a year.

We went on a happy wedding journey to the national capital where before leaving we were invited to the White House and presented to President and Mrs. Grant. We stopped at the Army and Navy headquarters, where I met many friends of both services. As all this was new to my dear girl wife, the novelty was most pleasing to her and I assured her we would come back some day and make Washington our home.

He was twenty-nine at the time, she was twenty-two. Of the courtship all that remains is an empty envelope on which he has written:

Mary Ethridge from John Carmody
Yew twig from the grave of Heloise and Abelard
Père Lachaise, Paris 1871

The yew twig tells us something of the light in which he regarded himself in his new role. But of Mary we know nothing except through the words of others. Of her girlhood, nothing. No wedding picture. Although resting there on the bookshelf in the upstairs hall in Pelham is the tiny oval photograph of Mary as a little black-eyed girl. She's perhaps five or six years old, dark hair parted in the middle, corkscrew curls tumbling on either side of her face.

Is this not the most baffling thing of all, the bodies of those lost ones, the hair springing from their scalps, the teeth in their heads? Because, after all, it was these bodies so like our own, bodies waiting to be touched, these sweating suffering exulting bodies, whose shudders washed us up on shore.

IV

With antecedents,
With my fathers and mothers and the accumulations of past ages,
With all which, had it not been, I would not now be here, as I am.

Antecedents

My very dear wife was the daughter of Mr. and Mrs. Robert Ethridge of Frankfort, N.Y., both mostly descended through several generations from the earliest Dutch or Palatinate settlers in the Mohawk Valley, dating from 1711. Robert Ethridge's father, however, Nathaniel Ethridge, was of New England or English blood. Mrs. Ethridge's father was Col. Weber and her mother was a Bellinger whose own mother had been a Herkimer. Both ancestors were possessed of immense landed property and were regarded with much respect by the community, filling all the important offices of honor and trust.

Without the Civil War, it's not likely the boy from the match factory, son of Irish immigrants, would have made such a connection. We can only imagine what attracted them to each other. Was she intrigued by his stories of the war? Did she love him for the dangers he had passed, and did he love her that she did pity them? Did she imagine a life of adventure awaited her on the arm of John Carmody that would carry her far beyond the confines of that *immense landed property*? Or was she fascinated by some quality that seemed to her foreign, his Irishness? What's certain is that in marrying Mary Ethridge he was marrying outside his tribe, outside his religion, which by that time he'd in any case almost certainly have left behind.

And in what light did her family regard him? Did her parents object to their youngest daughter marrying someone whose mother and father had so recently arrived from elsewhere? Although, it's true, the wholesale agony of the war must have done its work of softening the edges of these social pretensions, have also rubbed away the sharp outlines of his origins. What we do know is this: Mary's oldest sister, Catherine, had married someone named David Gregg who was pastor of the Lafayette Street

Presbyterian Church in Brooklyn. It was in their home that on January 25, 1872, John Carmody and Mary Ethridge were married. A newspaper clipping records this fact. It's quite likely that David Gregg performed the ceremony. There's no record, however, of the Ethridge parents' presence at a wedding where one of their daughters was married in the home of another.

And now, suddenly, mention of Mary Ethridge's older sister Catherine reminds me that Willie—on that summer's day in 1896 when he met Deirdre's train in Jersey City and traveled with her across the river and then to Grand Central Station—took as a sign of Deirdre's interest in him her suggestion that he come to see her, on her return from Utica, at her aunt's house in Brooklyn. Furthermore, the name, "Gregg," recalls something else as well.

Of course neither Charlie nor Maddie nor I ever laid eyes on Deirdre or Rob: all the Carmodys were lying in one kind of grave or another by 1923. But how could I forget our being taken, as children, to see two very old women at Christmastime? Two old women who I now think must have been the surviving children of Catherine and David Gregg? Yes, their last name was certainly Gregg, the name was in the air, but we called them Cousin Catherine and Cousin Margaret. Perhaps because Deirdre had taught Kate as a little girl to do so? Who they were, exactly, I never clearly understood. But now I think they must have been Deirdre's older cousins and might even have been present as small children at that winter wedding in January 1872. They lived just off Washington Square, in a building that looked down on Washington Mews. It was on our way to One Fifth Avenue, driving down the West Side Highway, that Charlie and Maddie and I were given our first view of the Chatsworth.

They lived in an apartment with a dim front room from which you could peer out at a tree blooming with all its lights in Washington Arch. I see the room, the waning winter afternoon, lamps set out on tables overflowing with papers and books. It is Cousin Margaret who opens the door. She is wearing a dress that flares somewhere above her ankles, a blue dress to match her eyes, probably, for it's clear she thinks of such things, her gray hair is set in waves about her face. She gives us a brisk welcome and we enter to see Cousin Catherine rising slowly from her chair.

Cousin Catherine is another case entirely in her black silk skirt that reaches almost to the floor, her long glinting chain from which hangs a round gold watch. As she rises she holds onto the watch with a hand that is paper thin, delicate as old ivory. Two gray braids wrap her head like a halo, and she bends on us a luminous gaze. For a long moment, after catching sight of us, strong emotions forbid speech and she can do no more than extend a fine white hand. It is clear to us that Cousin Margaret regards her older sister with the slightest shade of forbearance. Cousin Margaret has seen the world, in midlife she has married an Englishman and survived the London Blitz, indeed has written about it all in a pamphlet extolling the virtues of cheerfulness and industry in times of duress. She speaks in accents that recall her life abroad. It's only after her husband died that Cousin Margaret returned to live with her sister, who, in the end, never married anyone at all, has spent her entire life in this city "doing good," and who as one given to sudden bursts of feeling is surely, Cousin Margaret's glance tells us, not quite so capable as herself.

While Kate sits leaning on her elbow, listening to her cousins, while Bert rests a little apart in a chair beneath a lamp, picking up a book, putting it down, we wander restlessly from window to window, looking out onto Fifth Avenue and the beautiful white Washington Arch that frames the tree nodding with lights in the dusky afternoon. Charlie explains to Maddie and me that the tall marble figure standing at the base of each column is Washington himself: Washington in peacetime in front of the west column. And there, nearer to us, Washington leaning on his sword in time of war. From the window in the bedroom where we have left our coats we look down into the Mews. It must be that it is time to leave at last, that we are putting on our coats, for Cousin Catherine comes slowly into the room and stands at the window behind us: "It was in the stables below, don't you know, that General Washington kept his horses." And now we are at the door where they both stand waving us off, Cousin Margaret turning away a bit impatiently, a bit abruptly, wanting no further part in this farewell: the excited hand-fluttering, the lingering gaze her sister bends on us until we finally disappear behind the sliding doors of the elevator.

These two old women must have known them all: John Carmody and Mary, Deirdre and Robert, and almost certainly their own grandparents, the whole illustrious, landholding lot, descended from Bellingers and Herkimers. For all I know, it was proceeds on the land that paid the rent at One Fifth Avenue. Land acquired, probably, by practices not unlike those by which his wife's forebears—John Carmody suggests—had acquired animal skins:

An anecdote has been handed down regarding one of the early ancestor's methods of dealing with the Indians in the purchase of fur skins. He was popularly known as "King" Weber from his arbitrary manner. It appears he bought the peltry by weight, using on the

126

scales his hand as a five-pound weight and his foot for ten pounds.
He salved his conscience by claiming that the less money the Indian
had, the less rum and whiskey he could consume. A case of the ends
justifying the means. I will not vouch for the truth of this story
reflecting on your venerated ancestor as the same has been told of the
original John Jacob Astor who laid the foundation of his fortune by
dealing with the guileless savage.

Did these cousins tell stories of their own childhood? Of Mary Ethridge or John Carmody? Bored, edgy, on the roam, we listened during these visits to very little of what they said. But without question they would have remembered from their childhoods a New York echoing with the clatter of horseshoes on stone, a New York in which voices in drawing rooms fell with a distinct cadence, perhaps even with the intonation, the accent, of certain characters from the novels of Henry James. Of Catherine Sloper, for example, living just around the corner in Washington Square.

Even as children we recognized the voice of Cousin Catherine as that of another time. I think now it must have been the voice of one very small segment of the American population during the second half of the nineteenth century. She spoke rapidly, breathlessly, using hard *R*s, clipping short her vowels. Her tone was intensely *sweet*: there's no other word for it. It was impossible to imagine Cousin Catherine sounding aggrieved or angry. Decisive, yes. Even emphatic. But always the nod of deference, the inquiring glance darting from one of us to another from beneath her brow. "Margaret dear," is the manner in which she addressed her sister, as if to anticipate, to avert, any criticism; and then the expression we mocked mercilessly on the way home: "little mother dear," referring to the long-dead older sister of Mary Ethridge.

One stray comment I do remember. It was Cousin Catherine who observed in the midst of what conversation I can't imagine: "When the British took Rhinebeck, we packed our things and moved to New York." We vaguely guessed she wasn't talking about an event that she remembered herself. But now I imagine that these words, perhaps exactly these, had been handed down from one generation to another in the tribe to which she and Cousin Margaret belonged. Perhaps these words were repeated to Mary Ethridge as a child. Perhaps they were even repeated to Deirdre. In any case, the word *we* implied that what had happened to the ancestors had happened to oneself; but not to others, not to those not born to the tribe.

V

Fast-anchored eternal O love! O woman I love!
O bride! O wife! more resistless than I can tell, the thought of you!

The Husband's Sacrifice Is Greater

During the fall of 1873 I was granted sick leave while on duty in New Orleans where I had found little change in the people of that city's adverse feeling toward northerners and fully as unreconciled to the radically changed condition of affairs, such as the freedom of the slaves and their enfranchisement. I made haste to join my wife at my father's home in Mohawk where, to our supreme joy on the 10th of November, there was born to us our dear baby boy Robert.

A little more than a year later, in December, 1874, the order came like a bombshell into our own quiet household, sending me without delay to the <u>Monocacy</u> *at Yokohama, Japan, which meant a start within forty-eight hours. This separation was something new and painful for my dear wife to bear and distressing to myself.*

The Navy would be a Paradise were it not for these cruel separations but it strikes me the husband's sacrifice is the greater as he leaves wife and babies and relations and must fight alone his loneliness. It may be said that the husband has the attractions of foreign lands and strange sights to divert him, but these soon pall on the mature officer and become commonplace when his memory is constantly reverting wherever he goes to his home and family and fireside.

Gazing back to take a last view of our house in Mohawk that contained my dear ones, I saw little Robert on the veranda held up in the arms of his mother, which made a pretty but sad picture for me to take on my long journey across the American continent and Pacific Ocean, some eight thousand miles. I do not recollect the exact date of my departure, but know it was the latter part of December, for I passed a most dreary Christmas crossing the bleak plains of the great West.

Does he not sound, here, like Captain Harville at the end of Jane Austen's *Persuasion,* asserting his own greater claim, when he and Anne Elliot are arguing as to whose love is more constant, man's or woman's?

"Ah," cried Captain Harville, in a tone of strong feeling, "if I could but make you comprehend what a man suffers when he takes a last look at his wife and children, and watches the boat that he has sent them off in, as long as it is in sight, and then turns away and says, 'God knows whether we ever meet again!' . . . I speak, you know, only of such men as have hearts!" pressing his own with emotion.

And advancing his case, earlier:

I do not think I have ever opened a book in my life which had not something to say upon woman's inconstancy. Songs and proverbs all talk of woman's fickleness.

As outsider, reading with a squint, Anne sees it differently, tells him so:

Men have had every advantage of us in telling their own story. Education has been theirs in so much higher a degree; the pen has been in their hands. I will not allow books to prove anything.

Had the pen been in Mary's hands, what story might she have told of herself! And what's not mentioned at all is that her husband left her pregnant, this time with Deirdre, who was born a little more than three months later, on April Fools' Day, 1875. John Carmody didn't return from his travels for two years, and even at that, his tour had been reduced by a third.

How she passed those years remains completely unknown. But I see her alone, emphatically alone. In the Mohawk Valley, in the village of Mohawk itself: a town like the neighboring ones of Herkimer, Ilion, and Frankfort strung along the river and the Erie Canal which parallels it. Towns all now in a state of collapse featuring boarded-up factories, vacant and peeling Victorian houses, abandoned railroad stations. But the train running between Albany and Utica still follows the tracks beside the river, its long mournful whistle spilling over the banks on either side and flooding the villages and towns.

Low Hangs the Moon

I picture her on a warm spring evening a few weeks after Deirdre's birth when snow still lay in patches on the leeside of trees and peepers trilled in the pond. Once more she is on the veranda, but this time she is holding the infant Deirdre against breasts pricking with milk. The pure wash of April light is clarifying the world she sees before her, the cows standing in the water meadow, the sooty black of elm branches touched by points of savage green. The green—indistinct a few weeks ago, a mere smudge against the sky—surprises her, wounds her. Things are coming to leaf and she wants him, she wants him with her now. She remembers the recent birth, the tearing in her loins, the moans breaking from her as if she had been a gored animal, sounds that at Rob's birth she'd imagined at first must be coming from elsewhere. And she wondered this time as she had before why the wandering male should have the delight—delight she knew she'd shared fiercely, greedily—and then go his way and the woman be left with this. But that grievance had passed and it was simply wanting that seized her now, brute wanting, and the young May moon slicing the sky was a hook in her heart.

It had been there all day, the pale white moon, crossing the sky in the path of the sun, but she could see its sharp silver rim in the west only now as the sky went from pale blue to indigo, as night fell. They'd agreed the moon would be for each the sign of the other, for while apart it was only the moon they could share, the moon that new or full appeared the same in the sky from wherever one looked, from this veranda in Mohawk or— he'd written her—from the deck of a ship in Japan with Mount Fuji rising in the distance. And she tried to think yes, as with the moon, so with him, he accompanies me even now when I don't see him. In the dark I'll look and he'll shine the brighter. Gleam palely throughout the night like the necklace of coral beads he'd given her when they were married—a fitting gift from a sailor, he'd said, something hauled dripping from the sea—the necklace she'd vowed the day he'd left not to wear until his return, the necklace now hanging from a nail in the wall beside her brass bed. And yet, she thought, even at night, even when the moon is loose in the sky, sublime and serene, it may disappear behind a bank of clouds, may rise too late to be of any use—that was the low-hanging moon, the dying moon, as in the lullaby she sang to the babies—or vanish altogether for a day or two before it appeared again like now a shining sliver in the west.

No, there was no end to wanting and when she was with the very people who were supposed to have been a protection against loneliness—couples with their babies, husband and wife—a fierce yearning took hold of her that felt like possession, she could think of nothing else. The days were too many to count, she passed each in a kind of stupefied longing, and it seemed unspeakably cruel to her that he should be so far away and for so long. Every night when the babies were at last asleep, she took from a drawer the little daguerreotype in its lead frame, the one taken of him during the Rebellion wearing his Union cap with the eagle pinned in front. He'd given it to her soon after they'd met, he'd wished her to see how he'd looked before he'd been stung by fever on the *Yantic*.

But in truth, she thought—examining the likeness closely beneath the steady flame of a candle—she could see little difference between then and now: the gray eyes sloping down at the corners which almost immediately she'd loved for their sleepy look and whose lashes she'd soon wanted to taste with her tongue. The high-arched nose, the young full mouth that had by now swallowed her own often enough. Every day she carefully showed the picture to little Rob who was not yet a year and a half but it was clear that Rob was fast forgetting his father. And sometimes, staring as hard as she might into the face she had come to know so intimately, she wondered if she herself could summon the living moving breathing man and if her longing hadn't turned him into someone she didn't know, a phantom, as if she had been making him up, almost as if he'd been someone she'd once read about in a book.

But then she was so often adrift, so tired—awake at every hour with the baby, trying to make up to Rob for the loss of his father, Rob who clung to her skirts and wanted to climb into her lap always just when she was sitting down to nurse Deirdre—that she might imagine anything. Indeed, these fancies had begun even before the infant's birth, during those days at Christmastime when he was first gone and she, lying in the dark alone feeling within the nudge and turn of limbs still secret and untouched, thought she'd divined in the still cold air a plaintive crying and decided to name the baby Deirdre: Deirdre who, he'd told her once, according to an old Irish story of his father's, had been heard weeping in her mother's womb and when born was seen to be beautiful beyond compare so that the king himself despite all prophecies had wished to marry her. But not so beautiful as herself, he'd added gallantly, and he the ardent king waiting to unbind her own dark hair.

Yes, her imagination went anywhere, had the strength of a team of horses, and sometimes she had complicated dreams in which waves were breaking over the prow of a ship, pounding its deck mercilessly, the roll and pitch of the ship washing sailors into the sea, she could hear the timbers creaking, the howl of the wind, and when she came gradually to herself in the dark, dizzy with relief—and *Relief* was the name, wasn't it, of the ship on its way to France that had survived such a storm—she reached for the tiny white-limbed infant who was opening her mouth in the gasping frantic way of newborns but also in a clogged weeping all her own. Or no. It might not be little Deirdre at all who had woken her, but Rob himself who sometimes called out wildly in the midst of his own terrifying dream from which he always found it so hard to awaken, some dream of falling, he'd tried to tell her, falling down, down.

She would go inside now with all the lovely April night unfolding

around her—soft cooings and scents and moons and secret harmonies—
and cover the sleeping Rob with a blanket and sit in the rocking chair
and nurse this new creature who was beginning to stir against her. But
before she dropped into bed she would look east to see if she could find
the Swan, her favorite of all the constellations. Last night it had seemed
to her to be pointing northeast and so flying away from where it must
go, beating counter, as if dragged by the feet unwilling across the sky, and
then she'd realized no, of course not, its neck was long, its wings toward
the back where the brightest star shone steadily and so it was, after all,
flying due west with the flow of the Milky Way at its back.

It was then she saw that direction was a matter of perspective and
one might beat one's wings frantically against the pull but arrive at one's
destination regardless. Because it wasn't a matter of will it was a matter
of where one was placed in time and space and everyone disappeared at
last over the horizon like it or not. She was twenty-four now what people
called young and would live she knew not how long but like the Swan
would drop out of sight. And knowing this in the midst of this violent
storm of longing, this terrible extremity that she must after all weather
alone, felt a stern and solitary sense of some new life budding within, a life
she could only call her own that would flower as it would.

Yokohama

*Finally we sailed and after a passage of thirty days reached
Yokohama on February 22nd, 1875, a crossing which should have
lasted seventeen days but for some six or seven distinct adverse
storms. On our arrival we barely had fuel enough to creep into
Yokohama.*

*We found that the Pacific Mail officials were very much alarmed
over our delayed arrival and were about to send out a steamer
to hunt for us. We were of course delighted to make port after
our tedious trip and appreciated the crisp, sunny morning that
welcomed us. The harbor was studded with shipping dressed with
bright bunting and flags of many nations in honor of Washington's
birthday and as a picturesque setting for the background stood the
volcano Fujiyama in the distance.*

The Monocacy *was an old-fashioned sidewheel vessel, a product
of the Civil War, and was quite roomy and comfortable for all hands
and well adapted for river service but not very comfortable outside
owing to her light draft.*

By the next mail steamer after my arrival I was happy in
receiving letters from my dear wife, and thereafter, on every steamer
I counted safely on their coming. In the latter part of April 1875 a
most important letter came announcing the glad tidings of the happy
birth, on April 1st, of your darling mother, my only daughter, and
as is customary that evening at dinner my messmates pledged me
their hearty congratulations and good wishes for the young lady and
mother in the best wine the ship's locker afforded. As this occurred
on Saturday night, the regular toast to sweethearts and wives was
not omitted:

To our sweethearts and wives,
may the former soon be the latter,
and the latter always the former.

About this time we were treated to a view of the Mikado, or
Emperor, of Japan who came to Yokohama from Tokyo to visit a
new man-of-war which had been purchased as a starter for their
modern navy. It was the first time this Mikado had presented
himself to the public. He was a slight pale-faced young man of
about twenty-two years, who appeared quite awkward and stiff,
owing doubtless to his first appearance in European naval uniform.
There must have been a hundred thousand of his subjects present
to see his Majesty embark, while all foreign war ships present,
including the <u>Monocacy</u>, fired a royal salute of great guns in
his honor.

A Gilded Buddha

We spent several months in various ports, Yokohama, Nagasaki, Hakadata, Kobe, and Osaka, and parties were made up from the ship to visit interior cities, among them, Kioto, the great southern capital, where but very few foreigners had visited and where we had the good luck to be present during a great fair of beautiful silks, wood carvings, ceramics, etc. It was here I purchased a gilded Buddha that has now come to rest in our house in Pelham.

Homeward

Sometime in October, '76, a young pay officer, attached to the flag-ship as assistant, came to me and said if I wanted to call it a cruise and go home he thought, as the Admiral was friendly toward me as well as himself, it could be arranged. I was of course agreeable to the idea of cutting down the length of my cruise one third and especially so as it was not of my solicitation. By this time our ship had proceeded to Peking and subsequently gone into dry dock in Shanghai in order to receive new boilers. The Admiral readily approved the transfer. I lost no time in starting homeward where I arrived on November 6th, after a pleasant passage across the Pacific in the steamer <u>Belgie</u> *and comfortable trip overland from San Francisco, an altogether more happy journey than outward bound.*

It was after dark when I reached home but bright lights and warm hearts greeted me. The darling babies were roused from their sleep and gazed with wonder on their wandering father, while their fond mother looked on with joy, tears beaming in her lovely dark eyes.

VI

Who was to know what should come home to me?

Paradise of the Pacific

Never again will John Carmody sound so perfectly content as both traveler and family man, the two united in this moment of return. The hero of his hearth, the *wandering father* welcomed with tears of joy. A turning point, of sorts. When he leaves again, Mary and his children will go with him, a departure of a wholly different order.

Our reunited family spent the winter most happily, and with the coming of spring, 1877, I was ordered to duty in charge of naval stores at Honolulu, Sandwich Islands, which was done at my own request as the conditions permitted me to have my family with me.

We were given accommodations at the Royal Hawaiian Hotel, which occupied the centre of an ample park-like site in which were also built, separated from the hotel, several attractive cottages one of which we occupied, taking our meals at the hotel. In the grounds there grew an abundance of tropical plants and rare trees, among the latter Royal and coconut palms, breadfruit and papaya, mango banana etc. There was also in the grounds an ornamental bandstand where the Royal band played several times a week and always at night when the Australian and California steamers were in port: then the hotel grounds were brilliantly illuminated with countless Japanese lanterns, which with the sweet music, mild climate, and happy throngs presented a most impressive scene. We could easily imagine we were in the "Paradise of the Pacific," as Hawaii is called. However, the departure of the steamers and their passengers wrought a wonderful change and, until the arrival of the next, a profound quiet and monotony descended on the community.

Our sojourn in Honolulu was quite a pleasant experience, but as I had so little to do officially, it became rather monotonous despite its tropical allure and friendly, hospitable residents; so at the end of two years I did not hesitate to apply for my detachment and orders

home for examination for promotion to Paymaster, which had
come due. After our return, during the summer of 1879, I bought
a well-trained, gentle pony and basket phaeton which added much
to the children's summer enjoyment of the beautiful country of the
Mohawk Valley.

How not to notice the dread word *monotony* twice creeping into his account of Honolulu? *The Navy would be a Paradise were it not for these cruel separations,* he wrote on his departure for Japan. But *Paradise,* in his own lexicon, applies to a life of storms at sea, of adventures in lands with foreign names. It does not apply to cottages on hotel grounds, to ornamental bandstands.

VII

Passage, immediate passage! The blood burns in my veins!
Away O soul! Hoist instantly the anchor!
Cut the hawsers—haul out—shake out every sail!
Have we not stood here like trees in the ground long enough?

Bow to Fate

As time passes and John Carmody acquires babies and a cottage on the grounds of a hotel, does he wonder what has happened to the era of *light hearts and lighter baggage*? Certainly there's a falling off after he comes to rest in Washington, D.C., which is soon enough where they all find themselves. The further he advances into his life, the more elliptical his account. Is it because he's grown tired of telling his story and life is long? Because, dipping his pen in the inkpot, he's now an old man come to live with his daughter in a strange house where his only business is to die?

Or perhaps, too, in the end, sitting by the spitting radiator, listening to a low rumble high on the roof turn into a whoosh of snow that thundered past the window and landed with a heavy thud on the ground below, it did seem to him that the war—and the world he traveled afterwards, the world the war opened to him—had burned with the brightest blaze. That it was this brilliance he wished to bequeath to his heirs.

Who can doubt he believed he was chronicling travels that had snatched his life from the field of the ordinary? That the world he was describing—but for the war—would have remained as far from his knowledge as Yokohama from Mohawk. And so as he moved into middle age his tale became in his own eyes less *venturesome,* less a thing to relate and embellish, parting ways as it did with his early supreme desire like Ishmael's *to sail about a little and see the watery part of the world.* His travels, if they didn't exactly provide a plot, gave him at least a story.

—And did the travels you mentioned earlier, before your arrival in New York, give you a story?

A story, yes, that was simple. I married Martin at the same age Mary married John Carmody, twenty-two. We lived in Africa, where our children were born. Then we lived in France to avoid returning home during the time of the war in Vietnam. Eventually we settled in New York. That's the story. But a plot requires a character, a protagonist, someone whose fears and desires, hidden even from themselves, have consequences. Oedipus, for example, blind to the fact that the root of the kingdom's suffering lies within himself. Antigone, torn between imperatives that cannot be reconciled.

—Did you, like John Carmody, feel your travels had constituted the most memorable part of your life? And did your travels protect you from having to address the questions that might have yielded a character?

For some time, I felt the most compelling fact about my life was an escape from the house in Pelham. I had lived elsewhere, known people I'd never expected to meet, fallen into unimagined landscapes that even today haunt my dreams. But yes, my travels postponed my addressing certain questions. What within has been the cause of suffering to myself, to others? What imperatives in my life are irreconcilable? But perhaps these are not the questions of youth. And of course it's far from certain I would have entertained these questions if I'd never left my own country.

—Are these the questions you are entertaining now?

They are. How can I soothe the pain I've caused the people I love? The pain that was laid down within myself by former generations. An inclination to reticence. A fear of the scorching word. How reconfigure a family that will now include the ancestors? And what of these irreconcilables? A need for solitude as palpable as a need for air. And against that a need to love, be loved. To at all costs avoid rupturing the life-saving connection.

—Questions perhaps best contemplated in solitude. Did you sometimes remain at home as did Mary Ethridge while John Carmody was away? And if so, was that time the beginning for you of an independent life, propelled by suffering?

Sometimes I remained at home alone. But then sometimes I traveled alone, as well. Which it seems Mary did not. But the critical fact is that I imagine John Carmody and Mary Ethridge married for love as did we. Some force between them held. Some bond vulnerable to injury, to hurt. The time each of them lived without the other forced a knowledge no travel could achieve. Because it's there, in the bond, that it settles, the longing and the need, the fear that the connection will be broken. And in the children that spring from it. For a long time I felt I had grown up. I'd traveled, had quite consciously forged a life different from the one Kate and Bert lived in Pelham. But no. Kate's death revealed the depths of an earlier, consuming fear.

—Did you, like John Carmody, feel some glory had passed when the traveling was behind you?

The settling in one place seemed a compromise, a failure to realize the *venturesome* life that had beckoned so strongly at an earlier time. An end to youth. But of course, like those others, we realized the children needed to go to school, to be established in a place they could call home.

> *I was greatly surprised one morning after our return from Honolulu to wake up in Mohawk and find I had been elected Secretary, Treasurer, and Manager of the Navy Mutual Aid Association, whose object was to provide life insurance on the mutual plan for the benefit of officers' widows and children, a position which would require me to take up my home in the national capital.*
>
> *This was also very agreeable to my wife and children, the latter having reached school-going age and the educational facilities in that city being most excellent. We arrived in Washington and I at once secured a desirable building site at 1220 Sixteenth St. (now called Avenue of the Presidents), where I built a comfortable home, your mother and her brother going through the ceremony of laying the corner stone with a little box of records beneath. Standing on the sidewalk in front of our house, we could look down Sixteenth St. to the White House and up to an equestrian statue of General Scott. This home our family occupied most happily for twenty-five years.*
>
> *In 1886, my tour of duty at the Association having expired and feeling run down in health, I asked for and obtained orders to the* Vandalia, *a splendid corvette, fitting out for sea at Portsmouth, N.H. Having cruised about the Atlantic coast and the West Indies*

*for twelve months, my health continuing precarious, I concluded to
go before the medical examining board of surgeons who advised my
retirement on account of physical disability contracted in the line of
duty. This recommendation was approved by President Benjamin
Harrison on April 9th, 1889, substantially ending my naval career.*

*I need not say that my retirement was a disappointment to me,
but active sea service is no work for a man with broken health and so
I bowed to fate.*

.U.S.S. Vandalia.

Indeed, the year on the *Vandalia* must have been a cruel one: his failing
efforts, his attempts to disguise his waning powers. Perhaps some younger
men alert to his difficulties devised ways to relieve him, thus hastening
his shamed retreat. Perhaps the bow to fate involved some bitter personal
disappointment or humiliation. But what could life have been to him
afterwards? If he were to continue his story in any detail he would have
to give us more of his inner life. Which he does not. Did he consider it
an exercise in egoism, indiscretion, to enlarge on events that might be
described as personal? Or perhaps it was simply fatigue, soul-sickness,
that claimed him.

*Finding my idle time hanging very heavily on my hands after
my retirement I became identified with the business and
social interests of Washington as Treasurer and Director of the
Washington Loan & Trust Company; Vice-President and Director
of the West End National Bank; Treasurer of the Public Art
League of the United States.*

John R. Carmody Esqr.,
1220 Sixteenth Street,
Washington D.C.

VIII

Nothing remains to tell us of his final years as a bureaucrat. Except perhaps this: in the late nineties—the typed, lightly edited manuscript is dated 1898, the year she turned twenty-three—Deirdre wrote a very short story, a story within a story, called "The Desiccated Clerk." To my knowledge it's the only one she ever wrote.

The following story was told to me by a chance acquaintance, a Naval Officer named Young, whom I met one morning after breakfast in the office of a Washington Hotel, where I was stopping over night. I had been delayed on my way to my home in West Virginia by a terrific gale that had struck the Capital the day before. The morning papers were full of its havoc, and I had only to glance from the window to verify their reports—everywhere tin roofs, trees, lamp-posts and broken glass met my eye. My sea-faring friend, who approached me as I was still gazing from the window, was a kind-faced, sincere looking man with every mark of the gentleman about him; but for that I might have doubted the truth of his tale.

"Did you hear about that remarkable incident of the storm yesterday?" remarked my acquaintance quietly, stepping up to the window. "It was the most horrible thing I ever heard."

I replied I was a stranger in town and had heard very little news except what I had seen in the morning paper.

"Well, this won't be in the papers," he remarked confidently. "The government authorities will be very careful to keep it hushed up."

I here write truthfully and honestly as I was told, the following story:

Anson J. Whipple, a clerk in the State Department, was sitting at his desk by an open window on the previous morning when the gale had struck the City. A sudden gust of wind had taken him from his chair and blown him several feet away, where he fell with a heavy sound, causing clerks in an adjoining room to hurry to the scene. Upon attempting to raise Mr. Whipple, the body, to the horror of those present, fell apart and crumbled into dust. It was necessary to close the doors, windows, transoms etc. to prevent the lifeless remains from being distributed throughout the office and corridors. Clerks from all over the building soon collected in the room and were discussing the subject and examining the empty suit of clothes which remained on the floor.

Mr. Whipple had always been considered a most efficient clerk and was specially noted for the reserved and dignified manner which distinguished the accomplished and industrious force of that Department. He was said to be the uncle of Daniel Webster and on his mother's side an aunt was once engaged to the English Earl Warburton. In fact, his merits had been so fully recognized, that he had received two promotions during the past seven years.

In speculating and commenting upon the mysterious case apparently no one seemed able to recall any interchange of conversation held with the deceased in recent years, although the whole official force agreed in speaking well of him and his modest, unassuming manner. He was known to be somewhat rheumatic, for it was noticed that his two daughters drove him to office every morning, assisted him from the carriage and tenderly deposited him in his chair, invariably calling for him again shortly before four every afternoon.

Someone immediately volunteered to acquaint the Whipple household of the mysterious death. Arriving at the modest little home (in the suburbs of Mt. Pleasant) the door was opened by one of the daughters who cautiously admitted the messenger to the sitting-room, where her sister was busy dusting and putting *the room to order. To the surprise of the informer, his sad news appeared to call out more humiliation than grief in the rigid faces of the elderly ladies. Finally, upon being questioned closely about the mysterious phase of the case, they broke down completely and, sobbing, confessed that their poor father had died eight years before when it seemed that all source of support would be cut off from them and their invalid mother, who was fast dying of some dread disease. They prayed only that they might have money enough to keep their mother's last days comfortable. Their prayer must have been answered, for it came to Matilda the younger of the sisters (whose husband, when living, had been a skillful undertaker) how they could keep their father with them, and also his salary. It seemed a horrible thing at first, but their courage strengthened when they reassured themselves they were doing it only for their mother, and that when finally she died they would bury their parents together. Mrs. Whipple had now been dead several years, but their strategy had been so successful and the monthly salary so necessary that the daughters ceased to feel any compunction in continuing the practice of their deceit upon the government and dutifully continued to drive their father to and from his daily round of perfunctory duty.*

I shuddered when the narrator came to the end of his story. Glancing around the office I fancied every face I saw might be that of a dead man. Saying goodbye to my Navy friend, I ordered my bag from my room and left by the next train, more than ever convinced of the superior ingenuity of the female mind and with heightened admiration for that fascinating field of government employment which has attained such fixed tenure and automatic perfection that even grim death itself is powerless to interrupt it.

—Deirdre Carmody, 1898

From early on, apparently, long before her speech to the club members, Deirdre had slyly noted the relentless workings of the social machine, had looked around the offices she entered and seen dead men everywhere. Perhaps she'd already listened to Willie's tales of the business over which Mr. Hyde presided? Had for some time considered her father's tenure in the bureaucratic world of D.C. a kind of death in life? It may be she saw John Carmody at the time of her writing as a husk of the younger father she remembered, enfeebled, propped up by the women in his family. Perhaps it seemed to her a gust of wind would blow the remains away.

IX

Year that trembled and reel'd beneath me!
Your summer wind was warm enough, yet the air I breathed froze me,
A thick gloom fell through the sunshine and darken'd me,
Must I change my triumphant songs? said I to myself.

Heartbreaking Blow

My dear son Robert, your uncle, proved his title to the fighting
blood by volunteering on the breaking out of the Spanish War,
in the United States Marine Corps, in 1898. He performed his
duty so satisfactorily that in the following year he was awarded a
commission as first Lieutenant in the regular service.

But alas his promising career soon came to a grievous ending. In
May 1899, he was ordered to Guam, one of our island possessions
in the Pacific, going by way of the Suez Canal. In October he was
stricken with a fever, a disease of that country, and with others was
sent in the transport Relief to the Naval Hospital at Yokohama.
Early on the morning of the 23rd of October, he was missed from the
ship, having been last seen coming over the deck from a bathroom.
It is thought in his weakened condition he may have been thrown
overboard by the pitching and rolling of the vessel. Two days later
his afflicted mother and myself received by cable the heartbreaking
blow.

A monument to his memory now stands in the National
Cemetery at Arlington, Va. May he rest in peace, poor boy!

No wonder John Carmody is reluctant to take up a story that leads
inevitably to this moment! And then the terrible correspondences with
his own life: the name of the ship, *Relief,* for one, which tipped Rob into
the ocean. And Yokohama! When he received the news, did he revisit
that night almost a quarter of a century earlier in this same port when
he'd unsealed the letter announcing the news of Deirdre's birth and his
messmates had drunk to the infant with the best wine the ship's locker
afforded?

He sets down no more words concerning Rob. For John Carmody,
thoughts of his son may have flowed like water, attaching nowhere. Writing a few words may have seemed to him indecent, given the fact—I can
only suppose—he'd spent years after this catastrophe looking at Rob's

short life from every angle. It may be there were scenes he helplessly returned to again and again, unable to resist touching the hollow place that throbbed, wracking his memory to see if *this* time he might not recall some small fact, some word or gesture, that would convert a moment of crushing sorrow into one of benediction: his boy delirious, struggling up the sharp incline of the deck, then soon enough the answering plunge, the deck falling away beneath his feet, the drop sheer and clean, the waves rising to meet their honored guest. Salt in the mouth and nostrils, the appalled clutch awake, the effort to raise his hand to brush the water away as if it had been a cloud of bothersome mosquitoes, the letting go. His dark hair streaming up from his head as he sank further and further. Or perhaps, most horribly, glimpsed from the corner of his eye—and here the imagination falters—a flash of fin.

So John Carmody turned away in order to complete his *ruminations and recollections*.

> *On October 25th, 1905, a memorable event occurred in our family in the marriage of our dear daughter Deirdre to her good husband, Mr. William Conroy of New York. I had favorably known the bridegroom and his family for many years so your mother's separation from her old home did not fall as heavily on her parents had her husband been less known. Nevertheless, her departure for her new home in New York left a very sad void in our little household.*
>
> *I must proceed to the closing chapter of my dull narrative which to me is the saddest of my whole life and to which I never can be reconciled: I refer to the death of your sweet and gentle grandmother, my devoted and faithful wife of thirty-six years, who departed this sad world on May 24th, 1908, after an illness of six months. Grief, due to the loss of our son Robert, doubtless affected her heart and undermined her previous excellent health. Her remains now rest beneath the monument erected to the memory of her cherished son in the National Cemetery at Arlington, Virginia.*
>
> *"Oh! For a touch of the vanished hand and the sound of the voice that is still."*

Saddest Chapter

It may be he held himself responsible for Robert's death to which there was no witness. For his wife's who he believed died of grief. Because here we're at the mysterious intersection of plot and character, that crossroads so perplexing in ourselves.

—But why should you suppose he'd have held himself responsible? Do you feel responsible for the sufferings of your grown children?

I do. Particularly if the suffering is great. It is for this reason I find it hard to listen to stories of their troubles. I imagine that if on one October afternoon or another I hadn't been distracted by the turmoil of my own life, by my own internal wanderings, if I'd held my daughter a little closer, then perhaps she'd have a reserve of comfort that would have spared her. If I'd had the courage to speak what I knew, to risk the loss.

—And what of Kate? Did she hold herself accountable for your sorrows?

She never said so, but I think she intuited my need, my refusal to be consoled. Perhaps she saw it as akin to her own raging refusals.

But I may be altogether mistaken about John Carmody. He says he *bowed to fate.* Living in a pre-Freudian age, he may not have held a parent—himself, his mother or father—accountable in the ways we do now. He speaks as if fate were a mere twist of plot, following on the accident of his having contracted the dengue all those years before in the West Indies. Indeed, in his retirement, his terrible break with life at sea, he doesn't seem to consider at play his own personal qualities.

Still, it's possible he uses the dengue to disguise the fact that he had come face to face with a tragic discovery: the knowledge that the two things he desired most in the world—a seafaring life and a home with his wife and children—were irreconcilable. Did he become irritable on land, *growing grim about the mouth*? Within his soul was it *a damp, drizzly November*? Perhaps he read the first page of *Moby-Dick* and thought it written expressly for him?

And did he blame himself bitterly for all that followed: Rob's disappearance in the grip of a fever that he imagined, against all reason, had been contracted through his own dengue? The blow to the health of the *afflicted mother*? He writes that to the death of Mary Ethridge he *never can be reconciled.* Wouldn't that seem to suggest mysteries of which he cannot speak, images that float free in his dreams and deprive him of rest?

—Do you think that he became at last the protagonist of his own life? A life with a plot as well as a story? And what about you? What do your researches into his life tell you about your own?

I think he became a character at last by virtue of his suffering. A suffering he accepted in his final years in the house in Pelham. I hear the measure of it in the letter he addressed to Deirdre that day of the driving snowstorm in February only a few weeks before he died, in his efforts to console her, to assure her she would not be forgotten. Perhaps it was in those very efforts he returned to himself, fully, the character whose destiny had been settled long before he was born. Completed reading the book of his life in which that fate was written, recorded silently, tirelessly, every instant from a time already years before that first day of school in Mohawk when he was sent home in disgrace for striking a girl with his overshoe, the book in which was inscribed his own intense shimmering shadowed life.

As to the other: perhaps my own research tells me life is over only when it is. That I too may finally read the book of my life and find myself written in it.

—And this: in the book of John Carmody's life, how did they figure, the people he knew best? Rob, for example. Or Mary. What sort of character do you suppose his imagination made of his wife? I mean later on, after the days of delirious separation had come to an end.

Mary? Oh I think she presented to him an inner life that rivaled his own. And so was for him the most complicated, complicating, figure of all.

—And why is that?

Because it's only the people we love best who escape our easier inventions, whose inner lives compete with our own in their vast and mysterious purposes. We're driven to wonder and suppose; to turn the person we know we don't know every which way in hopes of seeing more clearly. The more we care for a person, the less we can say: he's this, he's that. No, the whole project collapses. The contradictions, the ambiguities, the conflicting forces: *that's* what we come to know. And then the nameless regions within the other closed to us entirely: dreams, fantasies, hidden desires, all hidden, all beyond our reach. The beloved turns to us a face like the one in the mirror we can never quite see. It's the passing stranger on the street who might supply us with quite an entertaining sketch.

—I would have thought it's love that illuminates and clarifies.

So it is. And now it's you I'm thinking of, you whom I know so little about. Who are you who speaks to me? Whose voice I hear as just now daring me to reconsider, to remember what I know? Who provokes and baffles? Whom I listen to as I would a self set free from the burden of

146

self-consciousness and fear? You are closer to me than my breath, the companion of many a solitary hour. And yet—and I hope this won't strike you to the heart—it's not after all your voice I hear in the furthest reaches of solitude where houses and people and wars have passed into nothing, where words have finally broken open and scattered their seed on the air. In that place of hushed expectation, of ever-expanding light, it's all rushing wind and cicadas whirring in the afternoon. It's the ripe green hickory nut hitting the ground with a sound like the heavenly silence that follows the breaking of the seventh seal.

As for Rob

On errands of life, these letters speed to death.

—"Bartleby the Scrivener"

*Oh! Ye whose dead lie buried beneath the green grass; who standing among
flowers can say—here, here, lies my beloved; ye know not the desolation
that broods in bosoms like these. . . . What deadly voids and unbidden
infidelities . . . that seem to gnaw upon all Faith, and refuse resurrections
to the beings who have placelessly perished without a grave. . . . But Faith,
like a jackal, feeds among the tombs, and even from these dead doubts she
gathers her most vital hope.*

—Moby-Dick

Her brother Rob went out to the island of Guam with Captain Leary of the Navy who was appointed first governor of the island when the U.S. took it over from Spain in 1899. There he was stricken with fever and was invalided to the Naval Hospital at Yokohama, Japan. October 23, 1899, two days out from Guam, he disappeared from the steamer and it is supposed that he jumped overboard in his delirium. Letters and presents for Deirdre and her mother arrived for a month after they'd received the telegram. When Mary Ethridge died she left the request that his last letters be buried with her next to her heart, and it was done.

At the time of her brother's death, Deirdre was her mother's constant companion and comforter, and had it not been for her, I fear her mother would have lost her mind. She ran the house, relieved her mother of much of her responsibility and, with a readiness to face sorrow with resignation and a smile, made life as tolerable as possible.

—Willie's life-account

Who can help noticing that, according to Willie, Rob *jumped overboard in his delirium*? In John Carmody's account he was *thrown overboard by the pitching and rolling of the vessel,* the possibility of a jump surely unbearable to a parent. Yet Willie can report only what he'd been told, almost certainly by Deirdre. What's more, Willie goes on to state quite explicitly that the letters and gifts arriving after Rob's death were for his sister and his mother. Why does he not mention Rob's father as well?

It might seem a mere oversight on Willie's part, an expression of his unconscious feelings, if we didn't already know from Kate's little diary that Deirdre, lying mortally ill with a view of swelling hickory buds in the window, called Kate into her room and told her the story: how after Rob's death, when his things were returned from the Philippines, they'd found he'd marked a gift for everyone, everyone except his father. And so because, after the last package had been opened, there remained a single article without a tag—an ivory knife with elephants lumbering along its edge—John Carmody had taken it for his own. A letter-cutter after all the letters had been opened. A gift by default.

Of course, it may all have been a mistake, a moment of confusion on Rob's part; he may have been at the very point of writing his father's name on some scrap of paper—to include with the rest in the package he intended to send home—when suddenly he fell ill: a skewering headache, a shiver along the skin. And yet the delay itself, if that's what it was, seems not without meaning.

Because a puzzling episode must find its place in this story. Records show that on September 11, 1891, Rob received an appointment to Annapolis. Four months later, having recently turned nineteen, he withdrew.

Your resignation as a Naval Cadet in the U.S. Navy, tendered in
your letter of the 27th ultimo, is accepted this day, February 4, 1892.

Why he attended the academy for no more than four months is matter for speculation. But the fact that nothing at all is heard of him again until more than six years later—when he appears at the outbreak of the Spanish-American War—gives one pause. What was he doing? And why is the silence around him so profound? After his babyhood, Rob breaks into John Carmody's narrative only as the lost son. He is not given a history of his own. And so we are left to make it up. Could it be that out of courtesy to his father—*a naval hero* and so forth—Rob was permitted by the authorities to resign as a means of avoiding the shame attached to a dismissal?

The facts are as irretrievable as any object fallen into deep unforgiving waters. But we can imagine that all the years of Rob's growing up, the house on 16th Street breathed stories of the Civil War, engagements on this river or that, the siege of Mobile, tales of the yellow fever, the pale young Mikado appearing for the first time in Western dress, tales of sailing the high seas on the *Yantic,* the *Monocacy,* the *Relief.* And then the assumptions, the jolly asides from his father's friends, that with such a father a son's greatest wish would of course be to follow in his path. No question put to him: "And you, Rob? What are *you* thinking?"

So, with all his instincts in revolt, Rob did what was expected of him. Then, a few months later, when gross incompatibilities had become apparent to all, endured his father's eyes on him, the look of shamed disappointment, of puzzlement. A spark of anger, as well, quickly quenched. His mother also watching, but sorrowfully, protectively, assuming a cheerfulness that deeply worried him.

Afterwards, six years of watching, being watched. Then, when any fool could see that the navy so revered in his house had set up an absurd cry for war, Captain Mahan and Theodore Roosevelt enflaming a situation that diplomacy might very well have solved—Spain having agreed to every condition, offered every condolence for the loss of lives on the

Maine even though there'd been no proof it had been responsible for the explosion—he thought only to escape. And did, at last, into the waters of the Pacific.

But it's hard not to wonder why Deirdre, on her deathbed, should repeat the story to the sixteen-year-old Kate of the packages that arrived bearing gifts for everyone except her father. Why should she have wanted to pass on this particular fact? Of course she herself may not have attached any special significance to the exclusion and told Kate the history of the elephant knife only by way of fixing for her the serendipitous manner in which this object was now falling into her hands. Or, as Deirdre knowingly approached her own death, her dreams were filled with Rob, her first friend, her brother, and everything to do with him had become a matter of preoccupation, her words spilling, unchecked.

There's a little photograph of Rob that Deirdre may have kept near her— not in uniform of any kind, distinguishing him at once from his father, who is never officially photographed in anything else—wearing the high white dress collar and loose tie of his day. He is strikingly good looking, very dark like his mother, with a full moustache that hides his upper lip and large eyes that droop a little at the corners. That slight droop seems the only thing he took from his father. His expression is alert, withdrawn. Knowing, you might say.

II

John Carmody bears his exclusion as he can. He sits, I seem to imagine, one leg crossed over the other, cradling the bowl of his pipe, trying to appear unconcerned as the packages are opened, their contents distributed, tokens specially addressed to this one and that, gifts that have become— en route—memento mori. But conceive his soreness of spirit when there is no longer anything still to be unwrapped, anything tagged with his name: a mariner's compass, for instance, of which he might say—taking it from his pocket, showing it to a friend—this, *this* he meant for me, yes, sent home specially to me, his father, thinking, you know, as an old seaman I might want it. Then his attempts to pass it off lightly before the others, this striking and tender omission, at last taking in his hand the letter-cutter and making a joke of it, inquiring of the room at large, staring from one to another: is this a dagger I see before me?

And Mary. Think how, watching him sit there forlorn and left out, she would have tried to cover the loss, to persuade him that Rob would naturally have thought of him in connection with the elephant knife, a bit of carved ivory, something very like the scrimshaw he himself had acquired in the past, pieces whalers had sold to him years before. Would have tried to reassure him that Rob, finding himself in the Pacific, would have for a certainty remembered his father's earlier passage through those same waters, have wanted to tell him so with the gift of the knife. Yes, she may very well have said something of the kind, half-believing it herself.

It's true, of course, I'm making up the character of Mary as I go. I have only Willie's account: that Deirdre's company alone prevented her from losing her mind, that she requested Rob's last letters be buried with her. And then John Carmody's assumption that grief for her cherished son *affected her heart,* accounted for her untimely death, at the age of fifty-eight.

But I harbor some notion that a shadowy version of Mary's grief has been passed down to me, infusing my own sorrowful moments, as it did Deirdre's and later on Kate's. While there's no evidence of this, it's the undying quality of Mary's grief that leads me to believe that some bitter, unspoken fact has been left out of the story. The silence surrounding Rob. The lack of photographs, of mention.

Aware that the day is already inclining toward dark, that yellow elm branches are moving on the other side of the window, I map my own fear of losing a child onto Mary. Because a child may be lost in a number of ways. None compete with death. That is a given. But if I cannot listen to the tale of her sorrows, do I not also lose my child? And what of this: did Kate lose me? If I was consumed as a child by efforts to elicit Kate's own stories of loss, loss of Deirdre, her mother, was I not hoping to hear Kate tell my own story? A story I couldn't have named if my life depended on it? The story of a child yearning for an absent mother? Because Kate's face was hidden from me. Or rather her gaze was directed elsewhere.

And in my preoccupation with Kate's loss of Deirdre, with my own unmourned loss, did I turn away from my daughters? Refuse to hear their stories just as Kate had refused to tell me her own? I could neither hear Kate's story nor listen to any other. Because it was only Kate's that might have restored me to myself, allowed the fear to drop a little. Put a human face on the stranger. Allowed the measure of peace required to listen.

So now I wonder if there was not some unspoken story, some story silenced, denied, reaching back as far as Mary Ethridge: the loss of child to mother, of mother to child. Or even back to the generation before, of whom I know almost nothing.

From a very early time, I believe, Mary Ethridge worried over her son's unhappiness in a manner that John Carmody, whatever his qualms, did not. The night of his return to Mohawk from the East, it was Mary who'd watched through her own tears of joy the three-year-old Rob hang back from his father, observed his answering uncertainty when he tried with a show of heartiness to take his little son in his arms. So that she hadn't been surprised later when he'd confided he'd seen a reproach in the boy's eyes. She'd quickly reassured him, thinking it the sensible thing to say, that in a few days' time all would be right, they'd be at home with each other.

Yet even then, amidst the relief of her husband's return—the delight they'd taken in each other's bodies more intense than at any time in the past, the elation she'd felt waking in the night, his hand on her breast, his mouth at the nape of her neck—she'd been afraid. So that as the days went by and his father had attempted to toss little Rob in the air, gallop him up and down on his knee, and Rob had cried to be let down again, had come to her sobbing, she'd felt uneasily that some premonition was being fulfilled. Some price must be paid for the bleak cast of mind that had taken hold while her husband was away and given her no rest.

Because during the months that followed Deirdre's birth—as spring yielded to the heavy leaves of summer and she'd watched the full moon in July rise like a call to some dull throb within—she'd at last given room in her imagination to the fear that had plagued her even from the time before he'd left: that while he was away from her, separated by half the world and ever-lengthening periods of time, in some port or other along the coast of China or Japan, he'd take pleasure with another woman.

In the abstract, of course, she'd known from the beginning this might very well be the case. But as the weeks went by her mind had entered a state of dull rebellion. She'd been tormented by images at the most unlikely moments, images that drained of spontaneity even her tranquil time with the babies, baths and melting bedtime moments when she gave them the butterfly kisses with which her mother had once soothed herself and her sisters. And though his letters were full of love for her, there was a current of bitter self-recrimination flowing beneath his words that made her wonder.

So when he'd returned and had immediately seen reproach—for that was the word he'd used—in their child's eyes, she knew her fears were justified. She never asked, he never offered, but she knew. And as the months passed, and finally the years, and Rob continued to be shy of his father, in fact timid with everyone, her husband, whom she'd always loved for his gentle, lively spirit, showed signs of imposing rules that seemed to her severe. She knew that he was acting out of fear for Rob, that he thought to toughen this son who clung to her skirts. But she knew too that Rob's mere presence was enough to provoke in him a sense of having failed them all. All except Deirdre, of course, whose eyes were clear when, not quite two years old, she'd first gazed on him, a complete stranger.

Still, their bond, their sexual bond, held. From the first this had been their way to each other, and when all else failed they had learned they could rely on a kind of quenchless appetite for each other's bodies. Mysteries, all of this, where desire takes hold and why. Before they were married he had obliquely let her know that life at sea had afforded him opportunities closed to her, that from the time he'd enlisted at the Brooklyn Naval Yard and found himself on the *North Carolina* living with seamen of all types, a rough, knockabout crowd—whalers and man-o'-war's men and sailors from around the globe—he'd been educated in ways that went unmentioned in Mohawk. But when he left for the East—so quickly, he was gone within forty-eight hours—and she'd stood on the veranda holding Rob up to him, Deirdre in her womb, she had been mutely making an appeal: you are free to do what you will, but think of us!

Later on, after her husband's return, after she'd observed and pondered the trouble between him and their child, she'd bitterly regretted using Rob in this way, knowing her husband felt he'd betrayed the boy. It was as if, in her husband's eyes, Rob had become her protector where he himself had failed, as if Rob had become the worthy one, the righteous one, the judge. And if Rob in fact had been a different kind of child, if he'd liked the rough and tumble of play, if he'd listened eagerly to his father's stories or at least with some show of interest, perhaps things would have slowly worked themselves out. But no, Rob kept his counsel, his thoughts were his own. It was this she could see tormented his father.

As for Rob, Mary Ethridge no more than her husband knew what he was thinking. She'd stood by, unsure, when his father had insisted—or rather by a certain unyielding manner forbidden dissenting discussion—that Rob attend Annapolis. Into this mix—and here she had trouble sorting out one thing from another—she knew that her husband's insistence sprang from his own disappointed hopes, his conviction that the teeming life of the sailor finally denied him should by rights belong to his son. It had been clear to her for a long time—since their sojourn in Honolulu where all had been strange and wonderful to herself—that her husband was never as at home anywhere as when he was away on the high seas, away from domesticity and from the people she had no doubt at all he loved best in the world. He ascribed to the dengue he contracted in Haiti

so long ago these spells of melancholy, these *fidgets,* as he called them. And although she mistrusted the bursts of patriotism that suddenly gave him reason to be up and gone, she knew it came to him as an unequaled blow, a personal calamity, when life at sea was forever closed to him.

While her husband had been away on the *Vandalia,* on that final voyage, his absence had been a source of pain to her but not of unceasing torment as during that time long ago in Mohawk when in late spring she'd seen the Swan taking flight across the sky. No, it seemed that her earlier suffering had been translated into some complicated concern for Rob, who, in his father's absence, had taken to wandering she didn't know where.

But it wasn't Rob alone that preoccupied her during the months her husband was away. Some old solitary impulse had risen within her that she remembered from those years when she'd been alone in Mohawk with two babies. Some stern sense of self that had followed its own stubborn course and now seemed to have centered—so strangely, she thought—in an object familiar to her from the first days of her husband's return from the Orient and that now rested on the sideboard in the dining room.

For she had gradually become aware—as she sipped her coffee after Deirdre and Rob had left the house for school—of something too new, too inchoate, to easily put into words: become aware that some fierce absorption in her own life had discovered a source of rest in the Buddha, the gilded Buddha that gathered the morning light in his robes. He sat cross-legged on his box with the inlaid figures raising smiling swords to each other, sat with eyes half-closed, upright palms pressed together in front of him, looking within to the place where everything had already happened. It seemed he was looking straight through to a point beyond the end of their lives, the end of everyone's life, of this world so familiar to them all—16th Street with its horses trotting smartly along and children driving hoops and gaslights hissing in the night—gazing beyond at a woodland pond reflecting a mild blue sky. She'd immediately imagined it that way, a place of glassy water where clumps of goldenrod were leaning in the sun and needles of white pines were shooting light in every direction.

But it wasn't till one night, waking from an elusive dream, that she understood she was remembering a pond she knew very well, the pond to which she and the man she'd only recently met, the man who would be her husband, had wandered away from a picnic that summer she was twenty. Had escaped without ever saying to each other that's what they were doing. It was there as they stood amidst the delicate lavender Michaelmas daisies with the bees droning round them, the fern springing and spilling at the water's edge, the silver trunks of the birch gleaming in a cluster there beyond, that he'd told her of his brush with death. In the heat of the moment she'd realized that this man would take her away from everything she'd known, that she was quickly falling into spaces that terrified her, realized that when night came and she was home alone again with her parents and sisters and the katydids began their crashing rattle in the night she would be thinking only of how she wanted him, she would be suffering her desire, dying of it. As they stood there gazing not at each other but into the pond—they hadn't touched yet, hadn't spoken—she felt that all the longing she'd ever endured was funneling into this moment and that for the rest of her life she'd remember this: this pond with the cloud shadows passing slowly over it in whose dim smooth waters she'd glimpsed a place where the force of her wanting would drive her straight through time and into eternity, a place where their lives that were only beginning would be already gathered and spent.

One night in the early summer of '89—as she and her husband were walking along 16th Street, their backs to the White House, returning late from a gathering they'd attended at the home of one of his old mates from the *Cincinnati*, a party much animated by talk of the forthcoming wedding of General Sherman's daughter to which they'd all been invited—her husband had remarked, in a manner she knew he hoped would strike her ears as entirely by the way, that his friend's son, who they both were aware had undergone some stormy school days, seemed now to be thriving on a seagoing life and what a satisfaction that was to his parents. Yes, he remembered his own early days in Mohawk when before the Rebellion he'd been just Rob's age, fifteen, and pulling at the reins with all the skittishness of a young colt. Then, as if to distract attention from his remarks, as if she weren't to imagine he meant anything particular by them, he'd stopped in their path and raising his stick to the sky commented how bright the Northern Cross was tonight, how clearly it could be seen there stamped amidst all the other stars. At first she didn't know what to look for, a constellation named the Northern Cross. But then, after he'd pointed out to her more precisely where he was looking and told her that at sea they'd often taken their sightings from those stars, she wonderingly realized that he was calling her Swan by another name.

She remembered then how in that terrible time in Mohawk of missing the man beside her—whose arm she held now in her gloved hand—she'd pictured the Swan dragged unwillingly across the sky, dragged like it or not toward the horizon, and how she'd looked again and there it was, flying full tilt ahead, on the path of its own setting. And now—remembering that she'd thought then it was a matter of perspective, the way things appeared to you—she perceived in a flash that it was indeed a cross as well as a swan. Looking at it in her husband's company, heads thrown back, eyes fastened on the same point in the wide sky glittering with stars, she thought of the cross he was pointing out as an emblem of marriage: there was the line flying straight across the sky like a flaming arrow, the arrow of desire, the line you chose when you married someone, that forward line, a matter of will, of wanting; and then there was the other that crossed it, a line almost invisible at first—one you had perhaps glimpsed but certainly not distinguished with any clarity—the line you'd never have chosen but that in time came to seem inextricably bound to the other, the line that crossing the first made an intersection at the middle where you were pinned to suffering.

A few years later, after her husband's expectations had been disproved, after Rob's return home from Annapolis, she'd felt a searing consciousness that all her joy had turned to sorrow. Yet something had altered. In odd moments she knew—and here she thought of the Buddha contemplating spaces where time had fallen into nothing—that the lock that wouldn't yield had to do with herself as much as with her husband, with the privilege she allowed herself in her internal argument with him. It wasn't that she thought she should give over her own vision of what was happening or deny what she saw as his exacting posture toward their son. No, not at all. Her husband, a mild and gentle man, with Rob was harsh. This she knew to be true. It was rather that she felt the angle from which she herself looked at things was too narrow. For the horse in the street, blinkered to preserve his plodding course, she felt a shamed sympathy.

But what was it she didn't allow herself to see? What? And for the hundredth time she reminded herself that the thing she was incapable of seeing was exactly that: a blind spot. It was not a matter of will. It was a matter of vision, some gift of sight. She felt obscurely that while at an earlier time she would have gladly given her husband the benefit of the doubt, found a way if not to excuse what he was doing, at least to show him she hadn't forsaken him entirely, now she withdrew into herself and permitted herself to become his judge. It was this that threw him into a state of panic, she knew, causing him to harden his line. In effect, she had allowed what she imagined to be Rob's version of his father to become her own. While she readily found excuses for Rob, over and over, she would not extend the same leniencies to his father. In her mind he'd been replaced by someone from whom the worst might be expected. His virtues counted for nothing, his faults bloomed like nightshade.

But she couldn't replace her intimate knowledge of her husband's struggles and regrets without denying a younger self that had first of all yearned to embrace him entirely, and then, when she began to see how difficult that would be, at the very least to meet him in the place of his confusion. Now she judged him in exactly the same way that she silently, bitterly, accused him of judging their child and—living from day to day in the bleak light of her self-regard, of a wan and stricken virtue—she slowly became aware she'd placed herself in the regions of ice. They came together as always in the middle of the night but there was an air of desperation about it all, the urgencies of panic and loss replacing those of desire.

It was the word *forgiveness* that turned in her head like a wheel. She had no idea what the word meant. She reached a moment during those late summer months of 1892—Rob had been out of Annapolis for half a year—when she came to believe that the unhappiness she was enduring would never be loosened so long as her heart lay in her breast like a stone. For how could she receive the mercy for which she yearned—the release from self-hatred which she had decided was the other side of what had become her habitual tendency to censure her husband—if within herself all was flinty wastes of rock and shingle, howling wilds of pebble and scree? And how could she forgive him for whatever it was if her own heart had not first been softened by a grieving knowledge of her own stubborn inclination to stand apart?

It was at about this time that they went together to Utica to attend a fall wedding. The daughter of her husband's sister, Elizabeth, was marrying a young man from Frankfort, the son of old friends from her school days. Standing there in the church of St. John's listening to the exchange of wedding vows, remembering how she and her husband had pronounced the same words in the Brooklyn parlor of her own sister and brother-in-law twenty years earlier, she looked up into the high windows and saw saints draped in sunlit robes of scarlet and emerald and blue. She supposed they were saints, for she wasn't familiar with these gilded domes and painted statues and figures carrying staffs and lilies and lambs. On every side she half-listened to the others murmuring words she couldn't understand, praying this and that, the priest singing one thing and the others calling back something else, and then all at once, spoken amidst the monotonous flow with a distinctness she wouldn't forget, a prayer separated itself from the rest: "Take my heart of stone and change it into a heart of flesh."

Remembering the words spoken by those around her at the wedding in Utica, she took steps that she might hear them again: if she herself wasn't able to ask that her heart be made human and forgiving, then she wanted to stand in silence amidst those who would pronounce the words for her. But she didn't tell her husband of her decision until the last moment. She had no idea what he might think—this being a religion he'd left behind, although, unlike her own family, he was always tolerant of it—and when she informed him of her intention he was at first astonished. He said little but she saw from the few things he did say that it was abundantly strange to him that she—whose own family was distinguished by wealth and property, by the freedoms these conferred—should want to join a church of immigrants, the church of his own struggling parents.

She wondered if he perhaps felt betrayed that she'd secretly followed a course he'd known nothing about, informing him of her intentions only at the eleventh hour. She hadn't been able to tell him that she'd kept silent because she'd been afraid her resolve might be broken by discouraging remarks. So at last, uncertain and again fearful that she was wounding him, she'd remarked impulsively—perhaps because it had been a source of satisfaction to them both that she got on well with his family—that she hoped to return to Utica for her baptism, hoped that his sisters would agree to accompany her to the church of St. John's.

In fact this proposal did seem to soothe him. Was it, she wondered, that she'd given him a way of thinking about her new undertaking, a story he could tell himself? Or anyone else who might inquire? That he could describe this unexpected turn of events not entirely to his liking as after all only something concerning women? Something that the limitation of their lives—children and home and aging parents—created a hunger for? Something that might even provide a sense of adventure, of the unknown, that men could more easily find in the larger world they were accustomed to travel?

She spoke to Deirdre of her intention one evening in early December when a cold rain was lashing against the windows, a night when both Rob and her husband were absent from the house. Earlier, at dinner, Deirdre had been talking about a prize she hoped to win at school, the art prize, for one of the paintings she'd recently completed: an oil of a listening girl holding a shell to her ear. At seventeen, Deirdre was in her final year and almost every semester awarded some distinction or other which she claimed almost as a matter of course. But she knew Deirdre would not have chattered away as she had this evening if the others had been present, not only because she was sensitive to Rob's unhappiness and would not have talked before him of her own successes but also because she was fearful of eliciting her father's approving remarks from which Rob was so conspicuously excluded.

Now she and Deirdre had settled into the remainder of the evening, Deirdre with her back to her at a desk across the room, herself on a little sofa piecing together a shirtwaist, her silver thimble pushing the needle stitch by stitch through the length of billowing white cotton required for the huge mutton sleeves recently come into fashion. She had been observing the fall of Deirdre's dark hair down her back—vaguely wishing that tonight Deirdre had worn her hair up as she had begun to do sometimes so that the sight of the hollow at the back of her neck, hidden for so many years, might jog her own memory of the baby who had once sat on her lap, the long lovely rise of infant neck—when it occurred to her that this lone night with the rain running down the windows might be the occasion she'd been looking for. Dropping her work she bent her attention on making it happen, the moment when as so many times before, just when she most wanted it, Deirdre would turn to her. And indeed Deirdre now turned from the desk with inquiring eyes, glancing out from beneath into that place, it always seemed, where you were waiting. By way of answer, she'd patted the spot next to her on the sofa and when Deirdre was beside her had taken her hand and tried to tell her in the simplest possible manner of her decision, of her fervent longing for a more forgiving heart and how this desire had led where it had. She'd been startled by the sudden tears, the look of dazzled bewilderment, but when she'd asked what the matter was, she'd seen in Deirdre's eyes something abashed, confused, as if she were attempting to contain a sudden overflow that had taken her entirely by surprise. It was then, watching the tears run down her face, that she'd remembered she'd named her little daughter after the Deirdre in her husband's story, the Irish Deirdre who'd been heard weeping in her mother's womb.

—And Rob? What did he think of these goings-on? Why is it that you can give only the briefest account of Rob during the years he was living in the house on 16th Street? Why are you able to imagine nothing of what Rob may have thought or felt?

I've asked the same question of myself and can say only that it seems to be Rob alone who turns his back to me. Is it that unlike the others he found some means or other before he died of expressing his grief? That is, in some intimate fashion, some manner closed to the others? To a friend? To a lover? Did he compose a poem, a prayer, a letter that has been lost? As he hurtled over the railing into the waters did he give a great cry that gave voice to everything he'd ever suffered and known?

—Perhaps Rob will suddenly, in some unexpected moment, turn and show you his face?

The mere suggestion frightens me.

—Could it be then that it's not Rob himself who turns his back on you but you who pass by without recognizing him?

It may be. For now, all I can do is acknowledge the empty spaces within, the fertile hollows presently clogged with fear. Prepare for appearances, for visitations. Continue my story with the hope of things to come.

—But what of Mary, who prayed for a forgiving heart?

She would have recognized him, of that I'm sure. But then her heart was to undergo changes. First a little at a time. Then all at once.

When the bolt struck that late October morning in 1899, the morning sun had been flooding the room in which Mary and Deirdre sat, reaching into the deepest folds of the Buddha's robes, bringing their hidden gold to light. The shadow of the Buddha's shoulders and long sloping neck had been stamped against the wall so that he was there twice: once gilded and wooden and discreet, and then a second time elongated, abstract, as if a more mysterious presence than the first were announcing itself. She'd been sitting with Deirdre eating a ripe peach, one of the very last, they'd agreed, of this lingering summer. Her husband had been turning over papers in a room nearby. At first she could not be made to understand what the death cable was saying. She'd closed her eyes and instead of letters had seen a sphere whirling faster and faster, a wheel to which she herself was lashed, a burning wheel of fire. It was only weeks later that the wheel showering sparks had finally fallen apart and drifted smoking and smoldering into spaces where she could no longer follow.

After Rob was lost, her husband's attempts to comfort her became occasions of exquisite pain. Her heart yearned over him, she woke sometimes from her own dream of fire to see him walking distractedly up and down the room. She guessed at the voices in his head, at the involuntary return, perhaps, of long-forgotten images of sea deaths, of bodies slipping beneath the waves. She could see him at a loss, wandering, and knew when he cried out in his sleep, or when—as they sat silently together—he dreamily raised a hand and waved it as if brushing aside mosquitoes, that he was afflicted as grievously as herself. Then, with a sudden rise of blood, she wondered angrily if he were measuring the cost of war differently now or if he deemed Rob a kind of hero ennobled by his death at sea. And just as suddenly she didn't care, it was all one to her now that their son was gone.

One dreary November afternoon about a month after the arrival of the telegram, when rain was in the air and blood-red oak leaves clung to their branches, she walked with Deirdre down the high flight of steps and along the street and saw for the first time a child that Deirdre would recognize only years later, in the wake of her own loss. Mary saw him disappearing around a corner, the boy with broken boots and a jacket too small for him. He'd looked back at them for a moment and she'd been startled by the black hair falling over his forehead, the quizzical look in his bright black eyes. He'd been carrying newspapers under one arm—later on she went over these details carefully—a boy of perhaps nine or ten. At the sight of him a trembling had overtaken her, and Deirdre, who was holding her arm, had stopped and asked if it wasn't time for them to return. Deirdre hadn't seen him, she was sure, because if she had she, too, would have been stricken. For it was uncanny, the likeness, even the quick look from the dark eyes sloping down at the corners, the shoulders slouched slightly forward. She said nothing but a few days later—this time a shining day, the last leaves hanging in sunlit scraps of pounded gold—there he was again, at a different corner, and as she looked he rounded the corner and disappeared.

This time Deirdre had noticed him as well but she hadn't seemed moved in any way except by his ragged condition, wondering aloud as she had often done at the number of children who lived destitute on the street. Perhaps it was Deirdre's remark that struck into awareness some memory or perhaps foreknowledge, because suddenly the streets were filled with children she hadn't seen before, huddled in doorways, standing in the cold, selling a flower or a match or a newspaper, children crowding the edges of her vision. She saw the children of her own childhood coming down in wagons from the hills into Frankfort, children from starving Ireland, her parents had told her. Each child she glimpsed stirred something new, something forgotten, but it was only the first ragged boy with the dark hair and eyes—leading her like an angel into these abandoned territories—in whom she'd seen her own child.

On Christmas Eve, the last of the century—a mild afternoon when a sky of pale washed blue filled the tops of the windows and she was alone in the house wrapping the gold watch she'd found for Deirdre the summer before in a little shop down a street, a watch with a spidery second-hand dial—she heard the front door open and then swing shut and knew her husband had returned and gone into his study. In a rush she remembered Christmases past: the one after Rob was born when she was sewing a long white dress for him and as she stitched could look anytime she liked into the cradle and see him sleeping sweetly there beside her; the one when her husband had only just left to join the *Monocacy* on a high tide of excitement and fierce parting, was on a train making his way across the plains to San Francisco and she careening, not knowing how she was going to find a path through the next days, not to say years; and then the next when Deirdre was an infant nine months old, a Christmas that although at the time she was sick with longing now seemed to her fringed with wonder because Rob waking in his sleep with bad dreams could be comforted with a song of the moon:

> Low, low, breathe and blow,
> Wind of the western sea!
> Over the rolling waters go,
> Come from the dying moon and blow,
> Blow him again to me;
> While my little one, while my pretty one, sleeps.

As she sang the words to herself now in the afternoon with her husband on the other side of the door, she imagined all the homes where happy families were even now gathering, the children assembling, where in the early dusk the candles on a tree were leaping to light and a dinner on its way to one kind of perfection or another, oysters or a little puny hen, and she imagined the black-eyed boy wherever he was, she hoped, around some fire warming his fingers and perhaps who knows with some special cake to nibble. And then her heart broke open and she thought but this is my life, this is my life, and why would I want to exchange it for any other, this one with my name written on it, the Swan on its flight across the summer sky, the cross driven with a stake into the ground, a sorrow all my own this Christmas Eve cracked open like a pod from which shining spores are spilling, drifting weightless around my head?

In the embrace of this knowledge that her life was in full flight toward the horizon—rising in its own time and setting, too, particular, perishing—she opened the door of his study and found him sitting in his chair, his back to her, holding in the hand resting on the arm of his chair his unopened letters, in the other dangling beside him the elephant knife, sitting motionless, as if stopped in his task for want of energy or will. Looking at the backs of his hands, the dark hair glinting on them, she remembered what she had known all these long years without ever saying it to herself: that of all things he wished her to come to him of her own will, without his asking, as she had that day after they had stood in long silence by the pond, turned to him at the same instant as he'd turned to her with the bees droning round them in the warm afternoon and for the first time inhaled his strange male scent, felt the scratch of his side whiskers, the rapid beating of his heart beneath his cotton shirt. So now bending over his shoulder she rested her face against his and at once felt tears, his tears, on her own cheek. As he raised his hand to encircle the back of her head she understood that from now until her final breath any consolation she would know, any release of spirit, would have to include this man who alone of all people on earth understood her grief as his own.

But Christmas Eve was only a beginning and whatever knowledge had been given to her that afternoon slipped away time and again. She tasted its impermanence almost immediately when after a little Deirdre returned from delivering gifts to friends and the three of them sat down in the early twilight to face as best they could the absence for which each in an unspoken way felt someone must be held responsible. Someone.

When a few days later Will Conroy came to visit Deirdre, mercifully muting the centennial which they overheard hilariously celebrated on every side with speeches and bands and fireworks, she was grateful to him for covering up the bare places in the house with his stories of Ireland. They'd heard these stories before, certainly: how the night before landing, as the ship neared the port of Queenstown, he'd glimpsed the light on Bull Rock; how he hoped one summer before long to go in search of "his people" somewhere near Drumsna, not far from Carrick-on-Shannon; how his friend Stuart Chambers had traveled with him and was now studying in Rome for the priesthood. Yes, he'd told them stories of this one and that, taking on the voice, the particular accent, as he talked, of County Cork or County Galway. She could see that Deirdre was stirred—just as she herself had been by the stories her husband had told her after the Rebellion—and she found herself liking him very much, this young man who was unsure of himself and who talked, she thought, as a way of surrounding himself with other people, other voices: who took his watch out of his waistcoat pocket to check its accuracy when the grandfather clock that had come to her through her mother's family bonged on the landing. She thought him unknowing in a manner that in other people sometimes disturbed her, although in him she felt his simplicity not so much a defense against knowledge as a straining toward some inspiration, some example, she could only distantly imagine. And of which he himself might be ignorant.

She understood, through stray comments and gestures and asides, that Willie struck her husband as baffling. On the one hand, when had he not known Willie's family? And hadn't he—in the spirit, almost, of kin—written to Willie a few summers earlier asking if he'd meet Deirdre when her train came into Jersey City? The Carmodys and the Conroys were all lying together high above Ilion beneath Celtic crosses in the same corner of the Catholic cemetery, a cemetery that she, growing up, had never even known existed, having herself attended funerals in the much older Protestant one in Herkimer. And then of course her husband's sister Elizabeth was married to Edmond Roche, business partner of Willie's oldest brother, John. On the many visits she and her husband had made to Ilion and Mohawk when Deirdre and Rob were children, she could remember Willie as a young boy behind a high desk in his brother's office in Ilion, keeping the accounts.

But she knew that her husband—watching Willie now—considered his hesitations and feints, his erratic comings and goings, not altogether comprehensible, having conducted his own courtship with an ardor and impatience neither of them could forget: she had only to remember the sprig of yew plucked in Paris from the grave of Heloise and Abelard that had fallen from one of his letters. After all, wasn't Deirdre, in her own person, more than worthy of Willie's attentions? Oh yes, there was the money, they all knew that. Willie had alluded more than once to his "lack of means" without ever mentioning Deirdre in connection with it. But neither she nor her husband could have imagined waiting so long for a guarantee. Meanwhile, Deirdre herself said nothing.

Yet she felt Willie trusted her. Her own ancestry was so different from his it was odd they should understand one another. Or perhaps that was it: Willie felt confirmed in his own traditions by her conversion although she had beliefs she suspected he would find surprising: the fires of hell, for example, were claptrap in a story meant to frighten children. At the same time, when it came to her husband, she wondered if Willie felt his lack of enthusiasm as a silent critique of their common ancestry.

Whatever the case, in January 1903, Deirdre suffered an attack of appendicitis and sent Willie, on the eve of her operation, a telegram asking for prayers. During Deirdre's convalescence her father at last sprang into action, organizing everything, convinced that a trip in early summer would return his daughter to full health as well as bolster his wife's failing spirits. And indeed, the telegram to Willie seemed to have disturbed his complacency: he'd sent flowers, cables, cards, and as soon as Deirdre was well enough had visited Washington, his eyes alternately shrouded or ablaze. When the Carmody family sailed from Philadelphia on the *Haverford*—at nine o'clock in the morning the sixth of June—Willie had made a point of traveling down from New York on the fifth and spending the night so that he might see them off.

III

And did the trip to Ireland restore Mary Ethridge's spirits? Give her new hope? Although it offered consolation of an unanticipated kind, it did not. Initially—during the late winter when Deirdre was mending from appendicitis—the prospect of a trip to Ireland, a trip to anywhere, had caused Mary to suffer a dread she couldn't name. Then one night she'd dreamt of a wheel spitting sparks, a wheel that came to a halt with a final faltering click click click. At that moment when she could count the spokes, note their bright glitter, the residue of ash, she understood that

Rob was irrevocably dead and that her great fear had been that she would once again fall into a pit of false hope. Any removal from Washington, she'd suspected, would in some manner revive her belief that he would be miraculously found, that he'd secretly stowed away, swum to shore, been picked up by someone and kept these long years in captivity. Because without a body how could there be any certainty?

It was this new understanding that she was battling a fear of misguided hope that allowed her at last to embrace Ireland for Deirdre's sake. Arriving in Queenstown, driving out to Blarney Castle, taken in jaunting-cars and coaches to witness the much-proclaimed beauties of mountain passes and lakes: all this was tolerable. But it was only when they were staying in Kilkee for a fortnight that she realized she was at last where she wanted to be, at the very edge of an ocean. It was precisely these weeks she had most dreaded, the inescapable view of restless waters; but as the days passed one by one, and she and her husband walked along the strand or warily traced the edge of the cliffs—while Deirdre wandered off by herself or sat in the cottage over her watercolors, looking out at that rocky shelf that jutted into the sea, the one they called George's Head—she'd come to experience a kind of solace. For where were they to visit Rob's grave if not here by the ocean? And didn't George's Head end abruptly in what looked to be a chiseled face, a face of timeless, enduring grief?

It was this flinty profile she found herself glancing at, through the windows of their cottage, walking on the high path. Aware she would think of it at all hours of the day or night with the waves breaking against it, she was consoled by the knowledge that Rob indeed had a memorial worthy of him. She could scarcely guess her husband's thoughts as he walked beside her, but as together they watched the swelling waves that ran up the shore to their feet, raised their eyes to the seagulls screeching overhead and on a clear day the sunlit Cliffs of Moher beyond, she felt pity for this man who had been so strangely punished for his love of the sea, whose great passion had become the agent of his greatest grief. Then she thought perhaps that's how it always is, and thought again of the cross where the line of desire is intersected by the line of suffering.

Can we know how they might have appeared to a stranger, this couple? In fact, a snapshot exists, presumably taken by Deirdre. The backdrop is the sea, a choppy white and black sea. John Carmody is wearing a straw hat with a stiff brim, a boater, the kind in which Willie appears as a young man. What we mostly see of him is his back: a slight man walking with hands clasped behind him. Mary is in the foreground and is not walking at all. She's dressed in black and is drawing in the sand with the point of a black parasol. But unlike her husband, she's become aware Deirdre is standing there with a camera and looks out at her suddenly from beneath the brim of her hat. Her dark eyes are intent, as if she'd been caught in a solitary moment and hasn't had time to adjust her expression. Unquenched.

IV

It was more than two years after their return from Ireland—on October 25, 1905, a date chosen perhaps to ease the anniversary of Rob's disappearance on the twenty-third—that Deirdre and Willie finally married, leaving Deirdre's parents at last alone.

And how did they fare? At first the wheeze of the grandfather clock in the empty house, the chimes and muffled bongs, the profound silence following the announcement of the hour that opened to yet further regions of silence, left them each wrapped in private distress. Immediately after Rob's death the presence of Deirdre—her dark eyebrows, exactly like his, the manner in which she also threw back her head to laugh when something seized her as ridiculous—had evoked Rob's absence in ways that had sometimes seemed unbearable. What they hadn't realized was that over time Rob's shadow rising just behind Deirdre as she moved about the house consoled them for precisely the same reasons it had once caused them exquisite pain. Now they missed Deirdre for herself, for her kindness to each of them, but without her comings and goings from the house, the empty spaces filled up with a silence from which Rob emerged, just himself. The front door opened on a November afternoon and shut again. The echo of his footsteps sounded in the hall, his hasty manner of taking the stairs two at a time, his feet crossing the floor of his room just above their heads. And then there he was before them, in the mirror over the fireplace, dressed for the evening, white collar and tie, black hair parted and combed, moustache almost covering his upper lip: she could see him again, fresh, alive. All her old grievances toward her husband revived, and so with a return of the same bitter heart she had consciously to remind herself of what she'd learned but so often to no avail. They sat to lonely dinners, the Buddha in his old place, shadowed in the early evenings.

Then one night as they sat there silently, lingering over the remains of their late-season pears, picking at scraps, he'd slowly risen from his chair and standing by her side had reached for one of her hands, had taken it from her lap and raised its palm to his mouth. Immediately she'd felt mercy fall around her like rain. Rising from her own chair she'd noticed again his gray eyes sloping down at the corners, thought that for all their years together he was still as strange to her as he had been that day when they'd stood by the pond in the September afternoon listening for what would come next, to the silence of the trees, the rush of blood in their veins. Here it was again, then, the old pulsing need, and leaving their napkins scattered on the table behind them, helping each other up the stairs, they went directly to bed, and so it all began once more, the hunger, the unslaked desire. The first time they'd trembled with eagerness, with fear. Now it was the same, although when at the same moment sobs broke from each of them they found themselves together at the bottom of a sea, the taste of salt in their mouths, adrift in waving seaweed and coral reefs and the stray anonymous bone.

She'd always known she carried an air of something that came from the fact that there had never been a time in their life, ever, when her husband had not desired her. She knew in the way other men looked at her or held her hand an extra moment that they felt whatever it was that came from her secret life with him. Now her renewed consciousness that his love for her had sustained itself over the entire span of her adult life filled her with a gratitude that she couldn't voice in words but that found expression in a patient and lingering tenderness she could see he felt and understood. And when she became ill, when she was seized by fever and chills and her final anguish was upon her, then night after night she was sheltered by the circle of his arms, and at the end the length of his body pressed against hers was the last thing she knew.

So Mary Ethridge too went down into the ground. By keeping Rob's letters on her person, after her death, she ensured they would never be picked up by anyone of a future generation. Also ensured her son would never be remembered by his own words.

It may be that Mary Ethridge alone was free of this preoccupation, this obsession, with being remembered. Didn't trust it, this blind confidence that words or paints could snatch the living moment, the beloved, from the burning wheel of loss. Or didn't trust the good will of strangers who might eventually pick up the letters with cold fingers and read them. As indeed why should she? There must have been a kind of fierce possessiveness at work, extending straight down into the grave. By keeping what was left of Rob to herself, she may have thought to spare him.

Or perhaps it was only that she felt the letters belonged there, for all eternity, next to her heart. Laid on like a poultice. May have held out some hope that—as his body had never rested in the soil, never found peace at last in any plot of earth nor been changed into coral or pearl but rather tossed by wandering currents until even his bones had been ground into pebble and shingle and shell that lay lifting and turning on the floor of the ocean—yes, she may have held out some hope that here at last deep in the earth where the seed could not refuse to break, the nubby root to grope upwards toward the sun, something of him might yet enter the unending cycle of decay and regeneration, of dissolution and renewal.

In Search of Deirdre in Kilkee

Gold light on sea, on sand, on boulders.

And so I crawled toward the edge of the cliff on my hands and knees, and when I got closer, pulled myself over the grass on my belly. The green turf was soft, like moss, a spongy heath. Looking far up the coast of County Clare, I could see Connemara in the distance, could count its twelve Pins. And there, laid out in the preternaturally clear air, the Aran Islands:

Inishmore, Inishmaan, and Inisheer. The bay of Kilkee is shaped like a horseshoe, and I was walking, or rather crawling, at the far end of one of its prongs. The Atlantic glinted below. I had taken the path that wound up past the golf links to the farthest bluff, a path with little stations along the way where you could stop and gaze into the far distance and read a placard telling you about the rocks, the sea life, the flora and fauna. Everywhere, bright flowers were blowing in profusion, long-stemmed pink clover, daisies, yellow buttercups, tiny star flowers I don't know the name of. And grasses, golden grasses, throwing off the light.

It was the longest day of the year, the summer solstice: mild, limpid blue. It must have been about five in the afternoon, but then the sun wouldn't go down till after ten. Here, on the west coast of Ireland, the sun sets later than anywhere in Europe. Except, of course, points farther north.

—And did you peer over the edge?

I did not. Nor indeed even reach the edge, or anywhere near it. It was clear that the mossy turf broke off suddenly, in thin air. Even thinking about the drop below made my head spin. And yet, if I'd stood, say, a foot or two from the brink, why should I imagine I'd fall? Where was the danger? Why should I, flat on my stomach, have feared its pull?

Because I might lose consciousness, looking out over the precipice; knowing myself on *the dreadful summit,* I might faint, might stumble forward and plunge.

But how hard to give any idea of the fascination! To describe the bright blue water observed from such a height. Blue like the water pictured on a calendar photograph of Corfu or Santorini, blue like the Mediterranean when you're looking down on it from Vence. Blue-green, with currents of dark, true blue, almost purple, running beneath. And wet black rocks rising in soaring arches and vaults, waves dashing against them, trailing foam. Waves drawing out slowly and in their own good time tumbling back in. And then as far as you could see, the vast waters of the Atlantic.

Today Father, Mother, and I took a long walk to the rocks which surpass anything I have seen in the way of grandeur. They are wild and take the form of caverns, arches, cathedrals, amphitheatres, etc.

So Deirdre describes them in her journal. At low tide the rocks could be seen clearly from farther down. Earlier, I'd seen young parents sitting there on the flat ones while their children played in little pools and crevices. It was beneath the bluff where I was crawling that the caverns and arches rose out of the ocean, soaring cathedrals.

—So you were thinking of the vacationing Carmodys as you beetled close to the edge?

No. I was simply tunneling through the air like an animal through dirt, driven by some dim instinct, not a thought in my head. But that night in my room in the Strand Hotel with its full view of the bay, a familiar dream visited me. I was falling from a great height into water below. From one of the cliffs, perhaps. As I fell I wondered if I'd be dead on hitting the water, whether I'd dash my brains out as on concrete or slice neatly through the waves like a knife. Then I was alive, I'd survived the fall, I knew it, could look up through depths of clear blue water shot through with rays of light. But it was plain to me I'd plunged so far below I'd never be able to rise fast enough to catch my breath.

—Rob?

Yes. Although waking in the early morning with the rain drumming against the windows it took me a moment to remember where I was, even to remember who. I was merely an intact body breathing in a bed.

—Could your dream have been the visitation you were preparing for? The visitation from Rob?

Probably not. Although the dream tells me that when he jumped or fell from the ship he had some moments of knowing he would die. But no, it wasn't a question of either jumping or falling. Of one or the other. It was something else. If, in the grip of fever, deprived for a time of the *sovereignty of reason* that throws veils over our truest desires, he'd simply looked down into the ocean and longed for the unattainable, then why wouldn't he have slipped over the railing? Put one leg over, then the other, before realizing what a distance it was from the deck to the surface below.

—What of those visitors who'd preceded you? Did they too crawl to that place where, finally, they were unable to look down?

Mary and Deirdre would have been confined by long skirts. And John Carmody? Not likely. However, I'd already found myself standing in a spot, in exactly the same spot, where Deirdre had once stood, holding a camera in her hands.

How do I know? From snapshots pasted into Deirdre's travel journal. From lining up, precisely, the angle of vision from which her picture had been taken of the row of houses where they'd stayed. Because I had her journal with me, carried it everywhere: my guide to Kilkee, my letter of introduction.

The mottled black and white cover, hard cardboard, is no match for the lovely soft suede of the fawn notebook. But the inside pages tell another story. The watercolors are dazzling, more worked than those in the fawn notebook, more painstaking. Small jewels.

"Oh, the treasure!" people exclaimed when I opened the book along the way, showing them the likeness of a house, a road, St. Senan's Well, asking where I might find it. People were amazed to find in a watercolor painted one hundred years ago a publican standing in front of a recognizable establishment dressed in the gear of his time: britches, a tall black hat and loose cravat, clay pipe in his mouth, canny black eyes looking straight out from the page; the silver water of the bay of Kilkee rushing up a beach encircled by painted cottages facing out beyond the seawall. And stuck between the pages, wisps of golden grass, long-stemmed, a single desiccated clover blossom. As always, her firm, flying handwriting. But here the written commentary decidedly takes second place:

> *Thursday, July 2*
> *We are comfortably established in lodgings on MacDonnell Terrace in a pretty green two-storied cottage overlooking the broad Atlantic from our sitting room window. Here we are to remain two weeks.*

> *Tuesday, July 7*
> *We have our breakfast and lunch in the cottage, and go out for our dinner to the West End Hotel. Kilkee reminds me of "Spotless Town." Sapolio, Pearline Gold Dust and everything that is clean. It is white-washed until it fairly glistens in the sun. The lodges and villas are all painted various colors—red, pink, blue, orange, green, buff, canary, and grey. The ocean, or strand, as they call it, is very fine, and there are also bath-houses where hot salt baths may be had for a shilling. At the West End Hotel the other evening a red-haired woman playing the harp sang one of Thomas Moore's melodies: "Believe Me If All Those Endearing Young Charms." When I spoke to her afterwards, saying how much I'd admired her song, she said in that case I might like to hear it at my own wedding!*

—And do you know this song yourself?

I do. From time to time Kate sang it and always with a kind of mocking fervor by way of hiding—I think now—some depth of feeling attached to it. Perhaps Deirdre used to sing it to Kate? Or Willie's friends, glasses aloft, bellowed it out around the piano? In any case, Deirdre continues:

Thursday, July 9
We have been in Kilkee a week today and think it lovelier than ever. We took a long drive this afternoon to Dunlicky Castle and were entertained all the way by our driver Michael McIvearny, a native of Kilkee. The drive sticks close to the sea, and the view of the rocky coast with its arches, caverns, and small islands is magnificent. There are numerous legends connected with the rocky coast. Bishop's Island takes its name from an old bishop who in time of famine departed for this island with all the "grub," as Michael McIvearny told us. Later when good times came he found himself unable to get back and so starved to death, bad luck to him!

Did I record this incident on an earlier page? An Englishman riding on the coach that brought us to Glengariff remarked to the Irish driver, "Why do you name so many of your places after the Devil? He's been dead for years." "Dead, sir," remarked the driver. "I did not know that, sir." And reaching into his pocket he handed the Englishman a shilling. "What's that for?" "Oh, sir, when a man dies in these parts, we take up a subscription for the orphans."

Sunday, July 12
As perfect a summer's day as I have ever known. We three went to the rocks this afternoon. The day warm and bright and the atmosphere so clear we could see the Aran Isles and the Cliffs of Moher nearly forty miles away off Galway Bay. I read and took a nap, Mother ate candy, and Father did nothing! It was a lovely lazy time.

To illustrate the scene, an ink sketch of a man and a woman, a box of candies beside her, both with their backs to us, gazing out at gulls and sea and sails. And then a reclining figure at a little distance, slumbering, book in hand, hat pulled down over her face.

—And so this is what you'd come for? To see the spot where Deirdre had recorded the progress of their days?

I'd come to Kilkee for something more particular. In two days' time, on June 23, I was scheduled to fly back to New York from Dublin. Waking the morning of the twenty-first in Dublin, I'd decided at the last moment to make a flying trip to Kilkee. I couldn't leave without seeing for myself the seascape Deirdre had painted across the spread of a double page, inscribed at the bottom: *View from our sitting room window—George's Head.*

Below, stretching straight across the bottom of both pages, in watercolor, is a low stone wall, all crevices and shadows. Beyond, whitecaps fly across a cold sea, tumbling against the rocky face of the Head that stares out—across the spine—at a white expanse of page devoted entirely to sky and boundless sea. A line of sea birds, penciled in, flap from the tip of the brow out over the waves, probably because the great rocky bulk needed something to balance it: something to prevent the picture from toppling off the page in one direction, like an upended seesaw. Yes, Deirdre must have made that decision later on, when squint-eyed she was contemplating her work.

And why should I have wanted to come to Kilkee for this particular view? Because it was examining the page one April morning near my window overlooking Morningside Park—looking down on ginkgo branches frosted with green—that I experienced one of those rare moments I'd come to recognize; a moment when, caught from beneath, I am suddenly, blessedly, in the presence of Deirdre, as close to her as I am likely to get. Here, the table with the box of watercolors lying open, the brushes in the glassy jar pluming the clear water black or green. And here Ireland, here the sea, the town of Kilkee where for a fortnight the world once again offers itself.

What happened is this: on my arrival I walked into my room at the Strand and dropped my bag on the floor. Then I looked out the window, dumbstruck. There was the bay and the ocean beyond. And there, leaping in through the window, George's Head. Immediately I opened Deirdre's book, comparing the view she had painted with the one before me. From where I stood I could see the entire green sweep of cape that ended in the Head. That made a difference, of course; the proportions were altered. And the rocky face at the end of the Head appeared blunt, as if Deirdre had imagined a sharp profile I couldn't see at all, a grim receding forehead, a sad mouth open to the waves breaking against it. But yes, certainly this ledge of rock was the George's Head I'd studied in the book.

—And the town of Kilkee, was it as you'd imagined?

Not at all! It was the town itself I was having trouble reconciling to some blind notion. It was as if the lights had suddenly been turned on, as if I'd been confronted by a world in bewildering, eye-drenching color: the water laid out in streaks of inky blue and azure, like that glimpsed from one of Matisse's open windows in a room where a goldfish circles a bowl, the sky cloudless beyond lace curtains. The Strand was located at the dead center of the horseshoe and below me the bay glittered in the sun, waves gently rolling in, children on the other side of the wall playing in the sand.

My surprise was the measure of my disbelief in the earthly existence of Deirdre. Had I suddenly been forced to see that everything I'd said and thought and understood had been wrong? That all along I'd taken it for granted that the past was not as highly colored as the present, that caught between the pages of a book it existed only in half-light, in a make-believe world of shadows?

—What did you do to correct your vision?

I left my room in search of something to eat. In a pub around the corner, under the pretext of trying to find out where the Carmodys had stayed, I opened Deirdre's book to the eyes of someone now living in Kilkee. As I ate my tomato sandwich and poured my tea, I showed the young woman who'd given them to me a photograph Deirdre had taken of a curving row of houses opposite a seawall, captioned *Picture of our cottage on MacDonnell Terrace.* She examined the photograph carefully and said she thought MacDonnell Terrace was out near the rocks, waved in the direction of the other prong of the horseshoe, the prong facing the Head. "But where did you find this book?" she asked wonderingly.

Soon enough I was passing low cottages, each painted its own color, pale yellow, rose, tan, green, passed a sign naming this stretch along one side of the bay Marino Paradise. I stopped to ask directions to MacDonnell Terrace of a woman sitting on the seawall, occupied in gazing out at the Head, a sleeping infant in a stroller beside her. Yes, yes, she answered, regarding me with green eyes, keep on just as you are. But when I directed her attention to the book, to Deirdre's watercolor, she stared: "The very likeness! But what will become of this? Do you have someone to leave it to? A daughter?"

Imagine how irresistible to demonstrate to the only people in the world who could appreciate it properly, the accuracy, the wonderful detail, of Deirdre's work! Here was her perfect audience and I had only a few hours to create it. In fact, no one seemed to think it odd that I should open the book to them: each seemed to go into a kind of trance at the sight, to be utterly spellbound. "Carmody!" someone said when I told her Deirdre's name. "There's an old woman named Deirdre Carmody living right here in Kilkee, someone who's lived here all her life. You must take the book and show it to her. Ah, she'll be delighted." But there wasn't time, simply. If I'd had another day in Kilkee, I'd have taken the road along the coast to

Dunlicky Castle, tried to find old Deirdre Carmody. My own Deirdre had no old woman waiting within her, although of course she didn't know it at the time.

_seen ___ on every hand, & the Irish greeting in celtic_ —

Céud míle Fáilte

(_hundred - thousand welcomes_) _& waving over the entire city_

At an old-fashioned sign that pointed the path to St. Senan's Well, I stopped to inquire directions of a man making repairs at the side of the road, a young man wearing an orange jacket, and he smiled and waved me along: "Yes, yes, farther on, then, a few houses." The road had begun to incline upwards, to extend farther out toward the bluff. At yet a farther point I inquired again of two men walking down, thinking they must have come from the place I was trying to reach, producing my book to show them the sepia-tinted photograph.

"Christ!" one of them said, "Where did you get this?" He was elderly, silver-haired, his left eye permanently closed, and he introduced the other, a younger man, as a "historian of Kilkee." The row of houses I was looking for, they said, was just there around the next curve, a little farther up, I'd have no trouble at all.

These two fell headlong into Deirdre's pages, wanting to scan each entry. When I read aloud the story of the old bishop—who in time of famine had departed with all the grub to what had been named Bishop's Island and later, when good times came, starved to death—the younger one shouted with laughter. "Bad luck to him!" he cried, and I felt as pleased as if Deirdre had been standing with us and had pronounced this irreverence herself.

It was he who pointed to a large house with bay windows up the hill a little from where we were standing and said that in one of its incarnations it had been the West End Hotel. And then remarked—perhaps thinking still of death by starvation—that Kilkee's first road, the road on which we were standing, the one that followed the line of the bay, had been built during the Famine, was one of those Relief Committee ventures that killed more people than it kept alive. We stood looking down at the road beneath our feet, and then I thanked them for their help and they wished me Godspeed.

But before taking leave, the one-eyed man raised an arm to point to Connemara in the far distance, said we could count each of the Pins. And there, pointing again, the Cliffs of Moher.

"A day like this is rare," he said. "Nothing to interfere with the vision."

Wind of wild air of seeds of brightness.

I don't think I've mentioned that as I walked farther out on the arm of the bay I'd noticed that the rocky face of the Head had begun to take on a craggy, indeed, a human look. Now I could make out a wild stricken countenance, grass combed back by the wind from its receding brow, mouth wide open in amazement. The likeness between Deirdre's watercolor and the scene before me was not exact, but I could see a face emerging. And then I rounded the bend and knew immediately that here at last was the row of houses that Deirdre had photographed, houses curving up in the direction of the golf links and the cliffs that later on I'd find myself clinging to, each house with its bay window and chimney pots, its little gate and garden.

Picture of our cottage on MacDonnell Terrace. But which cottage was it? There was nothing to tell. Green, she had written, but now it could be any color at all. And where had Deirdre stood to take the photo? A photo that included a boy walking toward her wearing knickers and a cap, and the back of a man in a black bowler, a wicker basket on his arm.

Through a break in the wall, I saw a grassy slope slanting down to the sea, a flight of stone steps to an embankment where you might sit on a cast-iron bench and gaze your fill. I thought I knew where Deirdre had stood, just there on the sidewalk next to the opening in the wall where the steps began. But something was still slightly askew. And then I realized that if I moved down onto the top step of the descending flight, I had the photo exactly.

It was here, then, that Deirdre had stood, exactly here, on this grainy flat slab where my own feet were resting. The brief shadows of the boy and man angled west, so it must have been mid-morning when she'd found the spot. Now, late afternoon, a wedge of shade ran the length of the wall, spilling east onto the road. Here she had once looked down into the eye of her camera, a box camera held carefully between hands that for all I knew my own resembled. And then, abruptly, I had a chilled sense of myself as intruder.

—Why intruder?

Because I was stalking Deirdre. And she without the least say in the matter. I was trying to feel within my own body what it was to be Deirdre Carmody standing on a step one morning in early July.

—But wasn't this to be your project from the beginning? To unearth the lives of an earlier time, to find words for the unspoken?

Yes. But surely, if asked, which one of them would have agreed?

—Their consent was never part of the arrangement. In any case, Deirdre is quite safe from your intrusions. The further we go, the clearer it becomes.

That I'm making it all up as I go?

—*To God alone does the soul reveal itself.* She no more than the others will release her secrets. But you say Kate suffered from the same enthrallment?

It was Kate's silence that made her own preoccupation with Deirdre so riveting. If Kate had related homey little anecdotes about her mother, Kate herself would have been a different person. We might very well have grown up in a different house.

—You say Kate's gaze was turned toward Deirdre? Distracted by Deirdre, she scarcely saw you?

Scarcely saw me! But wouldn't that be too strong! Surely she saw me. I'd prefer to say that Deirdre stood in the center of the frame, blocked the light.

—You wish to wedge between? To nudge Deirdre out of the way?

No, no, not at all! I don't wish to turn Kate's eyes away from Deirdre. It's rather that I want Kate to discover me standing just behind. I want her eyes to take in both of us at once.

—Even now?

Neither Kate nor Deirdre has anything to do with time. Is it preposterous to imagine that in Kilkee it was Deirdre herself, released from every constraint, who threw sudden lights in my path? Urged me to open my eyes to what was in front of me? The wave, for example, that as it slowly drew back spread across the sand a light film of shining water that for an instant gave me the sky? The blue sky in the mirror of the sea, in the thin glaze on the sand? Assured me it wasn't so much a question of her life, the accuracy with which I conjured it, but rather the burning world itself: *seaspawn and seawrack, the nearing tide, that rusty boot.*

Standing there on the step where I knew she had preceded me, I wanted above all else for Deirdre in her kindness to point the way to the cottage in which she'd passed a fortnight, to lead me to the iron gate she and her parents had opened and closed. I passed along the road slowly, the book open, looking up, looking down, examining each cottage, at a loss.

At the farthest house I glimpsed the path down to the same rocks where it might be they'd all passed as perfect a summer's day as Deirdre had ever known. There they'd sat, somewhere just below me. In her sketch a couple of sailboats floated in the distance and a gull flew by. I heard the screech of the gull, felt on my own skin the warm bright air. Lifting my eyes, saw across the bay the profile of the rock face Deirdre had painted so painstakingly: its sad underlip, its low brow and massive nose.

Yet again, exactly as with the photo until I'd found the single step from which it was taken, there was some slight jar.

But then, I thought rapidly, she hadn't painted the Head from this precise spot. Not from just here. In a moment I was back again on the stretch of road that ran in front of the cottages on MacDonnell Terrace, inching along, trying to match the face before me with a single house, a single bay window. In the gardens red and pink roses blew brightly against the black wrought-iron fences. The afternoon of flooding light seemed endless and, as I crept along, the face in Deirdre's book seemed to be coming more sharply into focus.

And then, suddenly, the likeness was exact. The mouth of the rocky face across the bay gaped wider than I'd thought, I could see the waves gathering and rising in front of it, see them crashing against its parted lips, observe the precise curve of the steadfast nose, the patient brow. The upper part of the face expressed plaintive resignation, just as Deirdre had painted it. But the mouth gaped, aghast.

I looked up to see a blue two-storied house, the bay window gleaming in the afternoon sun. Soon I was walking through the little gate of the cottage and knocking on the door. A woman opened it and when I explained my mission, showed Deirdre's book to her, she said I must come in, she was the owner of the house and together we'd look. A tall thin woman with a loop of black hair twisted at the nape of her neck, she spoke rapidly, repeating herself, as if she feared her words might not convey all she intended. I followed her into the front room, past the television in the corner, past a table with photographs arranged on it, to the window, its sill foaming with red geraniums.

She'd taken the book carefully into her hands. Looking from the page to the rocks and back again, she slowly nodded. Yes, she agreed, beyond a doubt, George's Head as it appeared through the pane of glass was precisely the one Deirdre had painted. "Ah, so it was here she sat," she said, turning to look at me with dark blue eyes. "And who could say it was not at this hour, half-four?" A hopeless expression overwhelmed her, as if she despaired of finding the words she needed. She pointed at the edge of the watercolor to an opening in the wall and then, looking out the window, made a gesture to a spot I'd noticed earlier. There it was, precisely as Deirdre had placed it, the break in the wall—an old man now passing in front of it—and there below, the cast-iron bench on the grassy embankment where someone might rest if they liked and watch the churning sea.

At the door, I thanked her, tried to say how glad I was it was she who lived in this house. Taking my hand in hers she again looked at me, speechless. Again the deep blue eyes, the stammering speech. Then, at last, "Ah, but how she must have loved all this! Loved it!"

Across the sands of all the world, followed by the sun's flaming sword, to the west, trekking to evening lands.

It was as if a deep shadow had fallen across a bright day. Was it the ghosts crowding? The woman struggling across a sharp divide? I closed the gate of the house behind me and set off toward the cliffs, pausing again at the top of the path I supposed they'd followed down to the rocks. Perhaps it was at about this hour, when the sun was inclining west, that they'd gathered their things and decided to return to the cottage to rest or write letters or read before making their way to dinner at the West End?

Then, in the face of the shining day, I thought I saw them moving slowly up the path toward me, Deirdre in the lead, her legs moving beneath a long dark skirt, the ends of a black tie flying in the wind over the shoulders of her white blouse, a gold watch hanging almost to her waist. Mary followed, dressed entirely in black, tapping her way with the tip of a black parasol. At first John Carmody's slim back was all I could see of him because he had stayed behind a moment to stare out over the sea, but he soon turned and followed the others. As Deirdre drew near, looking down at the path, I could see she was carrying the familiar travel journal in one hand, holding it against her breast. I thought I surprised a look of bafflement in her gray eyes as she passed the spot where I stood, the identical book in my own hand also clutched against my breast. She paused and looked over her shoulder as if brushed by some knowledge that the life she was writing down in her book was already complete.

In a moment, Deirdre had passed by and then Mary too paused as she approached, looking behind her. John Carmody quickened his step and caught up with her, taking her elbow and guiding her up the path to where I was standing. As they drew near, Mary turned again and I could see she was gazing back at George's Head. I looked across the bay, then, to follow the line of her vision and saw that the tide was rising, that the waves gathering slowly and crashing against the face had almost reached the lower lip, were drawing back slowly, then surging forward, flinging themselves against the rock, scattering foam in the long rays of the sun. When I turned again the three of them were gone. I made my way up to the golf links and then out onto the cliffs where I gathered a long-stemmed pink clover to join the one Deirdre had already pressed in her book.

Only this more. Sitting down a few hours later for a dinner of salmon and new potatoes at a large window in the Strand's dining room that faced the entire bay, I looked up and again saw George's Head clearly before me. Not as I'd viewed it from the high ledges I'd just come from, but as I'd first seen it hours before, with its face turned away. Far in the distance I could see the cliffs I'd recently clung to for fear of falling and, below, the houses high on MacDonnell Terrace. It must have been nine o'clock. As

I sat watching, squeezing lemon on my salmon, the long row of windows on the Terrace suddenly ignited. Yes, the sun was at last sinking and the high bluffs were aglow.

I felt I had not a minute to lose. Quickly finishing, I set off again, once more retracing my steps. The waves running up the sand were gray now, flecked with white. Here were the painted cottages on Marino Paradise falling into shadow and across from them the wall where the woman had sat with her baby looking out on George's Head. Racing along, I reached the West End Hotel and paused, remembering the one-eyed man and the town historian. I thought of the starving men who'd carried the stones for this road, wondered where they'd been stopped in their task by death: stopped, for all I knew, on even such an evening as this. They too had heard the waves' dull roar below, heard the long outgoing murmur before the rush back in, the heavy pounding against the rocks.

Then all at once I knew what it was, the reason for my haste. The setting sun ablaze in the many windows of the Terrace—observed from my dining table at the Strand—had seemed to me a sign, a summons. Of course they must be expecting me, these others I'd spent the day pursuing. It was their turn now and they would be eagerly looking out from their high point for my arrival. Because why must I bear the loneliness of being without them an instant longer when I might simply knock on their door? They must want me as I wanted them. It was so simple. They were here with me in Kilkee close as air. I'd sat at their window, put my hand on the latch of their gate, looked far out to the Aran Islands just as they had. Even now, what was to prevent their standing at the door of their cottage? Welcoming me with cries of joy and relief?

By the time I'd turned into MacDonnell Terrace, the flame had disappeared from the line of windows and the panes were taking on the dark gleam of night. The sun, no longer too bright to look at, was quickly tipping down toward the horizon. I passed the step where Deirdre had stood to take a morning snapshot. As for the cottage where the stammering woman had taken my hand, where Deirdre's absorption in her task may have provided some bulwark against her own loneliness, the windows were unlighted. The roses that bloomed at its door had taken on a ruddy cast, were gathering in.

Farther on, people were sitting on benches, standing about, talking, come to witness the slide of the sun into the sea. Was that a seal out on the rocks, a man asked, lowering his binoculars, pointing to a long ledge of rocks in the distance. Was it someone cut off by the tide? I couldn't make out the figure they were talking about but, glancing over at George's Head, I saw that the rising tide had now covered the lips of the rocky face and was quickly hiding the nose as well. Wouldn't it be as well if they alerted the rescue squad, a woman asked.

The man who'd raised the concern in the first place again lifted his binoculars and declared that what they were looking at was a seal: there wasn't a doubt in the world. The first woman said it was rarely as clear as it was tonight. There were clouds gathering overhead, but look at the bright band of light, look at Connemara, at Inishmaan. Look there, at the Cliffs of Moher.

The sun was slipping fast and I turned my head for a moment to glance at George's Head. The entire massive nose of the rock face was now below tide level. When I turned back I saw a quick flash of green light on the horizon: the sun was gone.

Part Four

IRELAND
in the 1840s

DONEGAL LONDONDERRY ANTRIM

TYRONE Belfast

FERMANAGH DOWN

ARMAGH

LEITRIM MONAGHAN

SLIGO CAVAN LOUTH

MAYO ROSCOMMON LONGFORD
Strokestown

WEST- MEATH
MEATH

DUBLIN

GALWAY

Galway KINGS Co KILDARE

Dublin

QUEENS Co WICKLOW

CLARE CARLOW

Limerick TIPPERARY KILKENNY Enniscorthy

LIMERICK WEXFORD

KERRY WATERFORD

CORK

Cork

Spirit Fires

Will my soul pass through Ireland?

Oh! Sogarth Aroon, sure I know life is fleeting —
Soon, soon in this strange land my poor bones will lie,
I have said the last prayer and received the last blessing
And if the Lord's willing I'm ready to die.
But Sogarth aroon can I never again see
The valleys and hills of my dear native land
When my soul takes it flight from this dark world of sorrow
Will it pass through old Ireland to join the blest band.
Oh! Sogarth aroon sure I know that in Heaven
The loved ones are waiting and watching for me,
And the Lord knows how anxious I am to be with them
In those regions of joy, amid souls pure and free;
Relieve the last doubt of a poor dying soul
Whose hope, next to God, is to know that when leaving
I will pass through old Ireland on its way to its good goal
Oh! Sogarth Aroon I have kept through the changes
The thrice blessed shamrock to lay o'er my clay
And oh! it has minded me, often and often,
Of the bright sunny valley so far, far away.
Then tell me, I pray, shall I ere again see
The place where it grew on my own native sod?
When my body lies cold in the land of the stranger
Will my soul pass through Ireland on its way to our God!

Denis O'Sullivan.

191

I

Oh Willie, what wrong have I done you, what grudge nursed with stubborn resolve these many long years? What injury turned in my mouth, savoring its bitter taste of dandelion leaves? Leaves that in May sprang up all over the grass and that Charlie, when he was twelve or thirteen, harvested and took to the cellar to make into wine. Was it my loyalty to Charlie, once again, that was at the bottom of it all? Did I witness some harshness toward him, some dark observance of the disciplinarian about you I could not forgive? You were indulgent when it came to me, the child named Carmody in unspeaking memory of Deirdre. But Charlie? Did you look at him through glinting lenses, watch him fling himself on the floor in some display of temper that recalled you to a forgotten self? The boy flogged by a mother who had known the scratch and bite of hunger, who recognized the difference between wishful thinking and the consequence of things?

So now at last it seems time to reckon with you, Willie, the one I've made up, made into the villain, my intimate foe. You who first brought tales of Ireland into Deirdre's life very unlike those she recorded in her notebook in Kilkee. Because you were a true if bristly member of a tribe to which Deirdre felt only a starry allegiance. It's your vengeance I've feared striking from a blind sky, you I've waged war against in fiery exchanges within myself. And in skirmishes with others, too, those I've propped up in your place—friends and strangers alike—who've proved useful to me in appeasing intolerable feelings of humiliation and shame. It's you I've fastened on for reproach, not John Carmody or Mary Ethridge or Deirdre. Nor even Kate or Bert. And in turning on you alone, Willie, I've no doubt spared each of these others. But not, strangely enough, myself. For in battling you so tirelessly, I've declared hostilities on a shadow self I've vehemently wished to disown.

Yesterday I went by the house, saw once again as in a dream the chimney pots, the blank windows in a misty April rain, the hickory still innocent of swollen buds that make such a display each spring. Saw the steps up to the front porch you climbed when returning from Deirdre's funeral. Saw, too, the walk leading up to the steps, remembered a snapshot of you standing there in your waistcoat and jacket, staring at the camera as if it had been a dog you were determined to intimidate. The same walk where Deirdre, on another occasion, is photographed bending down over tulips that might have been staring up at her and she anxious not to ignore their gaze.

But never you and she together, no photograph of the two of you standing side by side or more intimately with arms linked. No evidence that you occupied the house at the same time, that you came and went through the same door, anticipating whether with pleasure or fear or sudden apprehension the sight of the other in a room upstairs. No, none of that is there to see.

I asked Kate, once: "Do you remember the two of them together at all?"

"No," she said. "It's strange, isn't it? But no, I don't seem to."

Or was it that the light hurt your eyes, Willie, that you hated being instructed to stand full-face in the sun while someone took your picture? In the shade, your short-sighted blue eyes swam alarmingly behind pince-nez, that I remember. And remember, too, your mouth set in the same grim line that I would sometimes glimpse on Kate's face in moments of bitter resignation or anger or fatigue and that now, passing a mirror, I sometimes catch sight of on my own. It's not an expression I'm proud of, not a look I would willingly put before the world for what it reveals of my determination to have my own way, of my self-righteousness and pouncing judgments. Because how could I have condemned you for so long and with such unswerving dedication were this penchant for conflict and accusation not my own exactly?

In the beginning it might have been self-protection on my part. An instinct to denounce the thing I feared: the smack on the leg, banishment at the first show of temper. And yet I have not a single memory of your so much as speaking sternly to me. No, it's much more probable that Kate, even before you appeared, grew fearful you'd think us ill-behaved for not observing your own long-held principles of discipline and control. Principles she could scarcely pretend to be unaware of, having endured their lash in her own childhood, intimately, searingly, and what's more, in these same rooms. Oh yes, Kate herself had been known to have a will of her own and had been chastised by you, who knows, with the razor strap that hung from a hook on the back of the bathroom door; she'd been turned on your knee, afterwards known fits of wild outrage, of blistering humiliation.

So it's easy to imagine Kate would have been in some conflict when it came to applying your methods on our backs in the house where she now must play the adult. And Deirdre? At the very end of Kate's life, in response to a question I'd put to her about your character and Deirdre's, Kate said that she thought her mother had been "gentler, livelier" than her father. But went on to say that later on you'd become less stern. No, she didn't think she'd had that impression because she was older and so less vulnerable. She thought you truly had become a less difficult man.

Yet mustn't one wonder about Deirdre herself, what behavior of yours she closed her eyes to? Was this the order of the day, the mother storing up accounts of misbehavior to be settled by the working father when he returned home at night? The shivering child left to await the sound of the front door slamming closed behind the figure of fear? All this so that the image of the gentle mother might be protected from any taint of blind anger and retribution?

And so my undying resentment may have had to do with Kate and her own confused and terrified withdrawals when we behaved before you in a manner she knew had once elicited the strap. It could be said you removed us from Kate, our kindly if overstretched mother, caused her to doubt her own instincts and gave us a frightened mother in her stead. And why? Because you, Willie, were known to have had a fiery temper yourself and as a child were sure to have been chastised often enough.

But by what forces were those others shaped, the ones who'd disciplined you? The ones disciplined by hunger.

Yet none of this seems adequate to explain the peculiarly bitter taste of the grudge I hold against you. It's only the last possibility, that you removed Kate from us, that seems to bear the least semblance to the baffling truth. So now at last it's time to make a stab at putting down my single recollection of you—you who died a few days before my fourth birthday—transcribe it with a good deal of anxiety that something is going to be taken from me. Because how can we return to a wordless moment once it has been dressed in words? Or, after a vain attempt to translate it into language, feel along our nerves the seductive authority of the unspoken?

On this afternoon that is all I have of you it is summer and you've come to the house to visit Kate, to visit us all, presumably. Who knows, perhaps you'd woken the night before in the city and remembered the evening of Deirdre's death, the patch of sun that had appeared on the back stairs like a summons. You've taken a train out from Grand Central and walked up to the house from the station, climbed the steps of the front porch, stood looking through the screened door into the silent house. Turned the knob and entered, accustomed as you were to carrying the key in your pocket.

And then? Did you walk through the living room past the dreaming Buddha and out onto the porch, sit down in the white rocker, thrum your fingers on its arms? Listen to the cicadas stirring up a fuss in the trees? Then—but how likely is this?—did you find me wandering the house alone? Where, for instance, are Charlie and Maddie? Where is anyone else at all? I must have only just turned three because my birthday and your death day both occur in May: by the time I turn four the following spring you are already dead. So on this summer afternoon—one of your last, as it turns out—we find ourselves in the upstairs hall, tiptoeing along beside the books you've bought over so many years on your trips to Dublin. I don't know how to read and so the letters on the backs of the books mean nothing to me, but I already know the colors of their jackets, the look of their spines as they lean together on the shelves. I know their dusty smell, my nose often enough is in them. John Carmody is staring down at us from his gilded frame but we are oblivious.

Your finger is pressed to your lips, you are cautioning me not to make a sound. Your blue eyes, magnified by lenses, are looking straight into mine. I am imitating what you do: I have raised my own finger to my mouth, have perhaps only just learned from you this gesture of silence, this thrilling imperative. And why are we tiptoeing along in this manner, boon companions, silent conspirators?

Because Kate is resting this mid-afternoon, stretched on a bed in the room where you and Deirdre slept for so many years, the room that after her death you occupied alone an even greater number of years. This afternoon you wish to surprise Kate. That is the reason for our stealthy approach.

It is precisely here my memory fails. Do we peer through the open door? Call her name? The crystal scent bottles are throwing their rainbow nonsense on the ceiling, the windows and mirrors are bottomless pools of summer green. And Kate, does she raise her head? Feign surprise at the sight of her father and three-year-old daughter at the door? But what I soon understand—and wonder now if by chance I went to wake her and you sternly intervened—is this: Kate must be allowed her few moments of rest. They must under no circumstances be snatched from her. If she fails to raise her head or even open her eyes, then she is in a deep and healthful slumber and must not be woken.

The confusion is this: if we are not to disturb her, then why are we tiptoeing to her door? And what do you want, Willie, from me or from anyone else? Most especially, what do you want from Kate? Perhaps it's her company you're after, the old widower now living in the city, the comfort she will undoubtedly bestow, this daughter who has pitied your loss, has gone so far as to imagine herself and Grace among your most poignant difficulties. Oh yes, the poor man left with two daughters; and of such an age! Just as if she had not her own sore heart to consider. But what a dilemma must be yours, Willie. How are you to claim the solace you require without waking Kate from her sleep? When it comes to that, why are you tiptoeing to her door at all? Why do you not wait downstairs and allow her to wake in her own good time?

For the fact of the matter is this: Kate is not well. No, she is barely making do. During the last months she has been trying to regain her strength after a long season of illness, a bleeding ulcer, to be precise. While Kate is in the hospital and then later on—while she is recuperating in the quiet of your city apartment, Willie, during the spring months—we her children have been left in the care of Nora McHugh. Kate has vanished without a trace; Bert comes and goes, spending a night in the house with us, a night in the city with Kate. But Nora is with us always.

I have come to love Nora dearly, Nora who reads my fortune in the leaves at the bottom of my cup of milky tea and who tells me that when I am six years old she will take me with her to Ireland. "I'll take you home again, Kathleen, to where your heart has ever been." This is the song she sings, her head on the pillow beside mine, when I am going to sleep each night. Is there another home, then, before this one? A place where someone is longing to be? She will take me to visit her old mother and her old father and her brothers who work the farm in Galway. "Near Tuam," she says, pronouncing a name that starts with a sound like the beginning of the word *church*. In fact she takes me with her to Mass, we sit in a pew and look up at St. Catherine with her beautiful long hair alight in the sun, we look at the lamb, the gentle lamb with three drops of red blood on his snowy breast. Nora tells me that although the wicked emperor tried to break holy Catherine on the wheel it was not Catherine at all but the emperor's wheel that broke in the end. That is why Catherine stands there with her hand resting on it, to show that she was not hurt. Nora's eyes are gray, dark lashes all round, and she gazes at me with affection, although sometimes I anger her, refuse to get out of the bathtub, and then to my overwhelming shame she whacks me on the backside. But my love for Nora is such that I am afraid it is supplanting my love for Kate. With guilty apprehension—after Kate has returned to us, after she is in the house again but scarcely on her feet—I confess to her that I don't know whom I love better, Nora or herself. Kate rests her weary green eyes on me and says she's glad I love Nora so much. But is she glad? Does she say what she does only to relieve my fear? Is she struck at the quick? These are the questions that haunt and frighten me.

Yet Kate has left me, God knows, left me alone and afraid, so who is to blame if I have come to love someone else in her absence? I have already learned that a gaping heart attaches. And now, for the first time, I'm wondering if Kate too, in Deirdre's absence, had come to love someone not her mother and if my question to her as she lay in the room where Deirdre too had once watched trembling rainbows on the ceiling didn't evoke memories of betrayals of her own.

So also wonder if this scene of conspirators tiptoeing down the hall wasn't one of Kate's own first memories of the house. If she too wasn't instructed to creep silently along past the bookshelves at those times when Deirdre had thrown herself on the bed to gather her strength before making her weary way downstairs. Did you, in an effort to still your own urgent need—for you must have yearned above all else for Deirdre's sympathy, you who had been offended at work by some chance remark, you who had a temper that leapt like a flame—instruct Kate firmly in the need for stealth? Teach her this imperative to stifle the cry that burned in her throat? So that at last she came to look out at the world and identify the sufferer not as herself but as you, Willie: in fact, as anyone at all other than herself.

Because it's entirely possible that by the time the five-year-old Kate first stepped across the threshold of the house in Pelham—fast following little Mary's illness and death—she was already engaged in a fierce predicament. How was she to silence the howl that if she opened her mouth would certainly break from her? How ask for what she must at all costs receive from Deirdre, the source of all tenderness, when her cries might fatally sap her mother's strength at its root? You may have helped things along by your confusing injunctions, but the unanswerable question must have already lain heavy within. In any case, the clamor of your need separated mother from daughter, that's clear.

When Kate had finally left behind the last vestiges of childhood— having for years scowled and looked threateningly beneath her dark brows at you or another, having stopped her words and clenched her fists—just at that moment, just then, the source, the spring, the fount of delight, sank back into the earth, leaving behind a dusty desert soil crisscrossed by the dark purposeful shadows of birds.

My own memory breaks off at this point with our arrival at the door of the room where the invalid lies resting, the door with the glass knob, the knob of sliding silver depths, of dissolving planes of suggestion and possibility. And so the moment remains a fragment where all is anticipation and suspense, where nothing is resolved or understood, where the beloved mother might open her arms to her father and to her child, rise in health from her bed, delighted. Where she might feign sleep, or stretch out her arms only with reluctance and terrible weariness. Or not respond at all.

That you became a gentler man, Willie, Kate was at pains to let us know. Could it have been by way of illustration that she told us a story? Or did the story itself make the point, relieving her of any need to be explicit. During the summer of 1924, exactly a year after Deirdre's death, you and Kate were traveling in Ireland together: Kate having only just turned seventeen, and you—on your last birthday—fifty-five. That she felt uneasy in your company, wasn't used to spending time alone with you: all this was part of the story. As well as a predictable aside that she'd come to think more recently that you must have been trying to get to know your daughters better because in similar fashion, the following year, when you'd traveled again to Ireland, you'd taken Grace with you.

Why were you a stranger to your children? We might have asked but didn't because Bert similarly came and went, preoccupied with his work, and like you was named by Kate "the poor man," at least in connection with her own illness, exactly as you had been in connection with Deirdre's.

Far away in the background there might be some obscure mention of unforeseen costs, of large expenses. Of unspeakable stresses.

So there you are, Willie, and there is Kate, an uncomfortable pair, in Dublin, a city where mannequins appear in shop windows. One day you and she pass a shop—perhaps even Brown Thomas—and suddenly a dress catches Kate's eye, a green dress, as she describes it rather exactly, with a silver sheen on it and a low, exposed back, the kind that fashionably dips to the waist. The neck falls in loose Grecian folds, the skirt is cut very short. Kate sees the dress and is immediately taken with it, exclaims spontaneously that she'd like to have it very much.

And what do you respond, Willie, when Kate declares the wish of her heart? You speak to her sternly, tell her she's thinking only of herself and that she'd be better occupied in looking out for a gift for Grace. And then tell her, as a kind of afterthought, she'd only make herself ridiculous dressing up in that grown-up fashion.

Kate doesn't describe the walk back to the hotel, the bruising silence that must have fallen between you. She says only that a little later on you'd said you were going to step out for a moment. She hadn't known where you were going but soon enough you'd returned to the hotel with a box in your hands. And inside it—and here her green eyes fill with tears—is the dress.

Why, as I record that afternoon and your part in it, do I find my own tears rising, as if I too might repent of my obduracy and quick judgments? Yes, this must be recorded as well.

Kate's story is concluded at this point. But we can't help wondering what happens that afternoon in Dublin after you place the box in Kate's hands and she opens it, catches a glimpse of the shimmering green material from beneath layers of filmy white paper. Of course she must try the dress on. She must see if it fits. And so she disappears for a few minutes to change and when she walks through the door you're looking at a creature with long ungainly legs, with dark hair and brows like Deirdre's: someone you're not sure you recognize.

I think it might be at this instant—when Kate, still a schoolgirl, appears to you as an unknown woman and when for the first time you represent to her the source of tenderness she thought she'd lost forever in her mother—that Deirdre begins to vanish from the scene, that her image begins to be erased.

Of course Deirdre's death prepared the way for this moment. Without it there would be no story. But thoughts of her may have intruded on you, Willie, as you and Kate walked back in silence to the hotel, as your quick anger—of which you were immediately ashamed—lapsed into confusion when you remembered Deirdre's own love for beautiful clothes which this elder daughter seemed to have inherited, remembered both your pride in Deirdre's elegance as well as the part you'd come to understand money played in it. Marveling that here was Kate with the same quick eye for color and line putting added strain on your pocketbook just as her mother had done. And recalling with chagrin an occasion when you'd responded to a request from Deirdre in just such a manner, wishing you could undo—too late!—a meanness around money you knew you had to struggle against.

And then suddenly called to mind, perhaps, how Deirdre had once told you she thought your anger acted as a smoke screen for any strong emotion you weren't sure of, just as what you advertised as lack of means served as a pretext for holding back when you didn't understand the source of your own reluctance. At this point, Willie, you may have been suddenly overcome: missed Deirdre sharply, achingly, realizing no one would ever again both know you as she had done and at the same time extend toward your weaknesses a kind of sheltering patience. And so you came at last to remember with pity this child whom you knew above all things Deirdre would have wanted you to treat with kindness. For her sake, then, in the late afternoon you retraced your steps to the shop and discussed sizes and so on with a saleswoman who became quite energetically engaged in your project and so returned to Kate who was reading, head down, and didn't look up when you came in, and then when you extended to her the box, lifted her eyes green and sad, uncomprehending, until she opened the box and, with a torrent of tears, understood.

So now I return to the house we both know and to the child, of one generation or another, who on a warm September afternoon is biding her time in a room upstairs where she is supposed to be taking a nap. She has grown tired of sitting on the bed turning the pages of a book, trying to make sense of a picture of the sickly old king who has turned a deep shade of green beneath his little golden crown. With a crayon she writes at the bottom of the page the first two letters of her name, the only ones she's learned. Then she gets off the bed and stands in the middle of the room. Without the least warning, the head of an elephant appears in the open window. Yes, the wise old eye of an elephant is staring straight into hers. They exchange a long tender look and then he puts his trunk through the window and confidingly wraps it around her hand.

But then—just as she is beginning to lose herself in this enduring embrace—she starts with fear. Suppose the elephant takes it into his head to slam her up against the wall. Wraps his trunk tightly around her waist, carries her out through the window and away. How can she be sure he is not concealing some fury, some spite? That soon his ears will not fan back and forth, that he will not lift his trunk in a loud trumpeting, a shriek? And so, to her undying sorrow and regret, she turns her back on the elephant and leaves the room.

But who is this child, Willie? And why do I think now of the radiant promise at the end of the hall, of the sweetness of Kate's arms? Think too—as this vision of happiness hovers just out of sight like the shining moon about to sail free over the rim of the hill—of the turning aside, the finger pressed to the sealed lips, the caution, the sense of danger, of lurking mal-intent. A few seconds, a mere nothing, in the scope of both our lives. But those few seconds are everything I have of you. And within their brief and timeless span I am all yours, your conspirator in silence, your helpmate. Your fellow traveler, your would-be friend. I am yours most truly, most ardently, in deprivation, yours in exile.

II

Turn over the weedy clods and tease out the tangled skeins.
What is he looking for there?

I was born in Ilion in 1869 and as long as I can remember have
been given work to do. For years we kept a cow and as soon as she
was put out to pasture in the spring I was up at six o'clock in the
morning to drive her home, milk her, and drive her back to pasture.
When the pasture time ended she was kept in the barn and had to
be milked and cared for there. As soon as spring came the garden
was plowed and I helped with the planting, hoeing, and weeding.
I helped with the mowing of the lawn, the cutting of the field, and
the stowing of the hay in the barn. Then with fall the leaves had to
be raked, the fruit picked and put away, and most of the year there
was churning to be done.

    For three weeks from about the 10th of June a half dozen of
us boys in the immediate neighborhood would get up at half past
three and go up to John Devendorf's on the Barringer Road to pick
strawberries for the market. We would begin to pick as soon as it
was daylight and be back home in time for school at nine o'clock.
Some boys could pick 60 to 75 boxes of berries in a morning but
the most I could do was from 50 to 60; we received two cents a box
for this. When the strawberry season was over we went for wild
raspberries, then black caps, then black long berries. So the summer
was covered.

    In the winter coal had to be brought up from the cellar for three
stoves to heat the house, and the ashes removed. Winter would last
from November to April and we would have from 90 to 100 days of

sleighing. I recall it was 36 degrees below zero once and it was not uncommon for the temperature to drop below zero for a week at a time.

This is the way your life-account begins, Willie, with a catalogue of chores: the first words from your pen. And the next:

My father, Michael Conroy, was born in the parish of Creve, near Elphin, County Roscommon, Ireland, December 22nd, 1823 or '25; he was uncertain of the year and there were no registrations of birth there at the time. His parents died when he was small and he was put in the care of an aunt, a sister of his mother, who brought him up. He had a brother who came to this country as well and was in New Orleans at the time the Civil War broke out. Before the war my father used to hear from this brother occasionally but afterwards he never heard from or of him and always thought he had joined the Southern Army and been killed.

At the time of my father's childhood, conditions in Ireland were hard and opportunities for education were meagre. He was born before Catholic Emancipation which was not established until 1829. He was born during a time when a Catholic had no political rights at all and was merely allowed to live, and many were not allowed even that. Schools were forbidden, learning took place in hiding, in hedge schools. But my father had a fine mind and now that I am an adult and able to appraise him I feel that if he had had the advantages he might have gone far.

Of the details of his early life I know nothing except that as he grew up he worked on a farm and came to this country when he was about twenty. He arrived in New York, remained there awhile, and then went up to Herkimer County where there were many neighbors from Roscommon. He found work on the farms in the town of Litchfield among the "American" settlers, many of them from Connecticut. And later found employment a little way from Ilion on the Remington farm in the Gulph or the Gorge, as it is now called. This is the family that made the name famous.

Eliphalet Remington took my father into his shop and taught him all he knew. Then Remington moved from the Gulph down to Ilion because it was on the Erie Canal. He took my father with him and for a time he lived in the Remington family.

My father was a man of about five feet six and weighed about 135 pounds, but had broad shoulders, was strong, quick, agile, very light on his rather small feet and could dance the Irish dances with a good deal of grace. He had an even disposition and loved to have company at the house.

His tastes were what we call "nice." He was fond of music, of reading, of flowers, of fruit trees; his pleasure was to experiment with the raising of flowers and fruit. And his experiments were often successful because he loved the task and was ready to do much work to accomplish his object. His favorite pastime was raising pears. I remember we had a tree that produced a very early, yellow, sweet pear that I have never seen elsewhere. Pick these pears when they were just ripe and they were the best I've ever eaten. Leave them a few days and they would get soft. Then the tree would be so infested with bees, hornets, and wasps that you would not dare go near it.

But this man who dances so nimbly on his little feet is my great-grandfather, a man from Ireland! And how eloquent you are, Willie, remembering the lovely yellow pear, not to be left a moment too long. There it is, hanging in the sun, you reach up and break its stem from the branch, turning the warm fruit in your hands, biting into its sweet flesh, juice running down your chin.

There, too, in the little orchard, moving about, is Michael, the man who planted your pleasure. But now it's dawn on a mild June morning very near the solstice and you, the youngest of his twelve children, are long gone, are already up on the Barringer Road picking strawberries. As he prunes and plucks and looks for the first sign of fruit—now that the blossoms he so carefully protected during a late May cold spell have scattered—Michael is remembering how as a boy he too had been up early, had shivered in the dawn walking across meadows of tall grass blowing with yellow buttercups, had tried to take the chill from his fingers before milking by holding them up to the cow's warm breath. But no, he thinks, he's forgotten, as he has so much: in Ireland, at the feast of St. John, dawn breaks earlier than it does here in the Mohawk Valley. It would be broad daylight already at four o'clock in the morning and he setting out, the hawthorn threading the hedges, the curlew calling from the woods. He remembers again the day he left it all, how little he knew then that it would be the skies he'd think of most, that vast overhead banked with fast-moving clouds, spots of blue appearing here and there between, pale to white or turquoise or a deep true blue, clouds that seemed always about to break open, silver moving at their edges, yes, a light on the meadows, a shine.

Now, as he watches the tips of his dewy trees touched by the first sun, as the branches lift out of the shadows into a tranquil summer morning, he returns to the little pear trees of his childhood. The only thing of his father he remembers are his hands: tucking a fiddle into his waist, beneath his chin, slicing down with the bow and the air filling with the rushing sound of water; his touch on the bark of a tree like this one, the dusty gray bark split in places to show a deeper bronze, remembers how as a very small boy he'd thought the dust would come off on those rough fingers, remembers them delicately touching the pointed leaves of the pear trees, the deep crease down the middle of the leaf, a delicate ruddy pink in fall.

So as a kind of talisman, to prepare for the rest, tales of unspeakable deprivation and loss, I linger for a moment on these contrived and surely fanciful pictures of ripening fruit and plenty. There you are, Willie, born in 1869, exactly twenty-six years later than John Carmody, your future father-in-law, growing up in a town along the Mohawk River that neighbored his. And yet, strikingly enough, no barrels of apples, potatoes, and turnips for you, no sides of beef or ham, no woodhouse piled chockablock with stove wood so that you might bid defiance to the winter's siege. Your earliest memories read like an ode to industry; John Carmody's like an evocation of abundance and safe harbor.

Why? Here we're at the mysterious crossroads of naked spirit and the circumstances with which it must struggle: that perplexing intersection. Perhaps it wasn't in John Carmody's nature to see himself in the light of insufficiency. Or yours to see yourself in any other. Perhaps your older brother Frank—who was said to have sat reading in the station, so engrossed in his book that the train came and went without his looking up—carried within a sense of life's bounty, even overflow.

It may be that John Carmody's younger sister Elizabeth recalled her childhood as rendered miserable by perpetual cold and want. Or could it be that things might have been different if your father—instead of finding solitary amusement in fruit trees—had like John Carmody's always been ready for a romp with his children? Or if extremity hadn't so early and so intimately touched your mother's bones?

Because what in the end causes a human being to be one way rather than another? What accident of history or temperament makes the difference? What buried childhood memory of cruelty or mercy or kindness? What tender light? What sudden blow from behind? And what, finally, do we know of each other?

III

Rain is falling on the Burning Bush
Where God appeared.

The years of the Famine were the beginning of the emigration from Ireland that reduced the population in a few years from 8,500,000 to 4,500,000. County Roscommon, the home of my people, was to provide its share of these emigrants and Ilion, Frankfort, Mohawk, and Herkimer was a settling ground for them. These, the common Irish, came there in considerable numbers and their descendants still live in the area.

It was among them and from them that I was born and raised and it is to this environment that I attribute my love for the Irish. Not that I do not admit their weaknesses as well. But looking back to my boyhood days, I can estimate the character of these good people. None of them were learned. Cromwell said he would drive these poor Irish to hell or Connaught. Well, my ancestors went to Connaught. They were not permitted to practice their religion or to own land. The Mass could be celebrated only in secret. Schools were few and under ban of the law; people were very poor. But their loyalty to each other was great. If there was sickness in a family, the women would take turns in attending the patient or doing the housework. In case of death, everyone turned out.

The cemetery on Oak Hill at Ilion has resting there many a one who helped in life. I think no more beautiful character ever

*lived than old Patrick Carney and his dear old wife, Kate; Frank
Brennan, true as steel; Frank Grimes and Paddy Lynch, John and
Hugh Owens, Tom and Nick Fagan, Luke Crosby, John Gleason,
Jim Butler, Tom and Ed Powers, Martin and Pat Kavanaugh, and
I am not going to leave out my own father. In Frankfort the John
Dowd family were always active in the community life. There used
to be a saying up there, "The best funeral people from the Dowds
out," a word of praise for people who were faithful in attendance at
the funerals of their Irish neighbors.*

I can't help notice that excepting Patrick Carney's *dear old wife* there's not
a woman named. But in this matter you'll correct yourself soon enough.

*In 1846 and '47 the Famine occurred due to the failure of the potato
crop and thousands starved. The British government helped the
misery along by doing nothing, indeed, worse. Grain and cattle was
exported out of Ireland to England under heavy guard. Landlords
drove the starving from their cottages, tumbled down the roofs
over their heads so as to clear the land. People died on the roads, in
ditches, large numbers were buried in common graves. My father
emigrated before the Famine had fairly begun. My mother's family
emigrated during the Famine itself. First some of my uncles came
out. One came by ship to Quebec, was taken sick there and died in a
hospital.*

    *In 1846, my mother's father, that is, my grandfather Patrick
McDonough, who at that time held a leasehold of a farm in Ireland,
near Cloonfad, in County Roscommon, and who paid his rent I was
told at the big house in Strokestown, decided to come to this country.
He went to Frankfort, Herkimer County, leaving behind his wife
and children until such time as he could establish a holding.*

    *Patrick's wife, my grandmother, Bridgit Fitzmaurice
McDonough, who lived with us when I was a child, was born in
Roscommon on February 1st, 1799, and had a reputation for being
a remarkable woman, both physically and mentally. This I know
from my own researches undertaken when I was in Ireland. It was
in 1902 that I went out by train to Carrick-on-Shannon to find
some relatives of my grandmother's named Fitzmaurice, and drove
from Carrick to Hill Street, a farming hamlet some ten or twelve
miles distant, near Drumsna.*

    *There I was told that she was still known in her old home by
reputation. As a young woman she was able to take a barrel of flour*

(196 lbs.) from the back of a wagon and set it on the ground, a feat few men would attempt. She was spoken of as having been a woman of great intelligence and business, one whose advice and counsel were sought by all her neighbors. Indeed, I remember her myself as a tall woman of large frame, thin from old age, with a face that made me think she must have been a fine-looking woman in earlier years. Her white hair was combed down smoothly and parted in the middle and she always wore a cap or hood that covered her head, with a frill or ruching around her face. She lived in our family for many years and taught the children their ABC's and Catechism.

So we can imagine young Bridgit, tall, bare-footed, hoisting a barrel from the back of a wagon onto her shoulder, setting it carefully down; imagine her in the pre-Famine years of rising debt and evictions and land seizures advising her neighbors in rents, tithes, and leases, in deeds and conveyances, calculating payments to agents of the Crown.

But as to Patrick McDonough. After looking over the prospects for himself and family in the new country, my grandfather took a lease of a farm up in the hills south of Frankfort and sent word to his wife, Bridgit, to sell the farm in Ireland, settle up their affairs and bring over the rest of the family. This summons came during the fall of 1846. His wife disposed of such household effects as were not to be brought over, and set out by wagon for Dublin to board the ship.

In those days crossing the Atlantic in winter was no pleasure trip. The crossing was made in sailing ships, the traveler had to provide beds, bedding, and everything beyond the bare necessities in the way of food. As I recall from what my mother told me, the trip took six weeks and on the way across the good mother's hope of happiness in the new land was dampened by the death of a child, Bridgit, of ship's fever. She was buried at sea. After undergoing the terrors and hardships of a transatlantic voyage of that time, they at last landed in New York. From that city they immediately set out for Frankfort and arrived there on Christmas Eve. A heavy snow was falling. Patrick met them at the station and they went by wagon to the farm up on Frankfort Hill, at Cranes Corners, there to begin in their new home and country.

The couple had high hopes of happiness, and the conditions seemed to warrant such hopes. But these were not to be realized. On the night Bridgit arrived with the children, Patrick, who had got chilled and wet waiting for the train in the snowstorm, developed

pneumonia and in six weeks had died and been buried in St. Agnes
cemetery, Utica. At that time the Catholic cemetery on Oak Hill
had not yet been established.

My grandmother continued to work the farm with her sons and
daughters to the end of the lease, at which time my mother married
and she came to live in our family.

Is it possible to imagine at all? The children alighting in the snow, Patrick looking among them for small Bridgit before his wife gave him the news, sealing her lips even to him when it came to the small figure loose in the icy waters. Then the rattling ride in the wagon up the rocky hill to the farm, the squeak of the iron wheels turning in the snow, the lantern hanging from the axle throwing uncanny shadows through the unfamiliar trees, the horse straining in the dark. Patrick throwing over his wife and children whatever he had by way of covering, trying to fix his dead child's face in his mind. The next day, Christmas, the chill, the fever, the rattle in his chest, the cough. The cow to be milked, the path to the barn cleared of snow.

But no. Here Bridgit's forbidding shadow falls across the page and the imagination falters. The grandmother who lived in your house all the days of your youth, Willie, must have revealed to you very little. Almost certainly a mere bleak recital of selected fact. And why do I think so? Because you make a point of saying the crossing was no *pleasure trip*. But surely that's an absurd understatement! As if the coffin ships of sixty years before the time of your writing might have been improved by a few modern amenities. What muted version could Bridgit—or your mother, a child of twelve at the time—have chronicled of the ragged emaciated crowds sleeping on deck, the waves washing over them, the terrible thirst, the filth, fever, dysentery, diarrhea, passing from one to another doing their work.

Yet the death of the child is recalled and recorded, the child for whom the prayers for the dying would have been said, the child who found her grave in a shroud—stitched round probably by her mother although the rock inside was surely placed there by another.

If as you assert, Willie, Bridgit and her children did leave Ireland in the late fall of 1846 at the beginning of the severest winter in living memory, they'd have already seen the failure of the potato crop a second time. In the summer of 1845 only a patchwork of fields were infected. But the summer of 1846 saw weather rarely suited to the spread of the blight: torrential rains, washing the spore of the fungus from the leaves down into the soil, infecting the underground tubers. By August the fields were black, the stench nauseating. A scene of medieval horror: a plague, a scourge, a visitation. On that same Christmas Eve when the reunited McDonough family was enjoying a brief stare into each other's faces, Captain Wynne, an officer of the Board of Works who oversaw the poorhouse in Carrick-on-Shannon, was sitting down to write a letter to a friend:

> *I ventured through the parish this day to ascertain the condition of the inhabitants, and, altho' a man not easily moved I confess myself unmanned by the intensity and extent of the suffering. I witnessed this more especially among the women and little children, crowds of whom were to be seen scattered over the turnip fields like a flock of famishing crows, devouring the raw turnips, mothers half naked, shivering in the snow and sleet, uttering exclamations of despair while their children screamed with hunger. I am a match for anything else I may meet with here, but this I cannot stand.*

It seems Bridgit's fierce shadow casts a wedge: on one side the acceptable eyewitness account, the documentary report; and on the other the forbidden attempt to violate the intimacies of the sufferer by intruding on that last refuge, the self in hiding. For surely you'd have heard, Willie, as have I, that it was not uncommon for the starving to hide a shame against which they were helpless, to shut themselves away inside their cottages so as to die decently, unobserved?

Can we know at all what was left behind? What living connection was severed?

This: the unspoken, the timeless bond of not one generation to the land or two or three but of generations time out of mind, who set stones in a ring and a passage for the dead, lit bonfires on the hills and plotted the course of the sun. Watched the full moon rise above a lake, leaving not a stain, not a joggle of light, but something else entirely: a gleam that appeared to lift the lake into the night, to render the land and the sky mere backdrop, as if the light at the back of things had glimmered for an instant before vanishing.

And how do I know?

Because I saw it all for myself, Willie, when—out of frustrated love for you, out of some blind need to make good Nora McHugh's old pledge—I followed you to Ireland, followed you from Carrick to Drumsna and at last to Hill Street where I found a crossroads with a single pub waiting on the corner, meadows all round, crows flapping overhead, a stone bridge arched above blowing grass, a green river running with bright flowers scattered on its waters. Undertook your own pilgrimage and—although a hundred years had lapsed since your passage through and I found no one who remembered Bridgit Fitzmaurice, even by reputation, heard no mention of sacks of flour lifted from the backs of wagons—in Cloonfad encountered an intense young man in muddy Wellingtons named Brian Fitzmaurice, lanky, with a thin face and deep-socketed eyes blue like the shirt he was wearing, and nearby in a field a brown mare who stood and watched us from a distance. When I called out to her from the fence, reached out my arm, a trembling overtook her. Summoning her, then, with soft words and pleas, as fervently as I might have invited my own wandering spirit, I continued to call while step by step, cautiously, reluctantly, she came forward, legs seized with tremors, halting, stopping in the tall grass—over and over taken by the spasms, the shaking from her limbs of the fear this encounter inspired—until with many starts and stops she made her way to me from that distant place and lowering her soft nose at last into my hand, breathed into my palm, and when I looked up into her wide brown eyes gave me back my gaze, shining.

And now, Willie, I confess to you—as you are perhaps the only one who might understand it—my own hunger for what was left behind, for what I do not know, will never know, my entrancement with these silences; as if I imagined all losses might be restored if it were possible to return to that moment when the turf fire was extinguished on the hearth, when the wagon lurched into motion leaving behind once and for all the devastated fields of Cloonfad, when above a rushing stream blackthorn branches wound with rags and beads startled away and were gone, when, with the wind in the sails, the green hills seen pitching and rolling from the deck of a ship were swallowed by an immensity of water.

Because tell me, Willie, where did it come from, this ferocious urge— in a graveyard, beside a heap of gray stones: the single standing wall of an ancient friary, its high narrow window framing in small the whole windswept expanse of scudding clouds and splintered light—where did it come from, this imperative one June evening to embrace the earth, to fling myself on it, arms outstretched like a lover lying across the grave of a beloved?

And there with my face in the grass, my ear to the ground, heard—as from some distant place—oak leaves thrashing in the wind, the cuckoo's song, boots tramping, wheels turning, the dull thud of hoofbeats, made out an indistinct and continuous murmur, a chorus of muffled voices whispering, groaning, chanting, imploring but through it all the high wail of a pipe, a wail of hunger, wail of separation, separation unendurable from the beloved land, land of hedges and roads and lakes, of turf and moss and stone, land of holly and hazel, of rivers and wells and springs; listened ear to earth for the lost voices of all those whose bones have been laid here or at sea or in another land entirely, a land of strangers that became home at last and yet the oldest love carried in the marrow of the bones, bones that finally crumble to dust, the wind carrying that fine silt to the leaves of the alder, the willow, to the apple tree turning silver in the light rain, to the reeds at the rim of the lake.

So then what must I do?

Record the clouds racing gray and shining across the open sky, the blighted fields traveling counterwise beneath, the yew's dark flame flickering on the white page of devastation, the hawthorns shaking in the wind. The black hollow of the gaping mouth, the keen that rises and sticks in the throat, the tears swallowed and stored, the sorrow consumed.

IV

The cattle are out on grass,
The corn is coming up evenly.
The farm folk are hurrying to catch Mass:
Christ will meet them at the end of the world, the slow and speedier.
But the fields say: only Time can bless.

> *Life on a farm in those days up there back in the hills was hard.*
> *There was plenty of work and little enjoyment. I have heard my*
> *grandmother tell of milking the cows in the morning of a Sunday*
> *and then starting off to walk to Utica to Mass. And the children*
> *went too. It is ten miles from Frankfort to Utica and the farm was*
> *several miles back in the hills from Frankfort. They would walk to*

*town and if luck favored them they might get a lift on a canal boat
that was at one of the locks. If not they walked the whole distance
and walked back in the afternoon in order to be home in time to
milk the cows in the evening.*

I have heard my grandmother tell: Is it not strange, Willie, a story straight
from Bridgit's own lips! If she was silent about the Famine, about the
crossing, she nonetheless wanted you to know that distance, children,
cows in need of milking, counted for nothing when it came to making the
journey to Utica *of a Sunday.* But then Bridgit was a child in Hill Street
before Catholic Emancipation and so would have had memories of hedge
schools, disassembled chalices, priests wandering about in disguise saying
Mass in ruined monasteries beneath the open sky.

Perhaps Bridgit found not only hardship but some release from
homesickness—those Sunday mornings—in the chanted prayers, the
whispered words of bread broken, wine transformed, and afterwards in
the voices of neighbors speaking in tones familiar to her from the old
language, words she'd heard from her mother and father; words she'd
taught her children to say when they touched first their forehead, then
their breast, left shoulder, right.

> In ainm an Athair
> Agus an Mhic
> Agus an Spioraid Naomh
> Amen

V

These men know God the Father in a tree:
The Holy Spirit is the rising sap,
And Christ will be the green leaves that will come
At Easter from the sealed and guarded tomb.

*My mother Mary Elizabeth McDonough was born on March 1,
1834, in County Roscommon. I understood she lived on the farm
with her parents near a place called Cloonfad until she was twelve
years old when her mother brought her to this country with other
members of the family. It was her younger sister Bridgit who died
during the passage. She was married before she was sixteen and was
but four months beyond that when my brother John, her first child,
was born.*

On those Sundays when the children were trailing along after Bridgit or shooting ahead, did it ever happen, on the journey to Utica or afterwards—on the canal, suppose, or walking the long road to Mass one morning in late May when the apple trees were at last in blossom, or perhaps sometime around All Saints just after the cows had been brought in from the fields and a candle in a turnip set in the window—did it ever happen that Michael Conroy, meeting Bridgit the lone woman and offering help, had observed her eldest daughter, a well-grown girl of fourteen, carrying her small sister in her arms and thought suddenly to himself that it was time to marry? Was it the sight of her carrying the child that had roused his tenderness, the sleeping head lying heavy on her breasts?

Or it may have been that on a snowy Sunday afternoon in January, after coming from Mass in Utica, when a neighbor in Frankfort had invited some of them for a midday meal and the house was alive with the sounds of fiddles and whistles and drums, Mary Elizabeth noticed in the crowded rooms a young man with broad shoulders and delicate feet dancing with assurance and grace and suddenly remembered a summer night—before all that terrible time she was frightened to think about—a summer night around harvest when the moon was full and her own black-haired father had danced to the fiddles and pipes. And afterwards, when she sat alone, turned over in her mind the answer to the question she had asked a girl standing nearby: "Oh, that's Michael Conroy who works for Mr. Remington in Ilion."

> *My mother Mary Elizabeth was a tall, strong woman, and she kept house, bore children, and brought them up with the help of her mother and her sister Annie, later Mrs. O'Hara. A good manager, she insisted on running the house up to old age. She was a disciplinarian and her rules were obeyed.*

But what can you mean, Willie, by that last? And what memories sprang involuntarily to mind as you wrote? You don't risk a single word of criticism in regard to the forebears—as indeed John Carmody does not—so perhaps, in your estimation, to be called a disciplinarian is high praise. An effective one higher yet.

But at what cost? And what means did she employ to enforce her rules? Was it Bridgit she learned them from? These are the questions I'd like to ask. This woman who as a child almost certainly knew the tooth of hunger—who may have woken even as an old woman from terrifying nightmares of skeletons startling up from the side of the road, of a small sister thrown to the waves—with what words and attitudes would she have brought her twelve children sharply in line, with what punishments would she have sought to impress on them the unforgiving nature of the world? I ask, Willie, because it's just here—in my own obscure memories of the climate of fear you brought into the house, the stern eye of judgment with which you regarded Charlie—that I look for some understanding. Did your mother's childhood and the fear it spawned unleash your own? Kate's? In time, even ours?

That was faith, Bridgit walking with her children all those miles to Mass. Nowadays city Catholics think it hard if they have to walk a few blocks.

Yes, Willie, recalling your air of stern reproof, I remember the words—for the edification of generations to come—with which you finish off your account of Bridgit's valiant walk to Mass in Utica. But why the air of self-righteousness? Surely you don't number yourself among those *city Catholics* you're so firm in admonishing. And what do you mean by faith, anyway? Strict religious observance? Blind obedience? Or do you mean a craving, a hunger?

Or am I on the wrong track entirely? Perhaps for you faith meant practice under duress, was tied up in your imagination with a heroic age to which Bridgit belonged. A not-so-long-ago time when a desperate people from whom the "four beautiful green fields" had been taken declined to shake their fist at God. Because how could you have avoided knowing from an early age that the unbroken embrace of the faith brought to Ireland by St. Patrick was precisely what distinguished the Irish from their Protestant conquerors.

And one question more: did your notions of faith then include a strain of patriotic fervor? Did your unmistakable devotion to priests have something to do with their speaking out to Dublin Castle, to London, on behalf of a starving people? Father McDermott, for one, who denounced Denis Mahon, landlord at Strokestown, for promoting wholesale land clearances, evictions, forced emigrations, the same Mahon who was assassinated a few months later by his tenants, during the fall of 1847. Denis Mahon, to whom my great-great-grandfather, Patrick McDonough, would have paid rent. And then of course priests you knew later on in New York, Fenians who embraced the Easter Rising. Because I've heard it said that the Famine left a vacuum, a cultural vacuum, into which rushed the power of the clergy, the Church with a capital *C.* Oh yes, I think probably that for you, Willie, the rigorous observance of faith was bound up not only with ancient belief and ritual and piety but also with resistance, with holding out against the oppressors, against those who regarded your kind with the bitter contempt the occupier the world over regards those from whom it takes land and life.

As to Mary Elizabeth McDonough, whatever her own thinking, we know she said her prayers:

> *My mother was always kind and thoughtful to her children and grandchildren, and liked to have them around her. She also liked to have her friends come to our house. I remember when I was a child nearly every Sunday there would be from two to four extra for dinner, usually persons from Frankfort or Mohawk who had come to Ilion for Mass. With all her children and work what time did she have for the cultivation of her mind? Her reading was her prayer book or some other religious work, and it was not until later in life when she had the time to enjoy a book that I recall her doing much reading other than these.*

And here the *religious work*—oh miracle!—is in my hand, surely through your own agency: you, Willie, who liked to pick up books from here and there. You may have slipped it in your pocket the night after she died.

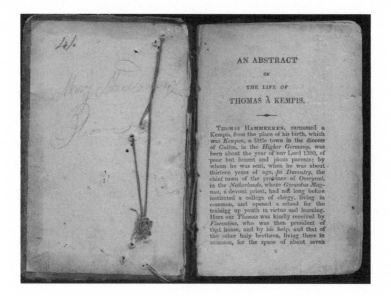

A tiny *Imitation of Christ,* that fourteenth-century Dutch classic by Thomas à Kempis, a marvel of austerity and enlightenment. A very little book, this one, five inches by two, perhaps, come unglued at the spine, patched together with a scrap of brown leather cut by an uncertain hand and sewn with coarse black thread to the fraying cover. And on the flyleaves, front and back, the name Mary McDonough, spelled out in pencil, the *M* curling up at the bottom of each end. And then, beneath: *Ilion.*

There can be no doubt that she bent her eyes to these closely written pages, now spotted with mildew and water stains and fingerprints. And, at one corner, chewed a little, as if a mouse had been at them. Some pages are much thumbed, but there is one page, brown and dog-eared, at which the book falls open of itself:

chap iii—Of a Good Peaceable Man

Keep thyself first in peace, and then thou wilt be able to bring others to peace. A peaceable man does more good than one that is very learned. He that is in perfect peace suspects no man; but he that is discontented and disturbed is tossed about with various suspicions; is neither easy himself, nor does he suffer others to be easy. He considers what others are obliged to do; and neglects that to which he himself is obliged. Have therefore a zeal in the first place over thyself, and then thou mayest justly exercise thy zeal toward thy neighbour.

And tell me, Willie, because presumably you would know: was it because Mary McDonough had herself a quick temper, a way of striking out, that she sought these words? In order to gentle herself? Did she readily find fault with those around her? Or was it not so much a matter of temperament as the low-burning pride of a humiliated people always ready to leap into flame, handed down from one generation to another, regardless of person or place?

And here a question of another kind intrudes. Could it be that the *farm up in the hills south of Frankfort* to which Patrick took Bridgit and their children that snowy Christmas Eve was one scrap of dirt in all that *landed immensity* John Carmody attributes to the family of his wife, Mary Ethridge of Frankfort? That it was from the Webers and their tribe that Patrick took his lease? That he in a manner of speaking vaguely regarded them in the light of English landlords?

Because I think, Willie, the dates would suit. But whom would Patrick have dealt with? It's almost certain he didn't put money directly into the hands of one of these Webers. There'd have been middlemen, go-betweens. Agents, of one sort or another. Who can say what the terms were? Or how fair they were, how just? Because we haven't forgotten the story of "King" Weber using his hand for a five-pound weight and his foot for a ten.

Would it have been possible, then—if the family of one great-grandmother leased a rocky ledge in the Frankfort hills from the family of the other—that these two girls encountered each other coming and going, these girls each named Mary? No, it would not, at least not when they were children. Because at the time Mary McDonough twelve years old first appeared on the street in Frankfort Mary Ethridge had not yet been born. By the time she had, Mary McDonough Conroy would already have been sixteen and herself caring for an infant named John. And here my heart stirs with longing for this one of my great-grandmothers who because her husband wrote no glowing words about her, because no lover's eye exalted her, I see only as an old woman bent over a tiny prayer book. Yet, do I not know her after all, even intimately, because at least I can say what words she chose to read? Touch my finger to the dark smudge her own left on the white page? Is it too much to believe that this knowledge gives me certain privileges, allows me to imagine that at the hour of death when her life was passing before her—the stench of potatoes rotting in the fields, the hands idle on the loy, the glimmer of light always at the edge of the clouds, the silver sheen, the piper's shoulders pressing forward one, then the other, to deliver a lament that must last a lifetime—at that extreme shore she saw a lake glassy and glittering in the dawn with white swans swimming on it and for each swan a reflection of its own in the quiet water? And remembered, then, Blessed Cellach's prayer, Cellach who had been imprisoned one night in the hollow of an oak tree and was awaiting death with the dawn:

> My blessing to the morning that is as white as a flame; my blessing to Him that sends it, the brave new morning; my blessing to you white proud morning, sister to the bright sun; morning that lights up my little book for me. It is you are the guest in every house; it is you shine on every race and every family; white-necked morning, gold-clear, wonderful.

Willie in Gotham

I

Come with me, Imagination, into this iron house
And we will watch from the doorway the years run back.

In a photograph of you and your older brothers and sisters, you are still a young man, Willie, maybe eighteen or nineteen, in a collarless shirt, open at the neck. You are standing in the last row of three, a little apart, the others filling up the ranks. Of all of them it is you I would be drawn to wonder about, who stares at the camera with stern intensity. You are not yet wearing glasses and your eyes blaze with an austere light. The others look more subdued, mild even, but then you're the youngest, your edges haven't yet been worn away. You don't look angry, exactly, but as if you had thoughts of a kind that would surprise.

And so I see you in those final days in Ilion.

In the spring of 1890, when I was a little more than twenty, my brother John decided I should come to New York and study shorthand in some good school and then, if I found a job, remain. To keep me occupied, he had taken me into his coal office when I was fourteen. I swept out the office before school, cleaned and dusted it. I went in again at noon and in the evening. John, who was a careful, thorough and accurate book-keeper, trained me in his ways.

I had graduated in 1887 from Ilion High School, the extent of education provided in that town, and had begun the study of shorthand. Three years later, on May 8th, I left Ilion, took the train to Albany and then the night boat to the city. I recall it was on this boat that I first saw an incandescent electric light. I arrived in New York on the morning of the ninth and at once went where I was told to stop, at the Murray Hill Hotel near Grand Central Station, the Murray Hill being a favorite stopping place for Ilion men. There I registered under the $4.00 American plan that included meals.

*The following day I went to Brooklyn by way of the new bridge,
the first steel-wire suspension bridge in the world, where I was
to study at the Ellinwood school. After six weeks I was told I was
qualified to take a job.*

*I went immediately to the office of the Hammond Typewriter
Co. and saw the employment manager. A day or two later he sent
for me and said a man was wanted at The Mercantile Safe Deposit
Company, housed in the Equitable Building, at 120 Broadway,
across from Trinity Church. He told me that I should go there and
ask for eighteen dollars a week and that I would get fifteen. He was
right. I met Mr. Lyman Rhoades, the President of the Company,
and started work on June 26th, 1890, remaining with the
Company, and its successor, the Chase Safe Deposit Company, until
I retired January 31st, 1935, a period of almost forty-five years.
I was named president of the Mercantile Safe Deposit Company
in 1908 and later on of the Equitable Safe Deposit Company. In
1930, when these two companies merged with Chase, I became vice-
president of the Chase Safe Deposit Company.*

*I was to be Mr. Rhoades' stenographer, but in addition to that
work I kept his personal books and did various other duties about
the office. At the time, the Company was putting in the South Vault
and there was considerable work given me. As Mr. Rhoades was
kind enough to tell me why things were done the way they were, I
had an opportunity of learning something about vault construction
as well as operation.*

*The stock of The Mercantile Safe Deposit Company was
controlled by Mr. Henry B. Hyde, President of The Equitable Life
Assurance Society. He also controlled the stock of The Missouri Safe
Deposit Company of St. Louis, and of the Security Safe Deposit
Company of Boston. One day Mr. Rhoades told me Mr. Hyde was
looking for some young man to do work of a confidential nature
and Mr. Rhoades had mentioned my name. It was Mr. Hyde who
showed me so much kindness.*

With what words would Lyman Rhoades have recommended you to
Henry Hyde? Did he say you were single-minded, diligent, eager to
accomplish what was asked of you? That you had a good head for figures
and kept scrupulous accounts? That you could be tight-lipped when it
came to matters of *a confidential nature*? Would he have mentioned that

you were Irish? Or would your name have been enough? What's certain is that they both must have seen that you were ambitious, driven by a desire *to go far,* as you would have put it.

*After January 1894, at Mr. Hyde's request, I made visits to St.
Louis and Boston at least once a year, to examine the companies
in those cities. In Boston I made the acquaintance of James Jeffrey
Roche, who was a cousin of Edmond Roche of Ilion, my brother
John's partner. At that time Jeffrey Roche was editor of "The Pilot,"
published in Boston, probably the most widely circulated Catholic
and Irish newspaper in the United States. It was started by a Patrick
Donahue years before and John Boyle O'Reilly was the editor.
O'Reilly published work in it by Oscar Wilde, Yeats, and Douglas
Hyde but had died just before the time of which I write. Roche had
become the editor with Miss Katherine Conway as assistant.*

 *It is hard to describe at this late day the position O'Reilly held
in Boston. He was born in Ireland and as a young man had joined
the British Army in a regiment known as "The Queen's Own." He
participated in the failed Fenian plot of 1865–66 and was sentenced
to be hanged, but the sentence was commuted to exile in the British
penal colony in Van Diemen's Land, now New South Wales.
O'Reilly was rescued from there by a party of Irishmen living in
America and brought to Boston. Later he helped organize the escape
of other Fenians aboard the <u>Catalpa</u>. O'Reilly had a fine physique, a
brilliant mind, and a charming personality.*

In the New England of those days the Irish were not well regarded. They were the hewers of wood and the drawers of water. O'Reilly changed all that and at the time of his death there was not a more respected or beloved character in Boston than himself. As a public-spirited citizen he was respected by everyone, and it is probable there were few men in Boston more popular with all classes of people.

It was into this situation that I was introduced in Boston. Roche took up where O'Reilly left off and kept up the fight for Ireland, for Irishmen in America, and for "The Pilot" as a paper. O'Reilly and Roche were both poets, they both had a love for musical language and the ability to produce it. They both had lofty thoughts and a sense of humor. Read Roche's Life of John Boyle O'Reilly and O'Reilly's poem "The Mutiny of the Chains." Read Roche's "The V-A-S-E and other Poems" and read his book Her Majesty, the King.

At the time of which I write, the Land League movement was still going on, and Boston had a number of intellectual, agitating Irishmen. Roche belonged to a club made up largely of Irishmen who met every Saturday for lunch and then spent the afternoon in discussion. Several times Roche took me with him and it was a treat to listen to the talk. Patrick Collins, who had been mayor of Boston, and later Consul-General in London under Cleveland's administration, was one of those who attended. It was about this time that I became a life member of The Society of the Friendly Sons of St. Patrick.

A heady time for you, Willie, careening between the seductions and patronage of the powerful Protestants, the "Americans," as your parents would have called them, and a counter group that seemed to turn your head entirely, a group looking for the disestablishment of the British Crown and church in Ireland. Yet it is the name Henry Hyde that runs through your notes like a bright thread.

In addition to these trips, Mr. Hyde gave me other work of a confidential nature, and in this way I became well acquainted with him and came to regard him with affection. His ancestors had been among the first settlers in New England, but he grew up in a village called Catskill on the Hudson River. He attended the Presbyterian Church at 11th St.

Elsewhere I have recorded how Mr. Hyde rewarded my diligence in obtaining information for him in Chicago by giving me enough money to cover the expenses of my first trip abroad in 1896, the trip I made to Ireland with my friend Stuart Chambers.

II

April, and no one able to calculate
How far is it to harvest.

And now, Willie, remembering again the intense young man in the photograph and those who crossed his path, I must tell you that on a recent July afternoon—much like that fateful one a couple of years before when I recognized my double in a mirror in the Chatsworth—I was once again in your old neighborhood, this time walking up the east side of Broadway, when I looked around and there suddenly was the Dorilton, that immense building on the corner of 71st Street, another Beaux Arts miracle. You must have been familiar with it in any weather: its high bays and balconies, the draped, vaguely classical figures looking down on Broadway, the mansard roof glazed with rain or sun; had only to lift your eyes as you stood on the southwest corner of 72nd Street waiting to cross Broadway to the subway station, knowing you'd be on Wall Street in twenty minutes flat, the same time the express ride takes today.

I stood thinking of you awhile, then rounded the corner and saw on the other side of the street a church with high steps leading up to it: the Church of the Blessed Sacrament, gold letters spelled out on a black marker.

With a start I remembered Deirdre's account in the fawn notebook of the procession you had all made—you and Deirdre and John Carmody and Lillian and the four-year-old Kate who had insisted on pushing the carriage with the twins in it—to a church on 71st Street, how you'd set out one warm October afternoon in 1910 because the twins were to be christened, little Mary wearing a gown stitched by Mary Ethridge for Rob's own christening thirty-five years before.

So this must be it, I thought, walking up the steps, the church where Stuart Chambers had baptized the infant twins just as he'd baptized Kate three years earlier and been named her godfather, as on another day in October he'd married you and Deirdre in Washington with John Carmody and Mary Ethridge and your own older brother, John, all in attendance: Stuart, friend of your youth, the one you'd first met—who knows how—a couple of years after arriving in New York from Ilion. For the first time saw that at least a part of the reason you and Deirdre were living in the Chatsworth was so that you might be a step away from Stuart and his church, that you might appear at the Mass he was saying any Sunday morning you liked. Or, if the hours suited, during the week as well.

Inside, the church was cool and shadowy after the bright day. It appeared empty except for two musicians standing not far from the altar, each with a black braid down his back, practicing for a concert of Venezuelan music—a notice in the back of the church announced—to be held that night. One was playing a wooden flute, the other a guitar, and together they made music that filled the space with a languorous triple-time. I had walked to the front to get a closer look when I glanced up and saw a plaque on a wall:

In Memory of
Rev. B. Stuart Chambers D.D.
His friends have placed this window
February 15, 1918
On the 1st anniversary of his death

So that you, Willie, on the first anniversary of his death, must have stood in wet shoes and dripping galoshes where I was standing now and looked up at an intricate arrangement of trefoils and triangles. At its center was a medallion, barely visible in the half-light, containing the silhouette of three black crosses.

I was wondering if Stuart had had a particular feeling for Calvary, if that was the reason his friends had chosen this scene, when I glimpsed a hand resting on the back of a pew to which there seemed nobody attached. Then I saw that someone was sleeping in the pew, his arm raised and resting against the back of it, and so continuing farther down the aisle saw someone else prone in another pew and yet another and another until I realized that Stuart's church, this summer afternoon, was the scene of a concert in which the privileged listeners were those who walked and slept in the streets of our city, citizens of sidewalks and benches and alleys, the unknowing audience of what may have been some lingering, deathless note of your friendship.

But it wasn't until I was out on the sidewalk again, walking distractedly up Broadway, that I stopped in my tracks. How had I missed something so obvious? Stuart had died during that terrible winter of 1917 only a week after John Carmody had sent his letter to Deirdre at 57th Street telling her of a driving snowstorm, died when the snow from that storm must still have been lying on the city sidewalks and roofs and water towers. Had, what's more, preceded John Carmody's own swift departure on March 17 by only a month. So that in missing the proximity of these two deaths so intimate to yourself, Willie, I'd proved as blind in reconstructing the past as the sightless face on the Chatsworth had ever been in foreseeing the future. And so in my ignorance had pronounced as unforgivable your escape to Atlantic City just before Deirdre's return to care for her dying father in the house in Pelham.

It was at that moment—standing stock-still in the dusty heat of Broadway—I saw you, Willie, walking up and down the wintry beach at Atlantic City, coattails flying, shouting into the wind. Wild with grief. And wondered, as people stepped around me, if this blow, Stuart's precipitous death from pneumonia, had not been for you the most severe of all.

Because how could I have overlooked your dearest friend? How could I have forgotten detecting on Kate's face—when she spoke of Stuart Chambers who'd died when she was ten—vestiges of the emotion with which you, Willie, must have remembered him aloud?

"A great friend of my father's," she'd say thoughtfully, standing at the gray Oriole stove, stirring soup in a pot. "He was a convert and soon afterwards a priest. It was my father I always heard who influenced him so strongly when they were young men." Or again: "He loved books, my father always said that. Loved the theater." And as evidence, for all of us to see, the many volumes—in the hall, on the landing—whose flyleaves contained words written in black ink, letters slanting backwards: *Ex Libris, Stuart Chambers.*

Lying at my elbow, at this instant, is a book inscribed with his name, a book with a dove-gray cover and embossed gold lettering: Oscar Wilde's *De Profundis,* a second edition published in 1909 by Putnam's Sons, The Knickerbocker Press. The only mark in it is a light pencil line drawn next to these words:

> To regret one's own experiences is to arrest one's own development. To
> deny one's own experiences is to put a lie into the lips of one's own life.
> It is no less than a denial of the soul.

But what could these words have meant to Stuart, Willie? And would you have been able to guess?

The Rev. B. Stuart Chambers DD of the Church of the Blessed Sacrament, Broadway and 71st St., died on Friday Feb 15 at the rectory after an illness of five days. The news of Dr. Chambers' sudden death came as a shock to his many friends in the priesthood and the laity throughout the city. The people of the parish were somewhat prepared for the news of his death because the announcement was made from the altar at the Ash Wednesday evening devotions that he was critically ill. His death was caused by pneumonia which developed rapidly from a cold he had contracted.

Dr. Chambers, a convert to Catholicity, was a highly-gifted, cultured gentleman, a devoted, earnest priest, and a preacher of unusual ability. He was a native of Lexington, Ky. where he was born Sept. 24, 1869. As a young man, he came to New York City and secured employment with the publishing firm of Harper & Brothers, where he remained for some years. The story of Stuart Chambers' wanderings that finally led him to the bosom of the Church of the Ages was written by himself fourteen years after his conversion:

When I was about twenty-three and an out-and-out worldling, ambitious above all else to make money, to be a successful man from the worldly point of view, I determined, with a happy inspiration like a rebirth of soul, to be a good man, to find my happiness in love, in the charity described by St. Paul in the XII Chapter of his First Epistle to the Corinthians. A capital idea in itself and pleasing to youth, but not easily realized because it means the daily, nay, the hourly practice of patience, patience which is charity's first ingredient. One must be patient in order to be kind. I tried again and again and failed again and again. At about the same time, by merest chance, I happened to form a friendship with a young man in many ways congenial, and a Catholic, practically the first I had ever known. We talked church a good deal as I was keen on the subject. I went to Mass with him once or twice on Sunday—to Solemn High Mass. It was about as interesting as a Chinese puzzle and quite as understandable. I determined, mainly from motives of curiosity, to find out what it was all about.

Dr. Chambers made his classical studies at St. Francis Xavier's College in Sixteenth Street, and then, firmly believing that his vocation was for the priesthood, went to Rome to make his theological studies at the American College. He was ordained in Rome July 25, 1902, being then thirty-three years of age, and remained for a year after his ordination to complete the degree of Doctor of Divinity. Father Chambers returned to New York in August 1903, and was assigned as an assistant to the late Monsignor Taylor at the Church of the Blessed Sacrament, where he remained until his death, serving faithfully and devotedly.

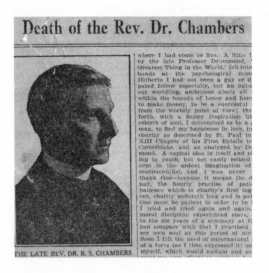

Death of the Rev. Dr. Chambers

where I had come to live. A little
by the late Professor Drummond,
Greatest Thing in the World,' fell into
Hitherto I had not been a gay or d
pated fellow especially, but an out-
out worldling, ambitious above all
within the bounds of honor and hon
to make money, to be a successful
from the worldly point of view; the
forth, with a happy inspiration lik
rebirth of soul, I determined to be a
man, to find my happiness in love, in
charity as described by St. Paul in
XIII Chapter of his First Epistle to
Corinthians, and as analyzed by Dr
mond. A capital idea in itself and pl
ing to youth, but not easily relized
cept in the ardent imagination of
sentimentalist, and I was never
thank God—because it means tho d
nay, the hourly practise of pati
patience which is charity's first ing
ent, charity suffereth long and is pa
One must be patient in order to be
I tried and tried again and again,
moral discipline experienced since,
in the six years of a seminary at R
can compare with that I practised
my own soul at this period of my
Soon I felt the need of supernatural
of a force (as I then expressed it) ou
myself, which would sustain and su

THE LATE REV. DR. B. S. CHAMBERS

The obituary, yellow, crumbling, folded in four, I fished out of the drawer of the chest in the sitting room where you must once have placed it, Willie, along with the black leather loose-leaf containing typed copies of pages from Stuart's journals, pages in which you appear, pages perhaps given to you after Stuart's death when his papers were being sorted. The words above make up only the first column of an obituary that goes on for two more and is accompanied by a photograph of a man still young, fair hair combed straight back from his forehead, a strong nose, a level gaze. You had recently each turned forty-eight, having been born, both of you, in the late months of 1869, a coincidence that when you first met, *by merest chance,* may have caused you to decide your friendship had been ordained.

But what could you have thought, Willie, reading this obituary in the early days of your grief, hunched over the paper with a scissors in your hand, trying to cut a straight line? What would you have remembered on reading those words in which Stuart referred to the young man *in many ways congenial* with whom he'd formed a friendship? You may have hidden your confusion and tears from John Carmody—himself marked for death within the coming month—as the two of you sat through solitary evening meals, the several clocks ticking around you, Kate and Grace already upstairs in bed. And between the wake and funeral you may have visited Deirdre on 57th Street, been secretly appalled to see that, far from being in any position to console you, she was herself in terrible need of a consolation you were wholly unable to provide.

It's possible that during those wintry days in Atlantic City, you knew of the journal Stuart had kept in 1893 soon after you'd met when together you'd *talked church a good deal.* Or perhaps it was only after his death that you learned of these pages in which he recorded his response to letters you'd written him during the summer of 1893: the summer when Stuart was in Chicago at the World's Fair displaying early copies of books published by Harper & Brothers and you in New York becoming blissfully acquainted with Mr. Hyde.

World's Fair, Auditorium Hotel, Chicago: Tuesday, June 13th, 1893
I bought a neat cigarette holder, made of olive wood which came from Jerusalem, from a rather beautiful woman, a native of the same Holy City, the woman from whom I bought a little cross from Bethlehem last week. I may send this cross, just a little thing, five cents, to Mr. Conroy. That was my intention in buying it.

Another one of his very neat, legible, and carefully prepared letters came to me this morning; his letters give me more pleasure than any I receive now; he is very persevering and energetic in carrying out his purpose, which is always well defined and good I think. His religion has done a lot for him it seems to me: that is, in certain directions.

In thinking of people or things that are congenial or attractive to me, I do always idealize them for a time, then afterwards inevitably cool. I fear I have already fallen into this weakness of idealizing Mr. Conroy; I will not be so severe as to call it a fault in my nature, this idealizing tendency, as it seems impossible for me to correct. I like the boy immensely at present and thoroughly appreciate his sterling qualities. As for his deficiencies, well it may be better that he has them. I was struck with a passage from Goethe: "It is only when a man knows little that a man knows anything at all; with knowledge

grows doubt." Although this is hardly applicable to Mr. Conroy,
for in a general way he knows a good deal, particularly of things
practical in their nature, nor is his religion by any means a case of
ignorance and bliss, his faith is childlike in its simplicity, and yet
perfectly preserved. May it never be broken.

With something like pity I wonder what you could have thought when you read these pages and realized that Stuart was clearly appraising you, recognizing the inevitable cool that would follow his initial enthusiasms. He was writing down his thoughts just as they came. But not all, Willie. Because what are these deficiencies he seemed to think might profit you in some manner? And how do they suggest Goethe's words? Did you surround yourself with little crosses? Did your faith depend on a simplicity incompatible with an inquiring mind, a restless curiosity? Is what he calls the simplicity of your faith perhaps a mistrust of the world you didn't know? Did you put on the armor of certainty to protect against self-knowledge?

But you must have thought your energy and perseverance well rewarded when a little more than six months later, just at the moment in early 1894 when you began your trips as Mr. Hyde's messenger to Boston and made the acquaintance of the intellectual, agitating Fenians, a photograph of Stuart was taken—at the Parkinson Studio, 29 West 26th Street—to mark an occasion at which you must certainly have been present: a photograph of a young man in a wing collar and black silk tie, white sprig in his lapel, his rather long hair parted in the middle; a photograph, signed on the back:

In commemoration of my communion to the Catholic Faith.
New York, St. Patrick's Cathedral, Patronage of St. Joseph, 1894.
The first rite in order. To my dear fellow-Catholic, William.

III

We are a dark people,
Our eyes are ever turned
Inward

In late June 1896, as you and Stuart set sail from the piers of the White Star Line Royal at 11th Street, as you hung over the rails watching the

Western Union Building, the towers of Printing House Square, and the steeple of Trinity Church slowly fade from sight, I wonder if you had any thought of Deirdre and the ride across the river on the Cortlandt Street ferry the summer before. And if, just as I am now looking back to you, you remembered your own grandparent, Bridgit, whom you knew so much better than I do you. Because after all Bridgit McDonough—who must have been acquainted with hunger, swiped by its claw—lived in the house where you grew up; she taught you your alphabet and prayers, years later you recalled the hood that covered her white hair, parted in the middle.

On that afternoon, as engines throbbed beneath your feet and tugs positioned your mail steamer for the broad sea, or more probably later on, during the long days out, did you encounter somewhere in those Atlantic wastes a dark stain in the waters, catch a glimpse of the wavering shadow of a ship that crossed paths with your own, one traveling so much more slowly, a creaking ship of many sails on which Bridgit and her children were passengers? Marvel that exactly fifty years later you were returning to the land the others had forever left behind?

You record no such reflections on the loose scraps of paper I have here before me, mismatched, picked up here and there, scattered sheets of writing paper with the name of the hotel stamped at the top from which they were taken: *The Imperial Hotel in Cork. Great Southern Hotel, Lakes of Killarney.* Written closely, painstakingly, in pencil, the words sometimes a little smudged as if you'd held the pencil too tightly, these few unnumbered pages might easily have drifted away and been lost.

G? SOUTHERN HOTEL,
Lakes of Killarney

TELEGRAMS:—
"CAPSEY, KILLARNEY."

All my hatred for England was aroused and my sentiments were not those of God save the Queen. But looking

As for Stuart's journal, I have no idea what it looked like, although it must have been familiar enough to you. I have only the typed copies of the pages you chose to preserve. But even these are many. I would guess that he—protesting all the while that his talents fell short—like Deirdre was bent on producing literary effects, wanted to make "a book." Perhaps imagined it passed around, read admiringly by others. Because I think—again like Deirdre—Stuart was accustomed to having his artistic efforts admired, perhaps was even a little vain in this respect. For a time, at least, he looked out at Ireland—at this landscape that was not American—and thought it picturesque, was put in mind of a pastoral poem, a stage setting.

For you, Willie, the land was real enough; you seldom enthused. And here once again my heart contracts looking at your smudged pages—certainly meant for yourself alone, a jog to memory—evidence of your small ambitions, your deference to those others whose superiority in these matters you seem to have taken wholly for granted.

Queenstown

Willie:

> *About 10 o'clock on the night of Wednesday, July 1st, we were called to see the light on Bull Rock, Ireland, the first point of Europe visible to the transatlantic traveler. We had just attended the concert given by the passengers in behalf of the Marine Charities of N.Y. and Liverpool and all was excitement. Stuart had sung "September" and "Funiculi-Funicula" to much applause. We saw the light and then about midnight went below to get a few hours' sleep.*

After sailing through Queenstown harbor we reached the city and at last struck terra firma. Stuart—as is always the case—captured the heart of the ladies, the first victim singled out by a woman with flowers.

Stuart:

I did not write yesterday as soon as we disembarked for on land I found myself more at sea than at any time during the actual voyage, trees, houses, tables, chairs, and beds moving around in the most intoxicating fashion. I was also very tired. When I came on deck yesterday morning I realized my whereabouts; that the rugged coast of Ireland was rising before me, beautifully foreign. I have since—but especially then—had to remind myself that it's nature I'm looking at and not a theatrical drop curtain.

A tender came out to take us ashore and we landed at Queens-town about seven o'clock. I was soon accosted by a woman who was determined I buy a flower for my buttonhole. "Indeed, son, you're too fine looking a young man to be without one," etc., etc. I left her talking, saying the same things to the next young man who came in my wake.

Willie:

We had our baggage examined and then went to the cable office where I sent a cable to Mr. Hyde, and went on to the Queen's Hotel for breakfast. I had always been told of the industry of the Irish by my father and mother, how they rose at break of day to begin work. Things must have changed between 1846 and 1896 for the hotel was hardly open when we arrived although it was seven o'clock. We were there for a few minutes when McGusty, an Irishman from Ballinasloe who came over with us and who possessed a fine rich brogue, came in with a rush as if he owned the place. In a short time he was after every servant girl and secured a promise of breakfast in a few minutes. We sat down to a breakfast of ham and eggs and tea in about half an hour.

At about 8:30 we took the train for Cork with Father Daly and some of the crowd. We reached Cork about 9:30 and were met by the head of the Imperial Hotel who happened to be a friend of Father D. He immediately introduced us to insure his attention and we drove through Cork on the top of the bus. We reached the hotel at 10 passing the statue of Father Matthew in St. Patrick Street.

Stuart:

We took the 8:35 train for Cork, riding second-class, which was quite good enough for anybody, I'm sure.

The beautiful River Lee ran along on one side of us and on the other a macadamized road, bordered with fine trees; here and there we saw cottages with neat flower gardens at the side and pots of flowers in the windows; then now and again immense iron gates swinging on splendid stone pillars, overgrown with ivy, behind which could be seen a winding drive, delightful to the eye in its light and shade as only occasional spots of sunshine could reach through the overlapping trees.

Glengariff

Willie:

At 11:50 we left Cork for Bantry by rail and passed through some fine rich agricultural land and plenty of bog. At Bantry we took a coach to Vickery Hotel and were astounded to be told that they had no fish prepared on Friday but would cook some. We certainly expected that in Ireland Catholics would have things their own way but found there were many Protestants who still had the run of things. From Bantry we drove by coach to Glengariff and arrived there at five o'clock at Eccles Hotel.

At this place we saw an unusual contest. A pig in a basket was attached to the end of a greased pole that extended out over the water. It was necessary to walk out on the pole to capture the pig. After several attempts which resulted in the contestants landing in the water, one nearly reached the basket when he fell, but in doing so he grabbed the basket and claimed the pig. However, two constables—ever present in Ireland—followed him and took away the pig.

From the hotel we took a short walk and saw Cromwell's bridge. This is a beautiful little spot of green trees and ivy. All along the road here we saw hedges of fuchsias and found arbutus and beds of forget-me-nots growing wild. The Irish daisy—my father's favorite—also abounds.

Stuart:

I feel if my cold, unsentimental heart were ever taken unawares it would be by an Irish girl.

Kenmare

Willie:

At 9 o'clock, the fourth of July, we left Glengariff and started for Killarney driving up through the hills and mountains of Cork and Kerry—wild, barren, rocky hills where only a few sheep can find sustenance. It is a dreary place and the wind was blowing hard. At noon we arrived at Kenmare and stopped for lunch, then walked around the town where we saw a good statue of St. Patrick in front of the parish church. We then continued through the mountainous region where we had an experience.

We had been riding all day with the Blackburns and Mrs. B. wanted to stop at the home of a family named Gaines as she had been requested to do so by a relative of the Gaines in Ottawa. Two or three miles out of Kenmare our driver called a lad from a house down below the road and when he reached us he said his name was Mike Gaines and he had an aunt in Canada. We all went down and beheld a spectacle such as I never have seen before and I pray I shall never again. I hope this is the only case of its kind although I fear it is one of many.

The yard was covered with manure and filth, the door was open, inside there was no floor, two coops of chickens, a bit of peat burning in the fireplace and seated or reclining on a box was a poor woman in the last stages of consumption.

Poor poverty-stricken Ireland! The land about would not produce sufficient for a family even if no rent were required. But alas, we were told that an eviction had been taken out but a few days before and this poor family with the mother nearly dying from 10 years' ravages of consumption was to be evicted.

All my hatred for England was aroused and my sentiments were not those of God <u>save</u> the Queen.

Stuart:

We drove all day, forty-one miles, stopping one hour for luncheon at the Landsdowne Arms Hotel at Kenmare where we had salmon fit for gods.

The beauty and grandeur of the scenery from Bantry to Glengariff, thence to Killarney with her Lakes, over the Prince of Wales route, is of course far beyond my power to adequately describe.

235

Magnificent mountains reaching far into the clouds, time-beaten rocks which are stone tables of history. Then the fresh valleys below, with their little rivers, lakes, and cottages all form a picture more ideal than the most spectacular stage setting or dream imaginable. "Dear me, dear me, isn't it superb!" is all I can say.

The wit of our drivers, like other Irish we meet, is truly wonderful, and they make me feel, Britisher by blood, hopelessly dull. And do not tell me the people are not refined or poetical, as some puritanical Americans are apt to think: the potted plants, never absent from the windows of the humblest hovel, refute the idea. I speak too of downtrodden, pauper, Catholic Ireland. The bright though often sad expression of faces, and the frank hearty good manners of the people everywhere, sometimes fill me with vengeful rage against the brutal government that has robbed, tortured, murdered, all but annihilated one of the most talented races on earth.

Had I the time I should describe one scene we incidentally came in contact with, of poverty, unimaginable Irish poverty, and English wealth, standing face to face in the interior of a tenant's hovel. It made me almost weep with sympathy and pity for the consumptive dying mother, crouched in a semi-nude position before a smoking fire of peat-bog, with her starving family, on one side, then boil with rage against the inhuman landlord, on the other. It was a scene never to be forgotten, it will haunt me for weeks I fear: and not inheriting the mantle of Goldsmith, nor of any lesser genius, but being on the contrary simply an American tourist, I can only give these rough, imperfect suggestions, not only of this but of all the unusual things I see.

Killarney

Willie:

At five arrived at the Royal Victoria Hotel. After dinner we took a stroll and went through the Cathedral and then to a public house where we found 3 English soldiers and an Irish civilian drinking. We joined the party but soon a fight broke out and we peacefully withdrew.

Tired out in mind and body we were glad at last to retire for the night without so much as lighting a candle and slept soundly until we were awakened in the morning by the bleating of calves in the marketplace.

236

Stuart:

I am so amused sometimes at the Irish tendency to "talk back" and have the last word. They have red-headed tempers, no doubt about that. We had just got into our room at Killarney from Glengariff after the long day's ride by coach, dirty and dusty. The chamber-maids dress as such characters do on the stage; skirts about down to their ankles, large buckles on their low-cut shoes, white aprons. A dainty head-dress with two long streamers behind, falling down below the waist. Will (Irish blood, you know) rang the bell, a typical maid answered it, red-headed:

"Did you call, sir?"

"Yes'm," he said, not very gently, "See here, we want a slop jar, there's nothing here to throw the water in."

"Yes, indeed, sir, there is, sir; there's a foot tub sir," showing us one under the wash stand.

"I don't want that," he replied, determined to carry his point, Irish against Irish (for the foot tub really would have done). "I want a slop jar, a regular slop jar."

"But there ain't none, sir, that's all you can get, sir."

"Then I'll throw the water out the window," he said.

"All right, sir."

"I'll throw it," his face reddening, "into the grate, the fireplace!"

"I don't care sir," and turning upon her heel, she left the room with a bang of the door.

And did your face burn, Willie, when you read Stuart's account of your brush with the chambermaid? Perhaps you trembled at what you blindly felt to be an unjust portrait of yourself. Wondered what else your friend might have noticed and left unsaid. Or did you—in your desire to put things in the best light—think no, he's only speaking of me affectionately as friends who are very familiar with each other do, laughing at each other's faults and flashpoints?

Because the dialogue Stuart writes is convincing, Willie, it seems he's caught the sound of your voice. As if you were taking lessons from McGusty of Ballinasloe who at the Queen's Hotel *came in with a rush as if he owned the place.* Took matters in hand when "the Irish" weren't fluttering about in the first dawn as your father and mother had told you was the case and all of you fresh off the boat and wanting your breakfast!

I confess that in this business of the slop jar you sound quite dreadful to me, not only quick-tempered but menacing in a petulant, absurd kind of way. As if you were terrified you wouldn't be taken seriously, would pass unnoticed. Which indeed may very well have been the case. You have none of the easiness of one accustomed to having his needs anticipated and met, none of the cool assurance of the high-born. But then why should you? It's Stuart who sings to applause, who's greeted by the woman selling flowers with compliments on his good looks, as he tells us himself. Yet what could this have been for Deirdre, and how well did she know you when she married you, a man who made scenes in hotels, who threatened to throw the water in which he'd washed into the fireplace?

And yet, Willie, whatever pride must have compelled you to veil your fiery temper in the presence of many, you didn't check your anger before Stuart. Nor did you all those years later, after his death, excise these pages from his journal. In relation to Stuart, perhaps, you were blessedly free of vanity, the vanity that would have burned the compromising pages.

Because this may have been one of the things you loved best in Stuart, his restless curiosity about his own inner life and the hidden lives of other people, a curiosity that wasn't particularly in your line. You may even have felt that his reflections in this instance gave you the advantage. Considered you now had Stuart where you wanted him, Protestant no longer, English with apologies. Although I'm asking myself if Stuart, in all the years to come, ever wearied of the bluff good humor, the underlying melancholy, of the many Irish priests he ended up living amongst, of these red-headed displays of temper not unlike your own in the hotel when you were offended—outraged!—by a foot bath having to do for a slop jar.

But just now, Willie—looking again through these travel entries written so long ago—I'm struck for the first time by something that may give the lie to everything I've supposed. And in exactly the same way that my tardy recognition of Stuart's death that winter of 1917, you'll remember, gave the lie to my earlier swift denunciations of your trip to Atlantic City. I confess that I've probably understood very little of your motives. And if I miss so much, you may ask me impatiently, why do I pretend to know you at all?

For it was on that day's journey of forty-one miles from Glengariff to Killarney—along a road that ran through Kenmare, a town where you and Stuart, at the Lansdowne Arms Hotel, enjoyed a lunch of salmon *fit for gods*—that you were confronted with a scene that jarred painfully on your nerves. Left you unsettled and upset. In fact, in a fury. Encountered a scene in a house down below the road reminiscent of an Ireland your mother witnessed as a child but had never described to you: at last, in the midst of all that extravagant beauty, the inside of a tenant's hovel, the first you and Stuart had entered.

And so later on, arriving that same afternoon at the Royal Victoria Hotel, were you out of sorts as you looked around the room you and Stuart were to share? Were you looking for a fight as relief to your overcharged feelings? Was that it? And so I may have been sadly mistaken in everything that comes before. *Poor poverty-stricken Ireland!* you write on paper taken from the hotel where you are to stop the following night, Great Southern Hotel, Lakes of Killarney. That evening in Killarney itself, after the long journey from Glengariff, as you poured water from a white pitcher into a large porcelain bowl, were you brooding bitterly on Ireland's past and your own, thinking savagely of England and its brutishness?

But how quickly the victim turns tyrant! And here's my final question for you, Willie. One of a different kind altogether. When you arrived in these travelers' rooms along the way, when you and Stuart dropped in exhaustion without lighting the candle on the long Irish twilight, did you and he, like Ishmael and Queequeg, sleep in the same bed? Did you, in the manner of Queequeg, throw an arm familiarly over your dear companion as he slept? Did you open your souls to each other, chat till dawn? Or is this a question only my generation would ask?

I confess I like your accounts, Willie, of fights breaking out in pubs and of pigs in baskets and your father's favorite flower, the Irish daisy. And to know, at so great a remove, of your parents' praise of Irish industry—perhaps by way of pointing out a contrasting way of life to their own children?—and your own need as a young man to argue with them.

As for Stuart, it's his desire to express the inexpressible I honor, his broken attempts in the face of inevitable defeat.

However unexpected the thought that comes to me now, I write it down if for no other reason than that it suddenly swims to consciousness. It's only here, in these pages seemingly composed for your eyes alone, pages written years before the more official records you so carefully composed after Deirdre's death, that Stuart is mentioned except by name. Why is it that in documents that make a scrupulous attempt to honor the dead you are without a single word on the subject of your dearest friend? Why, Willie, in all the pages you devote to picking berries in the summer dawn, the Ilion Irish, Deirdre, the world you entered after arriving in New York, do you write nothing of Stuart? And what occurs to me as sufficient reason is that it's not because you loved him less but because the mere mention of his name carried you away. It may have been that some unspeakable sorrow, some late matter for self-reproach or regret, stopped your pen. Or on the contrary you were struck speechless by an undying sense of your own youth, a shock to your nerves that seemed to you the great gift of your life. So that you winced from the mere look of his name in writing, like some fierce mourner afraid to open a grave for fear the wind will disturb the dust, erase whatever is left of the face already lost to oblivion.

Is it not strange, Willie, that now, more than a hundred years after you and Stuart passed through Kenmare on your way to an encounter that left its mark, I have learned—looking through one book and another on the subject of the Famine—that Friar John O'Sullivan, the parish priest of that same town, on the second of December 1847, wrote these words to Charles Trevelyan:

> Would to God that you could stand for five minutes in our street,
> and see with what a troop of miserable, squalid, starving creatures you
> would be instantly surrounded, with tears in their eyes and with misery
> in their faces, imploring and beseeching you to get them a place in the
> workhouse. . . . The landlords expect the Government will interfere, and
> the Government . . . say the land must support those who dwell thereon,
> but vae victis, alas the poor between both. . . . Whatever be the cost or
> expense, or on whatever party it may fall, every Christian must admit,
> that the people must not be suffered to starve in the midst of plenty,
> and the first duty of a Government is to provide for the poor under the
> circumstances such as they are placed. . . .

If, either then or later, you'd had a mind to, where would you have looked for the story of that time of which you yourselves witnessed a lingering version inside the tenant's hovel that same afternoon? Where would Stuart have looked? Stuart who read and spoke of books continuously and who may very well have been your inspiration in the purchase of so many of your own.

Now—as snow falls silently this morning on the stark bare branches of elm and ginkgo and ailanthus in Morningside Park below—I open one of your volumes, Willie— *The Well of the Saints: A Play in Three Acts,* by J. M. Synge, London: A. H. Bullen; Dublin: The Abbey Theatre, 1905—and see inside the cover, written crosswise along the binding: *W Conroy June 1909.* This, so far as I know, is the first time you inscribed a book with the date of its purchase and did so during a period when you and Stuart were living around the corner from each other on the Upper West Side, fifty blocks south of where I sit now, watching a peregrine falcon alight on a snowy branch. Kate had just turned two, the twins were moving toward conception, the house in Pelham was coming to gradual light in the imagination of an architect named Orchard. But neither you nor Stuart, had you looked, would have found any history of those years of Famine in this book's pages, despite Synge's own travels to the west where the Ireland of fifty years before would surely have been alive in the memory of old women on the Aran Islands, on Inishmaan, old women whose keening he heard and recorded.

Why did neither he nor any of those Irish writers of a later generation, laboring in the shadow of blight and ruin, leave an image, an elegy? Neither Joyce nor Yeats nor any of the others say a word about it? Why did Yeats prefer legend and myth? *Cathleen ni Houlihan,* the Poor Old Woman, and so on? Lady Gregory her tales of saints and sages?

Or Joyce his dear dirty Dublin besmirched with modernity, beguiled by song? In all the outpouring of Irish writing of the next hundred years where do we look? Not, it seems, in any of the books you and I crept past that afternoon in the last summer of your life on our way to a sleeping Kate. Not there. For both of us, an inheritance of shame. An inheritance of silence. And so perhaps it's in our own fears and feints and unthinking gestures that we must look for the story of the Famine, the finger raised to the lips forbidding words.

IV

I will not burn these rags,
The cast-off clothing of my soul

A new vault had not been open a year when we were in the midst of the Equitable Life Assurance Society scandal. Mr. Hyde died on May 4, 1899, and his son, James Hazen Hyde, having graduated from Harvard the year before, was elected Vice President. Young Mr. Hyde had a flare for Society with a capital S, was handsome, a favorite with the ladies, and sought and enjoyed attention and the lime-light. He was not sensitive about riding roughshod over the feelings of others. He was vain, something of a snob, and the type of man who could never be popular with most persons. James W. Alexander, who had been with Mr. Hyde from the earliest time, an insurance man of long experience, was elected President.

The result was a clash between the two men within the Equitable for control. The Counsel for the investigation was Charles Evans Hughes, who later became governor of New York, a candidate for President, and finally Chief Justice of the Supreme Court.

The inquiry spread, other insurance companies became involved, and a nasty public scandal became front page news. Such names as J. Pierpont Morgan and E. H. Harriman were linked with those of James Hazen Hyde and James W. Alexander. Both Hyde and Alexander were forced to resign from Equitable Life. None of these insurance men were prosecuted but they were shown to have had little regard for their responsibilities as officers entrusted with the management of vast sums belonging to the policyholders. Public clamor forced them out. Young Hyde went to Paris and stayed there.

January 9, 1912, a fire destroyed the Equitable Building and it was then I had the greatest experience of my life, one I wish never to repeat. Afterwards I was away four months, trying to get back my nerves and my strength. Of this I cannot speak.

No words attach there. But you make no secret of your feelings for James Hazen Hyde, whom you heartily disliked. If H. B. Hyde had come to seem an approving father to you—and if he in turn recognized in your own wild resolve some early expression of his own—you may have experienced feelings toward his son that partook of a sibling rivalry in which you were doomed to be the one less loved. Did his son James affront you with his blithe assumptions of privilege? When you complain he wasn't sensitive about hurting the feelings of others, was it possible you were remembering that on the few occasions you'd met he'd looked at you with a cold eye?

It's certain the scandal involving Equitable Life and other insurance companies was much in the news in the early part of the century, that there had been a remarkable misappropriation of funds. And in view of this, I can't help but wonder about your own Mr. Hyde and that *work of a confidential nature* he entrusted to you; those figures you rushed to Chicago to get hold of and for which he rewarded you so handsomely. Your loyalties to Mr. Hyde were absolute. Did you or others nervously consider where the line might be drawn between accepted norms of competition—fiercely exercised as they might be—and raw, devouring greed? Did it seem a matter of course that the funds entrusted to you by policyholders be transferred into the ready hands of J. P. Morgan or E. H. Harriman? And what of the handsome benefits, the swollen salaries, the extras, conferred on those who assisted in one way or another? The trip to Ireland would be counted little and certainly, Willie, it's clear you and Mr. Hyde both felt you'd richly earned it. But it was surely his power that intrigued you: he snapped his fingers and the money was yours. Quite simply, the funds were at his disposal.

It's probable that sundry compensations came your way, funds that made the Chatsworth a possibility. During the Hyde scandal of 1905—when Mr. Hyde was five years dead and his son pursuing the occupations of the rich and you at last arranging a marriage with Deirdre—did you confide your anxieties to Deirdre? It may have been her outrage at the manner in which the presidents of all these insurance companies were revealed to have conducted themselves that inspired the concluding words of her speech to the unnamed club:

God visits punishment upon a board of directors as surely as upon a secret society of assassins, though the first may have let the victim's heart blood out with a majority stockholder's note instead of with a stiletto.

If Deirdre recoiled in the face of your confidences, perhaps you felt betrayed. Vowed that next time you'd be more careful in regard to what you told her. Did you say to yourself—or even to her—that it was all very well for her to draw back her skirts in distaste when after all she herself was the beneficiary of your struggle to earn what money you could? As I myself am, hard as it is to admit, your money having purchased the books that filled the house in Pelham.

When you spoke together of morality, you and Deirdre, you may have spoken at cross-purposes. She may have had in mind the rich and the poor, the balance between. And you something quite different. Because it may have been that for you poverty was not something distinct from yourself; "the poor" were not people of another order, but instead identifiable as your own mother and father, close to you as the bones in your thighs. And so—feeling yourself obscurely the child of deprivation, whatever chances you were given, however much money you accumulated—it may have been difficult for you to see that you'd long ago come to be perceived by many as one of the impervious rich, impervious if only in your reluctance to imagine the sufferings of people who hadn't, like yourself, been able to find a way out of that place of want. Despite your arrival in New York the very year that Jacob Riis's *How the Other Half Lives* appeared, your close-up view of freezing children sleeping on sidewalk grates and in newspaper offices, despite your inevitable knowledge of Five Points and Irish squalor, your fear may have been so great of slipping from the curb and falling back into the mire that you could allow no commerce with it at all. Drew instead an uncompromising line that placed you firmly, back turned, with the Mr. Rhoadeses and the Mr. Hydes of the world.

Yet the difficulties involved! And here my heart again softens toward you, Willie, I who at this remove can only imagine the torments my generation has been spared. Because it may have been that if you'd been asked to acknowledge that, yes, you were indeed one of the world's fortunate, you'd have been overwhelmed by the sharp sense that you'd betrayed your parents in some unspeakable way, perhaps even felt toward your mother a shame not unlike that she experienced toward the lost little sister, Bridgit, who had disappeared over the side of the ship into icy waters below.

So I see you, Willie, on the horns of a dilemma: on the one hand, you could under no circumstances abandon your ancestral place of want and deprivation, alter your sense of solidarity with Bridgit McDonough, whose virtue was indistinguishable from her many ordeals. On the other, you were impelled to acquire means, to snatch yourself entirely from the fields of Famine, to taste and enjoy. To become a man of the world. And of course you must have lived, breathed, the awareness that this need to "succeed"—in what is called the Gilded Age when wealth conveyed a spectacular glamour—was not your imperative alone. For how could you forget that you, the youngest of twelve children, had been the one designated to leave home and seek your fortune elsewhere? You, elected by the firstborn, your brother John, almost twenty years your senior, who'd trained you carefully and sent you forth, who'd determined that it would be you, Willie, who'd make your way outside the Mohawk Valley with its tight communities of Irish immigrants, would stake your claims in Gotham where anti-Catholic, anti-Irish sentiment ran high?

Yet your path in some ways mirrored your father's: Michael Conroy who fresh from Ireland found work among New Englanders who found much to despise in the impoverished, papist Irish. Michael who even so discovered in Mr. Remington a patron and protector. So that when the cherry trees were in bloom—and, going up or down the stairs of the house in Pelham you glimpsed them through the French windows—you may have thought of your father's trees, of the sweet yellow pears that tasted when they were just ripe like nothing in the world.

Yes, the need to accumulate some money: that's the reason you give for deferring marriage so long. But the need to acquire means, to display your talents to Mr. Hyde and his like, may have been sparked first of all by a kind of pride, a long history of rebellion made current by your lunches in Boston with intellectual, agitating Irishmen, all in a fury about the suppressed Land League. Perhaps you, too, Willie, could not find it in yourself to submit to the pride of another race, the Americans, who had—a hundred years before the time of your childhood—themselves shrugged off a tyrant intimately known to your own grandparents but who looked on you and your kind as in no way desirable companions, whatever your achieved station, whatever the newly acquired depth of your pocket. Could not submit any more than those others known to you through story and song but much more powerfully through blood, through gestures you must have observed in your father, for example, attitudes of mind passed down through the generations inspired by some mix of crouching fear and overweening pride.

If you'd left behind your badge of poverty and allowed yourself to take on the attitudes and responsibilities of a man of means, it might have seemed to you that you'd not only betrayed your ancestors but also orphaned yourself in a world where you were neither loved nor wanted. Because a good part of Mr. Hyde's appeal was surely his patronage, *his kindness,* as you call it, allowing you to feel less vulnerable to the likes of his son. And so without quite stating it to yourself, you'd come to feel that Deirdre and Stuart—who knew you more intimately than did Mr. Hyde and had learned to care for you despite firsthand knowledge of your outbursts and peculiarities: aware, also, of your capacity for loyalty—were the people necessary to you above all others, as reassurance that you would not be abandoned, ever, to the James Hazen Hydes of the world. Come to feel that by virtue of having won the love of these two—Protestant-born, mysteriously at ease in circles in which you would perhaps always feel a stranger, Deirdre a convert to Catholicism with an American mother, Stuart of English extraction and likewise a convert—you'd escape staring into the glazed and hostile eyes of a stranger.

But at this juncture you might well turn to me and inquire about myself: what, you might ask, are your own attitudes toward power and money? How secure do you feel in your own skin? Do you think of yourself as an American?

Here I pause, wondering. How much easier to speculate on your shames than to admit my own! Yet it may be that my blind gropings in the dark corridors of the past are only an oblique attempt to dispel the shadows cast by my own lurking fears that have their source in yours. Because it's clear to me that I, too, would rather not acknowledge the money at my disposal, would rather project some image of myself as unable to afford, for instance, the occasional taxi. And yet, truth be told—and perhaps you were the same, Willie—on almost every occasion I do in fact prefer the crowded subway, the companionable bus, to the isolation of a cab. I prefer the faces around me, the bodies, an assurance that any time at all I am in the heart of my kind. In this confession of a need for the crush of people around me, am I perhaps stumbling on a motive for Deirdre's insisting on the El? Or for your delight that she did?

Bert was anxious about money in ways that Kate was not. Kate had notions that "one" did not talk about money or inquire what people paid for things, notions that were altogether foreign to the writer of your travel journals in which the price of a cup of tea is recorded carefully in the back pages. No, you'd raised Kate to lie abed in the morning—until the Depression sapped your funds and you thought again—even though she had to work hard enough, God knows, later on when there were no longer servants on the scene and her memories of the house as it had looked, once upon a time, condemned her to years of unceasing labor.

Here I catch myself in the very disguises I have been describing. For have I ever confessed in these pages that, yes, when Kate was growing up there was almost always a cook living in the house? And a maid as well? That the third floor included not only the large room with the brass beds—a beautiful room with windows looking in three directions, one into the heart of the hickory tree—but also two much smaller rooms half the size of the other, rooms that were stifling in summer despite the occasional glimpse of tulip leaves the deeply recessed dormer windows permitted? Yes, it was in one of these that Nora McHugh lived, rooms designed for "the help." And how do I know? Because the architect had finished them differently: simple plank floors instead of parquet, tin doorknobs in place of glass.

Yet there are moments, you might be surprised to hear, Willie, when I feel myself the shamed outsider. These moments sometimes occur among old true-bloods, those who have no sense of their ancestors as having come from any other place: except, of course, England. In this company, I am almost ashamed to tell you, I either avoid mentioning my Irish Catholic ancestry or else—conversely—make a great point of doing so. Yes, I am Catholic, born into a church of immigrants; make of that what you like. In this company I am ashamed to "pass," and also embarrassed by some old shame that you must have carried with you always. Or it might be that some old fire is ignited by a chance remark made by a friend belonging to any tribe other than mine, some oblique aside about "papists," "the Irish," and dazed, humiliated, I turn on my adversary, fists raised, ready for battle. And am immediately chagrined by my own outburst.

So it may be the house in Pelham that has proved the passage into a place where Maddie and Charlie and I call ourselves Americans. That you wanted Kate and Grace to hang on to the house, there is no question. It is under the gray-slated roof that each of us has found momentary shelter from the threat of eviction, of the open road.

One Fifteen Broadway
December 18, 1931

To my dear children:

 I am writing this letter to tell you of my wishes in the event of my death. I suggest you endeavor to keep together in the house. Three years ago I had ample to leave you in comfortable circumstances. Now I haven't as much. I hope there will be enough in all to keep you in a modest manner of living and I counsel you to practice economy.
 I urge each of you to prepare yourself to earn your own living. To keep your own money as property and under no circumstances to turn it over to any husband. Keep control of your own. It will make you more independent and in case of misfortune save you something on which to live.
 Prize your faith. Always guard and practice it. And in doing so don't forget to pray earnestly for the repose of the souls of your Deedy and

               Daddy

V

O cut for me life's bread, for me pour wine!

When the fourteen-year-old Deirdre saw you at the picnic in the Gulph, she may have noticed in your eyes those flashes of light visible in the photograph from about that time. And noticed them again when—

walking into your brother John's office in Ilion—she found you sitting behind a high desk, seemingly oblivious to her presence until John called to you, asking if you were aware that Deirdre Carmody had come through the door. In your letter to your daughters composed just after Deirdre's death, you say she'd teased you: that John had needed to alert you to her presence, that on your wedding day you'd fallen asleep on the train and snored most of the way to Martinsburg, West Virginia.

Could all this, Willie, be the studied bragging of the man who sees himself as caught but doesn't want to be thought eager? It's clear she took note of your reluctance. *I was not in a hurry to marry,* you say, pleading lack of funds. Perhaps Deirdre, through those long years of mourning in Washington, did indeed form an attachment to someone else. But pride would surely have prevented your saying so.

Who are you, Willie? In photos taken a little later—perhaps about the time of your marriage—you are no longer wearing the stiff-winged collars and soft dark ties of your youth, your collars are now deep and rounded, probably held together with a collar pin, your tie is tightly knotted. If you were wearing a hat I imagine it would have been a black bowler. I see the same eyes as in the earlier photos, eyes now looking out from behind pince-nez but still floating in some element of their own. They put me in mind of the eyes of James Joyce in photos taken at close range—bedazzled, vulnerable to light, surely—eyes that look straight into the camera and appear magnified by the shining lenses of his own pince-nez, too large, a little mad.

Obsessed, perhaps that's the word. What did you want above all else? And what did you fear? When you tell the story of Deirdre's teasing you about your wedding trip, I want to ask what is the meaning of your repeating the story. Perhaps you were embarrassed by it all, by the words of the ceremony, knew that people were thinking that tonight you and Deirdre would meet each other in bed. Perhaps you were aware of John Carmody's eyes on you. Aware, too, of the watchful presence of your brother John, still a bachelor in his mid-fifties—a man who allowed himself, you were certain, pleasures you'd denied yourself—who when you'd left Ilion fifteen years before had warned you against entanglements. The jolly time you mention at the reception may have involved some discreet but pointed toasts that you and Deirdre enjoy yourselves on your honeymoon.

And how would alcohol have figured in the mix? Did you drink to subdue the riot of your desires? To excite them? Did you drink because you had to? You were of a gregarious nature, your travel journals are filled with meetings, with convenings and partings. *The crowd,* you say, referring after you leave the boat and arrive in Ireland to your band of companions who reconfigure on land. These comings and goings were surely enhanced by rounds of drinks, by hearty toasts, by many an eager refill. As were your convivial dinners with the Friendly Sons of St. Patrick: a group, I imagine, that put a fair amount away.

In the house in Pelham, on a shelf in the kitchen, gathering dust, is your martini shaker, which I know from Kate you made free use of during Prohibition. Kate, who was never afflicted with a thirst, who would nurse a drink for hours, liked to say, proudly, that the house in Pelham had never been dry, as if this refusal to buckle were a badge of honor. A generous spill of gin, a measure of vermouth, a splash of bitters, and you were ready! Although I confess Bert used the same shaker freely enough in his day. As well as the martini glasses you and your guests must have fingered with some frequency: long-stemmed, wide-coned, a rooster blazoned on each one, a rooster flaunting a glossy tail of red and orange and green.

I will not pass this way again, Willie, choosing this word or that in the effort to give your story a shape. You and I will not meet I think after this intimate encounter. At least we will not meet in time, the element in which I am now trying—just as you once did—to make my uneasy way from one moment to the next. Snow is piled along the curbs and children are sleigh riding down the hill in Morningside Park. It is almost four o'clock on a February afternoon. The buds on the trees in the window may be a little swollen because it seems there's now something of a blur where only a month ago bare black sticks cut up the sky.

I'm moving toward the place where you are now, even as the afternoon advances, as the light reflected from the slipping sun, the backlight, falls on brick and branch and floating white gull. Dissolves far-off windows into pools of liquid gold, stamps purple shadows on the snow. Before long the children will return home and the city once again sink into the pure radiance of night.

And so I hover near in a moment that may for you have been a crisis, and for Deirdre as well. You and Deirdre are at last on the train heading for Martinsburg. Yet you, Willie, are sleeping, in fact you are snoring, perhaps recovering from a glass or two of champagne. So I like to think that for the moment I don't need to worry about you. But what of Deirdre? She has changed out of her wedding dress and is now wearing something suitably demure, gray perhaps, but new, certainly new, and chosen with this instant in mind. Which means that she has imagined it all beforehand, going off with you on a journey, the first of any length you'd taken alone together since that day on the ferry when you'd crossed the river and then walked up the many steps to the El. She thinks now—remembering the shadows lying in vivid bars on the street far below the high tracks, remembering how fearful she'd been that you'd felt obliged to meet her and how she hadn't wanted you to spend a cent more than necessary—that her worries at present are entirely different. The money, for the moment, is taken care of, both by your own swift promotions and by her father's generosity, his declared purpose of sending her every month something of what will eventually come to her so that she might be a little independent.

No, her fear now has to do with something entirely different. She is sitting next to the window of the train because you, Willie, have courteously placed her where you thought she'd most like to be. The day that she and her mother had so ardently hoped would be a fine one, a day of autumnal warmth and sunshine, has been gloomy. It has rained on and off since dawn and now the drops are running down the pane, the damp fields of Virginia are streaming past in the gathering twilight. When she turns from the window she cannot help observing you, Willie, and thinks that this is the first time she has seen you asleep. If she likes, she can look her fill. This guarded scrutiny unsettles her, as if she shouldn't be looking at you when you don't know it. She fears you might think she is judging you, which perhaps she is. Your restless hands are quiet, your fingers have ceased their thrumming, your pince-nez have been put away in a box that snaps open and shut and placed in an inside pocket of your jacket. She observes that your mouth is slack, indeed, that it whiffles in and out to the rhythm of your snores. For thirty years she has slept beneath her parents' roof and now she will sleep under yours. She's unsure what this new arrangement will mean, but feels she's had a glimpse of something in these few moments of watching you asleep.

When she turns her head and looks out at the rain sluicing down the windows, she remembers dashing in between the drops into the church, her father in full naval dress extending his arm, and then of you waiting there at the altar, Stuart by your side, book in hand, smiling. After she and her parents had returned from Ireland two summers ago you'd quickly let her know that Stuart, your dearest friend, was once again in New York, having returned from his studies in Rome. It was true you'd responded a year earlier with cables and cards when she'd been ill with appendicitis, also that you'd come down to see her off when she'd sailed for Queenstown on the SS *Haverford* from Philadelphia in early June. But it was only after the renewed presence in your life of this man she'd heard so much about that you'd been stirred to action.

She counted the change in you from the snowy day at her parents' house in Washington—more than a year after Stuart's return—when she and Stuart had finally met. She remembers you, Willie, making the introductions with some anxiety, looking through your shining lenses from one to the other. She was aware from the first moment that Stuart liked her and while you and her mother sat on the little sofa talking, as you were wont to do, and her father roamed restlessly about at the other end of the room, these two who had just been introduced had stood together before the oil she'd once painted while still in school of a girl holding a shell to her ear. Stuart had talked to her with so much understanding of what he saw and of what her intentions might have been that she thought—not for the first time—that you had chosen Stuart and herself at least in part because of what you might have called their "artistic" inclinations, talents that seemed to you in sharp contrast with your own more practical nature, a nature you felt obscurely to be necessary and good but somehow not as "fine" as the other. It was during that same visit that she'd shown Stuart another oil, hanging on another wall of the same room, a painting she'd only recently acquired of a pond in a snowy wood, the red light of the setting sun running all over it. When she'd tried, haltingly, to tell him that what had caught her own attention was that this startling pond in the still, white wood was undisturbed by anyone's knowledge of it, he'd nodded slowly without saying a word and continued to look long after she imagined he might have had enough.

Perhaps the thought briefly crosses her mind, this late autumn evening as you speed through the driving rain toward West Virginia, that she is sitting on a train with a man who, sleeping, she scarcely recognizes because another man, a priest, in fact, has looked on her with appreciation. And wonders how it would be if she were not feeling so alone and the sleeping man were instead awake and ardent and talking sociably with her about the day they have lived through together. Their wedding day, after all. And if she knows the slightest shiver of apprehension, I hope she quickly remembers a summer morning in New London a few years before when she had been sharply aware she'd stirred your senses, a morning when she'd dressed carefully, had worn a lavender dress and fastened a bunch of purple and white sweet peas into her waist. Walking along to meet you for Mass, walking beneath the elms that threw moving shadows on the stretched white silk of her parasol, she'd caught sight of you waiting there in the dappled shade, had taken note before you'd even become aware of her eyes on you, of the leaping fire, the blue blaze.

VI

The trees were in suspense,
Listening with an intense
Anxiety for the Word –

Yet I imagine Stuart only fleetingly in the house in Pelham, wondering if your remove from the city didn't loosen the tie, somewhat, as his duties as priest, as yours as banker and family man, swept you in different directions. When he returned from his studies in Rome, despite your great affection, did you look at each other across a distance? Perhaps it was to revive what you feared you'd lost that after your marriage you wished to live at only a few blocks' remove from his parish. It may have happened, despite efforts on both sides, that you eventually met only to repeat what had come before.

In my mind's eye I see Stuart walking up from the station to the house one Sunday afternoon at the beginning of October 1912, that first fall you and Deirdre are in Pelham. It is not his first visit—he'd come out to visit you almost immediately after your move, in May, and once during the summer: to become acquainted with the house, to see how you were doing, following your recent ordeal in the fire, and how the little girls and then Deirdre, especially, were managing—but it's the first time he's walked up from the station alone. He's told you not to meet his train, that he'd like the solitary walk to the house after coming from the noisy streets of the city. On this sunlit afternoon a single cricket is humming in the tall grass and the trees are only here and there touched with red.

He's taken the train from Grand Central where as usual he'd admired the constellations twinkling in the mild azure of the vaulting, the high-drawn figures of Crab and Hunter, taken the New York, New Haven, and Hartford line as he has done before. The train had emerged from the tunnel at Park and 110th Street and soon run briskly along tracks so close to the tenements of Harlem that he could look into the ill-lit rooms of people who like it or not had to endure the stare of those who had the means to remove themselves and their families from the city but not to break with it entirely. Sitting in his rush-woven seat by the window, book open on his lap, feeling the basic indecency of observing people's lives as spectacle— as if, he thought, the rooms he looked into had been illuminated stages—

he remembered how when he'd traveled to Ireland he'd been appalled by the poverty not because he hadn't encountered poverty before—he'd seen plenty growing up in Kentucky—but because it had taken such different forms from those he was used to. He remembered too how he dated his desire to become a priest, dim and shadowy as it had been, from that fourth of July when in your own company, Willie, he'd visited the cottage near Kenmare with the tubercular woman crouching half-naked by the turf fire. He'd been haunted by the sight for weeks and threatened by a melancholy he couldn't shake even after returning to New York and his job at Harper's, a distracted restlessness that lightened only after he'd become gradually aware of the course he'd in fact already embarked on.

Now the train—having stopped in Pelham—is on its way to New Rochelle and as Stuart walks to the house he admires the clumps of ragged goldenrod, heavy and stiff, the lavender Michaelmas daisies. On his birthday, a couple of weeks before, he was forty-three, a day made vivid to him this year as the first anniversary of little Mary's death. Taking note of the dappled sun spots on the sidewalk stretching before him, of the patter like rain of falling acorns, he is thinking how great the changes have been for all of you these past months and remembers the rainy day almost exactly a year ago, in sharp contrast with this fine one, when Deirdre had called to see him in the rectory on 71st Street. He remembers everything with extraordinary clarity, how he'd looked at her sitting there in her black skirt and waist, a gold watch hanging from a chain round her neck, the only spot of brightness, the gleam of that watch, in the ugly room with the picture of the Sacred Heart stuck on the wall. Remembers that in the silence, listening to the rain on the roof, waiting for her to speak, it had come to him that perhaps her greatest fear was that she would be ravaged by her own feelings, that she would not be able to survive them. And when she did begin to speak, hesitatingly, looking out at him with clear eyes as if from some place where she wandered alone, neither wanting nor expecting anything at all, he was reminded quite unexpectedly of the dying Christ's despair, of his sense of utter isolation, of disbelief, perhaps, that things had come to this pass. And because Deirdre like himself had not been born to this faith—and so would be untroubled by certain orthodoxies that he knew inhibited his speech with many others—he'd tried to tell her what he'd often thought: that despair's most intimate handmaid was shame, the humiliation of finding oneself broken down entirely when all the world was stepping briskly by on some unfathomable business you'd once pursued yourself, urging you to take notice, to pull yourself together, implying that your very suffering was in your own hands, that you could in fact come down from the cross if you only chose to do so.

She must not blame herself for her own unhappiness, he'd tried to tell her. But did not say what he was thinking: that strangely enough it was in her very agony that he glimpsed something inestimable he'd never yet discovered on the faces of the cheerful and content. And from there he remembers, again quite clearly—and wonders, walking along the sidewalk, if these recollections are flooding in the still afternoon because of the silence of the trees around him, the listening trees, tulips and maples and oaks—that his thoughts had run on from Deirdre to the good thief on Calvary. He'd sometimes imagined this thief had consoled Christ more than any other—yes, certainly more than the women and disciples standing looking up at him with tear-stained faces—because nailed to his own plank of pain, enduring the same flies and thirst and slow strangulation, he'd acknowledged in so many words that suffering at its most extreme and shattering could yield to vision.

Remember me, he'd said: and so, his breath cut off when in the end his legs had been broken, his heart stopped by an overflow of sorrow or joy, he'd been carried into the place of promise. Stuart had found himself telling Deirdre—his words tumbling forth without his thinking, as if he were trying desperately to find comfort for himself as well as for her—that she must look for the God who it seemed had abandoned her in the faces of those around her, those who however mistakenly or clumsily tried to show her their care and concern. Because Stuart had come to believe that the most fervent effort to comfort someone else was often inspired by something comfortless within oneself.

Here, Willie, he may also have been thinking of you, the silently bereaved father, his old friend whose limitations he knew so well, having long observed your lightning temper, your many fears and insecurities, remembering your burst of anger in the hotel in Killarney, and imagining now your own terrible sense of impotence in the face of the accumulated sorrows of the past year.

As he turns the corner into Loring Avenue and sees the house in the middle of the block, its chimneys rising among the trees, he remembers something else from that rainy October afternoon in the rectory: that as Deirdre got up to leave, buttoning her coat slowly and reaching out a hand to him, there had come a knock on the door and another priest was saying a small boy had come to the kitchen for soup and did he know if they had any clothes about the place that might fit a child of five or

255

so. Deirdre had accompanied him to the kitchen and crouching next to the little boy—who was sitting in a chair, feet dangling in broken shoes, hungrily tearing off pieces from a hunk of bread he held in one unwashed hand—she'd recited some rhyme to him about one misty moisty morning when cloudy was the weather, she'd chanced to meet an old man all clad in leather. Then as the boy stopped eating to look at her with wide eyes, his mouth a little open showing the place where his front teeth were missing, she'd taken his hand and shaken it nodding: "How d'ye do and how d'ye do and how d'ye do again!" Stuart remembers that in that instant he'd determined to apply for help wherever he could, among the rich of the parish—of which there were many—expressly so that the poor would at least for a little time to come find a hospitable refuge in this church on 71st Street where they might be sure of a bowl of soup, a piece of bread, someplace to stretch their bones.

But now the house is before him, its wide gleaming windows, the tulip branches above its slated roof touched here and there with yellow in the afternoon sun, and putting his foot on the first step he notices the bruised and broken hickory nuts lying all over the grass and thinks of his mother's home in Lexington and how far away that now seems. He reminds himself he mustn't forget to take the 9:05 train back to the city because as a younger priest he has the six o'clock morning Mass to say, and thinks isn't it strange that it's his old friend who lives in this house with the tall chimneys who'd written him those meticulous letters, urging him to a religion that has now become in one way or another his life.

And what then? Did you, Willie, open the door to him? Or had you in fact been standing all this while on the lawn in front of the house anxiously awaiting the appearance of the friend you were perhaps even now afraid of losing? You, Willie, sweeping back your blond hair in a nervous gesture with the palm of your hand. Perhaps the little girls, Kate and Grace, ran out to see what Stuart had brought them, a doll for each, a picture book. And when he entered the house, was it Deirdre's old father who first came forward, hand outstretched, and did Stuart think again, as he had that snowy day in Washington, that Deirdre had taken the melancholy eyes from her father, the stern dark brows from her mother? He may have glanced around for Deirdre, not seeing her at first, and looking up—just as the grandfather clock was booming three—seen her coming down the stairs, wearing a dress white at the neck that descended through every shade of gray until it floated black at the hem. Dressed in mourning, he might have thought, either way. Perhaps he observed, then, because his eyes were on Kate, his little goddaughter, that as Deirdre reached the bottom of the stairs and laid a hand on her head Kate sharply drew in her breath, as if protecting herself from her mother's distraction. You would all have gone into the living room afterwards where a Buddha sat on a box and on through to the porch. You, Willie, commenting that every advantage must be taken of the warm afternoon, there wouldn't be many more like this one.

It was only on the train returning to the city that night that Stuart recalled how Deirdre, following that rainy day last October, had sent to the rectory a package of clothing—small shoes and underclothing and woolen vests and jackets—that they'd given away as quickly as children had come to the door and how almost every month, since, she'd sent another. Remembers, too, listening to the rhythmic clacking of the wheels on the tracks, how riding back with you, Willie, to New York that snowy day on the train from Washington—immediately after he'd met Deirdre—you'd turned to him with an inquiring look, not liking to mention her name, to put the question. And remembers that he'd stared at you wonderingly, as if to him a question was unfathomable.

Looking out into the night, the lights sweeping by as the train jostled its way back into the city, Stuart—remembering the page from Oscar Wilde in the book he'd written while in prison claiming he wanted to regret nothing, deny nothing—thought sleepily that regretting the truth of one's own experience was a poverty all its own, an impoverishment of the spirit, to be corrected only by charity, the compassionate embrace of all that one was. And then, starting awake in his seat as the train wound round a bend and into a tunnel, wondered why he'd thought of Wilde's words just now. Who was the one forgetting? And what?

VII

I only know that I was there

In parting, Willie, I confide to you what I believe to be my earliest memory. If it is not the earliest of all it rises from the store of the summer I turned three, your own last summer, the one when you came to visit and we approached the sleeping Kate along a hall lined with books. The month is August, I know, because Charlie is six years old and we're having a birthday party under the cool trees. I think you are there among the other guests out on the lawn, one of the adults sitting in the wicker chairs that have been dragged out from the porch for the occasion.

I'm not with the children playing in the grass although I was with all of you a moment before. No, I've come in from outside. In a moment

I'll return but now I'm alone in the quiet house, going up the stairs. I'm wearing a middy dress with a blue tie and a white skirt, sandals, too, that have been whitened with a little cloth that Kate turns the liquid polish onto from its bottle so that it runs out, a chalky white that comes off on my fingers. But the astonishing thing is that the steps are falling away beneath my feet, I'm bounding up the stairs without touching them. The French windows on the landing are open on the summer afternoon and everything is waiting, the leaves and shadows, you'll all be there when I return and my joy is bearing me up on wings.

Part Five

The Horn of the Hunter

It is I who am desolate; I, Deirdre, that will not live till I am old.

August 1923

Dear Children:

That you may have from me, your father, the true story of your mother's last illness, I am undertaking to write the saddest chapter of our family life.

Easter, 1922, friends from Philadelphia were staying with us and guests were in for dinner. Earlier that day Deedy told me she wasn't feeling well and feared she would not be able to join us for dinner. But as usual, after resting awhile, she dressed and came downstairs. When I returned from work the following night she complained of feeling sick and on my suggestion went to bed. The next day she was still ill and we called a doctor. He said she had influenza and must remain in bed.

Wednesday, it was said to be bronchitis. Saturday, it was decided she had pneumonia. In a week or ten days, after what seemed an average case of pneumonia, she began to improve, her temperature was about normal and she seemed to be steadily improving.

Suddenly, after about a week, her temperature rose and she had attacks: first of chills, then fever and sweats. As she did not improve, specialists from New York were called in who said they feared some complication of the lungs. But none of them could diagnose the case. It was not until the last of June that the doctors concluded she was suffering from Hodgkin's disease of the glands. I was told the prospects for her recovery were not at all good and that she might live a year. Blood transfusions were tried three times, arsenic placed in the veins, and finally radium applied to the glands of the throat.

October 1st I took her to Atlantic City where I left her with a nurse. I went down to see her and there we spent October 25, our seventeenth wedding anniversary, which was to be our last.

She returned home the last of October and was able to be up and about looking after some of the housekeeping with help from the rest of us. The preparations for Christmas were made simple so as not to overtax her strength but we had many lovely presents and a Christmas made all the merrier by her eager participation.

On the advice of the doctors it was thought best that Deedy go to Florida to escape the cold weather at home, so arrangements were made and on January 16 we left together for Palm Beach. I saw her safe and comfortable in her hotel and then returned home, expecting her to remain at Palm Beach until the middle or last of March.

She was not anxious to go to Florida and I had to urge and encourage her to get her started. At Palm Beach, she felt improved in the warm weather and sunshine. She went to West Palm Beach daily to the little church over there to offer up thanksgiving for her improvement. She told me that the Sunday before she was again taken sick she had never felt better, was filled with the joy of living and thankfulness for her improved condition.

On February 2, I received a telegram from her saying her fever had returned, and she was alarmed. She called a doctor there who advised her to return home. Accordingly, she left February 4, arriving February 6 in the care of a nurse. The specialists from New York were again called in and under their treatment of radium and arsenic she began to improve so that by Easter she was able to be down at the table for dinner. She was up for a good portion of each day and was much interested in the garden. She bought wicker furniture for the porch and lawn and was looking forward to spending the summer in our house.

She had been in Pelham continuously from February so after Grace's birthday, May 12, she thought she would like to go to New York to spend a few days at the Murray Hill Hotel and to go out and see something new and different. She went on May 14 and at once had to go to bed. There, she began to fail and it was not until June 2 that we were able to get her back home. Once here, she seemed easier and better but that only lasted a few days. For the next two months she was in bed, steadily failing, and died a little after midnight, August 8th, 1923.

August 10th, a funeral Mass was celebrated at St. Catherine's Church, Pelham, N.Y., by our dear old friend Father Patrick Daly of St. Patrick's Cathedral, New York. After the Mass, we took her body to Utica and the next day, August 11, to Ilion and buried her in the little Catholic cemetery on Oak Hill where she lies, surrounded by her ancestors and mine, our relatives and friends, to rest amongst these dear ones until the Judgment Day.

This, dear children, is the plain story of the last sickness and death of your mother. It is the simple recital of events. The story of her sufferings, both physical and mental, of her courage, fortitude and patience and, above all things, of her resignation to the will of God, are beyond my powers of description.

In leaving this document of her last sickness I must tell you of an incident. Her birthday as you know was April 1. On that day in 1922, I awoke and at once reached over to her sleeping in her bed alongside mine and congratulated her on her birthday, wishing her many happy returns. To my surprise, she burst into tears and sitting straight up in bed, said, "In three years, I shall be dead and there will not be a one of them (meaning doctors) that will know what ails me."

I tried to console her and pass it off as a joke but she stuck to her statement. This was about three weeks before she was first taken sick but how true was her prophecy! She erred only in the number of years she had still to live. In less than seventeen months she was in the grave and I am not sure but that she was right too about the doctors.

When she was told she had pneumonia in 1922, I asked her if she wished to see a priest and she said she did. Our good friend Father Daly came out from New York. He told me then after talking with her for some time: "That woman hasn't a tie on earth except her children, but would like to live to bring them up." So you see, my dear children, what affection your good mother had for you. Always remember this, you were her heart's desire.

When the severe sickness developed, her sufferings were intense. Her chills would sometimes last an hour or two, so that the bed *was shaken, then a fever of an hour or more sometimes going as high as 105 and sweats that would wet the entire bed clothing. Her fortitude and courage in her sufferings and her bravery in taking the painful treatments administered excited the admiration of all the doctors. One of them told me he had never seen a braver soldier of suffering than she.*

Her ideas and mine in regard to religion and piety differed. Her conscience and mine differed, but I can attest that her faith was strong though she sometimes wondered if it was; her love of God and man was a fulfillment of the commandment to love God with all your heart, and your neighbor as yourself. She was naturally kind; kind in thought and kind to everyone. Her love for babies and her attention to the old was unlimited. Every baby she loved, and if the baby was poor and sickly, she loved it all the more.

Patient with my impatience and peculiarities, loving, consoling, and helpful, she was a model wife. As a mother, you well know her care. Her sole thought and interest was in you. In your sicknesses, she was constant in her attention. Your little interests and troubles were her own and touched her heart on all occasions. Cherish her memory. But what need have I to tell you such a thing?

II

To my surprise, she burst into tears and sitting straight up in bed, said, "In three years, I shall be dead and there will not be a one of them (meaning doctors) that will know what ails me."

There will not be a one of them: Irish idiom, distinctly Willie's rather than Deirdre's. Other words, perhaps carrying a slightly different meaning, floated up from her dream of death. The dream, however, claimed precision: falsely, as it turned out, erring as it did on the side of generosity. In a little less than seventeen months, *she was in the grave,* the grave a place, in those days, referred to in passing, the ground in which one was destined to *rest,* to return to dust, to dirt, to clay. To spread tap roots beneath the soil that would split apart the globe, touch its quick.

And Deirdre? The dream must have been a familiar one. How can one doubt it? It was Willie's "happy returns" that released the flood, the silent tears withheld too long. But how astoundingly sure she was. How blindly certain that she was dying and that "what ailed her" would remain hidden.

That whatever the diagnosis agreed on, the experts would remain in the dark. And yet Willie's parentheses give pause. Did she mean, as Willie thinks, that the nature of her trouble would in particular confound the doctors? Or was it that she was only stating her solitude, her conviction that not a soul on earth knew what she was dying of that birthday morning, that April Fools'? Did she include herself in that number? And was her solitude the greater if she did?

Or did she mean that she knowingly carried within as if it had been a burn the precise spot where death had touched her? But had kept silent so long that speech had become pointless. Dying of life, perhaps that's the way she would have put it if she'd cared to, dying as perhaps she'd come to believe each one of us does, of heart failure, of sweats and chills.

Or is there another way entirely of understanding all this?

And I am not sure but that she was right: Perplexing words. Willie tells us *the specialists from New York* at last concluded Hodgkin's: he tells us of the three blood transfusions, the arsenic placed in the veins, the radium applied to the throat. Despite all this did he have doubts? Did he believe her ailment—whatever name it was given—to be less pronounceable? There had been the removals to 57th Street, the familiar business of not feeling well, of lying down, of rising at last to dress and come downstairs to sit opposite himself at the table. God knows what else. Did all the eleven years in the house in Pelham, once her death had been announced as imminent, seem to him in retrospect to have been inevitably leading to an early exit?

Or was it simply that he believed the doctors didn't have sufficient knowledge, that their diagnosis was mistaken, that medical research hadn't yet caught up to whatever it was that troubled Deirdre?

> *He told me then after talking with her for some time: "That woman hasn't a tie on earth except her children, but would like to live to bring them up."*

That woman: Yes, that's what he would have said, Father Daly of St. Patrick's, who came out from New York, the same who in Cork during the summer of 1896 had conveniently introduced Willie and Stuart to the head of the Imperial Hotel where they were staying. How busy the Pelham station must have been with all that running back and forth, those specialists and priests! But did Willie's face burn, hearing—from this *dear old friend* in whom Deirdre had confided—that he, her husband, had not been counted as a reason to struggle with death? It was her children alone who constituted *her heart's desire.*

On the other hand, if Willie had felt ashamed of the poor part he played in Deirdre's confidences it's unlikely he would have quoted the priest. It may even have been that Willie was peculiarly equipped to understand Deirdre. Perhaps he was visited by recollections of an icy January morning when he lay beneath iron wreckage within a vault of his own making, the roar of fire in his ears, and recalled his own state of mind, torn between life and death. And yet the words he himself had spoken—which he could not remember pronouncing, although he had read them in the papers— had been "For God's sake, save me."

In any case, it's likely that both Willie and Father Daly understood whatever it was that Deirdre said as a sign of holy detachment. It was not that she wanted to die; it was rather that her attention had been directed elsewhere.

> *She thought she would like to go to New York to spend a few days at the Murray Hill Hotel and to go out and see something new and different.*

But no! See how wrong they all were. Close to the last moment of all, Deirdre's overwhelming urge was to live.

In late April, when the treatments were behind her and she was feeling somewhat better, she may have opened her eyes one night and been startled into wakefulness by the sight of the full moon in the window and there against it—as if held up for her inspection—a black hickory branch isolated in the perfect shining circle of light: the long late bud, the craggy twig, brought close as if in the eye of a telescope. This: look at this.

Next morning she'd woken with a sense of urgency. If she waited until Grace's birthday, the twelfth of May, always a day of peculiar strain, then soon afterwards she'd go into the city and stay. There were things still! Things even now she'd never tasted: a lover's impatience, for instance, perhaps such as her father's for her mother, Willie's long reluctance something else entirely. Yes, she'd always known that between her parents had burned some tenderness spawned in their youth that had sustained them throughout. She considered that it had been the loss of that lively, intimate bond to her mother that had been her father's greatest grief in this house, and that his death under this same roof hadn't come for him a moment too soon. But then, they hadn't waited, as was the case with herself and Willie, hadn't plotted and planned. And she thought suddenly of something she'd read about or perhaps heard described, a scene from the fire at the Triangle Shirt Factory, the fire so closely associated with her own sorrows occurring, as it did, on a Saturday afternoon in March not even four months before Mary's fall and less than a year before Willie's own ordeal by fire. A man and woman had appeared in a burning window high above the street, the man enfolding the woman in his arms and kissing her before taking her hand and stepping with her through the window as into another room. But before that: the lover's kiss on the mouth, the taste of desire. She wanted that, the intention, the deliberate fulfillment of something she didn't know how to ask of Willie who so quickly turned brusque when he was unsure. Of course she knew very well she was ill, but she didn't care: what she wanted despite everything was once more to surprise desire in the eyes of another human being—passing on a street corner, maybe, standing in front of a shop window—to see herself reflected as a creature for whom anything was still possible. Because what had happened to her these months was that a door, perhaps the same door, had slammed shut again and again each time she'd tried to leave the room she found herself in, a room with a bed where she was confined but was able to look out a window into a night garden where tiny white lights were strung in the trees and people were drinking wine and laughing and the heavy scent of jasmine hung over everything. Perhaps she was thinking of the island her father had spoken of, Madeira, a place of terraces and vines and high views of the sea with the red sun dropping into it. Or maybe a place she'd known herself when she was very little, Honolulu it must have been, where sometimes before they went to bed she and Rob had been allowed outside for awhile and there'd be music and palm trees and people dancing and far overhead the stars, so that she'd felt even as a little girl, now it's happening, right here where I am. Yes, the same sharp sense of things, the passionate delight she'd recognized years ago the first time she'd walked into the Murray Hill Hotel with Willie at noon and heard the strings playing some waltz or other and people passing back and forth between the potted palms, the fountain splashing, oh the pleasure of it, the shimmer of dresses, rose and pale green, the men with their watching eyes, the sharp click of heels on the mosaic of black and white tiles, and on the landing of the stairs the Tiffany window with the light streaming through. It was to there she wanted to return, even while she prayed your will not mine, thinking, it's all been given, this garden of earthly delights, this Eden flowing straight from the hand of God. Divine generosity, these tumbling fruits of the earth not in gleaming white stone as in that terrible place with the pink marble steps, but living, lustrous, whole, flesh you could touch and inhale, like the moist hickory leaf that in fall she'd laid across her mouth like a poultice.

But Willie was against this project. He'd said remember Florida, remember what happened there, and she'd said, yes, but that time it was your idea not mine; you know I didn't want to go so that at least now the choice should be my own. She was at a loss how to explain to him her conviction that if she could only leave all this behind, if she could get away from these rooms and these stairs, away from the French windows opening on the disturbing, the pitiless, push of spring, she might be well again, walk out of one life into another. But when he'd at last stopped objecting she understood it was because he was weary of the whole thing, but even worse that he'd at last given up and was treating her like one of the condemned who are allowed to choose whatever they like for their final meal.

And so it had been. And not even that. All she'd seen was the inside of a hotel room with its burgundy brocade that recalled the other and gleaming wood and brass fittings, seen even less than on that journey south in the dead of winter. But ever since her return from the city she knew she wouldn't visit again, her thoughts had taken another turn. As they had done, perhaps, after Florida when she'd lain in her bed watching the spring come so slowly, so imperceptibly, that she'd reflected how even the most enormous changes—like the transformation of a glistening ice storm into a green and billowy summer day—happen in increments imperceptible to the most attentive eye. It had been early February, then, when the doctors were with her every day and she'd lain in their hands trying to picture the high silver-sheathed branches of the tulip trees glittering in the sun, at night had listened in her sleep for their distant glassy chime. She'd reflected how although she'd looked out at the world and seen it pinned there to the precise moment in which she'd caught it, it was all spinning away like a child's top. No matter how hard you tried you could never catch things as they disappeared into the next, the shadows resolutely still as they lay there on the snow, refusing to budge, the sun fixed in its place between the limbs of the tree; it was only when you'd looked away then back that you could see that during this instant when you weren't looking the shadow had lengthened, the sun had fallen behind the hill. With what slow patience, she'd thought in her agony, everything is being accomplished.

And then, as the winter was at last giving way, it had seemed to her she was being drawn into the invisible motion of things, into the vast silent spheres: in this room, for instance, where silver mirrors and windows caught the watery spring light and threw it back and forth along the walls until she wasn't sure where she was, until it seemed the walls might be sliding open and she passing through into whirling spaces beyond, into obscurely familiar regions where the wind gathered her in, tossing her up and carrying her on the breast of its ferocious speed. She might fall asleep in the midst of that whirlwind; that's how deeply it would cradle her. But sleeping or waking wouldn't matter, because everything would be happening at once, the rose at the same time bud and blossom, the constellations shining above and below, the wave lifting and curling even as it ran silver up the beach, so that everything would be revealed at once, everything understood and forgiven, everything overflowing, like a love that cannot be exhausted but must be spent and spent.

But you had to get from here to there. You had to get to the other side. That was faith, leaping through the open window, and she thought again of those girls in the Shirt Factory trapped in burning rooms high above the street. The papers had said they'd jumped from the windows and fallen with a thud on the sidewalk below and that winter when she heard the snow sliding down the slate roof, the thud a moment later, she'd thought of them, prayed to them in her own hour of need. Help me when my time comes. Grant me the courage to jump. She'd thought of something like that as long ago as the May day eleven years ago when she'd walked into the house and from the bottom of the stairs looked up onto the landing where the French windows stood open: on what, she didn't know, having not yet seen the cherry trees in blossom, the nights shaken by a wind that made the stars shimmer like water.

Because even then, when they first came to live in this house her father had bestowed on her as his final Christmas gift, she'd been aware she bore a grief within her that would gradually fill one space after another. And so it had: first the spiraling back stairs where she'd tried to rest early one summer morning, then the closet in her father's room where she kept a lacquered box of letters, and not too long after that the cellar with its terrible slit of autumn light. Was this what they called despair? This sense that your life was stuck in one unbearable moment in time? She could never get the hang of the words Willie and the others seemed so sure of, Willie and his notion that sin was a deliberate attempt to thwart the will of God. She'd told him that she was a great sinner, then, because she wanted one thing only and that thing had been taken from her and she could not be reconciled. He'd tried, recently, to reassure her, tried to tell her that it had always seemed to him she'd struggled valiantly to resign herself to the suffering in her life, even if she doubted that she had.

Now she thought again of how her mother had struggled before her, God knew, had perhaps for reasons she would never fully understand struggled within herself even before that shattering sunny October morning in Washington when the cable arrived. Yes, and here she remembered the night in early winter some years before when the cold rain had been lashing against the windows and they'd sat together on the little sofa and her mother had said she was in need of a forgiving heart and was taking steps to learn what that meant. Yet she herself, on hearing her mother's words, had been astonished by her own flood of tears, as if the mere mention of the great questions of life and death that were never named in their home—the word *forgiveness,* for example—had unloosed within something secret, inconsolable, a yearning that she'd always felt to be unspeakable, to be shared in silence only with Rob. But then later, much later—after the Chatsworth, after the move to this house surrounded by trees where she now lay—she'd had time to consider her mother's word. It was not God she accused of her sorrows, or anyone else, for that matter, but her own oversight or delirium—the pull of her attention away from what was before her to something else—that she held responsible for a death she was certain she would have given her life to prevent. Perhaps even, by some kind of inverted logic, was giving her life for now. But she didn't flinch from the recognition that in failing to forgive herself she had failed to care for the people around her, or at least had not cherished them as they desperately needed to be cherished. However Willie defined it, in whatever language, she and her mother would have agreed that sin involved some failure of love. Like not loving the person sitting there beside you because you couldn't stop thinking about the absent one, the one who had been removed. But what were you to do? It wasn't always a matter of choice. Involuntarily, one face, one voice, one bright lock of hair replaced another.

So, in considering her own vain struggles to understand what it might mean to love someone, she thought again of the rainy afternoon in October when yellow ginkgo leaves had lain sodden on the sidewalk and she'd visited Stuart Chambers at the rectory on 71st Street. She couldn't immediately recall what he'd said to her, only that by the time she'd put up her umbrella and ducked back out into the rain—following the moment in the kitchen with the little black-haired boy who'd quite alarmingly made her think of Rob—she'd felt sustained by something in Stuart's manner toward her, an attention, a sympathetic reach, that she thought came from some loneliness in himself. She'd remembered, as well, what Stuart had said to her on another occasion, the last time she'd seen him, only a couple of weeks before he'd died of pneumonia that terrible winter of 1917, when she'd been staying at 57th Street and he'd come to see her there. Her greatest need had been to escape her own despair, the inner voices that tediously circled round again and again and accused her of not putting aside her own sorrows for the sake of those who needed her. He'd listened to her as she tried to say something of this and then after a silence in which they'd simply stared at one another without embarrassment or any need to turn away he'd told her that in a world where ignorance, a profound unknowing, lay behind even the worst acts of cruelty, we can be sure we've been forgiven already for all that we cannot accept in our lives, accept in ourselves. For after all to deny one's experience, he'd said, of whatever kind, was to deny one's very soul. And didn't Stuart on this same occasion tell her that as the dying Christ asked forgiveness for his tormentors he'd pleaded ignorance for us all, even perhaps as we inflicted harm on what was innocent in ourselves? Stuart had struggled with her despair as she knew only someone who'd struggled with his own could do, Stuart who had died suddenly at the age of forty-eight, the age at which it seemed she would die herself. What could this mean, that to each of them almost exactly the same number of days had been allotted? So—all at once remembering—she thought with tenderness of his earliest counsel, that she seek release from her unhappiness by looking for traces of God's goodness in the world around her, in the efforts people made toward her even if sometimes they failed to please: seemed misguided, clumsy. He was pleading for his old friend, Willie, she'd been sure, was mutely asking her to regard him with forbearance, knowing him almost as well as she did herself, having traveled to Ireland with him when they were young men and so surely having witnessed his sudden flares of temper, his refusals to back down. Yes, perhaps Stuart was trying to comfort her with his knowledge, trying to tell her that he knew her husband, knew his weaknesses, and loved him.

Oh but Willie! How she yearned over him these opening days of summer. How her heart contracted when—during a long afternoon at her bedside—she saw him nervously reach a finger into his waistcoat pocket to remove his watch, clicking the lid open, snapping it shut, or when he turned the poor blunt back of his head to her because, she knew, something or other had made him wildly impatient and he didn't want her to see. It was exactly those things in him that had once been the most difficult for her to accept that now caused her to feel a stab of pity. She knew how angrily he would have recoiled at the word but it didn't matter, that was the one she used to herself, and she wondered now if after all it might not be only one more name for what we like to call love.

Then there had been the night neither of them ever spoke of. She'd woken and he'd been sitting on the floor beside her bed in his nightclothes, staring into her face, deeply absorbed. His eyes without his glasses always seemed to her abashed, swimming in some uncertain sea. She'd noticed this even that first afternoon on the ferry, that when he took off his pince-nez and rubbed the place at the base of his nose where they pinched, dropping his head a little as if it ached, and then looked up in response to something or other she'd said, he seemed almost a different person, raked by doubt, lost, unsure. It was one of the things that had arrested her. And now, waking in the night and finding him there beside her, she suddenly understood—as if it had been given to her in the dream even then lingering between them—that his own most miserable fear, one he couldn't name even to himself, was that he'd driven her to this desperate pass, that he'd removed her a vigorous young woman from her parents' house and under his care and protection she'd fallen ill, that he'd been too much for her, simply too much, an irascible husband, demanding in small things, outraged by affronts to some stern inner code he was well aware she didn't share or want to.

But because he couldn't put words to this fear—just as he wasn't able to speak of the baby they'd left on that high hill—he couldn't ask forgiveness, or even ask her if it was true, that she'd received from him a mortal blow, that he'd fatigued her unto death. But when she opened her eyes and looked into his, he didn't flinch, didn't look away, but held hers with his own steady blue gaze, a long transparent stare that slowly brimmed until she saw that he knew she too was asking forgiveness for what she couldn't say any better than he could and then they were both smiling as the tears came and still smiling they gazed until there in the night with the sleeping house around them, weeping, smiling, they knew themselves absolved.

Of the children she couldn't think. Rather she felt each of them in the travails of her body. When cold seized her, when the icy hand of death snatched her up and shook her by the nape of the neck, then she recognized Grace's shivering as her own: Grace who—since her twin's death, since the removal of that warm flesh, both other and own, curled in womb and crib beside her for so brief a span—had seemed to be left in a permanent state of chill. That absence had done its harrowing work. She knew that what had made the devastation complete—and here her heart stopped, appalled—was that she herself, Grace's mother, had withdrawn the embrace that could alone set the blood flowing, warm her child straight through. She had tried and tried, God knew she'd grown ill with trying, but it wasn't the effort that counted, both she and Grace knew that. And so now, at the age of twelve, Grace hugged her elbows, chafed her palms together, draped sweaters over her shoulders. She'd acquired a stunned look, as if she'd been skipping along, flaxen hair afloat, when something

272

had suddenly risen in her path that had frozen her to the quick. And in this, this anguish of disbelief, this shock to the system, she, her mother, felt closer to Grace than to anyone on earth. She looked into Grace's face as into a mirror that threw back at her an expression of irreversible grief. Their loss had been comparable. They alone mourned and could not be comforted. There were even times, she thought, when they greeted each other in some unspoken recognition of this uncanny bond. But the point was that she was Grace's mother, Grace was her child, and she'd failed in the very thing that at birth she'd most wanted to give her, the knowledge that whatever trouble might come in all the years ahead, she'd been loved, loved in her bones.

So now, when the chills came and her teeth rattled in her head, when the bed itself was shaken with her violent shudders, she knew beyond all hope that she would never have a chance to make right this terrible wrong. And if not she, then who? Willie had tried his best, she knew that, but he himself had suffered some blow that had made him also a child of deprivation. How distressed she'd been, at an earlier time, when he'd been unable for reasons entirely different from her own to provide where she had failed. But so it had been and now she could only pray that Grace's name would save her: that someone would look into her eyes one day and immediately recognize as beautiful the refracted light that passed through their stricken blue, would hear her name pronounced aloud and know her once and forever his own, would hold her fast against the entire length of his body until the warm blood coursed into every part of hers.

But it was in the grip of spiraling fever, when without the slightest twitch of finger or toe everything she touched was instantly drenched—when continuing waves of heat ran along the surface of her skin—that she felt pass over her the fire of Kate's rage, Kate who had never liked summer, who always said she couldn't breathe, what with the hot still air and all the trees. Tatie, her firstborn, her beloved, whose furies even as a little child had puzzled and fatigued her. Whoosh, up went the flame and she would ignite, stamping her foot, throwing herself on the floor. Then Willie, from whom she took this, would be stern with her, would invoke discipline, would threaten her, and Kate would disappear into further reaches of fury that seemed to edge on despair. And yet, she thought, someday they would find their way, these two, with their brusque impatience and flinty love. It was Grace she feared who would be left outside.

One day in early June, only weeks after they'd moved into the house, she'd been able to do with Kate, during a tantrum, what had never been possible in that other place. She'd taken her outside under the trees and—

273

even though Kate had continued screaming, almost willfully, as if to show she would not be subdued by petty strategies—had talked to her quietly, walking about with her, describing whatever it was they were looking at, until eventually Kate subsided and stopped to listen. They'd crouched above the pool of purple violets, they'd examined the perfect heart made by their leaves, counted the delicate petals, five, exactly as many as Kate's years. They'd stood in the grass and looked up at the house, at its high chimneys and dormers, at the tulip trees reaching above, and she'd told Kate that this was their house now, the place they'd come to live. Kate had asked if they'd always live here, and she'd said she didn't think so, probably only a year or so. Then, before going in, they'd stopped to look at the rhododendrons, already coming into flower, the tight, green, notched cones, the buds of an intense, delectable pink that Kate had wanted to taste, and then the wide white flower, open, blowsy, and at large. They'd examined all these together, hand in hand, and the memory had come to her, swift and exhilarating, of the summer morning in Glengariff—before she and her mother and father had arrived in Kilkee—when she'd risen early and had walked down through the garden of the hotel to the sea, how everything had been drenched with dew, the hedges of fuchsia drooping there in the dawn, the climbing roses and the gleaming white blossoms of the rhododendron, how she'd been alone and thinking of Willie, and how she'd foreseen that they would marry at last and perhaps even someday walk together in a garden like this one. As she strolled about she'd been singing to herself one of Thomas Moore's melodies, the words so beautiful, she'd thought—"Kathleen Mavourneen, the gray dawn is breaking, the horn of the hunter is heard upon the hill"—and she'd vowed at that instant, making a promise to a future she wished to beguile, that she'd name a daughter, if she had one, Kathleen.

But now Kate had taken herself to the third floor of the house, she'd withdrawn in a manner no one could miss, she was sleeping in one of the heavy brass beds in the big room at the top. She would not be touched. While Grace's body even now acted on her nerves as a mute plea, Kate's, with its new breasts and long ungainly arms and legs, signaled a refusal, a bleak warning that if anyone had any ideas of approaching her, she was there to set them straight, she was not to be trifled with. In the last months she'd watched in Kate's eyes what she'd taken to be worry turn to fear, and fear to a kind of scraped anguish kept well hidden behind a veil of boredom. She'd always known Kate to be shy, as she herself had been as a young person, known that like many shy people she was given to self-dramatizing gestures, flinging herself into extreme attitudes because she didn't believe she could make herself felt in any other manner. Yes, she recognized all this in Kate because for a long time she herself had been able to write or speak only by way of exclamation, statements of exaggerated feeling, especially—as she had come to realize—on those occasions when she wanted to hide something from herself or from someone else or when she wasn't entirely sure what in fact she did feel, one way or another.

She'd been floating in a drugged sleep one day, bobbing somewhere between fevers and chills, when she'd known even in that far place where she was that it was time for her to open her eyes—then, exactly then—and with a supreme effort she'd roused herself to find Kate standing not far from the bed, dark brows drawn fiercely together, green eyes glowering. The hands hanging at her sides were clenched into tight fists, her hair was hanging dankly on either side of her face as if she hadn't combed it in days. With a start she realized that her own hair must be soaking wet, clinging to her scalp, and that Kate was looking at someone she could no longer claim as her mother, someone in whom there was nothing left to recognize. What force in the universe, she would be thinking, had taken this mother of hers and turned her into this creature, this fright, this thing nailed to a bed, hair stuck in dark wet strands along a naked skull. In that instant, like a drowning person making one last effort, she'd invoked whatever her wretched body had learned of suffering—the glands searing her throat, the blood plowing diseased through vein and artery, the sluggish thump, thump of her heart—and thrown into her eyes everything Kate might ever have known her by: every story, every lullaby, every endearment and riddle and joke, every explosion of anger, every scolding, every injustice and oversight, every embrace, every nonsense word, every neglect, every abandonment to desolation, every disappearance by day or by night, every absence, short or prolonged: had thrown into her eyes the words she couldn't speak: Oh here I am, Tatie, here, do not forget, this is where I am, here, here where you see me now, in this bed, in this hour. I am filling the house with the one you remember. And then her strength had deserted her, she could do no more, and she'd sunk back and back into waters far deeper than the ones from which she'd risen.

Already that day seemed to her only one more that had disappeared like a wave folding back into the ocean, one more that had swelled and subsided and slid into the rising surge of the next, perhaps into that day—or had that other come before?—when she'd given Kate the ivory knife with the elephants walking along the blade, the one her mother had removed from its wrappings still another day during that ruinous time soon after the telegram when the letters and bundles were still arriving. She and her mother had been sitting together after breakfast with the cups still on the table. The post had come and they'd recognized his handwriting at once, knew the package by the stamps and by the clumsy wrappings, and her mother had taken it in her hands and turning to her—fingers busy with the knot they were both exquisitely aware he'd tied himself—had said to her in a moment of rare self-disclosure, that right here is where she knew she belonged, right here in the place where she was, that this was the life that had been given her, the one marked with her name. Or perhaps it was another day entirely her mother had confided in her, but she clearly remembered that as she'd listened to her mother's words she'd thought how in the book of Job God had spoken out of the whirlwind, something like that, and how she'd seen a picture once of an immense crouching God above with a hand struck down from on high, pointing.

Recently she'd begun to feel something of the same, that this is where she belonged, here in this house where her own suffering had been great, where Willie and she had once hoped to find peace—setting out their poor pathetic props, table and beds and chairs—and where now she was able to admit to herself she'd known more anguish than refuge. The places where you've been in pain, she thought, become dear to you, like those in which you've been happy, and for the same reason: you've left parts of yourself in them, distillations of your own burning days that one by one have made up what you call your life. That precious ore, that quick-running drop of mercury. Even now all through these heavy nights the crickets were trilling wildly in the grass and trees, the leaves were casting their dark shadows. Far overhead the Swan was flying full tilt across a summer sky. The house in which she breathed lay beneath its dispensation, the house of tonight with all those sleeping in it as well as the house of years to come when others would lie down in its rooms.

When she was dragged beneath a wave of pain, when she was rolled and tumbled and left gasping for air, she thought of Rob and wondered once again if his life had passed before him the way they said it did before a drowning man. If he'd remembered those nights when they were little and had been allowed to stay up when a steamer was in and there was dancing in the park of the hotel, how they'd watch the sun drop down into the sea, and then when it was dark the band would strike up and they'd be wild with joy, the trees bright with Japanese lanterns and the people wandering beneath them, and then the moon would come up, so that the royal palm trees cast long dark shadows and they'd run in and out between the shadows, hiding from each other, dancing in the grass, agog, the scent of jasmine everywhere, and then at last the door of their cottage would open and their mother and father would come down the path, their father in his white uniform and their young mother in a dress with a low neck, wearing her coral beads, her hand on his arm, and then as they walked toward them, beaming, it seemed as if everything were beginning, the music, the moon, the night and themselves in it, all at the very brink.

Wind of Wild Air

I

The Color of the Grave is Green –
The Outer Grave – I mean –

I was not in the house at the time. But I'd been with Kate only an hour or
two before, and leaving to return to the city that night I'd observed the
dormers casting black triangles on the pale slate roof, an upsweep of leaves.
Because that's the way I pictured it a little after midnight when Bert called:
the November night, the trees moving in a strong wind, the moon flying
through a sky blown wide open. The next day would bring rain.

There was a wake, and then a funeral Mass in the church where St.
Catherine stood resting her hand lightly on a wheel. Afterwards we
drove up to Ilion and high on Oak Hill buried Kate at Deirdre's feet.
We threw dirt on her coffin, heard the words pronounced: "Grant that
we may not anguish in fruitless and unavailing grief, nor sorrow as those
who have no hope."

The others were all there in a place apart: Grace and Deirdre and
Willie. And of course Mary. A large Celtic cross engraved with a single
word, CONROY, marked the spot. Tiny cones were scattered at its base,
fruit of twin white hemlocks standing nearby, spindly tops distinct, lower
branches mingling in dense confusion. As for the longer-gone, they were
farther down the hill, against the side of the woods. We found older Celtic
crosses, one marked CARMODY and not far from it another, CONROY;
beneath them, following no particular design, small blocks of stones stood
in the grass, each engraved with worn initials, mostly illegible now. So

although at one time the town of Ilion could have given an exact account, it wasn't easy for us to tell whose bones lay where: Bridgit Fitzmaurice McDonough, Mary McDonough Conroy, Michael Conroy. Michael Carmody, Alice Quinn Carmody. Up and down the hill, more crosses marked with family names: Reardon, Powers, Daly, all those whose carts and carriages had once teetered up the steep winding path to see a body into the ground and afterwards—by way of remembrance or consolation or merely hopeless conviviality—raised a glass or two.

That's where we left Kate: Bert and Maddie and Charlie and I, our spouses, our children. Clouds scuttled across an immense silver sky and, coming and going, on the far side of the valley, on distant hills, gleams of light. From below, we heard the wail of a train making its slow progress along the Mohawk, the same river that over millennia had cut a path into the earth.

A week or so later the ground would have been frozen and burial impossible, Kate's body gone into a vault until spring.

—And the prayer said as Kate's coffin was lowered into the earth: "Grant that we may not anguish in fruitless and unavailing grief, nor sorrow as those who have no hope." Were these words you needed to hear? Were you despairing on that high hill?

I was not, and you'll see why after I've told the story of Kate's dying. It was only later, in the months following her death, that fear took hold.

—I remember your saying that although you'd imagined you'd forgiven Kate at the time of her death, this was not entirely the case?

I thought I'd forgiven her, yes. For swaddling our childhoods in silence. For erasing Deirdre from memory. Yet after her death I discovered I could not forgive her for something altogether unanticipated. I could not forgive her removal from the house. Because with her own translation into spirit the ghosts had moved in with a vengeance. And yet, despite my exposure after Kate's death to the terrors of the unknown, to the drop sheer and clean, I believe Kate had tried to prepare me. In asking me to read aloud words Deirdre had addressed to her when she was a child, words meant to console, she'd not only allowed me to stand in Deirdre's place, she'd opened to me her own vital store.

—And so it happened at last, what you once said you wanted above all else? That Kate take in both you and Deirdre in one sweep?

By way of answer I must tell the story of Kate's death. The story of the hidden letters.

II

Alone and in a Circumstance
Reluctant to be told

In the weeks before Kate's departure that windy night in November, there wasn't much to distinguish one day from another. Very gradually Kate was disappearing from the house along with the late yellow roses in the front hall, the rhododendron branches on the piano, the orange pits in the kitchen laid out on damp paper towels to encourage shoots. Bert had neatly piled the seed catalogues she'd received on her desk beside the ivory letter-cutter with the elephants lumbering along one edge.

During those days Kate was nailed to one spot, precisely to Deirdre's dying spot, in the room with the mirrors and windows. I'd arrive in the afternoon carrying groceries, make preparations for the dinner Bert and I would eat later on, sit with Kate as she lay in her bed. Bert would leave the house to take a long walk, return to sit by John Carmody's radiator, read. And invariably call me from Kate's room to observe the last of the sun-drenched tops of the yellow tulip trees. Because day after day the weather had been fine and most of the leaves were still on the trees, waiting for a heavy rain to bring them down. Charlie and Maddie and I came and went but seldom at the same time, trying as we could to provide company for Bert or to fill in for the hospice people; there was one nurse, Eileen Gallagher, from County Galway, who came to the house daily.

Kate was dying of a duodenal obstruction that was almost complete: you could say she was dying of starvation. Pain was a matter of course but she protested that morphine clouded her mind; she preferred not to take it, or only very sparingly.

So what did we do for her? We prepared food she couldn't eat. Cared for her body as if it had been the pearl of great price. Anointed her feet with lotion, combed her hair, massaged her neck and back. Sometimes when I was kissing her on the temple, the butterfly flutter with which she used to say good-night to us when we were little, I had the reeling sense of standing in place of that other who'd first anointed her infant limbs, who'd lifted her limp body to one shoulder when she wailed in the night.

Bert, who would be ninety on November 13, labored up the stairs and down, responding to Kate's call. He opened the door of the house to visitors. He sat in the room next to hers and read the Psalms, recited them to himself. And because he was now quite deaf and could no longer gauge the carrying sound of his own voice, Kate lying in the next room was often roused by his recitations, heartfelt, lugubrious: "How long, O Lord, will you hide your face from me? How long?"

Kate died five days after his birthday. You can imagine that everyone said she'd hung on for that. But it's true Kate's thoughts were of him at the end. One afternoon in September about two months before Kate died, Maddie and I sat with her on the screened porch, planning a party. "Lamb with mint sauce," Kate said, "he likes that. A cake, of course. Champagne. Myself, I wouldn't care about any of it, but he does. It must happen," she said, and looked from one of us to the other. It was a warm still day and squirrels were shaking the green branches of the hickory tree on the other side of the screen. I recall the clatter and roll of nuts on the roof, crickets thrumming. And on a slightly higher note a single one shrilling on, off: discordant, disturbing.

It wasn't long afterwards that Kate retired to her room to die. By October, we were already exhausted, running up to the third floor to root out some forgotten blanket, then back down a few minutes later to the kitchen and up again by the back stairs with an ice cube in the frantic hope that—wrapped in a washcloth and held to her mouth—it would relieve Kate's thirst, her terrible ravening thirst.

Yet each day had its own secret drama, its aftermath of dreams. One afternoon I'd gone down into the cellar to retrieve a wooden tray, into the inner storeroom where all the old things were kept: cast-offs as well as retired things of value. The door of the storeroom could be opened only from the outside by means of a special key that hung from a nail in the hall closet. The door was very heavy and the key difficult to turn. Standing outside this inner room in the half-light, trying to fit the key in the lock, I pictured all the lost and forgotten things looming within: a toy sailboat constructed once by Charlie with the help of Bert; a standing armoire containing flat silver that had belonged to Mary Ethridge; Maddie's old dressing table with the swinging oval mirror; fine-spun crystal oyster goblets, never used in our time; a round wicker table that appeared elsewhere only in fading photos of Grace and Kate as children taking tea on the grass; a Union flag from the time of the Civil War folded carefully in tissue paper; children's kimonos and little Japanese shoes, built up on stilts; a white cake plate with roses at the center that turned to the tune of "Happy Birthday."

But the point is that standing in front of the door of the storeroom I'd reached up to pull on the light and my hand had closed over a skate key hanging there at the end of a string. As with so much else in the house I had no idea when it first came to be where it was. Maybe it had once belonged to Maddie or to me who both used to roller skate on fall afternoons, keys hanging from our necks on white strings, just as on rainy days we'd played hopscotch on the smooth cement cellar floor where I was standing, grains of chalk even now ground into the crevices.

Or it may be that the key first belonged to Kate, may have entered the house with the skates given to her on that desolating tenth birthday.

That night I was visited by a dream: I'm in the house, at the top of the cellar stairs, standing behind the door that opens into the kitchen. But the door I'm facing is not the ordinary kitchen door. No, it's the heavy locked door to the storeroom that can be opened only from the other side. I'm standing in the dark and calling to Kate at the top of my lungs to come and let me out, to come and turn the key. But how will she be able to hear? How will she know I'm locked in? Because the horror is that even through the heavy door I can make out the unceasing din of the house, the to and fro, the clamor of Maddie and Charlie fighting in the kitchen, the phone ringing, Kate's own steps rapidly crossing in front of the door to greet Bert who is arriving home from work, the rattle of pots on the stove, the rain falling on the slates of the roof, the stairs creaking. And as I cry out more and more desperately from behind the locked door, yelling now, sobbing, I know with cold certainty that Kate will not hear me, the noise is far too great, my cries are for nothing.

Waking in terror, staring into the dark, I listen for a while to the pounding of my heart, to the clamor that for a time refuses to be stilled. For it seems to me—suspended there between waking and sleep—that I continue to hear people coming and going in the house: it is Willie now who is returning from work, the roar of fire in his ears, it is Deirdre who is crossing the floor to greet him. Kate and Grace are fighting in the hall with the grandfather clock looming over them, old John Carmody is passing by the Buddha, lamenting his lost loves, his lost lives. All the sounds of the house can be heard at once: the lonely knocking of radiators on a winter afternoon, the clatter of children's shoes on the back stairs, voices round the piano raised in "The Wearing of the Green," the suppressed sighs of Deirdre as she descends the stairs to the dining room, Willie's voice, irritated, chagrined, tender. And strains, too, heard only by dreamers lying in their beds: fiddles scraping as Michael Conroy dances on his little feet, the groans of freed slaves on the Mississippi levee as the boat passes them by, Rob crying when his father bends to pick him up the night of the return from China, Mary Ethridge singing the infant Deirdre to sleep:

Low, low, breathe and blow,
Wind of the western sea!

At first there are only sighs and lamentations, groans and clamor, lullabies and song. And then, as circles of sound spread and spread, each disappearing into the one that came before, a prayer: Oh to be released from this house! To be released! But how is the door to be unlocked? Who is to turn the key?

I've seen a Dying Eye
Run round and round a Room

Kate had become inexpressibly dear during those days of her dying. I confess she drew me like a lover, the scent of her skin, her eyes with their sudden lights, the bones I numbered with my fingers one by one. All those years of waiting, all for this, that I might lie beside her on Bert's bed in the silence of an October afternoon. I'd brought her a yellow hickory leaf, I remember; she'd held it to her cracked lips. "How it holds the wet," she'd said. Then: "Beautiful, isn't it," looking around, her huge green eyes open wide and beaming like searchlights first on one spot in the room, then another.

She spoke slowly, her parched mouth moving carefully. The trees were everywhere, the mirrors and windows turning the room into a strange underwater place of green light and gold. From the depths of the glass knob on the door, a silver gleam. A few weeks earlier I'd said to Kate that the room was like the bottom of the sea, green shafts of light streaming in from every side. But now all that was changing. The sun was throwing back and forth from window to mirror and back out again the bright leaves, filling the room with golden hickory light.

"She lay here, too," Kate said. "She too must have looked at all this."

Kate's words seemed to be making their way to me across a great distance, as if the sounds didn't cohere in any way I could make sense of. I was drowsily pondering the sea's floor—the reeds with rays of green light trembling through, little fish darting between, was lulled by the swaying reeds, the wily minnows—was falling through to a place where I had nothing more to fear, when I clutched and jolted awake: Deirdre.

I said nothing, waiting as I had for so long to see if she would say more. The long rays of the late sun were lighting up the deep red tones of Kate's mahogany dresser. Then, in the silent hum of the afternoon, I slowly became aware of a bright tangle of shadows flickering on the wall in a patch of sun.

I remembered that in spring the faintest play moved lightly over the face of the house, dark shapes flickering across the smooth surface. And just behind them, as if more distantly present—now distinct, now lost in the others—a mere suggestion of light and dark, a shimmer, as if something were leaving a mark not traceable to leaf or branch.

The distance that the dead have gone

It wasn't long after—on a hushed October afternoon, sunlit, breathlessly still—that Bert met me at the door, eager to set out on his walk. Kate had had a hard night and he'd just given her a Valium. I watched him make his way slowly down the steps and then pulled shut the shuddering door, felt at once closed in, chilled. How lonely the house had always seemed in the changing days of autumn, how contracted.

A terrible thirst was ravaging Kate. Soon she began to moan, at first very low, then sharply, her face crumbling.

"Wait!" I said, and in a panic ran downstairs and heated milk in a little pan, wanting only to escape a suffering I knew I could do nothing about, watching the blue flame in a daze of helplessness; then I rushed upstairs as if the milk had been morphine and would, entering her bloodstream, immediately tamp the pain. With a spoon I fed it to her drop by drop, whispering: it will pass, it will pass. Because sometimes the pain did pass as abruptly as it had begun.

Kate was lying on her back, face drawn, concentrating, her great green bat eyes revolving from spot to spot in their casings of bone. They moved in my direction and for a long moment settled on my face.

"The letters," she said finally, moving her lips very slightly.

At first I could think only of the alphabet, shapes floating before my eyes, an *A*, a *B*, a *C*. Or *Q* as the fat back of a cat, its tail curling behind. The letters when they were pictures of themselves, when they were seen only in silhouette against a light that quavered and shook. Or otherwise as the negative of a photograph, silvery figures staring out from dark frames, trees on a misty winter night rising like white candles in the swirling dark.

I remembered that a few weeks before when Kate and I had talked of what she called "afterward," she'd said, "No, not people, not as we've known them, but light; I think we'll be fused with light." And now, gasping a little, stopping and starting, holding my eyes: "The sitting room closet."

In an instant I was standing in front of the door of the closet, staring at a likeness in the mirror that might have been my own if I'd looked in time. Inside, Kate's winter clothes were hanging from a rod, coats and jackets and skirts that had never that autumn been taken out and aired, hanging there holding the shape of her elbows and knees. I gathered them in my arms, buried my face in them to inhale her scent, just as when I was a child I'd crept into this closet to hide from the sounds of the house, the creak of stairs, the ringing of clocks, had hidden here to find my way to the secret sources of comfort and love, sliding to the floor and sitting in the dark, at last resting my head on a black lacquer box that sat squarely in one deep corner, sometimes falling asleep and waking in a flood of peace. So now I knew where to look for it, the lacquer box with the mother of pearl figures playing across it. And guided not by anything as specific as memory but rather by instinct or need brought it to Kate as she lay there crying in pain.

I lifted the lid that fit tightly over the box and envelopes spilled out, fell on the floor and over the blanket that covered Kate, inked letters flying across each envelope: black letters with masts of their own, a fleet of ships in full sail. When they'd stilled—when they'd composed themselves sedately into words—I saw that the name written on the first envelope I picked up was Kate's, and the address of course 122 Loring Avenue. A two-penny red stamp was fixed in one corner, a white head of George Washington on a field of red.

At the top of the page the date had been written in the same firm hand: *April 9th, 1917.* And across the back flap of the envelope the address: *151 East 57th Street.*

Kate was eagerly watching me. I opened the envelope and drew out a folded page. In a voice I didn't recognize I read the words written on it:

My darling Tatie,

How I would fly to you if I could! In three days' time you will be ten years old and I will think of you when I wake in the morning and when I go to sleep at night. I have a plan and wonder if you will like it. At noon, when the clock in the hall is striking twelve, you in our house in Pelham must look out a window and I here in New York City will do the same and each of us will find a shadow. In my shadow I will look for you, and in your shadow you will know that I am very near.

I hope to be home soon, Tatie. Keep this letter and reread it. Remember that I am near and full of love for you.

Deedy

Her mouth a little open, Kate was moaning softly: Ahh, ahh. Her green

286

eyes, looking out over the edge of the blanket, were bright, a child's eyes.

The next letter I plucked from the blanket had been sent from East 57th Street as well and dated a few days earlier than the other: April 5, 1917. But I had to look carefully because the numbers at the top were partially obscured by what seemed to be spidery threads that had been fastened to the paper with a pin now black with rust.

My dearest Tatie,

You will see that I have not parted with the violets that we gathered only hours before I left home a few days ago. I have kept them by my side in a glass and every time I look at them I think of you. Do you recall how we went outside together to see if we could find any in that spot beneath the tulip tree?

Oh, Tatie, these violets would surely write the story of themselves, if they could. The story would begin with their blooming one April morning and then finding themselves on a train going to a very large city. And then they would have to continue their story to say how every day someone wakes up in a bed next to the table on which they sit in a jar of water and touches them lovingly.

Your ever devoted, Deedy

One of the stems fell into my lap, a thread, a bit of dust, nothing you would look at twice if by some remote chance you happened to notice it lying on the floor.

Folding the notepaper and returning it to its envelope I saw that Kate's eyes were closing so I quickly opened another, this one undated. Her hands, which had been holding onto the edge of the sheet, flexed and held, flexed and held. She was falling asleep.

Darling Tatie,

I am glad to hear you are knitting stockings for some poor soldier. There is much suffering in the world and doing something for someone else reminds us we are not alone. You write that you feel sad at school. You say you are often lonely and wish to return home. How well I understand you, perhaps better than anyone on earth. It seems only the other day that I cried and cried after leaving Washington on the train for a visit with my cousins in New York. I think I was about your age at the time. My home seemed inexpressibly dear, and I mourned it as if I might never see it again.

Oh Tatie, there is no disguising the fact that during these past months I have not been strong. It grieves me that when you and Grace return from school on the weekends, I am not always able to keep you company. How I wish to be to you a companion and friend! As you leave on Sunday evenings I often wonder if I will be able to wait patiently for your return. So you see we are the same, you at school and I here in our house in Pelham, longing for Friday.

Sometimes when I am opening one of your letters with the elephant knife that my beloved brother Rob sent from the Pacific, a memory returns of a spring afternoon when he and I went rowing on the Potomac. We found ourselves in a rowboat watching the trees trail their branches into the river as we passed. Rob was rowing and I was doing nothing at all, simply watching the smooth flow of the river, the way it carried us along. And then suddenly, Tatie, I knew what it was to see everything all at once. The day leapt out of its canvas, so to speak, and I saw it whole.

So I pray that you will find an overflow of joy someday when you least expect it.

Devotedly, Deedy

III

Not seeing, still we know –
Not knowing, guess –

Leaving the house that night, I turned to see—if not the low moon itself, just visible between the trunks of the tulip trees—at least the clarification of light, the sheen, on the slate shingles of the roof. Now, watching the Swan disappear into the dark bank of trees at my back, I was aware some new knowledge was waiting. During my adult life I'd been assailed by a silent shamed pity for Kate much more terrible than the old furies it had long ago replaced. Silent because I'd tried to hide from her my belief that she'd been pitifully deprived of all chance of another house, of another life, of other moons in other windows. And shamed because it seemed a betrayal, this furtive belief that while my life had allowed me to roam and enjoy, hers had condemned her to the same eternal spot.

Now, standing there in the grass, I saw that pitying Kate had been no more than a disguised form of judging her life and finding it lacking. Of refusing forgiveness, holding onto my grudges. Of keeping her fixed in place. But most of all it had been a way of ensuring my place in the locked room in the cellar.

Because hadn't the life I'd so long at once pitied and blamed Kate for allowing to slip through her fingers existed most of all as a figment of my imagination? A fantasy that allowed me to escape knowledge of my own? To obscure old regrets I preferred not to think about?

It occurred to me then that, in asking for the letters, Kate may have wanted me to know that, whatever I might think of the sorrows of her life, her passage on earth had had its own consuming force: like the orange seeds breaking open, like Deirdre's love spelled out in black and white, or for that matter like the pond in winter that through no agency of its own—no choice or high intention but simply by enduring—becomes the mirror held up to the winter sun.

Love – is that later Thing than Death
More previous – than Life –

Whether or not it was "seemly," as Bert put it, to have a birthday party in a house where death was hovering, we decided to go ahead with it in deference to Kate's declared wishes. I remember a couple of days before, thinking: she won't last, her breathing has changed. I lay next to her on the bed while Bert read in the sitting room and, putting my head beside hers, tried to adjust my breathing to her own. She took a single breath for every two of mine. I'd think: now she's exhaled for the last time, thank God it's over. But after a long pause, always, there'd be a sudden deep inhalation. I looked at the window and saw, blazoned by the afternoon light, struck into silver, Kate's own initials. And the date: November 18, 1918.

I decided to stay overnight, went to sleep in my old bedroom and fell asleep after eleven only to be woken by the clock in the hall striking twelve. Why only one chime, I wondered, becoming aware in the quiet house of the silence surrounding it. And so realized Bert must have given up fitting the key to its peg in the many clocks, winding up the springs and coils that drove the hands, both minute and second, was tending only to John Carmody's nautical clock, the one hung with cylindrical pendulums weighted with mercury to ensure the exact measurement of time against the roll and pitch of a ship. I heard it strike every half hour until four, and then at last was visited by the thought that finally allowed me to sleep: but this is the room in which he died, John Carmody, this is the room where on his own deathbed he called out, *Sweet Jesus, help me!*

When I woke a couple of hours later, I wasn't sure for a moment where I was. Then, slowly, I recalled waking as a child in this room on a summer's morning, an airiness filling the house, the windows wide open with screens in them, the trees cool and green on every side, the hour full of promise and beginnings. Kate might be opening the doors of the porch on a new day, Bert setting off for the station in a light suit, and getting out of bed we knew that nothing would be required of us, we could go barefoot all day long if we liked, could spend hours in the wicker rocking chair reading, the rhododendrons pressing at the screens, play Monopoly on the floor of the porch or poker using the red, white, and blue chips kept in a tin box. Go for a swim in the Sound during the long hours of the afternoon. Sit on the black rocks and watch the buoys slip about in the lapping waters, the tide move swiftly up the wooden pilings of the boathouse, catch sight in the distance of the lighthouse on Executioner's Island or the old Iselin house abandoned now in a field of weeds.

But most of all in the nighttime step barefoot in the grass, catching fireflies or, playing hide and seek, huddle behind a tree waiting to be caught, feet in the loamy soil where violets bloomed in April, the night when we knew ourselves strangers to the house, knew that our true birthright lay not in the rooms inside with their lights and beds and books but outside with the pounding cicadas, the leaves holding still in the dark, the little white mushrooms that had sprung up after last night's rain, the huge moon rising low in the trees.

Then something would happen in that day of dawns and beginnings, something to spoil it, a fight break out between Maddie and me, or Charlie raise a howl of defeat and lose his temper because he'd read in the paper lying on his stomach in the front hall that the Yankees had lost the night before, or the sky that had seemed so bright would inexplicably cloud over when we'd been counting on going to the Sound that afternoon to swim. Or—most terribly—Kate pouring milk onto the cornflakes would suddenly seem not so young as she had the day before, there was a new wrinkle in her forehead or in her brown hair a single strand of gray. Then a shadow fell over everything, the cicadas turned menacing, the trees oppressive, and there—into the house that had seemed wide open to breezes and idleness a moment before—entered the smell of fear.

Waking in the morning, I thought here is the death I'd always thought I wouldn't have the strength to survive. And perhaps because I'd dreaded its approach for so long and because now the moment I'd feared above all others had arrived and Kate was more intimately present to me than at any point in my life, I got up and joyfully went in to see her.

I found that during the night Kate had crossed over into a place where she was in constant distress. Despite Eileen's presence it had become almost impossible to leave her alone. I didn't return to the city till late afternoon. Maddie arrived, carrying the leg of lamb we planned to cook for Bert's birthday party the next day, a Sunday, and after going upstairs to see Kate returned to the kitchen where we wept in each other's arms. For hours afterwards we ran up and down the stairs, chopping garlic, peeling potatoes, putting extra leaves in the table, cutting the last yellow roses to arrange here and there. But mostly we were upstairs with Kate, who when she lapsed into sleep for a moment or two was tugged back, moaning. Oh. Oh. She would wake in alarm, eyes staring.

The next day, the birthday, was rainy and the leaves were coming down in clumps. I remember that because, sweeping for the guests a path that had disappeared beneath a mass of clotted leaves, I watched them falling fast from the highest branches of the hickory, flying black specks against a white sky. Sometimes a hand, a swirling stem with five leaves, rushed by before it hit the ground. Charlie and Maddie and I had arrived with our assorted families about noon. We put the lamb in the oven, the champagne in the refrigerator, put a cloth on the table, set out Willie's silver candlesticks. About three o'clock the guests came up the walk, cousins, grandchildren, two sisters of Bert, two brothers, the priest who'd anointed Kate a few weeks before.

A half hour later the rainy afternoon was already inclining toward dark. In Kate's room we delayed turning on the light from one moment to the next and then forgot about it altogether. We could see her face: nothing along the bone, the mouth no longer dry and flaking, but drawing back on itself, shiny and neat. The pupils of her eyes were dilated, the black overwhelming the green. And one eye veered off to the side, as if her eyes were beaming out to take in a wider scope. They raked past our faces, unseeing.

We heard the subdued voices downstairs in the hall, the clink of ice, the sudden involuntary laugh. Charlie, who had been moving restlessly all over the house, moving in and out of Kate's bedroom, up and down the stairs, put his head in at the door and withdrew it. Soon afterwards, one of my daughters came into the room and stood at the foot of the bed. The seconds ticked by, and Kate was so still it was possible to imagine we'd already witnessed her end when suddenly her whole body gathered and prepared to draw another breath. We all breathed with her, a single long laboring inhalation. And then out again. Ooom.

Leaving the room, I saw someone had turned on the light in the hall, the light dressed in the milky skirt and top hat; and there beside it in an oval frame Deirdre sat serenely with a sleeping infant in each arm, Kate in her little white-buttoned boots craning her neck to see. I went down the back stairs—bypassing the guests—and into the kitchen that was crowded with grandchildren moving the dinner along. It was this, I'd imagined, I'd come down to check on, the progress of food to table. But no, in the back of my mind all along had been an errand—parsley to soften the sight of the stricken lamb on its platter—that took me out the back door and down the steps into Kate's kitchen garden. The rain had stopped but the gutters were dripping, and the warm November night smelled rankly of molding leaves. A vapor was rising from the earth, from the ground on which the house sat, slipping up the trunks of the damp black trees. The garden was buried in leaves, but picking them off in wet matted clumps I found that hidden beneath—green and fresh and live—the parsley was waiting. For you, Kate, I thought, cutting the stems long, inhaling the dusk, the rain, the black wet earth that was still soft enough to turn in my hand.

Kate's room was dark now and it took a minute to see who was there: Maddie on one side of the bed, my daughter on the other, tightly holding Kate's hand, and there in a corner, standing quietly, one of Charlie's sons. His face was composed, impassive, even, but suddenly, as if seized involuntarily, his large shoulders heaved.

Kate's eyes were wide and staring. She lay still for what seemed an unendurable moment, and then once again gathered her strength, opened her mouth for a breath. We opened our own mouths and breathed in with her, a communal gasp.

The door cracked open, a sliver of light from the hall lay across Kate's bed, the tick-tock of the nautical clock resounded in the silent room. The priest from St. Catherine's appeared in the door, closed it behind him. When he'd arrived a few weeks earlier to give Kate the last sacrament, he had, entering, pronounced the prescribed words: "Peace to this house." To which we'd replied: "And to all who dwell therein." Now he said nothing. He stood motionless beside Kate's bed and soon enough had joined our chorus. Hot, alive, intimate, our breathing filled the room. In the long silent wait that followed each exhalation, the clock ticked on. Then, with a preliminary wheeze—like Kate's scraping at the bottom of her lungs for air—it struck the half hour.

Downstairs everyone was moving through the front hall into the dining room—we could hear the subdued hum, someone calling from the kitchen—could picture the long table shrouded in white, candles blazing, Bert standing at one end sinking the long fork into the leg of lamb, carving slices, placing choice bits, a sprig of parsley, on each plate, could picture the glistening green jelly in its dish going round, the mint sauce in its silver boat, the decanters of wine on the sideboard. Could see them sitting at last round the table, Bert in his chair where Willie once had sat and there at the opposite end—Kate's place until two months ago and Deirdre's before her—a chair left empty until the very last because no one wanted to sit in it tonight. Could anticipate all the rest, the cake carried in on a burst of song but without the customary ripple of piano, the splash of champagne in the glasses, the discreet toasts, the good-byes at last, the drift of guests away from the house and into the current of their lives apart.

But for now, the dinner only beginning, we were sealed off from all that, the scattered conversation, the vague uncertainties of polite exchange. We were safe in this dark room with Kate. We need not say anything at all. As the clatter below subsided into the hush that accompanies the business of eating, the priest bent low over Kate's bed, over her head, and pronounced slowly, distinctly, the words we didn't know we were waiting to hear: "You are surrounded by love in this house," he said. "Surrounded."

Kate, who hadn't seemed to have strength to draw breath, raised her arm and with the force of never-again pulled his head down close to her own. Into his ear, the words we barely caught: "I bless them. Every one."

IV

Out of sight? What of that?

One Sunday afternoon about a week or more before Bert's party, Kate was sleeping when Martin and I stopped at the house with Wang Hai Xiao, a friend visiting from Shanghai. His eyes fell on the Buddha as we walked into the living room and I explained to him that my great-grandfather had traveled to Asia. We lifted the Buddha from his place, opened the lid of the box, then the inner metal one, and removed the papers. "Made from cotton," he said, his long fingers carefully unfolding them. And could he read what was written there? At first he hadn't been sure, the system of writing was not quite the one used today; he could see it was a product of the Ching dynasty when syntax, idiom, colloquialisms would have been somewhat different. But he could readily make out that he was holding in his hands the *Shanghai Gazette* for May 25, 1876, a Thursday. And then, little by little, he managed to decipher the news of that day:

A public suit has been filed against a prostitute charged with purchasing small girls: Miss Chang, who has denied the charges, was said to have purchased Mr. Wang's youngest daughter.

Rumors are going round of a public dispute between China and Britain.

A government official has been put in charge of helping local people stop a flooding river. The people prayed that God would help them and their prayer succeeded in stopping the flood. They are now building a temple to the River God to give thanks.

People have been cutting off their pigtails, the pigtail that is the symbol of loyalty to the emperor, and have been threatened by the police with death. Some dishonest merchants are making money by offering magic potions that if swallowed would preserve life but such remedy is clearly ridiculous.

At 9 o'clock tonight at the Liberty Theatre "The Oxhead Mountain," a traditional opera set 2000 years ago that tells the story of the monkey king, will be performed.

Next Wednesday, May 31st at sunrise, a boat will leave by way of the East China Sea for Japan, from whence another boat will take all passengers to San Francisco.

The Mitsubishi Co. offers transportation services: you may rent a four-wheel car or a car together with a horse.

And notices of teahouses, a hospital equipped to help people stop smoking opium, auctions, a discount sale of old maps of Shanghai, a monthly paper for children, new medicine for hair loss, for coughing, a service by which one's name is inscribed on a personal seal. And the Remington Works, a factory located in the state of New York that specializes in making guns, armories, etc. advised any army officer interested to contact the office at 288 Broadway, New York City.

<h1 style="text-align:center">V</h1>

My period had come for Prayer –
No other Art – would do –

Yes, Kate died on the fifth day after Bert's birthday party, on Friday, the eighteenth. Indeed, at the same hour Deirdre had died, a few minutes after midnight. On the sixteenth, the doctor who'd come to give her a shot of morphine said she wouldn't make it through the night, her pulse had quickened. All day she hadn't responded to any of us except with a slight tightening of her grip on our hands: I am here, do not forsake me, I am here with you still, I know you are with me.

But on the morning of the seventeenth there was no grip at all and her skin looked almost like marble. Even her scent had changed, the strange scent I'd been inhaling and loving, the scent of her face, the scent I'd been rushing to: all gone. No, this was the smell of death, of corruption.

I remember this because on the night of the sixteenth an Indian woman from Guyana, sent by hospice for the first time, came into the room and, looking at Kate, swept her hands up in a circle, bringing them quickly together and down, palms upright at her breast like the Buddha: "Now we must pray," she'd said.

Then looking from Kate to myself and back again: "I can see you resemble your mother." And I, staring at the skull jutting from beneath the skin, the death mask, kept still.

The wind was blowing hard on the seventeenth, the skies gray, opening suddenly to patches of blue. The trees had been stripped of all but a few tattered remnants of color. Gone, the high-banked sunny splendor of the tulips, the choked maples blazing in the afternoon. Only a few remaining leaves hung from branch and vine, sun pouring through: blood-red ivy, shining russet oak, the tulip's sheeted gold. Like traces of another world, like silent appeals to remember it.

Charlie and I spent the last afternoon with Kate, Bert having set out on a long walk by the Sound. Charlie wandered between Kate's room and the sitting room; I—almost falling asleep—sat on a chair beside Kate and read aloud from the green cloth-covered prayer book she kept in a drawer beside her bed: the seven penitential Psalms, the long litanies of saints, the Latin prayers I remembered from my childhood: the *Memorare*, the *Salve Regina, Veni Creator Spiritus*—singing the ones I knew—the *Magnificat*, the *Stabat Mater*, and then finally the *Tantum Ergo*, hymn written by Aquinas and sung always on Holy Thursday when Christ entering the Garden of Gethsemane asked his friends to watch with him. I went on to read what the book called the prayers for the dying, as well as prayers for travelers in which protection was asked not only for the journey ahead but for that final one when we cross from time into eternity.

My eyes were closing over the book, I was falling into a dream of trains standing in a dark station, I was sitting aimlessly at the window of one train, my days passing like smoke, I was looking through the window at another also preparing to depart, and then—perceiving that the train across the platform was moving at last—in a moment was astonished to see a clear blue sky flashing in the window and dizzily realized it was not the other train at all but my own that had pulled out of the station; and so, beginning to sway and lose my balance, clutched awake, sat up straight in the chair.

I couldn't keep my eyes open and so stretching out on Bert's bed for a time watched the sun moving in and out from behind the clouds. Then I must have fallen deep inside the cavern of sleep because I was roused by Kate's drowning moans. She was calling urgently, insistently, but to whom? Even now: the flash from the deep, the slow sure rise to the surface, the gurgling in the throat, the wild knowledge that the waves were closing over and that this old companion the body was swiftly becoming a departing stranger and would soon be washed away.

Then Charlie was standing beside the bed—I saw him through the slits of my eyes—he was standing there, at last allowed a place, no busy sisters nearby, no father, and he repeated to her the words we had been saying day after day when there was nothing left to do for her, nothing: "We're here. We're right here with you." He hesitated, arms hanging helplessly at his sides, silently looked down at her.

Just then the patch of woven sunlight appeared on the wall behind him. In its web of shadows trembled the suggestion that it was Charlie who had spoken the last words she would hear.

After a while Bert returned from his walk and we sat drinking tea, he and Charlie and I, in the sitting room with its glinting glass doors closed on Dickens and Thackeray, its windows full of leaves making letters against the sky. And its massive chest with the little oil painting hanging above it.

Then Maddie arrived and she and I returned to Kate's room. By now—beyond the ring of light cast by the lamp near Kate's bed—shadows were rising in the corners of the room, up the long slippery mirror, and against the window that showed a last vivid thread of orange. When Eileen, who was to remain with Kate for the night, walked in we went downstairs and ate our dinner with Charlie and Bert, returning soon to Kate. We sat with her awhile and when we got up to leave each of us made the sign of the cross on her forehead with our thumb, imitating the gesture with which Kate used to say good-night to us as children. Eileen, looking on, pronounced the words we couldn't remember, had never known:

> In ainm an Athair
> Agus an Mhic
> Agus an Spioraid Naomh.

Not long afterwards we gathered our things and drove back into the city.

VI

I saw the wind within her –
I knew it blew for me –

Perhaps you'll remember that waking in the morning—after spending the night in the house, in John Carmody's death room, the one I called my own as a child—I went in to see Kate? The night I'd listened hour by hour to the striking of the nautical clock and realized the other clocks were still? When I entered the room Kate was looking out the window but soon enough the green floodlights swung round in my direction as I stood by the bed and settled on my face. And there it was, the great burning gaze of love. I didn't know what to say, where to look, and in a blind attempt to get out of the way laid my face against the bones of hers. For a moment we were silent. Then, from my own mouth, I heard the words: "I'll carry you. Always."

After a moment, very slowly, from Kate, in a thick whisper: "And I will carry you."

I was blown into confusion. What could she mean? But during the years since her death I sometimes think the world appears to be different from the one I knew, as if the unseen were slowly becoming visible. Is it for this reason I now imagine that my visit to Kate's bedside recalled her own rendezvous with the dying Deirdre? Because I have little doubt that Deirdre was present when Kate and I exchanged promises. Yes, their story may turn out to be mine as well.

—But is your story only that of the others? Will you one day read the book of your own life? Uncover its plot?

Reading Deirdre's letters aloud to the dying Kate seems to have altered some internal balance. This difference was not felt for a number of years—not until I'd encountered the ghosts more intimately—but these days it's plain: those who've gone before wait for me to fulfill their own lost moments even as my life spills into the next. For how can I forget it was Deirdre who needed me, that October afternoon, to speak the words of comfort Kate had asked for, words that Deirdre had herself written down on a piece of paper? Against every expectation my voice became the essential, the indispensable voice because it could still be heard in time.

As for reading the book of my own life, that's all still in the future. Sometimes I imagine that at the very last the burning letters in which our lives are written, letters fringed with fire, will appear before us as if on the black page of a night sky. We'll see a dazzling shower of light, a vast wheel in whose blazing compass our own story will be read as one in a cascading continuous sweep. And yet we'll be able to discern each spark as it flares and disappears: singular, outstanding.

The plot of my life is no different from John Carmody's, from anyone's: my greatest loves have been the occasions of my greatest sorrows. Yet something has changed. From the outside, my life looks as it did during those days of incapacitating fear when the towers of my city fell. Just as then, I drink my coffee in the morning with Martin, visit with my daughters. Sit at the table looking out on the trees that even now are moving toward fall.

—And during those visits with your daughters, do you have the impression that you've soothed and restored? Have you learned to listen to their stories?

I prefer now to let them speak for themselves. I know I cannot answer for them. But I clearly see my daughters' willingness to love, be loved.

Still, Deirdre's griefs stream through me. I try to reconcile myself to the possibility that there will never be a time when this is not the case.

—Have you learned to live with those griefs? And what is the change you speak of?

I have learned nothing. Yet I sometimes recognize the stranger.

—Have you any particular stranger in mind?

The stranger in myself, the one I cannot forgive. The one whose face frightens in the night. Who visits me in dreams. The one whose scourging attacks cause my earth to tremble, my house to go up in flames. Who tempts me to look out over the edge.

—And how did you come to this knowledge of the enemy within?

From old grievances addressed only very late. I know from Willie that deprivation carries with it a burden of shame, a shame bred of silence, of humiliation. A shame that is sometimes disguised by rage, a terrible turning on the self.

—Yet who are the people who have not inherited these lonely spaces, these deep pockets of deprivation?

Who indeed?

—Does this knowledge console?

It does not console. It illuminates. I believe the ancestors see my helplessness and forgive everything I can't forgive myself. After all, they know nothing of words, know only the nameless, the ringing, silence of eternity.

—But on what grounds does it rest, this belief?

On visitations that have only very gradually begun to reveal themselves to me. Do you remember the angel of the annunciation on that summer evening of the ginkgos? The dark-haired young man who swept out his hand as if bestowing the world itself? One night recently I woke with a pounding heart and knew the one I'd passed in the street had been sent by the one who'd mourned him most fiercely. Because I at last recognized the young man as Rob. Rob, who'd suffered a sea change, who'd sprung straight up from the bottom of the ocean to emerge as a creature of air and light, a visible emblem of hope.

If Deirdre's legacy is one of grief, it's also one of abundant joy. An overflow. I think now that our losses may sometimes be restored in unimaginable ways—but only when we've given up every expectation. For the present, all I can say is that joy seems a matter of sudden appearances. Rob. The daughter who waits on her doorstep, arms wide. Or the rhododendron to which Kate directs my gaze, the *rosa mundi,* on an evening in late June, sometime around the solstice. Long shafts of sunlight are slipping along the waxy dark leaves, illuminating the paler new leaves. Flowers float above, white petals dotted red, bees droning purposefully from one sticky stamen to another.

—And what of Bert, whom we last saw wandering the house alone? And what of the house itself?

Bert has disappeared into the ground. At his request, his ashes were placed in the earth just above Kate's coffin.

As for the house, it's all in the past. After Bert's disappearance from it, the house was sold, its contents distributed. Only the piano remained; none of us could fit it into our rooms and the new owners wanted it. Everything else was divided among us, children and grandchildren. Everything except the Buddha. We decided he belonged to no one, and so he moves from one of us to another, Charlie and Maddie and me, letting us know every few months, by signs we've learned to interpret, where his shadow will appear on a wall.

Throughout November, December—its having been promised for the last week in January—objects flew from the house like leaves from a tree. Closing the door one night, I promised myself a final visit when all the rooms were empty. It's the story of that visit I'm keeping for last. My plan was to return stealthily, alone, perhaps hoping to surprise the house when no one was looking.

And what of now that I can no longer walk through its door? Do I miss it? Perhaps this will tell. One recent hot night in July, I had an encounter. I was returning from visiting one of my daughters who lives in the city, returning not as usual on the subway but in a taxi—with Willie's blessing, I thought, stepping into the back seat. The driver was African, a man from Mali, and as we turned onto 120th Street with Morningside Drive lying just ahead, he said he considered this one of the most beautiful corners of the city. On these nights when the moon was rising over the park, he continued, he believed he'd arrived at the gates of paradise.

By this time we'd turned onto Morningside Drive and I'd paid him and got out. But I lingered a moment at his open window. Below, down in the park, the trees were rustling in a hot wind. "Do you hear them?" he asked. "Sometimes I imagine that sound is the sound of waves rushing up a beach. As if there were an ocean somewhere near. It is the sound of my home."

It was not until he'd driven away I remembered that Mali is in the middle of a desert. But it seemed to me, thinking again of Willie who'd directed me to this particular cab, of his mother and father, his grandparents, that the driver had been speaking for all those who'd left behind a home they could no longer reach, who everywhere recalled its voice in the stir of something they couldn't name.

Seeds of Brightness

Forever – is composed of Nows –
'Tis not a different time –

I visited the house for the last time on a day of bright sun and extreme cold, the third week in January, the day before it was to be turned over to the new owners. Getting out of the car I looked up to see the blond branches of the tulip trees reaching high above the house, pods gleaming in the sun like apple blossoms. Noticed, too, that a branch had fallen out of a tree and was leaning against the side of the house. Then I went straight up the walk, fit my key into the lock. The curtains that had covered the clear panes of the front door were gone now and I could look straight through.

I saw the newel post at the first landing on the stairs, saw it rise straight up in front of the French windows glinting in the bright morning light. Was it the novelty of looking in at the bare house from outside the door? Was it because I knew this would be the last time of all? Whatever, I was pierced by bitter regret. Why, only now, had I noticed how square and blunt it was, this post, noticed how it marked the spot where the stairs turned up again to another smaller landing from which the back stairs descended to the kitchen? But there it was, stubbornly in place, and having seen it, I knew I would suffer its loss.

Once inside I didn't seem to notice anything at all in particular. Perhaps it was that nothing now was framed in a small glass window. I looked around at the empty spaces in a sort of daze and then sat down on the piano bench, dropping my jacket on the floor. I'd brought a cookie with me shaped like a snowman, frosted white with a red scarf, buttons down the front. I unwrapped the cookie from its cellophane and as I sat there, taking a first cautious bite, looking across the top of the piano into the front hall and beyond into the stripped dining room, I heard it: a high-pitched keening that broke from beneath the boards of the house, a wail of sorrow that rose and fell like a boat lashed at sea, a fisherman's curragh lifted and tossed, or maybe like the waves themselves beating against a seawall, against the Cliffs of Moher, an ecstatic cry of grief lifting and breaking against a sheer rock face of shame and silence in a land where the children's mouths were making Os of desolation and hunger.

It seemed to be rising from beneath the boards of the house. And then—as in childbirth when I'd looked around to see where it was coming from, a sound I'd never heard—I realized that the cry was breaking from within myself. It was my own and not my own. Like everything else that happened to me while I was in the house that day, I acted not on my own agency, not as myself alone, but as one directed. It seemed I knew exactly what to do at every moment. I had only to follow a command that corresponded to my own deepest longing.

I carefully put down my cookie on the piano bench and proceeded up the stairs to the second floor and then straight up to the next and into the big room at the top. It must have been late morning, and the sun was slanting in from the east. Perhaps it was Maddie who'd placed a crucifix in the window: in any case the shadow of the cross marked a place in the long diagonal of sun spread across the parquet. I immediately lay down in the sun, one cheek flat on the floor, arms stretched straight out in either direction. I listened for the feet that had passed there but heard only the pounding of my own blood in my ear and a solitary knocking of one radiator or another from rooms all over the house. Lying in the flood of sun, I began reciting the names of all those who'd lived within these walls, summoned those nameless others who'd haunted their noonday hours. Called on those who'd entered the house as dinner guests or nurses or piano tuners or visiting children or undertakers or cooks. All those who'd washed dishes late and finally labored up to a room beneath the eaves on a sweltering night. Those who'd found joy in the house, those who'd been humiliated in it, those who'd left it behind with bitter regret. Those who between these walls had with terror or gladness known themselves on the brink of a great change. Those who'd slept soundly beneath its roof and those who'd woken to disturbing dreams, wishing for dawn.

Lying there in the sun on that day of fierce cold I felt warm. Blissfully. I remembered what Kate had said near the end, how she thought we'd be fused with light, and suddenly felt that I was being given a taste of that joy, of that place of boundless understanding. "Eye hath not seen" were the words that came to me.

I got up from the floor, then, and began walking the house, imitating the gesture that the Indian nurse from Guyana had taught me, sweeping my hands up in a circle above my head, then bringing them down together, palms upright at my breast like the Buddha. I walked into the room with bare plank floors where Nora McHugh had slept and that had later on been Charlie's when as a teenager he'd wanted to get away from the rest of the family living below. I saw his old tie rack nailed to the wall and wept for any harm, any misery, he'd endured in the house. I looked out into a sky of dazzling blue. Next I visited the bathroom where the tub standing on claws still held the captive light, the same tub where I'd been spanked by Nora for refusing to get out, observed the toilet that when I was little had been flushed by means of a chain. Then continuing to make the prayer circle I walked down the stairs into the hall on the second floor where a new bright place on the wall marked the spot from which John Carmody's portrait had been removed. Empty white bookshelves stretched below, the paint deeply cracked, and on one of them quivered a single patch of rainbow light. But from where did it come? At the end of the hall, the sun was streaming in due south, was hitting the glass knob of a door and settling on a shelf. Could it be, then, that every sunny January morning a patch of color had played on the backs of Willie's books? A rainbow, unseen by us all, muted and swallowed by the paper covers?

I walked then into the room with the sunny window, Bert and Kate's room that had once been Willie and Deirdre's. Despite the strip of brilliant sunlight on the bare floor, how ordinary, how faded everything looked! It had all been a matter of mirrors, of deep silver pools reflecting light back and forth, of shimmering surfaces, of cut-crystal scent bottles scattering rainbow spots on ceiling and wall. I made the prayer circle slowly, pronouncing out loud the date etched by Kate in the west window: November 18, 1918. Made the circle on what I imagined had been the spot where Willie, years after Deirdre's death, had sat in his chair "like an emperor on his throne," hickory branches at his back, waiting to receive Bert who had come in pursuit of marriage. Then, lingering for a moment in the room where both Deirdre and Kate had prepared to greet death, I watched the dust floating in the shaft of light falling in a slim straight path.

In the sitting room John Carmody's black radiator clanked noisily, loomed like a phantom in a space from which had been removed Kate's little desk, the massive chest that had held the fawn notebook I'd discovered one February afternoon when icicles hung in the window. Gone, too, the oil painting of the pond gripped by a fiery red sun, the bookcase with glass doors and the little key that locked and unlocked them, the bound sets of Dickens and Thackeray and Gibbons. I made a prayer circle over all the stories that had been read or listened to in this room, all the words confided to paper, all the notebooks and letters and journals stored away in safe places. The beveled mirror on the door of the closet hung straight in the face of the sun, too bright to look into, and when I closed my eyes I saw blazing frames embracing a black interior, as if the edges of the world were streaming with the light that shines on the back of things. When I opened my eyes I found there'd been some shift and glimpsed my own reflection in the mirror, gave it a fleeting farewell. The rooms on the north side of the house were in shadow and so I passed quickly through, making prayer circles over the child Maddie as she lay in bed waiting for sleep on some long-ago Christmas Eve; over John Carmody shivering on a March afternoon and wondering if it was the dengue that had come to claim him at last, perhaps listening for the strains of Mary's lullaby as she sang to the western wind, soothing their infant son who would fall out of his bed and into the sea.

I then went rapidly down the back stairs, not sure where along its curving wall the yellow spot switched on like an electric light on early August evenings, shining down into the front hall for only a night or two, a few minutes at a time. The kitchen door stood open, the key in its lock, and so I made my way carefully down the rickety steps into the cellar, aware for the first time how askew they were, tilting this way and that. The wooden banister, however, was firm and smooth to the touch, silken with handling.

As soon as I reached the bottom I began moving from one spot to another, making a circle of prayer over the tubs and old washboard, the hands that had plunged sheets and shirts and nightclothes into hot water, the enamel table holding clothespins in its drawer, the steam from the first washing machine billowing forth in the cold air, the scrap of screen flapping in a high window. I passed then into a space where snow shovels and rakes and hoes and a whirling lawnmower had once been kept and where, in one wall, the door to the inner room that had always remained locked now stood wide open. In front of it the skate key still hung from the string we pulled to turn on the light, but I didn't touch it, instead made a circle beneath, and then stepped into the room. The high half-windows admitted not green light at all, filtered through hydrangea leaves, but the unblinking light of winter. It fell on a raw new emptiness, the warped wooden planks of the floor, the musty spotted walls, and, in one corner, three built-in shelves. The top one had been lined with a page from the *New York Times* from which looked out a dusty dotted image of FDR's face, eyes staring through pince-nez. Without naming anyone, I invoked the help of all those who had ever touched or smelled or laid eyes on any of the objects that had once rested in this room, the sandal maker in vanished Kyoto who'd fashioned in straw the children's stilted shoes, those who'd gazed at the Union flag with pride or with hatred or remorse, the silversmith bent over a teaspoon, the photographer taking a snapshot of Kate and Grace sitting under the summer trees at a small wicker table, all those who'd wound the birthday plate on its stem to set off a jingly "Happy Birthday" then lifted the cake and carried it aloft, candles blazing, to the one who sat waiting. I then passed out of the room and over the smooth cement and back up the rickety stairs.

In the front hall I made the circle over the spot where the grandfather clock had once stood, its climbing moon smiling down on the children playing on the floor, on Grace, flaxen hair falling back from her face as she looked up at its little hammer, waiting for the strike of two. Made the circle over Stuart Chambers hearing steps above, looking up to see Deirdre descend the stairs in a floating skirt. Then I passed through the living room, unlatched the French doors and stepped onto the porch. I shivered with the sudden cold, hugged my elbows and observed the rhododendron leaves curled into cones, the twisted stamens of summer flowers shriveled to fine rusted wire. Then, breathing a white cloud into the frigid air, I again began making the prayer circle, this time over the children crashing through the rhododendron as they rounded the house in a mad rush to the hickory tree that had served as home base; the same or different children hunting beneath the tree for violet and rose Easter eggs hidden in the pachysandra; the children squashing yew berries between two fingers, bayberries, seed pods of maples and elms, bringing a heel down sharply on a nut, sifting dirt through their fingers, peeling layers of mica from a stone.

I became confused on the porch, there were too many people to remember, so I made a circle over the cicadas whose shrill intensities had been heard by all those sitting there on a summer's afternoon, over the amber shells the cicadas had struggled out of and left behind on the bark of the trees, the tiny clinging legs, the bulging blind eyes, over the insects even now sheltering in the frozen earth. And then I left the porch, carefully latching the doors behind me, and walked through the living room and front hall into the dining room. There, on the shining bare floor, I noticed a brass button that a foot must once have pressed to summon a soup tureen through the swinging doors of the kitchen, a platter of sliced lamb lifted from a warming oven of the old Oriole stove. I made a circle over those who'd labored in the kitchen, peeling, cutting, stirring, basting, over the children and grown-ups and guests who'd sat at the table hoping for solace of some kind. Over all those who'd found some brief camaraderie, some lightening of heart in the company of others; over those too who'd sat ignored and forgotten. The absence of the clock from the mantel, the clock with the revolving pendulums, reminded me that there wasn't a single timepiece left in any of the rooms, that nothing remained to tell the hour. I made a prayer circle over the vanished minutes so precisely recorded in the house, over those who'd wound the clocks, kept them oiled and repaired and had moved their hands backward or forward in April and October. In the window, a fallen tulip branch appeared like a sudden misplaced shadow, the same branch I'd noticed getting out of the car. Peering more closely, I saw that what I'd been calling pods were not pods at all but dried winged seeds, the inner glossy heart of the flower that appeared like sunny spots of orange in the trees in May.

I turned then—pondering how it was only by chance and at the very last moment I'd seen what was before me, thinking how many things I would never see—and went back through the hall and up the stairs. I'd picked up my jacket from the floor of the living room, taken the frosted snowman cookie from the piano bench and jammed it in my pocket. At the first landing I reached for the post that had appeared framed in one of the windows of the front door, but instead of placing my hand on it, bowed over the first occupants of the house, the Newells, who'd endured one winter in these edged spaces before fleeing them and each other.

Shivering a little, then, I put on my jacket and continued up the stairs to the second floor where at the top I faced the milky skirt covering the bulb, the top hat twirling above it, the tog that had been used to turn up the blue flame when electricity failed. I remembered Bert's saying that in the days when gas was used there were always black smudges on the ceilings, made a prayer circle over the ghostly clouded glass and the blank space beneath where Deirdre in a gilded frame had held a slumbering twin in each arm. I made another prayer circle over Willie and my three-year-old self creeping along the hall on our way to a sleeping Kate and then continued up the stairs until I was again in the room at the top. The block of light on the floor had shifted. The sun was now flooding in through the two large south windows overlooking, from high above, the slated roof of the porch. It could have been the glint of pearly light on the gray slates far below or, as I stood at the windows, the sharp tilt of the eaves on either side, but for a moment the room seemed to pitch and roll, and looking down I imagined the slate-gray sea as it might have appeared to Bridgit Fitzmaurice McDonough when her own child was lowered into it, to Mary McDonough standing by her side, imagined the glint of sunlight rising to meet Rob as he plunged overboard in the early hours of an October morning. For a moment I swooned as if I myself had lost my balance, and sitting down abruptly on the floor summoned those who between these walls had ever imagined someone they loved falling from a great height, breaking a fragile skull on a compact sheet of water or on a pink-marbled step. I was about to attempt the prayer circle but was stopped by the image of Bridgit herself, head bowed beneath a black shawl, raising a hand to bless all of us who had ever feared death by vertigo.

Sitting cross-legged on the floor, musing there quietly in a patch of sun, I knew myself at rest but also gathering for what lay ahead. I thought of Kate, sixteen years old and scowling, sitting perhaps exactly where I was placed now, laying out a hand of solitaire, listening for the steps on the stairs that would tell her a dying Deirdre had at last been left alone. I thought of her creeping down to find her mother and rose to my feet as she had done, walking quietly out of the room and starting down the stairs, making the prayer circle as I went. In the hall the rainbow spot no longer wobbled in a corner of an empty bookshelf, the sun had moved from the window, the gleaming doorknob had fallen back into simple clarity. I stood there, uncertain for a moment, waiting for direction, and then I knew it was my turn to go down the stairs for the last time, to accompany those others who had undertaken this journey themselves. Making the prayer circle continuously now, moving my arms in wider and wider circles, I moved with Deirdre from one landing to another until I was staring down into the hall where I was confused by what seemed a crowd of faces waiting below. But after a moment the air cleared and I could see I had only to move through the empty hall as all the others had done before me and out into the changing light.

Literary Sources

The sources for quoted material are as follows:

Prologue

Troubling the Waters
Dickinson, Emily. *Selected Letters,* ed. Thomas H. Johnson. Cambridge, Mass.: Harvard University Press, 1986.

Part One

Inmates of the Air
Dickinson, Emily. *The Poems of Emily Dickinson,* ed. R. W. Franklin. Cambridge, Mass.: Harvard University Press, 1999.

The Sheeted Dead
Shakespeare, William. *Hamlet.* The Folger Library General Reader's Shakespeare. New York: Washington Square Press, 1958.

Part Two

In the Despairing Hour of Life
Dickinson, Emily. *Selected Letters,* ed. Thomas H. Johnson. Cambridge, Mass.: Harvard University Press, 1986.

Part Three

John Carmody Has a Word or Two
Whitman, Walt. *The Complete Poems,* ed. Francis Murphy. New York: Penguin Books, 1975.
Austen, Jane. *The Complete Novels of Jane Austen.* New York: The Modern Library, n.d.

As for Rob
Melville, Herman. *Moby-Dick*. Boston: Houghton Mifflin, 1956; *Billy Budd and Other Tales*. New York: New American Library, 1961.

In Search of Deirdre in Kilkee
Joyce, James. *Ulysses*. New York: Modern Library, 1961.
Shakespeare, William. *Hamlet*. The Folger Library General Reader's Shakespeare. New York: Washington Square Press, 1958.

Part Four

Spirit Fires
Kavanagh, Patrick. *Collected Poems*. New York: Norton, 1973.
Gregory, Lady Augusta. *A Book of Saints and Wonders*. Dundrum: Dun Emer Press, 1906.

Willie in Gotham
Kavanagh, Patrick. *Collected Poems*. New York: Norton, 1973.
Wilde, Oscar. *De Profundis*. 2nd ed. New York: Knickerbocker Press, Putnam's Sons, 1909.
Tóibín, Colm, and Diarmaid Ferriter. *The Irish Famine: A Documentary*. London: Profile Books, 2001.

Part Five

The Horn of the Hunter
Synge, J. M. *The Playboy of the Western World and Other Plays*. Oxford: Oxford University Press, 1995.

Wind of Wild Air and Seeds of Brightness
Dickinson, Emily. *The Poems of Emily Dickinson,* ed. R. W. Franklin. Cambridge, Mass.: Harvard University Press, 1999.

Acknowledgments

Grateful acknowledgment is made to the editors of publications in which earlier versions of parts of this book appeared: "Inmates of the House" in *Ploughshares;* "Ginkgos in July" in *Lumina.*

My deepest thanks to:

Louis Asekoff, Mary Gordon, Clifford Hill, Margot Livesey, Joan Silber, Emilie Stewart: essential readers.

Myra Goldberg and Jean Valentine. Also Andrew Balet: fact-finder, scanner of old photographs, companion in research.

In Ireland, Rosemary Kevany for her house and friendship and Vincent Woods for showing me the old places in County Leitrim and County Roscommon.

Annaghmakerrig, MacDowell, Ragdale, Yaddo; and in New Mexico, Mary Ellen Capek and Susan Hallgarth.

Mike Levine and those who work with him at Northwestern University Press.

My sisters Mary Safrai and Jane Kuniholm and my brother Bill Balet. Mary Safrai, again, for the use of her remarkable photographs of the nautical clock and the Buddha.

And to Clifford Hill for his unfailing interest and help of every kind.

About the Author

Kathleen Hill teaches in the M.F.A. program at Sarah Lawrence College. Her novel *Still Waters in Niger* (Northwestern, 1999) was named a notable book by the *New York Times,* the *Los Angeles Times,* and the *Chicago Tribune,* and was nominated for the IMPAC Dublin Literary Award. The French translation, *Eaux tranquilles,* was short-listed for the Prix Femina Étranger. Her stories have appeared in *Best American Short Stories, The Pushcart Prize XXV,* and *The Pushcart Book of Short Stories.*

View from our sitting room window